William Henry Harrison Murray

Adirondack tales

William Henry Harrison Murray

Adirondack tales

ISBN/EAN: 9783743467057

Manufactured in Europe, USA, Canada, Australia, Japa

Cover: Foto ©Andreas Hilbeck / pixelio.de

Manufactured and distributed by brebook publishing software (www.brebook.com)

William Henry Harrison Murray

Adirondack tales

"SHOOK HIS GIGANTIC FIST AT THE JUDGE." Page 277.

ADIRONDACK TALES.

BY

W. H. H. MURRAY,

AUTHOR OF "ADVENTURES IN THE WILDERNESS," "MUSIC-HALL
SERMONS," "THE PERFECT HORSE," ETC.

With Full-Page Illustrations.

DESIGNED BY DARLEY AND MERRILL.
ENGRAVED BY JAMES S. CONANT.

BOSTON:
THE GOLDEN RULE PUBLISHING CO.
1877.

BOSTON:
STEREOTYPED BY C. J. PETERS & SON,
73 FEDERAL STREET.

Franklin Press: Rand, Avery, & Co., Boston.

IN MEMORIAM.

CONTENTS.

LIST OF ILLUSTRATIONS.

Designed by Darley and Merrill.

Engraved by Jas. S. Conant.

THE STORY THE KEG TOLD ME.

THE STORY THAT THE KEG TOLD ME.

CHAPTER I.

THE KEG.

" There is society where none intrudes." — Byron.

IT was near the close of a hot, sultry day in midsummer, which I had spent in exploring a part of the shore line of the lake where I was camping, and the tortuous inlet which led into the same; and wearied with the trip I had made I was returning toward the camp. There was no motive for haste, and I was taking it easily. Indeed, I was in that quiet, contented state of mind, into which one easily falls in the woods, where his labors are dictated by his amusements and his physical necessities, and not by the duties which carry with them obligation; and I had done little more than drift with the lazily-moving current. The quiet inaction, slow as it was, corresponded with my mood; and I felt almost a regret when my boat floated out from between the shrubby banks into the open waters of the little lake.

It was a very secluded sheet of water, hidden away between the mountains, not marked on the map, and whose existence was entirely unsuspected by me until in my aimless wanderings I had a few days before accidentally stum-

bled upon it. Indeed, I doubt if in all the woods there is
another sheet of water so shut in from observation and so
likely to escape the eye, I will not say of the tourist and
sportsman, but even of the hunter and trapper. It was because of this fact that I had fallen in love with it. Here
was silence undisturbed by any noise of man's making.
Here I could escape the prying eyes of idle and provoking
curiosity. Here I could watch the habits of animated nature and study the mystery of her charm without interruption. And here the wisdom which man learns independent
of utterance — the wisdom of the unspoken and the unknown — might, so far as I was fit, be received by me.

The first day on the little lake I spent in paddling around
its shores, in close scrutiny of them. In every bay into
which I successively paddled I expected to find a hunter's
cabin. On every point I doubled I looked for a sportsman's
lodge. I circled every island in my sharp quest. But in
vain. There was not a cabin nor lodge, a charred coal nor
mark of a guide's axe or trapper's knife in the entire cir-
cuit. Astonished and incredulous, I devoted another day
to the examination. I even landed at every spot where
Nature had suggested a camp-ground, and searched, with
trained eye, for the evidence of man's visitation, but found
none; not even the least trace. Springs I found, cool as
iced water and clear as crystal; but neither mark of axe,
nor knife, nor fire.

Convinced at last, I paddled out to the middle of the lake,
feeling, as I watched the sun go down, the shadows deepen
and the stars come out, that I beheld what no human eye

had ever looked upon : a place unvisited by man from the foundation of the world. In such a place the sense of time passes from you, and the sense of eternity is experienced. The years you have lived, the years of the world, are as if they were not, and you seem to be co-existent with the birth of material things. For are not the mountains around you.as they were when God called them up out of the depths? And is not the sky above them the same? And the great round sun, what has changed it? Yea, and the water, is it not as it was when its parent springs first poured it forth? In such a place one realizes that it is toil and worry and the grief of living, and not years, which make us grow old; for behold, the years rest lightly on whatever is free of these. For that which does not work nor weep is forever young.

And so it came about that the feeling that I was the only man who had ever visited this lake was so forced upon me by what seemed indisputable evidence, that I accepted it as a fixed fact. The idea took utter possession of me, and became a part of my consciousness. There was not a sign of man nor of man's coming or going, on the shores, and therefore I knew man had never visited it. To me this was an absolute fact, as sure as life itself. Well, as I was saying, it was near sunset when my boat drifted on the current that flowed with easy motion from the little inlet, out upon the quiet bosom of the lake. The sun was already sinking in the west, and the peculiar silence which attends the close of a summer's day in solitary places possessed the atmosphere. The heat was fast leaving the air and the coolness of the coming night was growing perceptible to the senses. My camp was only a short mile down the lake, and toward it, with easy stroke of the paddle, I urged my homeward course. "To-morrow," I said to myself, as I paddled along. "I will leave the lake. It is too lonely even for me, and its steady, unbroken silence day after day is getting oppressive. I am undoubtedly the only man that was ever on· this sheet of water; even the deer here do not know what sort of an animal I am, and the rats will scarcely get out of the way of my boat. I will move out of this to-morrow, nor will I stop until I find some traces of my kind."

Thus muttering to myself I paddled along, watching the reflections of sky and clouds in the clear unruffled depths beneath, and thinking of the centuries in which they had received and reflected back the changes in the firmament suspended above them. I had already come to the point on the other side of which my camp lay, when my paddle, as it moved forward for another stroke, struck against something floating in the water. I might not have noticed it, perhaps, but for the fact that it sounded hollow as my paddle struck against it. Curious, because of the peculiarity of the sound, to know what it was, with a quick turn of my wrist I reversed my paddle, checked the boat in its course, and with a sharp stroke sent it backward along the line of its wake. As I repassed the object I reached down, and finding I could raise it, lifted it into the boat. I will confess I started as if an electric current had been shot unexpectedly into me. It was a KEG !

Now, finding a keg in some places would not be very sur-

prising: in a ship yard for instance, or in a cooper's shop a
farmer's cellar, or in a liquor saloon; for in such places
kegs are plenty and you expect to see them. Nor would it
have astonished me had I met it on a frequented river, or
in any place where men come and go; but to find a keg on
this lonely lake, where I felt man had never been — where
no living soul had ever existed — was, as you will admit,
reader, a startling experience. Nevertheless, there it was
— a real keg, with oaken staves and iron bands, with a bottom intact, and perfect in all respects save that the head
was missing. As I recall it now it is really laughable the
way I sat and stared at it. I rubbed my eyes to make sure
of my sight. I tapped it with the blade of my paddle and
rolled it half over and then back again, to make sure that
it was what it seemed.

Convinced at last, I sat and looked at it, questioning.
Where did it come from? How did it get there? Who
brought it, and when, and for what purpose? Where is he
who brought it? Is he living or dead, and where is his
camp? These and like interrogations I put to myself as I
sat in my boat on that lonely lake, in the growing darkness,
looking at that KEG. "Well," I said at last, speaking aloud,
as one quickly forms the habit of doing, when alone, "well,
sitting here and staring at it don't answer such questions,
nor satisfy my hunger, either; and I had better shove in to
camp and get supper."

When supper was over and the necessary wood for my
fire laid in for the night, I went out for a while, as was my
wont, upon the point, for a quiet smoke, and to observe the
appearance of the night.

Of the beauty of such a place and hour those who never journeyed beyond the haunts of men know nothing. The sky was without a cloud. The air was breathless. Even the pines had forgotten in slumber their mournful plaint, and stood like so many shadows, dense, motionless and dumb. The water was as moveless as the atmosphere. It received the heaven as a mirror receives a face. It stole and appropriated the lustre of the firmament, and borrowed from the bespangled sky an ornamentation for its blank spaces as glorious as the heaven's own. The sky was blue-black, and out of its cerulean gloom the pointed stars shot gleams of many-colored fire. The mountains, sombre and vast, rested on their broad bases as if their foundations were laid in everlasting silence. The odors of the forest filled the damp air like incense. A loon far down the lake, as if oppressed by the all-pervading silence, poured into the still air the prolonged sound of its mournful call. It entered into, and lingered sadly for a moment in the air, then passed away, making the silence that followed even more profound. Deeply affected by the spell of the lonely place and the hour, I rose from the stone on which I had been sitting, crossed the point, and returned to my little camp.

I busied myself for a moment or two in starting my fire, and when the flames of it rose clear and strong I seated myself with my back against a pine, and half reclining gazed off upon the lake. As I thus sat watching the reflection of the fire-light in the water, my eyes fell upon the KEG. It seemed, in some sort, a kind of companion to me,

IT OPENED ITS DIMINUTIVE MOUTH AND BEGAN TO TALK.   PAGE 13.

alone as I was; a visible bond binding me to my kind; a reminder of the life that men were living in the great, roaring, busy world outside and beyond the lonely lake on whose silent shore I then was lying. It reminded one of life, — or what men call life, — the getting and the giving; the saving and the spending; the loving and the hating; of the thousands far away. I fell again to wondering where it came from, and by whom it was brought over the mountains, and for what purpose; — wondering what its history was, and what had become of him who once handled it; — whether he were living or dead, and a hundred other things such as one might fancy in such a spot, in such an hour, looking at such an object so strangely found. It may be I was awake; it may be I was asleep; but as I was thus looking steadily and curiously at it, and wondering strange things about it, it seemed to change its appearance, and become different from a KEG; even a MAN; a little man; a very little man, — a man not more than eighteen inches high, with the queerest little legs, and the funniest little body, and the tiniest face one ever saw, — but still a *man*. And, then, standing bolt upright and looking straight at me with its little gleaming eyes, that glowed like glistening beads, — wonder of wonders! it opened its diminutive mouth, and began to TALK!

THE STORY OF THE KEG.

"I suppose," it said — and as it began to speak it leaned slightly toward me as a man might in lifting himself upon his toes — and its ludicrous-looking face took to itself a grave expression, funny to see, — "I suppose," it said, "that you are very much astonished to hear me talk, as a man can, and to know that I even have a mouth at all; but I have, sir, a very good mouth indeed, and a tongue inside of it, too, as you will learn before I have done telling my story. For I have seen and heard strange things, both before and since I came into these woods, and had many queer experiences, of which I propose to tell you if you will only sit still and hear me, and not go clean off to sleep as you seem inclined to do. O yes," it continued, "I desire to tell you my story; the story of the man who brought me here; why he did it, and what came of it; and how he lived and died. And it is a very sad story indeed; and it pains me even to recall it." And here the Keg lifted one of its little thin hands, and placed it with great emphasis upon its heart, "but it contains a lesson which it were well that all men, who strive to be rich and are growing to love money, should hear, and I trust that what I tell to you to-night, you will some day tell to them; and I trust it will do them good, and be a warning to them, and make them wiser than was the poor man who once owned me, and who died right here · on the point off which you found me, — peace be to his soul! and, indeed, I think he did find peace in the end, although he found it by a weary way, and a steep one, and one which lead him nigh into hell. But I will go back to the beginning and tell you all just as it happened, and the reason of things as I saw and felt them long years ago.

"The earliest remembrance I have of myself is of the cooper's shop where I was made; and a nice looking keg I

was then, too, although you may not believe it judging by
my present appearance. But that was many years ago,
and you must remember that years wear the life and beauty
out of kegs as much as they do out of men; and although
I look so worn and weakly now, yet I can recall the time
that my staves were all smooth and clean, so that the oak
grain showed clearly from top to bottom of me, and my
steel hoops were as bright and shiny as steel can be. I
have had many hard knocks since then, and seen hard
usage enough to drive the very staves out of me time and
again; but the cooper that made me, made me on his
honor, and took a deal of honest pride in putting me together, as every workman should in doing his work. And
I remember as if it were but yesterday — for I have laughed
over it many a time when I had poor reason to laugh at
anything — that when I was finished, and the cooper had
sanded me off and oiled me so that my side fairly shone,
he set me up on his bench and said to his apprentice boy:
'There, that keg will last till the Judgment Day, and well
on toward night at that.'

CHAPTER II.

"Some lone miser visiting his store
Bends at his treasure, counts, recounts it o'er."
Goldsmith.

"WELL, one day, a few weeks after, a man came into the shop and asked the master: 'Have you a good strong keg for sale?' And he put the question in such an earnest, half spiteful and half suspicious way, that I fairly started within my hoops, and opened my eyes wide to take a good look at him; and a very peculiar man I saw, too, I assure you. He was quite a young looking man, not more than forty years of age; of good height and strongly built. He was a gentleman evidently, although his face was darkly tanned and his clothes were old and thread-bare. His mouth was rather small than large. His lips were thin and had a look of being tightly drawn over the teeth — at least it seemed so to me. His chin was very long, and was joined at the base to large, strong jaws. His hair was brownish-black, and not over-abundant; indeed, I am not sure that he had not even then begun to grow slightly bald. But the remarkable feature of his face was his eyes. They were blue-grey in color, smallish in size, and set in deep under the arch of the eyebrows. How hard and steel-like they were, and restless as a rat's! And what an intense look of suspicion there was in them, — a half-scared, defiant look, as if their owner felt every one to be his enemy, against whom he must stand on his guard, and whom he might at any instant have to fight and kill. Ah, what eyes they were! and how they came and went to and from your face, and shot their glances at you and into you — aye, and through you, too. I grew to know them well afterward, and to know what the strange, wild light in them meant; but of that by and by.

" 'Have you got a good, strong keg to sell, I say?' he shouted to my master, who was hammering away at a barrel so that he had not heard the man enter, much less his question. 'A good stout keg?' said my master, as he turned around and looked squarely at the questioner. 'I should say that I had, Mr. Roberts; do you want one?' 'Yes,' returned the other, 'I do, but I want a strong one, — *strong*, do you *hear?*' — and he took a step toward my master as if he meant to strike him. 'Strong enough to hold the devil himself if he were in it, or a sinner's hope of heaven, either, if you like that better,' and he sneered the sentence out as if the blessed hope of Paradise were fit only to point a fool's joke. 'Well, I don't know much about the devil, Mr. Roberts,' rejoined my master, — 'not so much as you do, it may be; and as to one's hope of heaven, I don't build kegs to keep that in; but there's a keg,' — and my master tapped me with his mallet until I rang clear as a bell — 'that I made with my own hands, from the best of stuff, and I said to the boys when I finished it that it would last till the Day of Judgment; and I verily believe it will, if white oak staves and steel hoops can last that long.' 'I didn't ask you anything about the Day of Judgment, or anything else the long-winded parsons talk about and frighten their cowardly followers with,' snarled the other. ' All I want is a good strong keg—strong as can be made of wood and iron—and if that keg is what you say it is, I want it and will take it, if you won't cheat me at the bargain, as I dare say you would like to do; what is your price, eh ?' Well, the price was set, the money paid with a muttered protest, and Mr. Roberts hoisted me up under his arm and hastened with me out of the shop.

"Well, you can imagine that I felt very anxious about myself, and wondered as I was being hurried along, where I was being taken, and what use I was to be put to; but I made up my mind to do my duty and hold whatever my new master should give to my trust so that my maker might not hear ill of me; but I little thought what was to befall me, or what I should have to bear as the years went round. For I have seen dreadful sights in my time, and beheld things too awful to declare. For I have seen the undoing of a man, and the wreck of a human soul !

" Well, as I was saying, my new master hurried me along without stopping to speak to any one, although we passed many, and I noticed that no one of all we passed spoke to him, but looked at him coldly or wonderingly, and that he, whenever we were about to meet any one, whether man, woman or child, only clutched me the more tightly and hurried on the faster. At last we came to a common look-

ing sort of a house, set back from the road, with a very
high fence built clear around it, and a heavy padlock on the
gate, and great, strong, wooden shutters at every window.
Into this my master entered and set me down carefully
upon the floor. This done, he went back to the door and
locked it, and drew two large iron bolts or bars across it,
securing them most carefully in the sockets. He then went
to every window and examined them to see if each was
fastened. He carefully examined every room and closet,
even looking into the ash-hole and the oven in the chimney.
Then lighting a candle he went down into the cellar, and
after that up into the attic, carrying the candle in one hand
and a great club or bludgeon in the other.

"By this time I had made up my mind that I had fallen
into the hands of a maniac, and that my new master was
insane. Leastwise I did not know what to make of him, or
what was to be the upshot of his strange ways. After a
while he came back to the room where he had left me, and
took me up and set me on the table; and starting the upper
hoop proceeded to take out one of my heads. At this I
was thoroughly frightened, and kept my eyes on him wherever he went, as I wanted to see what his strange conduct
meant, and what he would do next. When he had taken
one of my heads out, he went to an old drawer under the
cupboard and got a large sheepskin, with the wool closely
clipped; and with a pair of large shears proceeded to fit
me with a lining of it. I must say that he did it with remarkable cleverness, and that when he was done with me
I was lined as well as any tailor could line me. But what

it all meant I couldn't guess; and so I watched and waited.
For you will admit that no keg was ever treated as he was
treating me, and that I had good reason to be surprised.

"After he had done lining me with the soft skin he
seemed more easy, and less nervous, and he put his hands
inside of me and felt of his work and was evidently pleased
at it; for he rubbed his hands together, and his eyes glistened, and he said to himself: 'There! I call that a pretty
good fit; I don't think old Tim, the tailor, would have done
it better.' And then he laughed to himself and rubbed his
hands together again as if he had said a very funny thing.
By this time it was well on toward night, and he kindled a
fire in the fire-place — a very small fire it was, only a little
thin blaze made of three or four short sticks which looked
as if they had been picked up in the roadway, and a handful or two of chips. But small as the blaze was he managed to heat a little kettle of water by it and cook a cup of
tea, which he placed upon an old board-table alongside of
a loaf of bread, and then he sat down by the table and began to eat the bread and drink the tea. And this was all
the supper he had, and I thought it very strange that so
large a man should be content with such a supper; but I
grew used to the sight afterward, and ceased to wonder, as
you will when you know the cause of his frugality.

After he had done eating, he wrapped the remainder of
the bread carefully in a piece of paper, and put it away
with the little tea-kettle in the cupboard. And then he went
to the door and re-examined the bolts, and looked closely
at all the shutters, while I stood and wondered what his

strange actions meant, and why he was so anxious that the doors and windows should all be fastened so tightly; for the neighborhood was a good one, and the people law-abiding, so much so that the doors of half the houses in the village were never locked of nights, even from one year's end to another.

When he had done all this, he brought the club or bludgeon that I had seen him carry up stairs with him when he went up into the attic, and laid it on the table beside me, and also a large thick knife, with a strong horn handle, which he had taken from the mantle-piece where it had been lying; and then he went to the ash-hole in the chimney, and brought the ash-pail, which was full of ashes; and he went to the cupboard, and brought an old earthen jar; and from under the bed he fetched a bag; and from a . chamber overhead he brought a small box; and from the cellar he returned with a sack, all damp with earth. All the while I kept my eyes well open, you may believe, wondering what it all meant, and what there was in the pail and the jar and the box and the bag and the sack. Well, when he had these all side by side near the table, he sat down and out of the ash-pail he took a small pot, and having blown the ashes off it with great care, he turned it bottom upward on the table, and — merciful heaven! what do you think was in it?

Dollars! Gold Dollars!

Then he took the bag and untied the cord that held the mouth, and emptied it upon the table, and it, too, was full of *dollars* — gold dollars! And then one after the other,

he opened the jar and the box and the sack, and out of
each and all he poured a great stream of bright golden dollars! Oh, what a pile of them there was! What a heap
they made! How they gleamed and glistened! How they
jingled and rang! How they rattled and clinked as he
poured them down upon the dark boards! And how his
eyes gleamed in their deep sockets as they saw the golden
stream, and how the thin lips drew apart as the dollars
flowed out, until his teeth showed their line of white back
of them, and his hands shook and trembled as if the palsy
was in them!

It was a dreadful sight to see him sit down, and leaning
over the table, run his hands under the yellow heap and lift
the pieces up so that the bright bits flowed over and out of
his hollow palms and ran down through his parted fingers
in shining streams. And then to hear him laugh as he
played with the glistening coin! How mirthless his laughter was — hard and sharp and ringing like the metallic ring
of the dollars itself. Oh, it was dreadful to think that a
human soul could love money so. And he did love it —
wildly, madly love it, — love it with all the strength of his
strong nature. And this he did not disguise nor deny to
himself; but admitted it, and gloried in it, too, with a most
wicked and blasphemous glorying, as the Arch Fiend himself is said to glory in his own sin.

He would take a dollar up and look at it as a father
might at the face of his favorite child, and pat it with his
palm, and smooth the surface of it with a finger tip as if it
could feel a caress. Ah me, 'twas dreadful! And then he

would take a piece up and talk to it and say, coaxingly,
" Thou art better than a wife," and to another, " Thou art
sweeter than a child," and to another yet, "Thou art dearer
than father or mother." And to the great pile of shining
gold, he would say, as he leaned over it, " O my beauties,
the parsons may say what they please, but you are better
than a far-off heaven." Ah, such blasphemy as I heard
that night ! How the sweet and blessed things of human
life were derided, and the things that are divine and holy
sneered at !

At last he fell to counting them, and by the way he did it
I knew he had done it often ; done it so many times that
he counted as men do things by habit,—mechanically. He
would say : " ONE, TWO, THREE, FOUR, FIVE, SIX, SEVEN,
EIGHT, NINE, TEN,—GOOD ! ONE, TWO, THREE, FOUR, FIVE,
SIX, SEVEN, EIGHT, NINE, TEN, — GOOD ! " And so go on,
faster and faster, until his breath was gone ; and then he
would catch it again, and start anew. " ONE, TWO, THREE,
FOUR, FIVE, SIX, SEVEN, EIGHT, NINE, TEN, — GOOD !" Oh,
it was awful to think of an immortal being loving MONEY
so !

For a long time he counted on ; counted until his hands
shook, and the sweat stood thick on his forehead, and his
eyes gleamed and glowed as if he were mad. And perhaps
he was mad, — as all men are who live for gain, and whose
hearts are fired with the awful lust for gold. So he counted
on. And when he had counted all, — even to the very last,
— the old dark boarded table was covered thick with little
piles of tens ; and he arose with a jump like a maniac,

and stood above the table and shouted until the old house
rang again :

" SIXTEEN THOUSAND, SIX HUNDRED AND SIXTY-SIX DOL-
LARS ! SIXTEEN THOUSAND, SIX HUNDRED AND SIXTY-SIX
DOLLARS ! "

Well, after a while he sobered down and became quiet,
and began to pick the dollars up and pack them away in·
side of me, — carefully, one by one, as a mother might lay
her children in their beds to sleep, — and this he kept on
doing until the last shining coin had been taken from the
table, and I was full to the very brim.   Then he put my
head in its place, and drove the upper hoop on snug, and
put me in the bed, and the great knife under his pillow ;
and, blowing out the light, lay down beside me and putting
one arm across me as if I were a child, fell asleep.   And
over the old house in which the miser lay clasping me to
his heart, I knew the stars were shining ; and beyond the
stars, with eyes that never slept, I knew that the great God
was looking down upon him and me.

CHAPTER III.

THE MISER'S FEAR.

"I greatly fear my money is not safe." — *Shakespeare.*

"Increase his riches and his peace destroy,
Now fears in dire vicissitude invade,
The rustling brake alarms, and quivering shade,
Nor light nor darkness brings his pain relief;
One shows the plunder and one hides the thief." —

Johnson.

WELL, things went on in the same fashion day after day, and night after night; but getting worse all the time. My master did little work, and of course earned little money, — only enough to buy his bread and tea, with now and then a little piece of meat. He seemed to have no desire to get more, but was only anxious to keep what he had. And about this he was so anxious that it kept him in a fever of excitement all the time. For days he would scarcely go beyond the doorway, and if he saw a man coming along the road he would come in with great haste, close the shutters and bar the door as if he feared the man was a robber and was coming to rob him. And indeed this was his feeling. He was never for an instant free of the fear of losing his money. He would mutter about it in the day time, and he would mutter about it in the night when he was asleep. Many a time have I heard him, in the dead of the night when the old house was as still as a tomb, suddenly break out and say, "Oh, you don't want my money, eh? You came for it, you know you did, and you hope by crying to get it out of me; but you shan't have a dollar of it; no not a dollar! D'ye hear?—if it would save your soul!" And then he would put out his arms and wrap them around me and strain me to him, muttering and murmuring about his "Beautiful dollars. My own, own DOL-LARS, they want to get you from me. I know them; but they shall never do it, for I would kill them if they tried." And he would grind and grit his teeth and hoarsely repeat the word, "*kill,*—*kill,*" as he sunk again into a heavy sleep.

It was bad enough to hear his muttering when all was quiet and peaceful, and his sleep was undisturbed; but when the night was stormy and wild, and the wind made the old house shake, and the rain was slashed in great sheets against the windows, and the timbers in the frame-work creaked and groaned; — at such times, he would toss and moan in his bed, shriek and clutch me with his fingers, leap up and strain and tug and strike as if he were wrest-ling with an unseen person, who was striving to carry me away. Indeed, waking or sleeping, he was tormented with a deadly fear; and the fear was born of the suspicion that some one would succeed in stealing me, and the treasure in me.

And this suspicion it was that had poisoned his whole life, and made him hate his kind, and driven him into the wretched strait he was in, when I came to him. And a more wretched strait no mortal was ever in; for what is worse than the suspecting of one's kind, even of one's wife and child; yea, and of the man of God himself, whose love for you is as God's, — the deep, steady, ministering love of the soul. And this was just his case, as I found out one day. And this was the way it came about: —

It was summer; and for the sake of comfort — for the old house was damp and close — he had left the door wide open, and, seating himself in his chair, had fallen asleep. Indeed, I was rather drowsy myself, and was fast dropping off into a nap, when I heard my master give a horrible yell, and leap with a frightful oath to his feet. My eyes, as you can imagine, came open with a snap; and the sight I beheld nearly upset me. In the doorway stood a man and woman; and by his dress I knew the man to be the old village pastor, and the woman I soon learned was my master's wife. For a minute my master stood looking at them, and then he said abruptly, "What in the Devil's name did you come here for?"

"John," said the woman, "your child, Mary, is dying; and I thought you, who are her father, might want to see her before she passed away;" and her voice choked, and I saw her breast under her dress heave with suppressed sobs.

"Dying, is she?" said my master brutally. "I don't believe it: it's a trumped-up story of yours to get me away from here, that you may steal my gold; but you can't fool me with your lying, and you might as well get away from here, both of you."

"John," returned the woman, — and as she spoke the

great tears came into her eyes, and her hands twitched con-
vulsively, — "John, I never lied to you, nor to any one, in
my life, and you know it. Mary is dying, as the parson
here can tell you ; and I dare not let her die, and not give
you a chance to see her ; for she was the last one born to
us, and you did love her before the cursed love of gold in
you drove from your heart all other loving. And I said the
father should see the child before she dies : it is his right;
and so I have come and told you. And besides, Mary herself last night spoke your name in her sleep, and talked in
her wanderings of you ; and this morning she said suddenly, 'I wish I could see father before I die. I dreamed
of him last night : it was an awful dream ; and I wish I
might tell it to him before I go. It might be it would do
him good, and win his heart from his dreadful gold.' And
so, John, I got this man of God to come along with me,
that he might bear witness to my truth, and perhaps speak
a word of wisdom to you."

While the woman had been speaking, my master had
stood looking at her with the same scowl on his face, and
the same hard, suspicious expression in his eyes. Not a
muscle changed, nor a line softened. So he stood a moment, glaring at them ; and then he said to the minister,
who was leaning on his cane, — for he was old and weak,
and his head was white as snow, — " Well, what have you
got to say ?"

" John Roberts," said the old man solemnly, " I have
much to say; for I bring a message, not from your dying
child, but from your living Lord. I remember when I bap-

tized you as a child at the altar, on the day your pious parents gave you in holy covenant to God. And I remember
when I married you to this woman here, your wife; and I
remember your early promise, and the happiness you had
yourself and made for others, until the lust of gold possessed you. And I have known your downward path, and
how that which God meant for good, became by your per-
version of its use, an evil to you, — yea, an evil which poisoned all your life, and changed the course of it; turned
you against your friends, made you brutal to your wife and
child, and brought you to the gate of hell, where you now
stand, — a miserable miser! All this I have watched and
seen and known; and all this I have warned you against
time and again in past years, and in the name of Him who
was sold to death by a miser like yourself. And now I call
upon you to repent, and by true repentance and deep con-
trition find mercy in Him whom you have sold out of your
heart and life, and in whose eyes you are another Judas,
yet lacking repentance. Repent, therefore, and return to
your right mind, lest a worse thing fall upon you, and the
curse of your life be doubled upon you in your death, even
that as you are now deserted of man you may in that
dreadful hour find yourself deserted of God. And as for
your child, as your wife has said, she is dying, and she has
asked for you. She bids you come to her before she dies.
For God has spoken to her in a vision, as he did to some of
old, and revealed to her what shall be if you repent not, —
a dreadful death, in a wild spot, with no one nigh, and a
darkness round about you in your death-hour like the dark-

ness that surrounds the damned, — all this she has seen
with eyes prepared by the mystery of the Unknown to see
it; and I pray you, therefore, as one standing between the
living and the dead, that you come right speedily and see
your child, and hear her message, lest she die, and leave
it unspoken, and what she has seen in vision be realized
in fact, and you be lost in death even as you are already
lost in life."

He paused, and his face shone as one who speaks beyond
the measure of the spirit of man — even by the measure of
the Spirit of God, — and his aged hands shook; and when
he had ended, his lips continued to move, as with one who
follows an exhortation with an inaudible prayer.

But my master remained unmoved. He heard the words
of his old Pastor, as he had the words of his wife, with the
same scowling, sinister look in his eyes; the same set, dog-
gedness of face, the same sneering expression on his lips.
He stared at them a moment, and then shouted: "You LIE!
both of you, — you want my money, you mean to steal it
from me. Everybody wants it; there isn't an honest man
in the world. All are thieves. All love gold. You do. I
know by your looks you love it. You can't fool me by your
tears and your preaching. You get out of this house or I
will kill you," and he swore a horrible oath, and stepping
back a step he seized the bludgeon and swung it round his
head, and stamped his foot upon the floor and swore at
them again; his eyes glowed like hot coals, and the froth
hung on his lips. The woman ran screaming from the
house, but the old pastor stood his ground, and faced him,
and said: —

"John Roberts, thou art a doomed man. Thou hast denied the truth and resisted the Spirit, and Satan hath thee in full possession. The lust of gold that destroys many is in thee strong and mighty, and only God can save thee, nor he against thy will. Repent, or thou shalt perish in a lonely spot, on a dark night, with none to help nor hear thy cries; and thy gold shall perish with thee." And so saying, he turned and slowly left the house.

For a moment my master stood, and then he rushed for the door and locked it, and slid the great strong bars into their sockets; and then he came and lifted me upon the table, and patted me with his hand, and laughed and said: "My gold! my gold!" And when night came he took my head out and poured the shining pieces upon the table, and played with them for hours, and then, as was his fashion, he fell to counting them by tens in the same manner as was his custom, saying: "ONE, TWO, THREE, FOUR, FIVE, SIX, SEVEN, EIGHT, NINE, TEN. GOOD!" until he had counted them to the very last one. As he counted the frenzy grew on him, and when his task was over, and the old dark-wood table was all yellow with the gold pieces lying in stacks of ten, he was wild in the joy of his terrible lust. He leaped and danced around the glistening coins, and shouted till the old house rang: "SIXTEEN THOUSAND SIX HUNDRED AND SIXTY-SIX!"

And then he put them all back within me, fastened my head in tightly, laid me in his bed, laid himself beside me, and, putting an arm around me, he fell asleep. And I knew that over the old house the stars were shining brightly, and that above the stars the Great God, with eyes that never slept, was looking calmly down on him and me.

But when he woke in the morning he was not as he had been, but more nervous and savage-like. He did not unbar the door during the whole day, nor open the heavy shutters an inch, but kept all closed and dark. And he was muttering and talking to himself all day. He had the look of one who was planning some deep plot, nor could I make out what it was; but I caught enough of his talk to know that he was more suspicious of losing his money than ever, and trusted no one, but was afraid of all men, known and unknown, and was thinking and planning how to make his money safe and get me to some spot where no one could steal me. Once I heard him say: " All men are thieves. I suspect them all. No one with money is safe among them. They will get it yet, unless I go where they cannot find me." And then he would curse his kind and swear.

At last he suddenly stopped in his tramping up and down the room, and shouted: "I'll *go*, go where they cannot find me. Go where I can be alone and can count my money as much as I wish, in the broad day, under the bright sun or stars, and see it glint and glisten in the bright light. Won't that be glorious! — to be alone with my money, where I can spread it all out in broad day and see it shine, and count it over and play with it, with no one nigh to scare me nor make me hide it away, for fear of its being seen and stolen. Men, curse them, are what I dread. I will go where there is not a man!"

CHAPTER IV.

THE MISER IN THE WOODS.

"Gold, gold, gold, gold,
Bright and yellow hard and cold." — *Hood.*

AFTER this he said no more, but packed up the few things he had, and rolled me up in a blanket and put me in a sack, so I could neither see nor hear a single thing that was done or said, and that is all I know of what happened for many a day, only I knew by my feeling that I was being *carried*, CARRIED, CARRIED, over rivers and mountains, and through forests that were wide and deep, until one day I felt myself put in a boat; and on we went, day after day, night after night, until one afternoon, I knew not when, neither the year nor the day, the boat stopped, the bag in which I was, was carried ashore, and, for the first time for many a day, I was taken out of it, and I saw the sunlight once more, and behold! I was on the very point off which you this evening found me."

And here the keg paused a moment, as one who is tired of rapid talking, or oppressed by mournful memories; and it made a motion as if it would sit down, but did not. But it put one little hand up to its chin and rested for a moment so, and I thought it fetched a little sigh, but of that I am not sure, for it might have been a puff of wind playing with the uppermost tuft of some neighboring pine, or the sputtering of the fire, for that matter; but in a moment it began again.

"You must pardon my stopping a moment, but I have not done much talking for many a year and it really takes the breath out of me; moreover one of my heads is gone, and that makes a great difference with a keg I assure you; for we are like a great many men who manage to get along with one head, but no one sees how they do it, and all heartily wish they had another in addition to the one they have, and a better one too. And besides I am getting rather old, and I doubt if I live much longer, for ever since I have been standing here, by the fire, I have felt that I might fall to pieces at any moment," and the keg cast an anxious look down over itself and then as if partially strengthened, at least, went on : —

"Well, things continued very much as they were at the old house for several weeks, and my master seemed happy in the thought that he had got beyond the reach of men and the danger of their stealing me, and what I had in me. Every day when the sun shone brightly he would take me down to the point yonder, from beneath the shadow of the pines, where the sun shines clearly, and pour the treasure out in one great pile and play with it by the hour. It seemed to please him greatly to see the yellow coins shine and shimmer in the bright light, and he would lie in the sand and watch the sparkling heap by the hour, and count it all over and over again, and laugh and shout while doing it as he used to do around the old table when we were in

"AND COUNT IT ALL OVER AND OVER AGAIN." Page 34.

the house. And it seemed more dreadful to me than ever before, for here every thing was so still and solemn, and the sky seemed so grave, the sun so strong and bright, and the mountains so vast and majestic, and all things so suggestive of God and Eternity, that it seemed blasphemy for a human being to be thinking so much of his money. Indeed, the sky and water and mountains, and even the trees, seemed to have eyes and to be looking straight down at him as he sat there in the sand counting his money, as if wondering what use it could all be to him.

But after a time I could see that a change was coming over my master. He grew grave and quiet, and moved about in a noiseless way, very unlike his old fashion of acting and talking. So, gradually, a change came over him until he was not at all as he had been. He left off counting his money for days at a time, and when he did count it, it was in a listless manner, just the reverse of his old-time fashion. He would even go away and leave the yellow heap on the sand unwatched, and uncared for, while he sat looking at the shadow of the mountain in the water, or lay stretched at full length on his back, a stone for his pillow, his hands crossed on his breast and his eyes gazing fixedly up at the heavens. You may imagine that I was very much puzzled at all this, and wondered what it all meant, for I could see that something was preying on his mind, and that a great change was coming over him.

One day he came, and packing the gold within me, put the head in with the greatest care; and when it was done he stood looking at me a moment and then said, "I think I

will never open you again," and he said it in such a sad
sort of a way that I was vastly puzzled. Indeed, I did not
believe him, but fancied that he was not feeling over-well,
and was low spirited like because of it, and that when he
came to himself he would come around and count what
was in me as happily as ever. But a greater surprise was
in store for me; for when he went to the camp, which was
in this very place you have here to-night, he did not take
me with him, but left me there alone on the beach. I did
not think much of it at first, for I said to myself, he will be
back by and by and carry me in with him to the camp as
he always does; but the minutes passed and kept passing
and still he did not come, and at last I gave him up and
decided that I must pass the night where I was, alone.
Well, as you can fancy, I felt very strangely in view of it,
and rather nervously, too, for I had never spent a night
alone by myself since my master owned me, nor outside a
house or tent either, for that matter; so as I have said I
felt a little nervous about it. But I made up my mind to
be as brave as I might and put as good a face on the matter as I could. But it was a very strange experience I had
that night, and one I have never forgotten. You see it was
the first night I ever spent alone in the wilderness, and it
made an impression on me I shall never forget, and although I have passed many nights since alone in this solitary spot, yet never has there been one to me like that first
one. The shadows of the mountains were so dark and
heavy that they appeared to burden the lake as with a ponderous bulk, and the very water that reflected their vast

sides seemed oppressed by their presence. The sky was blue-black; a grave and sombre sky it was. In it only a few stars shone, and those with shortened beams. The silence was like an atmosphere. It rested upon the mountains, brooded on the water, and slept amid the shadows of the still trees. And yet, dark as it was, I felt that in it was an eye, and, silent as it was, I felt that out of it would come a voice — an Eye that looked in steady but unwrathful condemnation upon me, and a Voice that spoke in solemn judgment, although with inaudible tones.

It seemed as if the sin of my master was being charged upon me, and that the whole universe was visiting upon me its contempt. O ! sir, I saw strange sights that night, and heard sounds that made me shrink within my hoops in fear. Bands of angels all robed in white, and flying on white wings, came and stood poised in the air above me, and pointed at me with their white hands, and as they gazed, their sweet faces dilated with horror. Devils, too, great black beings and shapes that were shapeless, whose faces were those of hell, and eyes bloodshot with torture, came, and poising above me, would point with their black fingers insultingly downward, and laugh with horrid mirth; then sai. away until their black wings faded in the farther gloom. And I heard moans in the air as of a woman moaning for bread ; and prayers as of a dying child, dying with a dread at her heart for some one whose sin lay on her soul ; and sounds as of many noises mixed in one: prayers and curses, oaths and snatches of hymns. And out of the stillness of the outward space — the stillness of the far-off and the far-

up and the beyond, I seemed to hear a great voice contin-
ually saying; "THE MAN THAT LOVETH MONEY OVERMUCH
IS DOOMED. THE MAN THAT LOVETH MONEY OVERMUCH IS
DOOMED."

"At last the sun rose, and right glad was I to see it, but
little did I dream when I saw it come up over the mountain
yonder, what would happen before it rose again. For of all
days in my life that was the most eventful, and I do not
expect you to believe me when I tell you what took place
in it; but I shall tell you the truth, nevertheless, and of
things just as they happened.

About ten o'clock in the morning my master came to the
point where I was, and his face was as I had never seen it
before. It was the face of a man who had suffered much,
and was suffering. His hair lay matted on his damp forehead; his eyes were blood-shot; his teeth set, and his mouth
white at the corners, while his hands were clinched as the
hands of one in a spasm. He came and stood directly over
me, and in a voice hard and strained said: —

"For thee, thou cursed gold, I have wasted my life and
ruined my soul."

This he said many times. Then he walked away and
stood and talked to himself; and I heard him say: "He
said, 'Unless you repent, you shall die on a dark night, in a
lonely spot, with no one nigh.'" And he kept repeating,
"On a dark night, in a lonely spot, with no one nigh." And
then he would look around him at the trees and the mountains and the solitary shores.

After a while he began to walk up and down the point,

and wring his hands and smite them on his breast, and cry
out: "Oh! if I COULD do it! Oh! if I COULD do it! Perhaps there would be hope for me: perhaps there would be
hope for ME!" And he would emphasize the ME in such a
plaintive, pitiful tone as was never done, I think, by man
before. Once he got down on his knees, and clasped his
hands together, and I wondered what he was going to do,
for I had never seen a man in that position before, and it
looked so queer; but in an instant he leaped to his feet and
cried: "NO, NO! It is no use. Forgiveness is not for me:
forgiveness is not for me."

And so the day passed, and a fine day it-was, too, for
though my master was in such trouble, and the grip of a
dire distress was on him, yet the sun took no note of it,
but shone as brightly in the sky, and the trees swung as
merrily to and fro as the breeze blew through them, and
the ripples ran laughing along the curved beach as if there
were never such a thing as human trouble in the world.

Toward night, just before the sun went down, my master
came, and taking my head out, stood for a while looking at
the gold within me; then he said slowly to himself: "Perhaps I may have strength to do it: perhaps I may have
strength to do it." And then he sat down on the sand and
gazed far off, as one whose thoughts are not in his eyes.
And there in the one spot, without moving, he sat, while
the sun went down, the shadows of evening settled slowly
and darkly on shore and lake and mountain range, until at
last night like a mantle lay darkly on the world. There, in
the stillness, my master sat, his face hidden by the gloom,

thinking — I knew not what. At last he moved; and, as if too weak to rise, crawled along on the sand to my side, and steadying himself on his knees, he placed his hands together, and lifting his face to the dark blue heaven above, found speech, and began to talk to One I could not see : —

"O Thou, who art the Lord of this great world; whose eyes see every creature thou hast made; and whose ear is open to their cry, see me to-night, and hear my prayer. Bound have I been, and bound I am, to sin. My soul, pursued by evil, knows not where to flee. My life has been a hell, and out of hell I seek deliverance here and now. Come to my aid or I am lost! Save me in mercy or I am doomed! Give thou me strength, for I am weak, and may not do what I would do, without thy aid. Out of this stillness speak to me. Here where no man may hear, hear thou my cry. Thou Lord of heavenly mercy, lend me thine aid!"

He paused, and rising to his feet, lifted me, and started toward the bushes where he kept his boat, and placing me in it shoved out upon the lake, and paddled toward the center, saying slowly and solemnly to himself: "Lend me thine aid, O Lord! Lend me thine aid!" At last we reached the center of the lake, and having checked the boat, he sat for a moment without saying a word; then lifting his face upward he said in a low, sweet voice: "Dear Lord, thou hast given of thy strength. I thank thee," — then raised me in his arms and —— "

A rattle and a crash, as of pieces of wood falling suddenly in a heap, and my eyes came open with a snap. My fire had smouldered down, and a thin column of blue smoke was rising, unattended by flame, in a wavy spiral through the air. The moon had found an opening in the pines overhead, and was pouring its white beams upon the whiter ashes. The keg I had picked from the lake, heated by the fire, had shrunken in its staves until the rusty iron bands afforded them no support; and shaken by the slight jar of a crumbling brand, or falling pine-cone, perhaps, had tumbled inward and lay in a confused heap. I rubbed my eyes, stretched out my chilled legs, and said to myself: "What a queer dream! I really thought that keg was talking to me. If it had kept on much longer it would have persuaded me that the old fellow, its master, or his ghost, is actually on this lake now. Egad! I think it would start even my pulse a little to see a man in a boat on this lake to-night."

Half laughing to myself at the silly suggestion that my fancy had made, I rose to my feet, stretched myself, yawned, and stepping down to the edge of the water looked off upon the lake. I am not ashamed to say that I started, and the blood chilled a little in my veins at what I saw. There, off the point, *within twenty feet of where I found the keg, was a boat and a man sitting in it—motionless as if carved from the air!*

CHAPTER V

" Nature's Nobleman." — *Thompson.*

WELL, I will admit that I was surprised, greatly surprised, for I knew that there was not a living being
on that lake at sunset—nor had there been for days, or
years for that matter : for there is no place in all the world,
save cities, where man can go and stay even a night and
not leave marks of his presence, and on all this lake shore
there was not a trace of any human being. Yet in spite of
all this evidence forbidding the supposition, there sat a
man, paddle in hand, in a boat, not forty rods from where I
stood. I knew that I was well concealed from view, for
the shadows in which I stood was as dark as the matted
branches of the rich cedars that lined the lake-shore and
projected outward over the water, could make it; and so I
kept my station without moving an inch, and watched.

For a full minute the boat lay on the level water as if it
had grown up out of it, and was a part of the lake itself,
so steadfastly did it hold its place; and I could well guess
what was passing in the mind of him whose form was as
motionless as the boat, but whose eyes I knew were searching every inch of the shore line, and whose thoughts were
as busy as his eyes. He had evidently come round the

point as little expecting the presence of man as I had an-
ticipated his, and some flitting spark, or the gleam of some
coal, — or likelier yet the thin filament of blue smoke rising
from the smouldering and ash-covered embers, —had caught
his eye and brought his boat to a stand as quickly as a reversed paddle could do it. In a moment the boat began to
move; so slowly, so easily, so steadily, that the eye could
scarcely detect the movement. I laughed silently to myself to see the familiar motion of ambushing a camp from
the water side, done so skilfully. For whoever he was, or
whatever his errand, the man in that boat knew how to
handle a paddle as only a few ever learn the art, — to perfection. His body never moved. The bent posture of it
never changed. His head kept its fixed position. The
arms worked from the shoulder-sockets, and were lifted
with a movement so slow and gradual that the eye that
could measure their extension and return must needs be
keen of sight, nor lose its observation by a wink. The boat
did not start — it simply ceased to stand still; but that
fraction of an instant at which it ceased to stand still and
began to move, no human eye could tell. Slowly, slowly,
so slowly that at times I doubted if it did move at all, the
boat came floating on. For ten minutes had it been moving, and yet it had barely covered as many rods. Then the
motion of the arms died out in the air, and the boat again
stood still. But the body of the boatman still kept its fixed
position, and the arms still hung suspended in the atmosphere, where they were when the will of the paddler had
checked them.

"By Jove !" I said to myself, "that man acts as if he wants to murder some one, or fears some one will murder him : but he understands how to do a job like the one he is at, and I would like to know how long it has taken him to learn that use of the paddle."

A few minutes passed, then the arms began to rise and fall again, and the boat stole slowly into motion. Again ten rods were covered; again the little boat came to a pause. It was now barely fifty yards away, and the full moon made it an easy matter to study quite closely both the boat and boatman. The boat was of the common build, sharp at either end, low-sided and light. In the bow was a pack-basket, while a hound lay crouched in the middle. A rifle was resting across the paddler's knees. Of his face I could discern little, because the moon was at his back. In a moment he laid the paddle softly across the boat; lifted his rifle as noiselessly from his knees, and rose slowly to his feet. All this had been done as only a skilled boatman and woodman could do it : not a jerk nor awkward motion in the process, but coolly, deliberately, and without the least suggestion of a sound.

"Few men could have lifted themselves from their seat in a boat like that in the style he has done it," I said to myself, "and few dogs would lie as that dog lies, in a boat manœuvred as that has been for the past twenty minutes, without stirring nose or foot. I wonder he has not scented me."

That very instant, even as the thought was passing in my mind, my ear caught the sound of the lowest possible whine from the hound; but his body never stirred, and his nose, active as it must have been, never lifted itself a hand's width from its resting place on the bottom of the boat.

"Hollo, the camp there!" said the man in the boat suddenly. "Be ye sleeping or dead, man or ghost, whom I find in this lonely spot to-night?"

"Not dead, nor asleep," said I, speaking from the dense gloom of the overhanging cedar; "but wide awake and watchful as it behooves a man to be, in a place like this, with a man ambushing his camp in the dead of night. Put down your rifle and come into camp if you want to. The sound of a human voice coming out of your throat makes me feel friendly, whoever you are. Come in, and I will stir up the fire and we can see how we like each other's looks."

So saying, I stepped back to where my wood was piled, and proceeded to thrust a dozen pitchy knots and a huge roll of white birch-bark into the embers. The few remaining coals beneath the ashes caught eagerly at the pitch thus thrust against them, and after an instant's sputtering the inflammable material leaped suddenly into a roaring flame. As the blaze shot upward, I rose from my knees on which I had dropped to give the embers an encouraging puff, and the man, leaning on his paddle-staff, with the hound crouched at his feet, stood before me.

For a moment we stood and looked at each other, as two men might, meeting for the first time, at such an hour, in such a place, — looked each other over thoroughly, from head to foot, and then satisfied, at least on my part, I said: —

"Old man, you are welcome."

"Thank ye; thank ye," replied my visitor. "I shouldn't have dropped in upon ye in this onseemly way, and at sech an onseemly hour, but the line of yer smoke took me onawares like as I turned the pint yender, for I didn't expect to find a human bein' on these shores, and I half doubted if a mortal man was here, till my hound got yer scent in his nose and signalled me that flesh and blood was nigh. And so I ax yer pardin for comin' in on ye as I did, more like a thief than an honest man; but I have memories of this spot that made me think strange things, and fear that all was not right. Young man, what may yer name be?"

"I am called, when at home, Henry Herbert," I said, "but you can split it in the middle if it would fit your mouth better in that way, and take it half at a time, and call me Henry or Herbert as you please; for I know one about as well as I do the other, and answer to either pretty readily; and since you are getting on in years, and are old enough to be my father, with a good liberal margin at that, you had better take the first half of it; and so, if you please, you may call me Henry for short."

"Well, Henry," said the old man, and there came a beaming look of good nature into his eyes as he spoke, with the least twinkle of humor playing in and penetrating the benevolence of it, "I *am* gittin pritty well on in years, and ye don't seem much more than a youngster to me, although ye have managed to git a pritty good growth in the time ye have been at it; and perhaps the comin' and

goin' of years has put some things inside my head that boys
can't be expected to git, while they have been whitenin'
the outside of it; so, mayhaps, it is well enough that I
should call ye by yer Christian name, as if I was yer
own father; although I have never had a boy of my own,
or a wife or home either, for that matter; onless ye can call
:hese woods a home; for I have seen sixty year come and
go sence I came into them, and the Lord has cared for me
in summer's heat and winter's cold through them all, — so
well that I haven't had a wish for other company than I
have found with the animils and things He has made, or for
any other home than He has builded for me by His own
hands." And the old man paused a moment, and looked
lovingly down at the hound which lay stretched at his feet,
with his muzzle resting on his paws, as if, in the dog, I
could see one of the companions which had supplied with
affection a heart that had missed the love of wife and children.

"Yis," he continued, "the woods have been a home for
me for the number of years that measure the life of mortal
man, and there is leetle in them I haven't seen, and few are
the noises that natur' makes that my ears haven't heerd;
and I know all their paths and their ways as well as a man
in the settlements knows his door-yard. But that ain't
neither here nor there," — as if he was conscious of having
fallen into a musing mood, and would check himself —
"that's neither here nor there," he continued, "and I am
glad to have run agin ye here to-night, although the seem-
in' of things was agin me. For I did ambush yer camp as

a thief of a half-breed might; but I was taken onawares by yer camp smoke, and startled, as ye would well understand to be reasonable in me, did ye know what I know of this spot, and the strange goin's on that has been here years agone, as I know them; and it seems queer to me to find a livin' bein' to-night, where I thought there was only a dead man's grave. But I am glad to have run agin ye, Henry Herbert, for I have heerd of ye many times in the last ten years, as one who loved the woods and the way men live in them, and knowed the proper use of a rifle, and how to handle the paddle as some born to the use of it never larn it; and I have heerd that yer eye was keen and finger sure, as a hunter's should be, and that ye let no buck run off with yer lead, but dropped him dead in his tracks where he stood — which is marciful and decent in a man who handles a rifle. And I have heerd, mor'over, that ye loved to be alone, and to find things out that natur' never tells to a company; and that ye boated up and down through the woods all by yerself, sleepin' where night overtook ye like an honest man, and I know'd that I should some day cross yer trail and jine ye; but I leetle thought to run agin' ye here to-night, for I'd no idee that mortal man know'd this lake, save me and him whose body I buried here eleven years gone this fall." And the old man paused, seated himself on the butt of a log, and gazed with a solemn look in his face into the fire.

I did not feel quite like breaking in on his meditations, whatever they might be; and so I stood and looked at him. In a few moments he began : —

"I ax yer pardin if it be axin' too much of ye, but I've fetched my boat through fifty miles to-day, and it's nigh on twenty hours senco I've tasted food: not but that I could have had enough — for I run agin a buck on Salmon Lake this arternoon jest as tho sun was goin' down, that was big enough to keep a Dutch parson in venison for a week, and that sizes him pritty big, as ye know, if yo over camped with one of 'em" — and tho old man opened his mouth and laughed a peculiar, good-natured laugh, that showed more on the face than it gave forth noise — "but I was in a hurry to git through here and couldn't stop to dry him, and I never settle lead into any cretur I can't use for meat, onless it be a fur-bearin' animil or a wicked panther. So I jest paddled up to him ontil I could flirt some water onto his shoulders, and I landed about two quarts on his back, and the way the cretur jumped sot my eyes swimmin'." And here the old man laughed again in his own peculiar fashion. "But, as I was sayin', I haven't tasted food sence the last day dawn, and feel sort of empty like; and somehow latterly the night mists seem to git into me more'n they used to when I was younger, for age thins the blood, and cools it, too, for that matter; an' if ye feel like botherin' yerself that much ye may cook me a pot of tea and give me a cold cake, if one be lyin' round; and if yo happen to have a bit of buck ye fear won't keep till mornin' I guess I could keep it for ye in a spot where I've put a good deal of that kind of meat in the last sixty year;" and the old man laughed again, in his hearty, noiseless manner, as if greatly pleased at his own homely and innocent wit.

"Old man," said I, "you just sit on that log a few minutes, and I will give you a drink of tea that will warm your
blood as if forty years had been taken from your record;
and as for cold cakes, I don't keep that article, but here is
some batter"—and I uncovered a pan standing a little
back from the fire—"that will make cakes so light that
you will have to hold them down with your fork; and lork
at that"—and I swung out of my birch bark cupboard a
roll of tenderloin steak twelve or fourteen inches long—
"I'll spit that for you so that it will dissolve in your mouth,
and go down your throat like honey; and you and I will
have a feast that will make us feel as full as a doe in the
lily-pads,—for I know whom I have for my guest to-night
as well as if you had told me your name, and right glad am
I to have the best shot that ever drew bead, and the best
boatman that ever feathered a paddle, and as honest a guide
as ever drew breath, in my camp, and there's my hand, and
you are welcome to all I have in my pack, and to all I can
do for you, John Norton"—and I stretched my hand out
to the old man, who met its palm with his own in a hearty,
hunter-like grip.

"Well, well," laughed the old man, as he re-seated himself on the log, while I bestirred myself with preparations
for the meal, "I sorter suspicioned that ye knowed who I
was, but I didn't know for sartin; for ye carry a mighty
steady face, and ye didn't let on with yer eyes what ye was
thinkin' about, as most youngsters do; but I take yer welcome in the same way ye give it, and if old John Norton
can do anything to make yer stay in the woods more pleas-

ant-like to ye, or larn ye any trick of beast or bird, or tell ye anything of natur's ways that ye haven't larnt as yit— ye may depend on it, young man, that he will larn it to ye;" —and so saying he relapsed into silence, but watched me steadily as 1 kept on with my work.

In a few minutes the bark that served for a table was put in front of him, with the plates and cups, the pepper, salt, sugar, and such other luxuries as my pack afforded, and I poured the old man a cup of the best that ever came from Formosa, while I kept on turning the cakes and the steak.

" Well, now, that's the best tea I ever tasted, for sartin," said the old man, as he sipped the stimulating beverage — " it's as smooth as spring water, and goes down a man's throat as easy as an otter goes into a crick. I never tasted drink that the Lord hadn't made, for sixty year of my life, but latterly, 'specially at night, or when over-tired, it does seem to me that a few leaves of tea, judiciously steeped as ye have done it, sort of strengthens the water and makes a kind of improvement on the Lord's own work, if it be right for a mortal to say so; leastwise," he added, as he took a deeper quaff, " this is mighty pleasant warmin' to the ribs, and sort of makes a man feel inhabited-like inside, and not empty as a shanty with nobody in it;" and the look of placid contentment that came to the old man's face was a picture to see.

By this time, the meal was ready, and we sat down on either side of the bark table, in the glow of the fire-light, to eat.

" Henry," said the old man, as he drew his hunting knife

through the tenderloin roll, and marked the ruddy juices
that oozed out, and the puff of odorous steam which ascended as the blade clove it, "this meat is cooked hunter-
like, and sort of encourages the teeth to git into the center
of it. I have often noted that cookin' was a kind of gift,
and couldn't be larnt out of books no more than holdin' a
rifle or featherin' a paddle properly can be larnt in the settlements. The Lord gives one man one set of gifts and
another another, and cookin' and huntin' are things of
natur', and not of readin', and they don't often go all of
them to one man, although in yer case, Henry, the Lord has
been very marciful and gracious-like in his treatment of ye,
— for I have heerd ye are a great scholar, and love the
knowledge that the schools give ; and I have many things
I want to ax ye of — things I have heerd, but that seem
onreasonable to me ; but, depend on it, Henry, the best gift
the Lord has given ye is yer love of natur' and the things
that go with it — a keen eye, a quick finger, a strong back,
and a conscience that can meet him in the solitude of these
waters and hills and not be afeared; for a wicked man can't
bear the presence of the Maker of those solitudes, as I have
good reason to know"—and here the old man paused a
moment and gazed steadily into the fire — "yis," he resumed, "it is wonderful that he should have gin ye the love
of books and of natur' both, but I dare to say, he has his
favorites, as I have often noted mothers have among their
children, and I can see jest how it may be with him; but
how he came to give ye the gift of cookin' with all the
other ones, is wonderful, and I can't understand it, but" —

A long, loud cry, beginning with a thin whine and swelling up into a terrific yell, arose into the still air, from the other side of the lake, held possession of the atmosphere for a full minute, then died away in successive echoes, leaving the stillness deeper than before the terrible sound disturbed it and broke suddenly in upon the old man's speech. For a full minute he sat motionless, with his fork half way between the plate and his mouth, and his mouth half opened to receive it, and not till the last mimic imitation of the frightful scream had died away along the hills that bordered the head of the lake, did a muscle of his figure move.

"Yis, I know the varmint, and an ugly one he is, too. I heerd him in the balsam thickets as I come down the inlet, and he trailed me for a full mile, as they will when hungry; but the cretur' was too cowardly to show himself in the mash where the moon would tech him, for a panther has a keen nose for the smell of powder, and he scented the muzzle of my rifle and knowed I had a wepon. I hoped he would show himself a minit, or that the swish of the mash grass as he tramped through it would make a line for me, for I thought I knowed his whine, and I said to myself, if he gives me half a chance I'll let light into him, and sort of square accounts with the cretur that's been some time standin' — but he is a cowardly chap and " —

Again the terrible scream leaped into the air, — this time wild and savagely fierce at the start, and so harsh that it seemed to tear the silence into shreds in very fury; and the last hoarse aspiration of it was so terrible in its wrathful strength that the trees, water and air seemed to shrink back and shiver in terror at its injection into the peaceful atmosphere.

"Aye, aye! I know ye now," continued the old man, "and a truer hound than ye murdered for me eleven year ago, come next month, never nosed a track or guarded a hunter's camp. Ye can yell till ye are hoarse, but if the Lord spares this old body, and my eyes don't get dim for another mouth, I'll look ye up some day and give ye the contents of a grooved barrel that carries a half-ounce bullet, and chambers eighty grains of powder, and ye shall larn the difference between a hunter used to the sights and a poor hound that has nothin' but his teeth and his courage to fight ye with. I guess," continued the old man, as he rose to his feet, "I had better bring up my pack and my rifle, for I noted by the direction the echoes took that the brute yender is trailin' down the lake, and he may cross the outlet at the foot and scout up this side, for his cry shows he is hungry, and he has seen our fire and may think that he can play his capers on us; but he will find the two liveliest morsels he ever tried to put his teeth into, the varmint!" and laughing to himself at his own thought he started for the beach.

"Henry," said he, as he stood leaning over the end of his boat, "come here and we will hist this boat into camp. I dare say I am foolish, but somehow I sorter feel that this lake shore isn't quite the spot to leave an honest man's boat on. I can remember when to have done it would have cost a man his boat and scalp, too, onless the Lord marcifuly kept his eyes open by dreams."

In a moment the boat was placed where the old man wished it, and setting his back against its side for a support, he unlaced his moccasins, and thrust his smoking feet out toward the fire. Taking a pipe from my pocket, I filled it with a choice brand of tobacco I had in my pouch, and proffered it to him.

"Thank ye, thank ye, Henry," said he, as he made a motion of rejection of the offer with his hand, "I thank ye for the kindness yo mean in yer heart, but if it be all the same to ye I won't take it. I know it is a comfort to ye, and I am glad to see yo enjoy it, but I have never used the weed; not for the reason that I had a conscience in the matter, but because the Lord gave me a nose like a hound's, and better too, I dare say, for I doubt if a hound knows the sweetness of things, or can take pleasure from the scent that goes into his nostrils. But he has been more marciful to man — as it was proper he should be — and gin him the power to know good and evil in the air; and smellin' has always been one of my gifts, and I couldn't make ye understand, I dare say, the pleasure I've had in the right exercise of it. For ye know that natur' is no more bright to the eye than it is sweet to the nose; and I've never found a root or shrub or leaf that hadn't its own scent. Even the dry moss on the rocks, dead and juiceless as it seems, has a smell to it, and as for the 'arth I love to put my nose into the fresh sile, as a city woman loves the nozzle of her smellin'-bottle. Many and many a time when alone here in the woods have I taken my boat and gone up into the inlet when the wild roses was in blossom, or down

into some bay where the white lily cups was all open, and
sot in my boat and smelt them by the hour, and wondered
if heaven smelt so.   Yis, I have been sartinly gifted in my
nose, for I've always noted that I smelt things that the
men and women I was guidin' didn't, and found things in
the air that they never suspicioned of, and I feered that
smokin' might take away my gift, and that if I got the
strong smell of tobacco in my nose once I should never
scent any other smell that was lesser and finer than it.—
So I have never used the weed, bein' sort of naterally
afeerd of it; but what is medicine for one man may be
pisen for another, as I have noted in animils, for the bark
that fattens the beaver will kill the rat; and so ye must
take no offence at what I've said, but smoke as much as
ye feel moved to, and I will scent the edges of the smell as
it comes over my side of the fire, and so we'll sort of jine
works — as they say in the settlements — ye do the smokin' and I'll do the smellin', and I think I've got the lightest end of the stick at that."   And the old man laughed in
every line of his time-wrinkled fare, at the smartness of
his saying.

CHAPTER VI.

THE OLD TRAPPER'S AMBUSH.

"I am out of humanity's reach;
I must finish my journey alone,
Never hear the sweet music of speech —
I start at the sound of my own." — *Cowper.*

SO we sat on either side of the fire, filled with that contentment which pervades the mind when the body has eaten its fill of hearty food, and the process of digestion is going forward under the conditions of perfect health and agreeable surroundings. For several minutes we sat in silence, too physically happy on my part to think; and the old trapper seemed to have undergone a change of mood, for the play of humor had left his features, and his countenance had settled into a solemn repose.

"I was thinkin'," he said at length — "I was thinkin' of things that happened here long years ago, when I fust come through this lake. I can tell ye, Henry, strange doin's have been done here, and my thoughts have been on the back trail for several days now, and I had a feelin' come to me that I oughter visit this lake, and sorter see how things looked; for there's a grave over there on the pint, that I made with my own hands, and I buried the body of a man in it that had no mourner at his funeral, onless me and my hound, there, might be counted as sech. And I thought I

would come through here and see if the grave wanted
mendin', although I dare say it lies quiet enough, and ondistarbed, for I built it up in good shape, and sodded it
over as the man gave me word to do;—not that he ordered
it, but because I knowed it was his wish, for he said the
day he died : 'I wish when I am gone my grave might be
sodded as they sod them down on the coast where I was
born.' And I said to him, 'Don't worry on that score, for I
will make it as ye tell me, so far as me and the hound can
do it;' and then he told me how he wanted it done, and I
will say he talked rational-like from the way he looked at
it, and I did it jest as he told me, as the hound there would
bear witness if he could speak; and somehow, latterly I
got the feelin' into me that I oughter come through here,
and sort of see to it, and that's the reason that I am here,
although sence meetin' you I have wondered if I warnt
brought here to meet the livin' and not the dead ; for the
Lord don't always tell what he starts us on a journey for,
or what we are to find at the other end of it, for the tar-
mination of things is marcifully hidden from the beginnin',
and the two ends of a trail never look alike."

While the Old Trapper had been thus moralizing, he had
risen to his feet, and turning round with his back to the
fire he stretched a hand out toward the lake, saying:—

"It is not often, Henry, that ye see so bright a moon as
that, even here in the woods where the air is as pure as the
Lord can make it; and it calls up memories. It is eleven
year this very night that me and the hound slept here, and
a solemn night it was, too, for the man had died at sunset,

and his body lay right there where the moon whitens the 'arth by that dead root.—God of heaven, Henry, what is that!"

The old man's startled ejaculation brought me to my feet as if the panther were on me, and glancing at the spot he had indicated by his looks and gesture, as the exclamation tore out of his mouth, I beheld only the scattered portions of the KEG. Not knowing what to make of the old man's excited action, I said:—

"That? that is only a keg I picked up in the lake this evening."

For a full minute the Old Trapper stood gazing steadfastly at it, and then he stepped to the spot where the remnants of the keg lay, and picking up a stave he contemplated it a minute or two in grave and solemn silence, and then returning to the fire he re-seated himself on the log, and still holding the piece of wood in his hand, said:—

"The ways of the Lord is mysterious, and his orderin's past findin' out; and some of his creturs are born for good and some for evil, and how he ontangles the strands in the end is beyend our knowin'. But perhaps in the long run, he brings the wrong to the right, and so makes the evil in the world to praise him. Ah me! ah me! what a load the man carried while off the trail, like a blind moose walkin' in a circle; but before he tired I reckon he struck the blazed line that led him to the Great Clearin'. Leastwise, it looked so." And the old man paused, gazing fixedly at the bit of the keg that he held in his hand. In a moment he resumed: "I have a mind, Henry, to tell ye the story of

the man who owned that keg once, as far as I know it, and
onless ye feel sleepy-like I will tell ye what happened here
years ago, and what I know of the man whose body lies
buried there on yender pint — for a strange tale it is, and a
true one, and the teachin's of it is solemn."

I was thoroughly awake, by this time, and urged the old
man to proceed. After a moment's silence, he began : —

" Well, it's now eleven years gone, that I was drawin' a
trail through the woods from east to west, and I did a good
deal of my boatin' in the night, for the moon was full, and
I always had a sort of hankerin' for the night work ever
sence I slept on the boughs; for natur' looks one way in
the day-time, and another way in the night-time, and no
one knows how sweet she can be to the nose, and how
pleasant to the ears, and how han'some to the eyes, onless
he has seen her face, and heerd her voices, and smelt her
sweet smells, in the night season. I've always noted
that those who knowed natur' only by day-light, knowed
only half her ways, and less than half, too, for that matter.
For in the evenin' she gits familiar and confidential-like
with one, and talks to him of herself and her ways as
she never does in the day-time. For natur' has a great
many secrets, and she's timid as a young faan, and ye've
got to creep into thickets, and lay yer boat up under the
banks of streams, and lie down in the mash grass when all
is dark and still, if ye want to hear her whisper to ye of
her innermost feelin's. The Lord only knows how many
times I have ambushed her in her hidin' places as a Huron
would a camp, and caught her at her pranks. Ah, Henry,

ye have no idee how many things I have larnt of her in the night-time, or how frisky and solemn, both, natur' can be betwixt the settin' and risin' of the sun.

Well, as I was sayin', I'd been over to the east boundaries of the woods, nigh on to the Horricon waters, where I did a good deal of my early scoutin', to sorter see how the brooks and wood-ways looked agin, but it was a sorry time I had on it, for the settlers had pushed in, and their mills was on every stream, and their painted housen stood under the very trees where I used to cook my venison with no sights or sounds around save those that natur' herself made. And ye can well believe, Henry, that I was glad to git away from what I went to see and be back here where my ears couldn't hear the sound of axes and the fallin' of trees — yis, I was mighty glad to git back where things was quiet and peaceful-like, and the cruelties and devilments of men that have no respect for things the Lord has made hadn't come to distarb the habits of natur'.

Well, as I was sayin', it was eleven years back, and in this very month, and well on in the night, that I came down the inlet yender into this lake. And the moon was nigh on to her full, and everything looked solemn and white jest as they do to us now, and the Lord knows I leetle thought to meet mortal man in these solitudes when I run agin what I am to tell ye of.

I was paddlin' down this side of the lake, keepin' well under the shore, list'nin' and thinkin', and happy in my heart as a rat in the water, when I heerd the strangest sounds I ever heerd come out of bird or beast. It was a

kind of murmurin' noise that run out into the stillness an'
sorter capered round a minit, an' then run back where it
started from. Ye better believe, Henry, I sot and listened
as a man listens scoutin' alone in the night time in these
woods, when he gits a sound in his ears that he can't make
out. Yis, I sot and listened ontil I was nothin' but ears,
and the very stillness beat on the narves of my head as I
have heerd the roll of the waves on the lakes beat on the
beach. But for the life of me I couldn't make it sound
nateral, nor tell what animil it belonged to, and it took the
conceit out o' me to larn that there was a cretur in the
woods whose mouth didn't tell me its name and habits.

Arter a while I got the true direction of it, for a sound
goes as straight from its startin' to the ear as a bee from a
wind-fall or burnt clearin' goes to its hole in the beech,
and I said to myself as I lifted my rifle to my knee, that I
would ambush the cretur and find out what mouth had a
language in it that old John Norton couldn't tell the meanin' of. So I laid my boat up in the direction of the sound
as if my life depended on the proper use of the paddle. I
hadn't gone more than ten rods afore the noise stopped,
but I'd fixed it in the line of a dead Norway and I knowed
I could put my boat inside of fifty feet of where the cretur
lay. I never acted more sarcumspectly nor fetched an ambushment more easy and sartin', and in a shorter time than
it takes me to tell ye I had my boat under the pint of that
bank there within ten feet of the shrubs, with my finger
on the trigger of a rifle that goes easy in an onsartin ambushment. There I sot a full minit knowin' I was inside

of fifty feet of the cretur, with my eyes and ears as open as they should be in such sarcumstances. Then I heerd a a kind of crawlin' sound as if the brute or reptile was trailin' himself along the sand; and I knowed if the wiggle of a bush would give me the line I could open a hole through him. It might have been ten feet that the cretur crawled and than he stopped, but I had fixed him well in mind and felt sartin I could drive the lead where it ought to go. I had got the breech of my rifle half way to my face, and my cheek was settling to the stock, when the cretur opened his mouth, and by the Lord of Marcy, Henry, *I diskivered I had ambushed no animil at all, but a mortal man !* "

Long before the Old Trapper had got to this point of his narrative I had become profoundly interested in his recital. For he told the story as men born to the woods tell their tales of personal adventure — with a natural eloquence of tone, feature and gesture which only those have whose experiences have been narrow but intense, and who speak from the simple earnestness of untutored and therefore unfettered power. His narrative had been told from the beginning in two languages; one verbal and the other pantomimic, and he had carried me along with his story as it advanced as much by that which addressed the eye as by that which entered the ear. He had gathered warmth and energy of expression as he had gone on, until I found myself moving in sympathy with the visible action of his features, body and hands; and when he reached the climax of his discovery, I shared to the full in the excitement of his pantomimic action, and doubt if the shock of surprise

which he had experienced eleven years before in his boat
under the bank, on the point which lay in the moonlight full
in view, was much greater at the startling discovery he had
made, than was mine. So we sat looking full at eacl other
across the camp-fire, our faces tense with mutual excitement, as if we were actual sharers in the astonishing discovery.

" Yis, Henry, a *man* was there, a man on that pint where
I expected to find only an animil; and his words, as they
came out of his mouth into the still air of the night, strong
and clear as a man in the rapids calling for help, were words
of prayer. I've been, Henry, in many ambushments in the
seventy years I've lived, and I've been in peril from inimies
behind and afore; and more than once have I met the rage
of man and beast and been brought face to face with death
onexpectedly; but never since my eyes knowed the sights,
so my life depended on the proper use of my faculties, was
I ever so taken onawares or onbalanced as I was under the
bushes, there on yender pint eleven years gone, when I
heerd the voice of that man I had mistook for an animil,
break out in prayer. It was of the Lord's own marcy,
Henry, that I was not a murderer of my kind, for my finger
was on the trigger as I told ye, and my eye was getting onto
as trusty a barrel as man ever hefted, when He opened the
cretur's mouth with the sound of His own name. For a
minute the blood stopped in my heart, and my hair moved
in my scalp; and then I shook like a man with the chills,
ontil I drew from the guard of my rifle a finger that had
never quivered before, for fear I should explode the piece
and distarb the man in his worship.

I sot and heerd the man from beginnin' to end, and I larned, under the bushes that night, how hard-put a mortal may be by reason of his sin. For the man prayed for help as one calls to a comrade when his boat has gone down under him in the rapids, and he knows he must have help or die. I've been a prayin' man, Henry, as one should be who lives here in the woods where the Spirit of the Lord is everywhere and in all things; but I never prayed as that man prayed, and it larned me that what is prayin' to one man isn't prayin' to another, for the natur' of our wants settle the natur' of our prayin', and the habits of our life makes the trail to His marcy level or steep. And this man was climbin' a steep trail, and his soul was strugglin' on a hard carry, I tell ye; and the words of his cry came out of his mouth like the words of one who is lost onless somebody saves him. It's dreadful for a man to live in sech a way that he has to pray in that fashion; for we ought to live, Henry, so that it is cheerful-like to meet the Lord, and pleasant to hold converse with him.

So I sot in my boat ontil he was done, and then I hugged myself close in under the bushes, for I heerd him coming down toward the shore, for I knowed he must pass nigh where I lay in the ambushment. And he did, — aye, so nigh that I could have teched him with my paddle, and he had something heavy in his arms, for he staggered as he went by, as if put to it for strength. In a minit I heerd him shove a boat out of the bushes onto the water, and gettin' in, he pushed off onto the lake. He led straight off into the center of it, and I trailed him in his wake, for the moon

had got back of the mountain here to the right, and I was
determined to see what his queer goin's-on meant. Well,
when he had come nigh to the middle of the lake he laid
his paddle down, and lifted somethin' into the air, and
turned it up endwise and poured what was in it out. I
larnt, afterwards, what it was he lifted into the air, and
what it was he poured out of it, for he told me with his
own lips, and under sech sarcumstances, and at a time,
when mortals are apt to tell the truth; for he told me on
his death-day, when he lay dyin', and I never knowed a
man, white or redskin, that didn't talk straight as an honest
trapper countin' his pelts, when he had come to the last
blaze on the trail, and his feet stood on the edge of the
Great Clearin'.

CHAPTER VII.

"Sagacious hound." — *Virgil.*

WELL, I didn't make myself known to him that night, for I felt onsartin' as to the natur' of the man; and beside, I conceited I had no right to step in suddenly upon a man in the midst of his troubles, of whatever sort they might be; — for it always seemed to me that a mortal had a right to have ownership of his own grief, and to shet the door of it agin' the whole world, as much as a hunter in his own camp has a right to shet the door of his lodge. So I shied off farther into the lake and made camp for the night, or what there was left of it, on the island yender.

Well, in the mornin' I bestirred myself, and started my fire ostentatious-like on the side of the island next the p'int, and it made as much smoke as if it had been built by a boy from the settlements, or a college lad in his first trip to the woods, whose tongues run to words, and whose fires are all smoke, — for I wanted to call his eyes over my way and let him know that there was a human on the lake, and one that didn't seek concealment like a thievin' half-breed on an honest trapper's line; for a fire here in the woods is 'like the little keerds that the gals in the settlements, I have been told, send round to their friends to ax them to drink

tea with them, or jine in a jig: a gineral invite to come in
and feel at home. So I piled on the timber in a wasteful
way, and dropped on a bit of punk now and then, until,
'twixt the blaze and the smoke, I warrant a hunter's eye,
even in peace time, not to say a scout's when the redskins
are loose, could have seen it ten miles away. But the man
on the p'int never took the hint, and well enough he
mightn't, for I afterwards larned that he never saw either
blaze or smoke, for he was lyin' in his lodge back there in
the swale, with his thoughts far away, and his eyes on other
lights than such as the hands of man build.

Well, I cooked my breakfast for the hound there and me,
and while we were eatin' it we both kept thinkin' of the
man on the p'int; for a dog of breedin' knows what his
master's thinkin' about, and I could tell by the movements
of the hound's nose that the Lord was blowin' knowledge
to him from the other side of the lake, and that his
thoughts were not on the meat he was eatin', but over
there where him and me had fetched our ambushment the
night before. So arter we had finished eatin', and cleaned
things up, we stood around awhile and kept our eyes on the
p'int for some friendly sign, and both me and the hound felt
sort of disappinted-like, and the least bit oneasy in mind
as to what it all meant; for it seemed mighty queer that
the man should make no sign, not to say show himself,
when he must have knowed that we wanted to be neigh-
borly. So arter a while I put off toward the p'int, determined to see for ourselves what sort of a cretur' he was,
whose behavior had been so mighty onusual the night afore.

And I paddled over straight for the bushes where I knowed his boat was, and, sure enough, there it was plain in sight, where I felt it must be.

Then I went ashore and began to poke around, and the trail was plain enough for a man from the settlements to follow with his eyes half shet; for it led from the boat straight up the hill, under the pines and down into the swale back of it. So I pushed along, keeping an eye open for the shanty that I knowed must be nigh, and soon sot my eyes on it, sure enough; but it was no shanty at all, only a mis'rable old tent. I will confess, Henry, that it rather sot me agin the man, whoever he was, when I saw him livin' shet up in an onventilated canvass bag, like a rat in his hole in the spring freshets, when he might have housed himself in a bark lodge, dry and airy, with one side open as a house always should be, arter my way of thinkin'; for it's a great blessin' to be able to see the bigness of the world in which you are livin', and breathe the air as the Lord blows it to ye fresh and strong from the slope of mountains and the cool water level. And I conceit that whoever lives in a canvas shed, that's damp and swashy as last year's mash-grass, must be a very senseless or wicked bein', who don't know how handsome the world is, or else wants to hide himself from the eyes of man, and of the Lord, too, for that matter; for an honest man in the woods builds his lodge so he can see and be seen by day and by night, because he loves the sun and sky by day and the stars by night, and has no reason to hide himself or his traps from the Lord, or from his own kind, — which is open and noble-like, as I understand it. So when I seed the mis'-rable and nasty old tent, where the bark was plenty and willin' to be peeled, I felt suspicious of the man, and conceited that his morals wasn't what they should be. But in spite of my suspicionin' I detarmined to go on and nose the man out; and I said to myself: 'What right have ye, Old John Norton, to sit in jedgment on a fellow mortal, and before even ye have seed him. It may be the man is ignorant of the ways of the woods, and knows no better nor a babe how to care for himself; or perhaps he has been onfortunit and needs help more than jedgment.'

So I pushed ahead and laid my hand on the rag of a door and drew it aside in a frank sort of a way, and, by the Lord, Henry, the man lay dead before me! Leastwise I thought he was dead, for his eyes was half shet and half open, as a dead man's should be who has died onattended, and his face was as white as the moss on the rock when the moonshine is on it. Well, Henry, it was a solemn sight I can tell ye, and one that made me ashamed of my sus-picionin' of the man, and I trust the Lord forgave me the wicked thought I had had of a fellow mortal because he hadn't showed himself on the p'int, or called on me at my camp, when all the time the hand of death was heavy on him, and his legs were as streugthless as the reeds on the mash when the frost has smitten them.

Well, I stood at the door of the tent and I onkivered my head, as a mortal should in sech solemn sarcumstances, for I verily thought the man was dead; but the hound, there, knowed better, for the Lord has given a sense in sech things

"I ONKIVERED MY HEAD." PAGE 70.

to a dog that he withholds from the master, for the hound
arter standin' respectful-like behind me a minit, as if he
would n̶o̶t̶ be too forrud, or shame me by his better knowledge, pushed in to the side of the body and put his nose to
the cheek and then just turned his eyes up to me and
wagged his tail. Ah me, it's wonderful what larnin' the
Lord has given to the creturs he has made, and how often
they know more than their masters; and here was a dog
who knowed the livin' and the dead better than I did,
though the body was the body of a mortal, and not of his
kind.

Well, when I seed the hound move his tail, happy-like, I
knowed the man was not dead, however nigh he might be
on to it; and so I stepped in quick as powder ever burnt
and histed the man up, and took him in my arms, and carried him out of the mis'rable tent into the fresh, cool air,
and laid him down in the warm sunshine on the p'int, and
fell to chafin' his legs and his wrists, and pressin' on his
chest, and sprinklin' water in his face; and I blowed in his
nostrils, and did as a man should in such sarcumstances to
one of his kind.

But he was mighty weak, and all the strength he had was
in his eyes, for he couldn't move hand or foot, more than a
buck with a bullet through his spine the mornin' arter he
is shot. And it was a very solemn sight to see a full-grown
man lyin' on the sand with all natur' lively around him, and
he onable to move a leg, or lift a finger; and it showed
that the body of a mortal has no more life in it than a las⸀
year's beaver's hide, when his sperit has left it; and it was

awful-like to see a fellow bein' dead in every member of his
mortal frame but his eyes, and all there was of himself
lookin' steadily out of them at ye. But I felt he would
fetch around arter awhile, for the sun was warm and the
wind fresh, and I bolstered him up so it would blow straight
into his mouth and nostrils, and I said to myself, if natur'
can't bring him to, nothin' can. And so I felt cheerful-like,
and pretty sartin that between the sun and warm sand and
wind we would get his members warmed up and agoin' agin
afore long; and the hound thought so too, for when the
man fust opened his eyes the animil knowed it was a good
sign as well as I did, for the cretur no sooner saw them
open naterally, than he scooted a circle round the body in
the sand lively as a young pup at play, and then he stopped
in his foolishness and let a roar out of his mouth that might
have been heerd over to Salmon Lake; and then he came
back and sot down on his hanches close by the man, and
watched him as arnestly as I did. Every few minits he
would look up at me with a happy sort of look in his eyes
and fetch a wag or two, with his tail; and it was mighty
cheerful and encouragin to see the animil act so, and made
me feel sort of chirpy myself, as I sot in the sand watchin'
the man, for I knowed the hound was a truthful dog, and
was wise in his gifts, and wouldn't lie agin the vardict of
them, and I conceited that the man would pick up and be
able to talk, if the dog said so.

" Well, arter a while the man begun to pick up for sartin, for the blood come back into his skin, and his fingers
begun to open and shet easy-like, and he put his tongue

out and wet his lips naterally as a man does arter sleep in a hot lodge. I sarched my pack and found some tea a city woman gave me the summer afore for a sarvice I done her on the Racquette, which was no more than any man would do for a woman, but which she said she should never forgit till her dyin' day, — and I guess she never will, for I found somethin' she had lost that lay near her heart, and I never knowed a white woman, or squaw, neither, for that matter, forgit a man who done them a sarvice in that direction; — well, as I was sayin', I sarched for the tea the city woman had given me, and steeped a cup of it for the man on the sand, and I made it strong as the leaf would make it, for I knowed it would help natur' to rally, and make him strong enough to take nourishment, and set his tongue goin', if such a thing could be by the Lord's appintment.

So I gave him the drink, and it took hold on him at once. It was really amazin' Henry, how the yarb put life into him as if it had the Lord's own power to call the soul back into the mortal frame and set the members of it workin'. Yis, it was a marvel to see the power that natur' had put into a few withered leaves — for the more he drank the better he felt, and by the time he had come to the bottom of the cup I could see that the man was nigh himself agin, and likely enough to begin to talk ; and sure enough, in a minit he made a effort to speak, and arter one or two trials he got his tongue used to the motions, and said : —

"Old man, who be ye, that has called me back from the gates of death and summoned me from the borders of the grave?"

"My name," I said, "is John Norton, and I be nobody
but a hunter and trapper who has done nothin' but live in
a nateral way and sarve his kind when the Lord gave him
a chance; and as for bringin' ye back from the border of
the grave, I think ye was pritty nigh onto it, and me and
the hound yender, and the tea I steeped for ye, did mayhaps give ye a lift in the right direction — though it musn't
be overlooked, if ye are cur'us in the matter; that the sun
and wind done their part to bring ye to; and I dare say the
Lord in his marcy has done more than us all, for ye sartinly
would have died if he hadn't given the hound the sense to
know the dead from the livin' and helped us in our endivers. And now, friend, what may yer name be, and what
game did ye have in mind when ye pushed yer trail from
the settlements into this lonely lake ; for I see from the
signs, that ye know nothin' of the woods, and I marvel why
a man of yer ignorance should leave the hants of yer
kind, and I dare say kindred, and risk yerself in these out-
of-the-way places, which be pleasant to those who know
them, but risky to them that doesn't; so I ax ye yer name,
and why I find ye here alone and unprotected as if ye
hadn't a friend on the arth."

"John Norton," said the man, "my name is Roberts,
John Roberts ; and I have not a friend on the earth, nor do
I deserve one, for I have forfeited the love of all that ever
loved me, by my evil acts, and the Lord has visited upon
me the punishment I deserved by separating me from them.
Yea, out of my sins has come judgment, and my evil
thought has been the pit into which I have stumbled. But

the marcy I had forfeited has been shown me, in my guilt, and the peace of the Spirit that made and lives in the universe has been breathed into me from these mountains and the sky and the majesties of nature in the presence of which, glad that my mortal life is ended, I lie dying;' and the man turned his eyes on the objects he named, with the look of a hound in them when he meets the pleased face of his master.

"John Roberts," I said, "I do not understand ye, for the beauty of natur' is sech as to make men wish to live and not to die, and though I trust I may be willin' to go when He calls, still I can't conceit of any place pleasanter or more cheerful-like for a human bein' to live in than these woods, and I hope He will let me stay here, scoutin' round, as long as His plans techin' me allow of; and, as for that matter, if He should forgit us altogether I don't conceit that me and the hound would be very onhappy or feel cheated-like, but would hold it as a kind of a marcy, and keep on enjoyin' ourselves and sarvin' Him in the way of natur's app'intment; and as for friends, I haven't an inimy in the world but a thievin' Huron I caught on the line of my traps, last winter, and shortened his left ear half an inch with a bullet, and a mis'rable half-breed or two I've larnt the commandments in a similar manner. But outside of these, me and the hound there are in peace with all the 'arth, and feel cheerful and pleasant-like toward every livin' bein', except the panthers, — yis, always exceptin' the panthers, that we keep a kind of runnin' account with, as the pedlars say in the settlements, and square up whenever we git a chance."

"Ye see, Henry," continued the old man "I wanted to chirk him up as much as I could, because he was mighty weak still, and I thought that low sperits would sot him back agin, so even the hound and me couldn't bring him to; and so I talked the least bit frisky-like, and took on as if I felt ondistarbed. But he knowed better all the ime; for he looked at me with his eyes fixed solemnly on my face and said: —

'Old man, I know you can't understand, because you have lived an innocent life, and according to the light you had you have walked in the path of righteousness, and the peace of the upright is in your heart, and the light of it is over all the world, and makes it desirable to your eyes. And I can well understand that you need no other life than the one you lead, or other heaven than the lovely scenes which your gifts and your manner of life have taught you so well to enjoy; and I can understand, too, how you cannot grasp the meaning of a guilt as those who sin against light feel it: the guilt of a man who has resisted God and hardened his nature by a cursed passion, and hated what he should have loved, and loved with lusting what he should have hated — for you have been as a child, and the Kingdom of Heaven has come to you with the years, because your aging took not the simple innocency of childhood from you. But I have lived so that memory is only fuel to remorse, and the earth a constant reminder of my guilt; and hence I would seek my heaven in the forgetfulness of death, and anticipate another land beyond the grave, in hopes of finding escape from what torments me here, and having ministered unto my life the boon of a new start. And you must know that there are those in the world beyond the grave whom I have wronged, and the load of their wronging lies heavy on my soul. I would find them, and on my knees ask their pardon; for, old man, even God himself cannot undo the structure of our minds, nor perform duty for us, and I feel that the forgiveness of Heaven cannot make me happy until I have the forgiveness of my wife whom I deserted, and of my child whom I, with curses, refused to see in her dying hour.

And you should know, old man, that I am dying, and I long to die; nor do I ask aught save that I may have strength to tell you my story, and give you a few directions; for it will ease my soul to talk while dying, and I know it will delight you to hear of the goodness of that God whom you, in simple reverence, worship, and to learn from the lips of a dying sinner that the woods you so love have been to him the means of his salvation. So sit you down, old man, and listen closely, for I am weak, and I will tell you the story of my life; — why I am here, and what you are to do with what is left of me and mine when I am gone from here, as I soon shall be, forever.'

"Well, Henry, I saw that the man was in solemn arnest, and I knowed the Lord was apt to give a mortal nigh death a foreknowin' of the time and order of things techin' his departur', and I conceited the man was right in his idees, and that it would be onreasonable to resist him; so I sot down on the sand by his side and said, 'Well, friend, I allow there's reason in your words, and John Norton is not the one to arger agin a dyin' man nor distarb his thoughts with foolish talkin'. And it may be ye have come nigh the end of the trail, as ye say, and if so I sartinly advise ye to onload yerself of whatever bears heavy on ye; for a man should enter the Great Clearin' with nothin' heavier than his rifle about him, and ready for whatever sarvice the Lord app'ints. And as to the directions, ye may give me as many as ye have to tell, and if it be within range of mortal power it shall all be done as ye tell me; for I have sot beside many a dyin' man arter the scrimmage was over, and heerd his words, and not one, white or redskin, friend or inimy, can rise in the jedgment and say John Norton didn't do jest as he was told to do. So ye jest go ahead and ease yer mind, John Roberts, and me and the hound will listen, and as we larn yer wishes so will we do, even if the traps aint sot on the line next winter, or the trail of your errand takes us into the ounateral noise and diviltry of the settlements.'

So I promised the man, Henry, and kept my word, as the hound, there, knows, for he heerd it all and seed it all arterwards, and it was done jest as the man appinted. And this is what he told me as he lay on the sand, with me and the hound listenin'.

CHAPTER VIII.

THE MISER'S CONFESSION.

"One impulse from a vernal wood
May teach you more of man,
Of moral evil and of good,
Than all the sages can." — *Wordsworth.*

"MY father, John Norton, was a miser, although the world never knew it; but he loved money, and all his life was spent in getting it. He lived to be an old man, and when he died he was buried from the meeting-house — for he was a deacon in the church — and the minister preached the sermon, and told the people of his thrift and economy, of his industry and sobriety, and held him up as an example, when I knew, and all his friends knew, that he was sober when others drank, simply because he was too stingy to drink, and that his industry was all selfish, and that his economy was miserly. I only tell you this to let you know whence I got my love of money, and how the lust of gain came in me. It was born in me, John Norton, as much as the power of scenting was born in your hound; yea, given me at birth from the miserly nature and habits of a father who was a church member, and whose character and mode of life were praised by the minister when they buried his body.

He left me all his property, for I was his only child; and no one save me ever knew how much it was, for it was largely in gold coin that he had hidden away, and which he told me of, and where to find it, by whispering it in my ear when he was dying. I was thirty years of age before he died, and the property fell to me; and until I had the gold myself, and had seen it and counted it, I had lived a happy life; for I was married to an angel, and had three children, and a happier family never lived than we were before the gold came to me. But no sooner had I gotten it into my possession than I began to love it. Yea, the sight of the coin started the lust for it in me, and woke to full life the awful appetite for it which was in him and which he had transmitted to me. And the love for that gold grew on me as I handled it; — and handle it I did, until it became a passion with me. I used to get up nights when my wife was sleeping and go down cellar where I kept it in a large pot, and count it over, and push my hands into it, and laugh to hear it rattle, and to see it shine in the candle light. And the love of it grew and grew and grew, until I loved nothing else. And with the growth of the dreadful lust in me there grew a suspicion of men and women, because I had got it into my head that they would steal it, until at last I grew suspicious of my own wife and children, even to such a degree that I drove them out of the house and forbade them ever to cross its threshold again. You say I was mad. Yes, I was mad — mad with the awful madness of one in whose heart is a terrible and wicked love; a love that entices him and seduces him from good unto evil, and

finally becomes stronger than conscience — stronger than
affection for wife and children — yea, stronger than his fear
of God. Yes, I was mad in that way, and the madness
grew in its fury until it became a continuous frenzy, and
my life one hell of raging fear, suspicion and hatred of my
kind. I need not tell you all, for you would not understand it; you could not understand it, for you have never
handled money nor known the love of it, and are as a child
in your knowledge of such an experience. At last I came
to these woods; came driven by the frenzy of fear lest
men should steal my money; came, not from the love of
nature, or the longing for a peaceful, quiet, innocent life;
but in order to be where my money would be safe, for my
money was my God, my life, my heaven, and I feared some
one would steal it, and so I brought it here because no man
was here. How did I bring it? I brought it in a keg; a
keg stout and large, and lined with my own hands; and
that keg was my altar, my shrine, my God. John Norton,
remember it's a dying man that is talking to you, when I
tell you that here, on this very beach where I now lie, and
you sit, I have sat in the bright sunlight and in the solemn
moonlight, too, and counted my money by the hour, and
laughed and danced around it as a devil might; yea, I, a
mortal man, have danced around a pile of money like a
heathen round his idol, with the great blue sky overhead,
and beyond the sky, the greater God looking solemnly down
with his all-seeing eyes upon me and my gold.'

And here the man paused, Henry, a minit, and he panted
like a young faan in her fust race with the hounds, for he

was overtaskin' his strength, and I feered he would die for sartin if he didn't fetch up a bit and git rested; so I thought I had better give him a lift in the right direction by talkin' a leetle myself, and I drawed at a ventur', like a man who sends the lead by his notions of the sound, when it's too dusky to get his eye into the sights, and said : —

"If I was in your place, Mr. Roberts, I would set down and rest a bit, for ye are travelin' with a big load over a rough carry, if I am any jedge, and ye are gittin' sort of shaky-like in yer legs, and ye will come down in a heap pritty soon if ye don't steady up a bit and take it a leetle easier; for me and the hound mean to fetch ye round yit that is, if the tea don't gin out, and the Lord's app'intments be not agin it. So ye jest hold up a minit or two, and rest while we stir in a few more leaves of the yarb, and steep it for ye easy-like, for tea can't be hurried no more than a slow hound in the beginnin' of a race, before he's got the scent warm in his nose, and his faculties workin'. No, the yarb is spunky and knows its own importance, and won't stand rough treatment; and if ye bile it a bit, its vartu' is gone, for a wallopin' pot spiles the tea; so ye give me and the hound time to do the thing up accordin' to the rules and practices of correct obsarvation, and we will give ye a lift that'll make ye grateful to us both.

I don't catch the pith of yer last sayin' about the eyes of the Lord bein' terrible as he was lookin' at ye ; and I can't conceit of it, nohow. Now, the eyes of a panther are terrible, sure enough, and I have lined the sights by them when they barnt a hole in the darkness; and I have had many a clinch

with a Huron in a scrimmage, when I was younger, when
the blood of his savagery was up, and his eyes was as red
as an adder's; but the eyes of the Lord, as I have seed
them in the works of his hand, have always been strong,
for sartin, but gentle and mild as a mother doe when her
faan is friskin' around her; and I can't conceit of the face
of the Lord as bein' terrible, nor understand how a mortal
could be afeerd to have them on him."

And all the while, Henry, I kept kindlin' the fire for the
tea. But the man broke in on me, and said : —

"Old man, leave off preparing that tea and hear me; for
naught that you can do will prevent my dying, for it is
written that I die this day, and I feel within my soul that
my hour is drawing nigh. Leave off your preparations,
therefore, for your efforts cannot save me from death, nor
would I have it otherwise if I could. I want you to listen
and hear my words, nor move again until I am done."

So I sot down agin, and the hound came and sot down
on the other side of the man, and then he began to talk : —

"John Norton, I came to these woods a miserable miser.
There was in all my life but one love, and that was for
money. Money I loved, loved it with all the strength of
my nature. For years I had thought of nothing else, and
cared for nothing else. For years I had no joy but the
fierce joy of seeing it and counting it. To me my money
was all there was in the whole universe worth loving, — the
one idol of my soul. Well, I brought it here because no
man was here, and hence knew it could not be stolen.
With it safe, I was happy. With it secure, I asked no higher

boon. I was not only a miser, but I was hardened in all
my nature. The lust of gold had eaten out all other crav
ings. All noble affections, all tender sympathies, all truthful qualities, all charities and fine emotions had been by
this all-absorbing passion, banished from my bosom. I was
only a shell of a man inhabited by one great devil. This
devil in me had his fierce joy, his tormenting suspicions,
his rending rage, his agonies and his pangs; but no trace
of humanity, no fiber of charity, no possibility of peace.
Thus possessed, I came to this lake. You must not think I
had not been entreated; for man and women had alike
been faithful to me, and with prayers, with tears, with
warnings and exhortations had they striven to deliver me
from the devil within, and bring me to my right mind. But
neither man nor woman, neither wife nor child, nor the
Spirit of God acting in and through these could make me
see the sinfulness of my sin, nor the emptiness of my passion, nor the vanity of my life. These I could resist and
had resisted. Man could not master the devil in me nor
drive him out of my soul."

" But here the demon was met by other agents and agen-
cies he could not resist, and here the devil in me was mastered. By whom and what? By Nature, I reply, and by
the irresistible majesties of God in Nature. Here the greatness of my surroundings made me small, and the immeas-
urable splendors above me at night, and the glories around
me by day, made my gold seem contemptible. Not that
these influences came to be felt at once; not that the conviction produced by them was sudden, for it was not; but

slowly, subtly, and in a way I could not fight; with a power I could not resist, out of the silence of space, out of the blue sky and the uplifted mountains, out of sunrise and sunset, out of the water and the air, out of the solemn nights and the succession of splendid days there came regeneration to my soul. Within me was born in this mystical way a sense of larger and holier things, and moods of worship, and generous thoughts, and longings for what was fine and far ahead ; so that, involuntarily, and before I was aware, a change came to me in my likes and feelings, and I beheld as with eyes newly opened the significance of things, the use of life and the true application of its lessons. I said that my eyes were opened; and they were, so that I who had never thought of the beyond and the coming, but had lived in the here and the now, was compelled by a force within me to look constantly up and ahead into the great unseen and unknown. And this force within me I could not resist. It was stronger than my will and mightier than habit, and, forced by its energy, I yielded. And then out of the unknown and the unseen there came forth, as the blaze of a beacon from darkness and distance, a vision, and it scared me at first to face it, but at last I was able; and the vision that blazed out upon me from the darkness and the distance, terrible in its brightness, was the *Idea of Immortality.*"

"John Norton, this idea haunted me. The idea of life beyond, stretching on forever and forever, unintermittent and endless, lay like a mountain on my guilty soul. And out of the conception came interrogations that searched me

through and through like a knife. And out of this searching, amid agony and pangs, was born a Conscience: a Conscience which pinched me like a vice, and wrung groans
and cries of remorse out of my mouth, until, at times, the
silence of the night was filled with my moaning. It was
the silence that did it, old man; for the silence was more
than silence: it was GOD. I could not fly from it; I could
not escape its rebukes; I could not hide myself from its
solemn upbraidings. .It condemned me for the life I had
lived; it upbraided me for the passion I had nursed; it
threatened me with the censure of a just and holy verdict.
Here, on this point, in the midst of the all-surrounding
silence, I found my Judgment Day. Here my mind lost
the petty measurement of time, and took to itself in perfect sensing the realization of eternity. Here I wrestled
with the Spirit that has not form, and strove with the
energy that can never be incarnate: the Spirit of Justice
and Love commingled with the energy of God. Here, old
man, I strove; here I was overcome; and here I yielded;
aye, yielded to a test. And the test was this: that I should
deliberately, with my own hands, empty into the waters of
this lake the gold I had loved like a devil; and to keep
which, without fear of losing it, I had been self-banished
from my kindred and kind and had come to this lonely lake.
Yes, I yielded; yielded to the power I could not resist; the
power of the Lord who made and inhabits these woods,
and whose presence I saw and felt in their beauty, and
majesty, and silence. And I cried unto Him to whom I
had yielded, for strength to do the test; cried unto Him on

my knees, with my hands on the keg that held the gold, for strength to deliver my soul from its horrible spell, and pour it — yea, every dollar of it, — into the waters of the lake. And he gave me strength, old man, — even in answer to my prayer did he strengthen me to do the deed, which, being done, delivered me from the spell of the power that had held me, and from the bondage to the terrible lust. And last night the battle was fought, and the victory won, and I was delivered from Hell. For I prayed unto Him, and he listened and heard; and I lifted the keg and carried it to my boat, and paddled to the middle of the lake. And there, with hell and heaven to see, I lifted the keg in my arms and held it out over the water, and poured the gold I had worshipped into its depths. And there and then, when the deed was done, the blessing of the Lord came on me, and His marvelous peace stole into my soul. It came to me from the air, and the water, and the sky; from the bosom of the white moon-lighted stillness; from the motionless woods and the shores; came to me from the nigh and the far; from the air around me and the infinite spaces above and beyond; came to me, Old Trapper, from the outbreathings of that God who is Spirit, and in whom the innocent and the forgiven live, and move, and have being."

Here the man came to a halt, Henry, and he looked into my eyes as if he wanted to see if I understood, and arter a minit or two he said, — -

"Old Man, do you understand me?"

"Well," said I to him, "I can't say that the trail of your

talk is altogether plain to mo, Mr. Roberts, but mo and the hound has kept our eyes on ye as ye blazed along on the line, and I guess we have got the gineral direction of it. I can see for sartin that ye had a rough trip, and a heavy pack to carry, and ye must have found it hard backin' at times. It seems to mo if ye had onloaded earlier ye would have fetched through in better shape and saved valable time, for ye look to me like a man who hasn't got over the carry 'til dusk, and can't bo of much sarvice to the camp 'til another sunrise; but I think yo have got across for sartin and are out of the woods, and that's a good deal to say of a man who has been lost and fooled away half his day by walking in circles, and I rejice that ye are where ye are, and know which way the trail leads arter this and if ye are sartin of the lay of the land ahead and know where the line yo are on leads to, ye oughter feel contented and happy like, as I dare say yo do, Mr. Roberts."

"Yes I do feel contented and happy," said he, 'happier than words may tell. My sin has been great, but the mercy of God is greater, and I feel I can trust Him here and beyond. I have lived as no man should live, but here, on this beach to-day, my life will end, and when I am gone you may think of me, as a sinner whose sin was forgiven and whose soul had found peace."

Arter this he didn't say much for some time but lay with his eyes lookin' up to the sky and a quiet sort of a look on his face. I conceited the man was thinkin' of things, and it may be of people, a good ways off, and that it wouldn't be right to distarb him in his meditations. But arter a while

I said to him, for I felt a little oneasy on the subject, for I feered he would forgit it, — "Mr. Roberts, ye spoke about some directions ye wanted to give me, and perhaps ye had better say what ye have in mind on the matter, so me and the hound may know jest what ye want done by and by; for we shall mind and do jest as ye tell us, if it be within the range of our gifts, and death don't overtake us on the arrand."

Well, arter a little while he turned his eyes on me and said: —

"I suppose it don't make much difference where or how my body is buried, after I am gone; do, you, Old Trapper?"

"Well, no, I don't think it does, Mr. Roberts, when ye git right down to the gist of the matter; but every cretur' is born with his prejudices, and has his own ideas of what is right and proper teaching things to be done; and I conceit the Lord allows a man to fetch his line about where he pleases in pints of parsonal jedgment: and if I was in yer place I should have my own way about my burial, and have everythin' did straight and systematic-like, accordin' to my own idees of the thing. Now, me and the hound there, has our own notions about the treatment the mortal frame should receive arter the speerit has left it, and we conceit that it should be treated as a Huron treats his lodge when he is about to move out of it forever. But we can guess our notions wouldn't suit ye nor seem reasonable-like, because ye was edicated another way, and I have always noted that a man sticks to his arly edication as a moose sticks to his gait. So we won't distarb ye with our idees;

but do jest as ye tell us to, even if it be agin reason, as me
and the hound understand it ? "

Well, the man seemed to be sort of encouraged to say
his mind out arter what I had said, and arter looking at
the sky awhile, with his eyes half shet, he said : —

" Do you know, John Norton, for days I have been
haunted with the fear of dying alone. I dare say it is
foolish of me, but I can't help it, nevertheless, and I praise
the Lord that He has sent you to me in the hour of my
need. The sight of your face helps me beyond what I can
tell, and the sound of your voice has banished the terrible
loneliness from my soul. Yes, I shall die happy, now that
the companionship of my kind is given me in death. When
I am gone I want you to give me a decent burial, as they
do down on the coast where I was born. And the way of
it is this : They dress the body in good clothes, and put it
in a coffin, and they read a chapter or two from the Bible
at the house where the man lived, and the minister prays
and the choir sings. Then they take the coffin to the grave
and bury it, and they generally have a prayer at the grave ;
and they sod the grave, and put a slab of stone at the head,
and plant flowers on the mound. I know, old man, that
you can't do all this, and you needn't try. Only do the best
you can, that is all ; especially bury me so the wolves can't
get my bones, and say a few pious words above the grave."

Well, arter this he said nothin' for a full hour, and I said
nothin' neither, for it was plain that his feet was on the
very edge of the Great Clearin', and I felt it was nateral for
a man standin't at the very end of the trail to want to look

around him in silence awhile; and so I said nothin', for I feared to distarb his mind as he stood lookin' into the etarnal world. By and by he said:—

"Old man, the hour is almost come when I must go, and the way ahead is dark. I see no light and no helper. What can I do?"

"John Roberts," I said; for I could see by the look of his face and the fear in his voice, that he was in trouble, like a boy lost in the woods, "stick to the trail and keep your eye on the blazed line of His marcy. Don't hurry, but take it slow and sarcumspectly and trust to the markin's. I have heerd said that the carry ye are on led through a valley, dim and dusky as a stretch of pine land by night, but that the man who stuck to the line would fetch through all right. And remember, that me and the hound isn't far behind, and sartinly the Lord aint far ahead; so stick to the line, and don't swing a foot from the trail, and ye will strike risin' land afore long and see light." And I moved close up to his side and lifted his head into my lap, so he could catch his breath easier; for he was laborin' heavily, and I know'd he couldn't stand it much longer.

So I sot in the sand holdin' his head, and the hound sot at his feet, and we both kept our eyes on the face; and arter our fashion I prayed for the man, and put the case before the Lord in a strong sort of a way, I can tell ye.

Well, arter a while a great change came over his featurs. He opened his eyes and looked into my face in a happy way as if he had seen a new sight, and a smile crept over his lips, and his countenance softened like the clouds arter storm, and he said:—

"Old man, old man, I see light ahead!" And then he drawed a long contented sort of a breath, moved his legs out easily in the sand, rolled his head gently over in my lap as if goin' to sleep, closed his eyes; and his sperit, without groan or struggle, stole out of the body in which it had lodged so long in trouble, and passed through the clear light and the air up to its Maker. And that is the way, Henry, he came to the eend of the trail, and I reckon he found the Lord of marcy waitin' for him at the edge of the Clearin'.

So I sot in the sand, with the head in my lap, closin' his eyes, and the hound, accordin' to his gifts, came and put his nose agin the cheek, and then walked down to the end of the pint, and sot down on his haunches, and lifted his · nose into the air and lamented."

CHAPTER IX.

THE DEATH WATCH.

"In vain the she-wolf stands at bay ;
The brinded catamount that lies
High in the boughs to watch his prey,
Even in the act of springing, dies." — *Bryant.*

WELL, Henry, I didn't do nothin' about the burial until next day, for I thought it looked more decent-like not to hurry the matter of the entarment, and, moreover, I conceited it was no more than reasonable that me and the hound should hold a council over the matter; for there's nothin' helps a man's jedgment more on any pint, whether it be a funeral or a scrimmage, than to set down and talk it over with a companion, and me and the hound has consorted so much together that we understand each other and never differ on the main pints of a case — although I do thiuk that he lost a panther last fall by gittin' the scent wrong eend to in his nose, and leading off like an unlarned pup on the heel of the track; but the hound thought otherwise, and mayhaps I was mistaken. So I went down. on the eend of the pint where he was lamentin' accordin' to his gifts, and put it to him that we had better camp just where we was, on the trail, and lay over till another day, and I give him the reasons for it systematic-like from beginnin' to eend, and made the pints plain accordin' to the natur' of

the case, and we both agreed to it. And we jined judgment, furthermore, in this, that the body oughter be carried to a camp and watched and not left on the pint, for
fear the varmints would git to it over night and spile the
corpse. So we went back to the body, and carried it to my
boat and laid it down on some boughs I had cut for it, and
the hound followed on careful-like and sot down at the feet
of the body, and I got in at the other eend and shoved off,
and so we fetched the dead over the water till we come to
this pine knoll, and here me and the hound come ashore
with the body, and sot about preparin' for the death-watch
we know'd we must hold over night.

Well, Henry, it was sorter new work, ye see, for me and
the hound; for though I have buried many a man in the
trenches arter the fight, and though I have kivered up a
good many redskins off and on in my life, yit I wasn't very
handy at the mournin' equipments of the settlements. But
I have seed many a gineral laid out on his bier, in the old
wars, with his uniform on and his sword by his side, and
the death sentries on duty, and the muffled drums all beatin'; and I conceited that though Mr. Roberts wasn't a gineral, nor even a privit in the ranks for that matter, that he
should be treated in an honorable way now he was dead.

So I cut some crotches and drove 'em into the ground,
and made a frame of small white birches, about the size of
a bier, and on these I put a layer of balsam and cedar
boughs, and over these I scattered pine tufts ontil I had a
bed fit for the dead or livin', gineral or privit, and I laid in
plenty of hard wood for my fire, and some pitch knots, for

I said to myself, 'if the animils come round I will have to shine up on 'em, and defend the corpse'; for I feared the panthers—for this lake is a great spot for the varmints, and 'leven years ago there was sartinly as many as there is now. And arter I had got the bier ready I laid the body on it, and bolstered th head up nateral-like, and then me and the hound sot down to supper with a dead man at the table. We didn't waste time in the eatin', for the sun was already down, and by the time we had cleaned things up night had come.

Well, Henry, I took my stand at the foot of the bier, and kept my death-watch, rifle in hand, steady as a sentry on duty, save when I stirred the fire or lighted a pine knot. For the animils was oneasy, as they always is when a corpse is round, and I needed the pine knots more than once, and some of the varmints got the tech of lead and the smell of powder that night, I tell ye, for they was full of their dev- ilments, and made me and the hound as wakeful as if we was surrounded by inimies."

" Did you really have to kill any thing?" I asked, speak- ing for the first time in an hour; for the Old Trapper had told his story with such naturalness of intonation and ges- ture that he had held me spell-bound by his narrative— for no one could hear him tell the strange tale he was tell- ing and not be carried along by the movement of it, — and now that he was evidently reaching the climax, I feared I should miss some detail of his experience which being omitted would mar the narration, so, hoping to hold his utterance to the line of actual occurrence, I said, "Did you have to kill any thing, that night?"

"Well, yis, I did," ho replied. "I bored a holo through a dog-wolf over thero on tho beach, arter I had borno his onnateral howlin' as long as a mortal could; and I dropped a cat from that dead cedar there, arter mo and the hound had stood the stare of her eyes for ten minutes or more, and about two in tho mornin', a litter of panthers crawled in on us ontil the bush seemed alive with 'em, and I lifted tho scalp of the biggest of the drove, arter ho had got within forty feet of the corpse and paid no more attention to the brands I pitched at him than if they was tufts of sod; so with a pine knot all afire, in ono hand, to show me the sights, I drove the lead in between his infarnal eyes in a style that taught 'em all manners for the rest of tho watch. Yis, Henry, wo had a solemn and lively time of it, for sartin, that night, and at times it looked as if there would be no funeral tho next day; leastways, nono that me and the hound would attend, onless we made ono for our-selves; but we stood to our post, and between the brands and the lead and tho help of the Lord wo brought tho body through safe 'til sunrise.

But it was mighty solemn watchin' by the body all by myself on the shores of this lake, hero that night; for at times tho animils would make tho air roar and scream, and tho mountains to yelp as if tho upper world was inhabited with cats and wolves and panthers, and then they would suddenly become quiet, and the world round about was nothin' but silence with tho moon shinin' through it: and tho dead man's face was white as the moon and still as the air, for his troubles was over and the marks of them passed from his featur's when his breath went away. And so me and the hound kept our watch by the dead, 'til the sun riz in the east, and the hour had come for the funeral."

CHAPTER X.

"And let there be prepared a chariot-bier
To take me to the river, and a barge
Be ready on the river." — *Tennyson.*

THE first thing to do was to fix on the spot for the grave, which took leetle time to settle, for it seemed natur'l that the body should lie nigh where it had lived; and natur' sartinly had made a fit spot for it jest up on the bluff, off the p'int; for it was clean and sweet there, and the pines was always singin' overhead. And if a man is to be buried underground, arter he is dead, which me and the hound hold to be onreasonable and heathenish-like, I conceit he should be laid in a sightly spot, with a good outlook to it, and not stuck away in a swale or mash as if he was no better nor a cat, or a root-eatin' hedge-hog. So I shaped me a spade from a slab I rived from a pine the lightnin' had leveled, and digged the grave deep in the dry sand under the pines, and filled it half full of pine stems, and cedar-twigs, and other sweet smellin' things that grow around; and on the green stuff I flung in an armful of white lilies I plucked in the bay, to make the bed look cheerful and fittin' for a mortal to lie in. When this was done I come back to this spot and did to my boat what I had done to the

grave : made it green, and sweet, and handsome, with the
growths of natur' that had pleasant scents in them, until
the boat was nigh on to bein' full. And then I lifted the
body and laid it at length, and put the hands alongside each
other on his breast, and, with the hound in the bow of the
boat and me in the starn, I swung out into the lake, and
with easy stroke, lined a course straight as an arrow could
go toward the p'int. And so, without the presence of wife
or child, or kin of any kind to attend him; without bell, or
drum, or priest, the man who had desarted his home and
fellow-bein's went toward his grave.

Well, arter a while the boat tetched the sand, and the
hound got out; and I shoved it up a leetle further and I
got out, and liftin' the body in my arms I carried it up the
p'int, and climbed the knoll till I come to the grave, and I
laid the corpse down on the pine tufts and the lilies. And
I recalled all the man had told me about the singin' and
the prayer and the Book, and I did the best I could under
the sarcumstances, to follow the trail of his directions, and
I knowed if I did the best I could accordin' to my gifts, the
sperit of the man would overlook the rest; but I felt sartin that somethin' oughter be said out of the ordinary run
of human talkin', or the man wouldn't be more than half
buried arter 'twas all ended. And the hound seemed to
jine with me in the idee, for he looked up in my face in a
questionin' way, as if askin' when the sarvice was to begin.
So arter a minit I got down on my knees and told the Lord
what I thought was jedicious. I think I can recall jest
about what I said word for word, for my mem'ry is good,

and a man don't talk overfast, Henry, in sech sarcumstances, and it has all come back to me sence I sot here to-night
as if it was but yesterday sonce I buried the man, and I
can give ye the words pretty nigh. Yis, I got down on my
knees by the edge of the grave and said : —

"Great Sperit, here lies the body of one of thy creturs.
His arthly ways was known to thee, and the wrong of his
wickedness was not hidden. He seems to have straightened the trail of his misdoin's in the cend, and fetched
through to the Great Clearin' as a mortal should. But me
and the hound know'd leetle about him, and jest how he
came to thy presence we couldn't see, but it sartinly looked
hopeful. Here me and the hound has brought his corpse
for entarment accordin' to orders, and the trail at this p'int
is onsartin', but we mean to fetch through to the cend
of this job with thy help. So jest give us a lift at this
talkin', that the corpse may have a sarvice as is becomin'.
Bless us in our endivers, and let thy peace, which is one, as
I understand it, with Natur's, come on this grave I am
buildin', and here rest until the Jedgment Day. Then
squar' accounts with the man, not by the line of give and
take, so much for so much, but by the line of marcy and of
overlookin' of scant skins in the man's count; and don't
forgit to reckon easily with me and the hound, for we are
rather onsartin' consarnin' the blazes on this line, and suspicion we may git wrong cend to before we fetch through.
So be marciful to us three ; — to the man because of what
he did, and to me and the hound for what we didn't know
how to do. Keep all varmints from this grave, — sech as

cats and wolves, — especially panthers: onless I am here to attend to them, in which case ye may let them come rampin' round as much as the creturs' please, and I'll agree to keep them orderly. Amen.'

"Well, Henry," said the Old Trapper, after a pause, "do you think I did the square thing by the man? I did the best I could accordin' to my gifts and I sartinly trust the corpse was satisfied."

I could see that the Old Trapper was troubled in regard to the matter more than he chose to confess, and knowing how impossible it is for one totally unaccustomed to forms of any kind to fall into the grooves of formal utterance, I could fully understand how profound must have been his embarrassment in attempting to conduct a funeral service according to the rules and methods which prevail in civilized, not to say fashionable communities, and as I looked into the simple, guileless face of the Old Trapper, which showed doubt, perplexity, and pain in its every wrinkle and furrow, I felt that I was authorized to go as far as I could truthfully in the way of comfort, so I said : —

"I think you did excellently, John Norton; and I doubt not the spirit of the man was well satisfied with what you did to honor his body at its burial, and I know that the Lord understood your circumstances and gave you full credit for the beautiful spirit of obedience to the dead man's wishes you showed in following his instruction."

"Well, I am mighty glad ye think so, Henry. I have felt oneasy on the matter for eleven years, for I feerd I had got off the track altogether in the sarvice, for I had a dim line to trail by, as the man's talk wasn't very plain to me to start with, and the hound was no more help in the matter than an unlarnt pup is to a hunter on a dry track. Yis, I sartinly feel easier in the matter arter what ye have said, and the Lord knows I meant only good to the man, and tried to be respectful to the corpse.

"Well, there isn't much more to tell ye. Arter the sarvice I put some green boughs over the body, so that the dirt wouldn't tetch it, and filled it up easy-like and as gentle as I could. And when the fillin' was all in I went and cut some sod with my huntin' knife, with the flowers all grow-in' in them, and made the grave as green and pritty as natur could be and than I took position soldier-like and let off my piece as a kind of farewell and the hound lifted up his voice and gave one lament; and the sarvice was over."

Here the old man paused, and as I stirred the fire the flame leaped up and brought the features of his time-beaten face in clear relief. And a remarkable face it was, and such as is seldom given to man save when nature produces her noblest work. It may interest some who have been in-troduced to him in these pages and who will meet him fur-ther on in many scenes, both of peace and war, and who will grow to love him for the purity of his nature, and the courage of his conduct when exposed to temptation on the one hand and peril and death on the other, to have a pen portrait of one of the most noted characters that the latter part of the last century and the early half of the present one produced.

John Norton was, even in his seventieth year over six feet in height, but so symmetrical was his proportion in his physical stature that great as it was, it was neither awkward nor ungainly. Temperate in his habits, and constant in the exercises which develop and retain muscular power, he was even at the time of our story a marvel of physical strength. But for the fact that his eye may have lost a trifle of its earlier brightness, and that his hair once black as a raven's wing was now sprinkled with threads of gray, it would have been impossible to believe he had reached the period of threescore years and ten, for his form was still erect, his step elastic and his voice clear and strong. His face was of that square, strong shape, such as you see in a few of the older men still living in New England but who are fast passing away, and with them we fear the type of self-reliant and indomitable character they represent. His eyebrows were large and abundant, and projected over the eyes. The eyes themselves were gray and changeful in color according to the method of the speaker. His nose was large, and straight and full at the nostrils and broad at the base. His mouth was firm and in a marked manner suggestive of power. His chin was round and handsome. Into this noble and remarkable countenance time had channeled many a line, and the years had spread the repose of age without weakening the aspect of determined strength. In color the skin was of course bronzed, but of so pure a tan that the blood showed almost as plainly as in an untanned countenance. And, as he sat at the close of his narrative gazing into the fire with his face almost solemn

in the gravity of its expression I said to myself as I gazed
steadily at it, revealed in its every line and wrinkle as it
was by the clear blaze, " I have never seen so noble and remarkable a countenance among men." I grew to love it in
subsequent years as a son loves the face of a father in
whom is no guile.

At last he started from his revery and said, " Henry, the
morn is comin', for I feel the changes in the air that tell
the beginnin' of day. Let us heave the rest of the logs on
the fire and stretch ourselves for a nap, for natur' has her
rights and must be dealt reasonably with. We will sleep
now, and by and by I will show you the man's grave."

I did as he requested and then, stretched at full length
on either side of the fire, we fell asleep.

The sun was high in the heaven before I awoke. I
rubbed my eyes to make sure of my sight as I started up,
for breakfast was ready, and the Old Trapper sat on the log
patiently waiting my waking. The old man divined my
thought, for he said: " Nay, nay, Henry, you need not feel
hurt because I got the start of ye; for sleep to the young
is sweet, and I could not wake ye till natur' was satisfied.
But the eyelids of the old rest lightly on their balls, and
the rays of the sun wakes me quicker nor a bugler's note
rouses a soger. So me and the hound have been stirrin'
about, and between your pack and mine we have got a
meal fit for a king. So jest take a dip in the lake off that
rock there, and we will try the vartue of the victals."

After breakfast was over, the Old Trapper said, " Come,
Henry, we will go to the grave, and I will show ye where

the body of an unhappy man lies buried. I warrant the hound remembers the spot as well as I do."

A few minutes brought us to the point where we landed. The hound being in the bow of the boat, had touched the shore first, and mounted the bank. No sooner had he reached the top than he lifted his nose into the air, turned around once in his tracks as a hound will when searching for knowledge, then started in a straight line for the bluff.

"Aye, aye, I know'd the dog would recollect the spot," said the Trapper, "and there he goes on a trail that's been whitened by the snows of 'leven winters as if he was arter a buck jest started from his nest in the moss. It's sartinly wonderful what sense the Lord has given to his creturs, sech as the beaver and the dog, and even a wolf in the darkest night can tell the toe from the heel of a track, and I have seen the wild hosses on the prairies act as sarcum-spect as if they was reasonin' mortals."

At this point the long, solemn cry of the hound rose into the air and rolled in mournful cadence over the lake. The Old Trapper halted a moment, and then as he turned to-ward me, he said : —

"You see Henry, the heart of the dog is true to his mem-ory of the spot. I have heerd many a dog give vent to his grief over the grave of his master, long years arter it was made, and it should larn us mortals to be true to what we have promised the dead, and keep their graves green and sweet arter they have gone. Henry, I feel a leetle oneasy lest somethin' of ill has happened to the corpse on the bluff. Come, let us go and see."

So saying, he started for the knoll, and I followed on.
We soon reached the upper edge, and the grave, with the
hound sitting on his haunches at the foot of it, was before
us. The Old Trapper's face brightened as he saw it had not
been disturbed, for, except that the mound had shrunken
somewhat, and that the green growths of nature were more
luxuriant, it was evidently the same as when it had been
fashioned eleven years before.

The Old Trapper paused as he reached the head of the
mound, and leaning on the muzzle of his rifle, said, "Henry,
the Lord has sartinly been marciful, and kept the grave on-
disturbed, and natur' has made it handsomer than it was
when me and the hound left it; and a sightly spot it is, and
a cheerful one for a grave to be in, for the view up the lake
is a good un, as ye see, Henry, and the pines overhead
keep up a pleasant sort of a darge. Yis, it sartinly is a
cheerful spot for a grave, and if me and the hound could
make it seem reasonable to us we would sartinly pick some
sech spot as this to lie in arter we are dead; but it don't
square with our notions of right and wrong, and we can't
make it nohow, though we have held many a council over
it. Still, a grave makes solemn and instructive company
for a mortal, especially for one as old as me and the hound;
and it may be, a leetle overhaulin' the pack, and goin' over
the count of the years we have lived sence we left this
grave, wouldn't do either of us any hurt; and as it is a
matter that the young and them that has long life ahead of
them aint much interested in, perhaps it may be as well
that ye go back to the camp and pack things up for a start,

Henry, for we will take to the boats when me and the hound has done with our meditations.

Appreciating the wish of the Old Trapper to be for a brief time alone, I retired down the knoll, and entering the boat was soon at the camp. As I stepped ashore, I cast my eyes across the bay to the bluff, and then I uncovered my head. The Old Trapper, with the hound looking steadily into his upturned face, was kneeling at the head of the grave, engaged in prayer.

THE MAN WHO DIDN'T KNOW MUCH.

PART I.

THE MAN WHO DIDN'T KNOW MUCH.

CHAPTER I.

THE BEAVER'S LODGE.

"For men like these on earth he shall not find
In all the miscreant race of human kind."
Homer, Pope's Translation.

IT was early autumn, and the woods were only just beginning to take to themselves the variegated colors
which make our northern forests a wonder to foreigners
and an annual delight to those who live within sight of
their glorious changes, that two men might have been seen
forcing their way through the underbrush of a tamarack
swamp, which divided two small lakes near the centre of
the wilderness.   On the shoulders and head of one was
balanced a birch canoe, larger than the average make,
while the other was literally loaded down beneath a monstrous pack-basket, which was not only full of camp and
trapping materials, but had tied to it a dozen and one arti-
cles for culinary and camp use.   In a few moments the
man under the canoe came to a halt, and laying it gently
on the ground, he turned to his companion and said : —

"Come, Henry, let's halt a minit and git breath.   This
is sartinly a tough carry, and ye are loaded like a sinner

at the Day of Jedgment, when as I have heerd the missioners say mortals will be summoned into court with all
their devilments on top of 'em. And while ye have nothin'
that an honest man need be ashamed of, even in front of
the Lord, yit I will say that ye are mighty heavily cum-
bered with the fixin's, for sartin, and yer legs must feel in
a rebellious state agin sech treatment as ye've been givin'
'em for the last mile; for if there's any thing that will set
the sinews in a man's thighs twitchin' and sort of knottin'-
up like, its fetchin' a carry through a tamarack swamp like
this, with a whole camp on his back, and no bottom worth
speakin' on under him. That's right, — settle down there
on that bog and squirm out of the straps and ease yerself
awhile. I'll bet the wales on yer shoulders are red as a
rat's hide when the meat has peeled with it; and as for yer
neck, the infarnal basket, Henry, has rasped it like a file.
How do ye feel inwardly, for I know ye smart outwardly?"

"O, I feel all right," replied his companion. "Of course
the straps have cut into me a little, and the basket has
worn through the skin somewhat, I guess, by the feeling
on my neck; but I am good for the distance between here
and the lake, wherever it is; and when we get through, if
it is a decent place to look at, we will take a rest and a
good strong meal too, for I am as empty as a last year's
gourd."

"I like the sound of yer talk, Henry," said the old man,
whom our readers will have easily recognized as John Norton, the Trapper, and his companion as Henry Herbert, "I
like the sound of yer talk," continued the old man, laugh-

ing; "and I can well believe ye; for ye have the look of a man whose loadin' is all on the outside and none of it in, and I should ventur' the opinion that a pound or two of that steak ye have in the basket there, jediciously spitted and eaten slowly, 'twixt proper allowances of corn cakes and spring water, re-inforced with a few leaves of the tea, would round ye out and make ye look sort of enhabited-like; for I have always noted that a man with no victals in him looks like a deserted settlement,—kinder lonesome, and a good deal as if a funeral was goin' on inside of him. But another good lift will bring us out of this snarl of tam-arack and put our feet onto the beach of as handsome a lake as the Lord ever made, even here in these woods, where he does seem to have did his best, and kept at it a long while, too; for I think, 'twixt trappin' and boatin', I've been on a thousand of 'em off and on in the last forty year; but a prittier one than lies ahead of us never had its springs set runnin', if I am any jedge. So crawl into yer straps, Henry, and I will give yer pack a hist, and we will see how soon we can fetch out of this devilment of bushes; for a tamarack swamp is the devil's own work in natur' for sartin; and if a man who is nothin' but ordinary, and hasn't been favored in pious edication, can bring a boat or a pack through one of 'em and not get sort of strong and arnest-like in his speech, it is because the Lord is on-usually marciful to him, anyhow."

So saying, the Old Trapper lifted the canoe on to his shoulders, and pushed determinedly on through the dense thicket, whose dried, thorny branches scraped and rattled

against the bottom and sides of the canoe, until the noise
might have been heard miles away.   •

At last, after twenty minutes or so of desperate struggling, in which the strength and temper of both must have
been severely taxed, the Old Trapper burst out of the opposing brush, and cast the canoe upon the yellow sands of
a beach which curved its line of gold around the northern
shore of a lake. In an instant, Herbert tore his way out of
the swamp, and without saying a word, settled, with the
pack still on his back, into the soft sand. His pantaloons
were seriously torn, his hair full of moss-dust, and bits of
dried twigs, while his face was fairly white with weariness.

"Well, Henry," said the Old Trapper, as he looked at
him, after having unbuckled the straps which bound the
pack to his companion's shoulders, "ye look as if ye had
been in a tussle that taxed ye, and yer breeches seem as if
they had got the wust of it for sartin. I have never liked
the tailorin' of the settlements, for I have never seed any
of their work that would hold when a man was in the center of a tamarack thicket, or a windfall, and got sort of
arnest-like in his feelin's. Summer afore the last, a man
from the coast, that I run agin in a mighty weak condition,
and sort of nussed back to life, sent me a box of stuff, and
it had for sartin a great many useful things in it, seeh as
traps, powder and lead, not to speak of tea and other yarbs
for medicine. Yis, he sartinly put in a good many things
accordin' to reason, and useful to a man of my gifts; but
he missed the trail entirely in one thing, for he sent me, all
done up as pritty as could be, and tied with red string, a

whole suit of garments that he called black cloth, or wide
cloth, or some sech name, not to speak of hat like the
chapeau the militia wore fifty years agone, and which I
could no more keep on my head in this bush than a beaver
could keep his fur in spring-time. But I felt sartin the
man meant it for good, and to sort of please his mem'ry,
and show proper feelin' in the matter, I sot apart a day to
celebrate the man's good-heartedness; and I got into the
things, hat and all, and if ye b'lieve me, Henry, when I
looked in the glass I didn't know myself. And I said,
'John Norton, be this you?'" And I marveled, Henry, that
a mortal could so change himself by a few clothes that he
should be strange in his own eyes. But the thing that
seemed queerest of all was that the hound there, that ye
know is a knowin' dog, and a obsarvin' one, too, who had
been foolin' around with a young faan in the thickets for
exercise, come in, and seein' me settin' in a cheer, hat and
all on, whirled his tail round and let a threatnin' roar out
of his mouth that made the cabin ring, and he showed his
teeth in a way to make flesh of a cowardly half-breed creep.
Yis, Henry, to think that a few city garments could change
a man so even his own hound wouldn't know him ontil he
heerd his voice, and actally got his scent in his nose. I
have spent a good many hours wonderin' about it, I tell ye.
Well, Henry, I never tried on the coat and vest and hat
agin, ye may believe, for they was useless to one of my
gifts, and made the hound onhappy; but I did think the
breeches would sarve me awhile, for they was roomy and
looked as fine and tough as a doeskin; and so I detar-

mined to give them a try. I put them on one mornin'
when startin' on a still hunt, and by the Lord, Henry, when
I got back at night there wasn't any breeches on me, leastwise nothin' to make a fair show on a man in the settlements. It was amazin' how they went to pieces. The
briers went through them as if they was paper. I left
them all along the line of my trail as a bear leaves the fur
in the beginnin' of summer. And it larned me a lesson
tetchin' the tailorin' of the settlements which I shall never
forgit. And ever sence we started on the trip I have felt
onsartin about yer garments, and though they have held
on agin all expectation, yit, sooner or later, I knowed they
would play a prank on ye and gin out sudden-like. And if
ye will take my advice ye will let me make ye a good pair
of buckskin I've tanned with my own hands, and I warrant
ye will never get a brier through them or feel oneasy about
yer appearance in company."

While the old man had been talking, Herbert had remained stretched at length upon the sand with his head
bolstered against the pack basket, recovering his breath
and gazing with eyes which drank in the loveliness of the
scene around him. It is doubtful if he had even heard half
the Old Trapper had been saying, so absorbed was he in
contemplation of what would seem to one unaccustomed to
such scenes, more like a picture from Fairy Land than an
actual landscape of the earth. The lake was perhaps a
short mile in length, and bordered with high hills both on
the eastern and western shores. The whole northern end
was in the form of a sickle, and ornamented with a beach

of sand of brightest yellow. The southern and eastern
shores were bordered with a marsh whose deep green grass,
brightened here and there with various colored flowers,
stretched far out into the shallow waters of the lake. The
shores were thickly wooded with evergreens, while here
and there a maple, far up the hillside, flung out its flame of
color as a royal banner, planted in some ivied recess of an
ancient castle, might wave its rich blazonry forth to the
passing breeze. At last, as if his soul had drunk its fill of
the surrounding beauty, Herbert rose to his feet, and still
gazing off upon the water, said: "John Norton, this is lovely;
by what name is this lake called, or has it no name? I
have never seen a sweeter sheet of water."

"I am glad ye think so, Henry," rejoined the Trapper;
"for I have always thought it was about the best the Lord
could do in this line, and many be the days and nights I
have spent on its quiet shores, for I have know'd it off and
on for fifty year; and the first time I ever sot eyes on it
was under sarcumstances kalkerlated to make a man remember it, I tell ye; for I was hard pressed by a pack of
redskins, and me and a comrade held our own agin 'em for
two days and two nights, and we put our marks onto the
biggest part of them in a way the Lord will remember in
the Jedgment, for they did awful murder here; and I sunk
in the water there, off that p'int, as handsome a body as
the Lord of Life ever made, if her skin was red and her
father the chief of the thievin' Hurons. And as for the
name, it is a name which the Indians gin it, arter what happened here in the scrimmage I've told ye of; for they say,

and there be white men who swear to the same, that in the
month of July, on the twenty-fifth day, jest afore dawn, a
white figger can be seen comin' up out of the water, and
that it walks over to this beach and then across to where
you stream comes in, through the alders there, and then
floats back abreast the p'int and sinks out of sight; and
they call it the ' Lake of the Lovely Spirit.' And I can well
believe the spirit is lovely; for she was lovely in life, and I
don't see why dyin' should mar the beauty of the Lord's
cretur's. Yis, it sartinly is a handsome lake, and its shores
are thick with mem'ries to me. And right on this very
beach, aye, jest here where we stand, I had a tussle with
half a dozen redskins which came near being my last, and
a life was given for mine, and another met the death that
was meant for me, here. But I squared accounts with the
last of the scamps thirty year ago, and that's sartinly con-
solin' to one who remembers, as I do, the cruelty of the
devils, and how they did murder without cause and agin
reason."

"Well," Herbert responded, "the lake is certainly beautiful and appropriately named, too, if what men say occurs
here, and I will make you tell me the history of your fight
on this lake fifty years ago, some day, and all about the
death of the beautiful Indian girl, if the memory is not un-
pleasant for you to recall. But now I am hungry and feel
as if the sooner we get a fire started and some meat cooking the better it will be for my feelings."

"Sartinly, sartinly," rejoined the Trapper promptly, " but
not here lad. Toss your pack into the canoo and I will pad-

dle yer over there to where yon stream comes in through
the balsam grove, and we'll find a camp all ready for us
there onless the snows has broken down the lodge poles, or
some onlarnt city man has stolen the bark off the roof for
kindlin's."

In a few moments the two were in the canoe which the
Old Trapper was urging with an easy stroke across the
glassy surface of the unruffled water, and shortly the canoe
was run ashore in the green grass at the mouth of the little rivulet which with a faint musical gurgle flowed through
the balsam grove under the alders into the lake.

"There, Henry," exclaimed the old man, as he stepped
ashore and cast his gaze around him, "This looks homelike for sartin. Many be the days and many be the nights
I have lodged here, both in winter and summer, and I have
never seed the time when the mouth of this little brook
didn't give me fish, or the shores of this lake didn't keep
me in ven'son. And as for ducks, and geese, and wild fowl
in their season, Lord-a-massy, Henry, the water used to be
black with 'em; and I've taken the head of many a duck
off with my bullets, sittin' right here in the door of the
lodge; and if ye noted the ledge back of here as I paddled
ye in, ye saw the home of more panthers than any other
spot in the wilderness. Many a night have I laid here in
my lodge and heered their cries and screams as they scrim-
maged with each other, or held their ugly feasting over the
body of a buck. Yis," continued the Old Trapper, as he
lighted a match and applied it to a bunch of dried twigs he
had piled in the fire-place, "I have kindled my fires here

by flint and steel instead of lucifer matches, and started a
blaze under different sarcumstances than we be in to-day.
Come, Henry, do ye fetch some water from the brook and I
warrant ye will find it cold as the iced drinks of the settlements, and we will have the pot bilin' and the steak cookin'
in no time."

Both men now applied themselves to their respective
tasks and in a brief space of time they were sittin' cross-
legged on the ground with a bark between them covered
with food smoking hot. Without delay Herbert addressed
himself to the eating with the quick, earnest motions of
hand and teeth, of a man who is desperately hungry and in
the enjoyment of perfect health.

The Old Trapper sat looking at his young companion a
moment with a look of broad, but benevolent humor on his
wrinkled features, and then picking up a corn cake he
placed a bit of the brown luxury leisurely in his mouth and
said : —

" It does my old jaws good, Henry, to see ye so familiar
and off hand like with the victals. A parson I guided last
summer used to think it ongrateful not to say grace afore
he tetched a morsel, and he lived up to his idees of right
and wrong, for sartin, for he never failed to say grace over
his plate afore he tasted it ; but he had a powerful strong
hold on language, and I used to conceit many a time that
he overdid the thing a leetle. Ye see, Henry," said the Old
Trapper in a low, confidential tone, as if half talking to
himself, "the man was chock full of words, and gave tongue
like a young hound on his fust track, and he sort of spilled

over because he was so full of 'em. The least chance to say something religious joggled him, and I do think I've heerd the man say his prayers so long over his plate that his victals actally cooled before he got to 'em, and that's what I call darned foolishness, put it any way ye mind to.

Now, Henry, I never cook a steak or bile a tater or brown a flapjack that I don't sort of have a pleasant feelin' inardly to the Lord for his marcy to me; and sartin, I never sot my teeth into the crumpy edge of a brown corn cake like this and didn't feel how pleasant and cheerful a thing it is to live; for a cake like this is toothsome eatin', and if the meal isn't too fine, there are chunks of the karnals lyin' around in it that the teeth git into, and the tongue intarprets the real vartue of the corn, in a way that sartinly ought to make a man grateful for the faculties the Lord has gin him, and the sweet growths of natur.'

But as for a man stoppin' to ontangle a string of pious words when his stomach is empty, and he feels like a cellar with no house over it, and the steam of the hot victals is strong in his nostrils, why, Henry, I must say that it seems to me to be agin natur' and reason. My idee is that the Lord knows all about our feelin's and can see the grace of the man's heart goin' up, as the victals go down, and that he loves to see us dip in hearty-like, and as if we enjoyed the smell and taste of the things He has made to grow for us; and if words must be said, I conceit that they should be said arter the man is full, and is ready to sit back and feel religious-like; but as to wastin' time in layin' hold of the Lord's marcies when they are all smokin' hot and afore ye, and the wind is coolin' 'em, I don't conceit that the Lord expects any such foolishness from men of sense and jedgment."

So the two men sat eating and talking in the wise, humorous fashion of American back-woodsmen, until they had satisfied the demands of nature. They then washed the dishes, and having re-packed the basket restored it to the canoe, and stood one at either end of it ready to launch it forth on the level water and resume their journey. This they did in a moment, and were soon on the bosom of the lake, whose unruffled surface reflected like a perfect mirror the blue sky and white clouds above, and the autumnal glories of the hills on either side.

"I tell ye for sartin, Henry," said the Old Trapper, as he lifted his paddle from the bottom of the canoe, and passed it with the easy motion of long habit into the water, "I tell ye, for sartin, Henry, that we shall have some fun afore we git through this trip ; I feel the comin' of it in my bones as a hound gits the fust stray whiffs of the true scent in his nose, and opens on it musical-like. I'm mighty glad ye are with me and can stay in, this year till the snow drives ye out, and later, too, if ye have a mind, for I must confess that I take to ye mightily, and the trail will be lonely and the old lodge empty-like, when ye are gone. Now, I have an idee that we had best swing across to the Saranacs and see what's goin' on there, for ye remember we heerd them talkin' in the camp we ambushed on the Cranberry waters, of a boat race that the city folks was gittin' up on the Saranacs. Ye see, Henry, ye pull a mighty clean stroke and a strong one too; and though I have held the paddle back of a good many men who was handy with the ash, I never felt a boat git away from under me as fast as ye make it when ye fairly put your strength onto the blades, and I would give the best furred beaver's hide I shall trap this winter to see ye cut out a stroke for two miles and return, with them cocky Saranac chaps; for they think they can out-shoot and outrow all creation, and it would be doin' the Lord's sarvice to take a leetle of their foolishness out of 'em, as I feel ye can do; and if they would only let me in, too, I tell ye, Henry, twixt you at the oars and me at the paddle we'd e'enamost drive the bottom-board out of the boat and show 'em what an old man and a young one used to the woods, when they jine works, can do," and the old Trapper gave a flourish with his paddle, and passed it into the water with an energy that fairly lifted the canoe half off the water.

"Well," rejoined Herbert, I like your plan, and we will push through as you say, for one spot is as good as another to me, and I would like to see the races and take a hand in them, too, if you wished; but I would like to see a beaver lodge before we go out, and you know you said I could see one almost any day."

"Sartin, sartin, I did," returned the Trapper, "and ye shall see one inside of thirty minits if the vagabonds have done their summer wanderin' and got back to their homes; for there's a lettle pond here, away to the right of the carry, twixt this and Mud Lake, from which I have taken many a hide, and I never skeerd one of 'em by careless trappin'

and so they keep comin' back every year, as they will if ye
don't distarb them by any foolishness, and I warrant a dozen
of the brown backed rogues are playin' in the water this
very minit. Aye, here we be at the carry, and we will
leave the canoe and see if we can ambush the pond."

A swift walk of twenty minutes brought the Trapper and
his companion to a point where the old man paused, and
turning to his comrade, he said in a whisper : —

"There, Henry, jest over that pine knoll is a bit of mash
with a pond in the center of it, and the grass grows tall,
but there's not a bush on the whole lot, and we must crawl
for it; and if there's any way ye can make yourself flatter
than another, I sartinly advise ye to try it, and if ye break
a stick as big as the stem of ye pipe, Henry, ye will see
no beaver to-day, for they be mighty timerous animils, and
their ears and eyes are as open as a Huron's in the midst
of an ambushment. So be keerful, lad, and if yer gifts be
as good at crawlin' as they be at shootin', ye shall be lookin'
into the eyes of a beaver within forty feet of ye inside of
ten minits. Now down to the arth, Henry, for we sartinly
have got to snake it."

So saying the Old Trapper sank to the earth, and being
followed in the action by his companion, the two began to
work their way noiselessly over the knoll and into the tall
grass of the meadow.

It would have been an interesting spectacle to one unaccustomed to exhibitions of woodcraft, to have stood on
that knoll and have seen with what patience and skill the
two men worked their way onward through the tall grass

toward the pond. Not a twig snapped, not a rustle came
from the withered grass, and scarce a movement of the
pendent blades revealed that two human bodies were passing onward toward the edge of the pond. Two-thirds the
distance had been covered, when the Old Trapper paused in
his course and noiselessly passing his hand backward along
his side beckoned with his fingers for his companion, who
had been trailing in his wake, to move up to his right. This
he did, and the two men lay stretched side by side, motionless as logs, in the tall grass. The Trapper put his lips to
the ear of his companion, and breathed, rather than whispered into it : —

"Yis, Henry, ye are a nateral woodsman, for sartin, and
ye can crawl like a Huron, and I rejice in yer gifts. Ye
remind me of a lad I had as a comrade in the old war, and
a truer hearted boy, though a redskin, never drove a bullet
into a grooved barrel. Many a time has he and me crawled
our way out of danger when the inimy was round us on all
sides, and athirst for our blood : but the boy himself couldn't
have fetched this trail stiller than ye have done. By the
Lord, Henry, I wish we had men and not beavers to crawl
onto, for this sort of business stirs memory and blood both
in me, and my hand has actally slid toward my knife handle more than once sence I started, as if there was a inimy
somewhere, lyin' close in the grass, when I know a human
bein' isn't within forty mile of us ; and there's nothin' more
harmful than innocent beaver in front. Now, Henry, let
your very breath go down into the sod, for the edge of the
pond isn't fifty feet away."

To these whispered reflections the young man made no reply save with his eyes, and in an instant the two bodies slowly, and without noise, began to move on through the grass.

Five minutes may have passed when two human heads moved slowly and partially out of the grass that grew with rank luxuriance on the edge of the pond, and hung pendant over and drooped its points into the water. Several beavers were swimming hither and thither in the water, while several others were busily engaged in mending the dome of their home.

The Old Trapper put his lips to the ear of his companion again, and said, "Ye see the activity of the creturs, Henry, and how they work wisely accordin' to the sense the Creator has given 'em. Do ye see the old fellow with the white patches on his sides and the light spot atween his ears. If he would only turn round, ye would see he had no tail, for he left it in my trap two years ago, and how he steers himself in swimmin' the Lord only knows. I would give the best horn of powder in the cabin to see him try to circle this pond once. I doubt, lad, if there be another man in the wood that could fetch himself through the grass to the edge of this pond, and not distarb the watchful creturs. I would like to see the man that could do it, for sartin. Jest stay where ye are, Henry, while I move a foot or two to the left to git a glimpse back of the lodge."

So saying, the Old Trapper rolled slowly over till his back was turned to his companion. He rolled over, but moved not an inch beyond. His face suddenly sharpened with excitement, his nostrils dilated, and his hand sought the handle of his knife in earnest, for there, not three feet from his face, was THE FACE OF ANOTHER MAN, AND A PAIR OF BRIGHT EYES WERE GAZING FIXEDLY INTO HIS!

CHAPTER II.

"Dressed in living green." — *Watts.*

"Thou comest in such a questionable shape
That I will speak to thee." — *Shakespeare.*

A FLASH of lightning is not quicker than was the motion with which the Old Trapper sprang to his feet, knife in hand, and, as he struck the perpendicular, he exclaimed: "Henry, lad, up with ye, and set yer eye into the grass here and see as fine an ambushment as a Huron ever made. Look at his eyes, boy, and tell me if ye can the name of the cretur', and what be the purpose of his devilments."

The motion of the Trapper was not quicker than that of his companion, as he rose from the grass to the old man's side; and certainly no astonishment could be greater than his, as following the direction of the old man's finger, he saw the gleam of eyes gazing, as it were, from the very roots of the marsh-grass into his face.

For a minute the two stood gazing downward into the grass where lay the body of the man, into whose very reach they had crept without the least suspicion of his presence. The countenance of Herbert showed only blank astonishment and surprise too great for speech, with such a startled expression as nature will bring to the face of one unaccustomed to such a sudden summons as the cry of his companion had been to him. The look of the Trapper's face showed neither astonishment nor alarm. If, on the instant of discovery, he had felt either, its expression had passed from his countenance, and in its place there had come to his features the look of profound curiosity. He was evidently studying, with the full force of his faculties, the trick or arrangement by which the man, whose eyes alone were visible, had been able to so conceal himself that even by those who were then looking downward upon him, not a square inch of his garments could be seen. In a moment the Old Trapper opened his mouth and began to laugh in his silent but hearty fashion. For several seconds he indulged himself in his peculiar, self-satisfying merriment, and then, turning to his companion, he exclaimed : —

"By the Lord, Henry, the cretur', whoever he be, has the gift of concealment, for sartin; and he has larnt a man, whose head has whitened on the trail, a trick the Hurons never dreamed of; and it might well take the conceit out of me if age had not larnt me the wisdom to know my ignorance. For here be I, a man who has never lived in the settlements, but lived accordin' to my gifts in the woods, and has seen a thousand ambushments, and knows all the tricks and devilments of the redskins, and the cretur' at our feet here has larnt me a lesson in hidin' whose vartue sets my eyes swimmin'. See, Henry, the cunnin' of the cretur'. Bless me, boy, if he hasn't woven the very grass into his breeches; aye, and into his shirt, and the hair of

his head, too; ontil the very mash is not greener nor more
like the arth than he. It's marvelous that a human bein'
could so convart himself into a bog, that a man with my
gifts and my trainin' might e'enamost have crawled over
him and not felt the shape and warmin' of his body."

"Come, friend," exclaimed the Trapper, as he drew back
a step and motioned toward the man at his feet, with a
hand that still kept its hold on the knife, "Come, friend or
inimy, whichever ye be, suppose ye hist yerself from the
bog and show yerself in yer nateral form, as the Lord made
ye, that we may see what sort of an animil ye be that has
crawled to the edge of this pond with the whole marsh on
yer back, and deceived the eyes of one born in the woods."

As the Old Trapper uttered this exclamation, the grass
upon which they were gazing, with eyes that lost not a motion, became agitated. A quiver ran through a section of
the turf at their feet, and then the body of a man, covered
from head to foot with grass and bits of sod, deftly woven
together in the semblance of a mantle, rose into the air and
stood upright before them; but the strange covering with
which he had clothed himself still clung to his garments, so
that it was impossible to discover the size and shape of the
man, or what might be his actual appearance when entirely
rid of his strange metamorphosis. But it was plainly seen
by the two men who stood staring at the astonishing figure
before them, that the man was of extraordinary height, and
that his arms, at least, were unusually long; but beyond
this, little could be guessed of his proportions or real appearance.

"HE SHOOK HIMSELF." Page 131.

"And now, friend," continued the Trapper, as he stood eying the wonderful figure before him, "if the grass isn't nat'ral to ye, and hasn't growed into yer skin so it would hurt ye to part with yer heathenish raiment, and especially if ye have got any breeches on, and yer ribs are kivered with a waistcoat, suppose for our knowledge and yer own comfort, ye sort of shake yerself free from what don't nat'-rally belong to ye, and show yerself to us jest as ye was afore ye stole the kiverin of the arth to sarve ye in yer cunnin', — that the boy here, and me, may know what sort of a man ye be; for though I have lived in the woods sence I was born, and have consorted with whites and redskins alike, nigh on to eighty year, and have seen all the tricks and devilments of Injin cunnin', yit I be ready to confess I never seed a man look as ye do, or onkivered, afore to-day, sech an ambushment as ye made for the beavers here on the edge of this pond. So shake yerself out of yer kiverin and show us yer nat'ral figur, or I shall sartinly lay hold of ye and see what's the color of yer hide myself."

In obedience to this exhortation of the Trapper, the strange being, who had not yet opened his mouth, but had remained staring at the two in front of him, began to quiver from head to foot. He shook himself as a dog shakes himself from extremity to extremity; the vibrations began at his head, from which, as the agitations grew, the grass spires and bits of sod began to fall in a shower, and as the motion worked its way down the body on its way to his feet, so did the strange covering fall away from him, until with a kick and flourish of his feet the last ad-

hering tufts and pieces of bogs and patches of swamp-
moss flew from his limbs, and a creature of astonishing
height, clothed in buckskin from toe to neck, stood forth in
plain view.

As the strange process of freeing himself from his un-
natural, but cunningly wrought covering, had gone on, and
while the agitation was at its height, and the air around
the man was literally full of the grass and sods and moss
he was shaking from himself, the Old Trapper yielded to
the sense of the humorous that was natural to him, and
beginning with a smile and a twinkle of the eyes, the expression of mirthfulness deepened and spread until it possessed his broad face and convulsed his stalwart frame.
He drove his knife into its sheath, and putting his hands on
his knees laughed a laugh that brimmed his eyes with irrepressible tears. In this laughter — from the very conta-
giousness of it perhaps — his companion joined, and had
there been a spectator to the scene, he would have perceived the strange spectacle of two men, standing on a
marsh, on the edge of a beaver pond, bent and swaying
with mirth, while in front of them stood a man, of immense
height and length of limb, but unusually lank in his proportions, and with a countenance that moved not a line,
nor changed a shade in its look of simple and almost solemn
gravity.

"By the Lord, Henry," exclaimed the Trapper, "if the
man isn't made up of grass and roots and yarbs! He is
nothin' more nor less than a section of the mash on legs,
and where there's depth of sile enough in him to support

such a crop is more than I can see, for he isn't thicker than a rived shingle, and another shake would send him into eternity." And the Old Trapper fairly surrendered himself to the merriment of his mood, and laughed and roared until the woods that bordered the marsh rang hollow to the sound.

Indeed, there was much in the appearance of the man, whoever or whatever he might be, in front of them, to provoke the mirth to which Herbert and the Trapper were so freely surrendering themselves, especially when taken in connection with the attendant circumstances of the scene. In height he was at least six feet and a half, but of such spare and extremely slim proportions that he appeared of even greater height. As for flesh, it could not with truth be said that he had much of any on him, for he seemed to be altogether made up of bones, skin, and sinews. His legs were of extraordinary length, even as contrasted with his immense height, and his arms fairly matched his legs. His hands were flat, with long, slim fingers and enormous joints and knuckles. His chest was narrow and his shoulders decidedly stooping. His face was beardless, and strange to say, well and regularly formed in its features. His mouth was rather small, chin pleasantly rounded, his eyes a light grey in color, his head fairly shaped and covered scantily with fine, light-colored hair. On his upper lip was a downy growth, scarcely discernible against the blonde skin that seemed incapable of taking tan or of receiving those characteristic lines which life and exposure bring to the average countenance. The dominant expression of his face

— and it spread its soft mildness over every feature, — was
a look of profound simplicity — the simplicity of one utterly guileless, and whose innocence is the result of passions
unexcited, and possibly of capacity too limited to receive
the temptations and seductions which are supposed to assail
and be received by the majority of mankind. Whether it
was the normal expression, a natural constituent of the
youth's countenance — for he could not have seen thirty
years — or whether it was because he did not understand,
and was pained at the somewhat boisterous mirth of the
two men in front of him, was uncertain; but over his face,
especially in the unsteady light of his eyes and around the
corners of his mouth, was visible the slightest possible expression of plaintive deprecation, as if he suffered in being
laughed at, and yet knew not why he was the object of
their mirth, and had not the strength of self-assertion to
resent it, even if he did know. It was the hurt, deprecating look of a loving animal, intelligent enough to receive
the pain inflicted by the ridicule, but unable or unwilling to
defend itself from the infliction.

The Old Trapper perceived what seemed to be passing in
the mind of the singular being in front of him; he checked
his laughter and his face settled into its accustomed gravity. He even made a motion that had in it the grave
significance of an apology, and, after gazing closely but
respectfully at him for a moment said, in the direct fashion
of a hunter's speech, and in a tone that had in it the vibration of astonishment, " Who be ye ? "

For a moment the man made no reply, but stood looking

first at the one and then at the other. At last his eyes
fixed themselves mildly but steadily upon the honest countenance of the Trapper and he replied : —

"I BE THE MAN WHO DON'T KNOW MUCH."

"Well," returned the Trapper, "ye are singularly named
for sartin, and I dare say honestly, but ye are the fust man
I've ever met on the arth, whether he was born in the
woods or the settlements, that would own up to his lackins,
or confess to his foolishness. And as to yer not knowin'
much ye sartinly know enough to ambush a beaver pond
when the water is alive with the rogues, and the top of
their lodge sentinelled by the father of the tribe, who larnt
the folly of carelessness in a way a beaver isn't apt to forgit,
when he left his tail in my trap two year agone; and that's
givin' ye credit for larnin' that few men in the woods have
to-day, not to speak of the parsons and other great men of
the settlements, who could no more fetch a trail across this
mash to the edge of this pond here and not skeer the critters than they could stop a wild pigeon in its flight with a
single bullet, with all the larnin' of their books to· help
them. And let me tell ye, lad, for it may comfort ye if ye
are short of larnin' and feel the lack of it powerful-like,
there isn't another man twixt the Horicon and the great
plains, that could so sink his body into this mash and kiver
it with grasses that old John Norton, when fetchin' an onsartin' ambushment, would crawl within reach of his knife,
if he was hostile, and lie within a yard of him for three
minutes and not know of his presence. And was it not for
the cunnin' of yer trick and the fact that years has larnt

me that the gifts and the larnin' of mortal man is imparfect, I should be kivered with shame at the thought that I actually rolled over agin ye afore I knowed the grass within reach of my arm was inhabited. So, comfort yerself, lad, for ye are sartinly gifted as few be in crawlin' and hidin', for ye have done what was never done afore by white or redskin, in peace or war, sence my eyes knowed the trail, or my nose larnt the difference twixt the smell of dead grass and the body of a mortal. And why are ye here, lad, and where are ye bound ?"

But the youth made no reply, but stood and stared at the old man, with mouth half open and eyes filled with surprise. At last, without answering the interrogation of the Trapper, he said : —

"Be you John Norton, the Trapper! I've heard of you since I was a boy on the farm, by the great sea, and men told great tales of you, and one man said you saved his life way off in the West, where the land is all flat and the Indians are thick as the grass. And partly because they laughed at me at home after mother died, and partly because I wanted to find you and live with you, I ran away and came to the woods here, where I've been these twelve years trying to find you. And now I have found you, and you said I did well in crawling onto the beaver here, I'm so happy." And the poor fellow paused as if overcome with very delight. And then he looked wistfully at the old Trapper, as if he would ask a favor, which he feared would not be granted, took a half step toward him and said timidly, "John Norton ! Please, may I take one of your hands ? "

"Lord bless ye lad, of course ye may. And ye needn't think its any great honor either, and if I can do ye any good, or give ye a lift in any way, I will do it for sartin, and there's my hand on it," and the Trapper stretched out his broad palm to the youth, who took it in one of his long bony hands and clasped his fingers round it with a closeness of grip that would have crowded the bones out of place in a weaker structure, while his face was absolutely radiant with delight.

"Aye, aye, shake away," exclaimed the old man, laughing as he saw the pleasure on the young man's face and felt the power of his grip, "ye've got a grip like a bear-trap, and if ye was as strong in yer back as ye are in yer fingers ye'd be a tough one to meet in a scrimmage when yer blood was up and the whoop of yer inimies was sharp in yer ears, and ye warmed to the work. And now, what can ye do and what can I do for ye, my boy? for tall as ye be ye seem no more than a boy to one who has seen seventy years come and go, and whose head is whitnin' with the snows of the winters he has lived."

"I can't do much," responded the other, "for I am not smart, but slow, and I never could learn at school like my brothers, although I got through my letters; and mother, who never scolded me because I was dull, learnt me to spell a good many verses in the Bible, and I haven't forgot one of them either. But I can work at almost anything you may put me at, and if you will only let me live with you I will do anything you tell me. And I had great luck at trapping last year, and I have as nice a boat as was ever built,

and a very good rifle, and traps enough to set a twenty mile
line ; and I love the woods and I love you, for I have heard
of your goodness, and if you won't laugh at me because I
am dull, nor blame me when I make mistakes, I will work
for you as long as I live."

While the poor fellow had thus been running on in his
entreaty, the Old Trapper had stood looking steadily at him;
and over the calm gravity of his features there came, as the
youth proceeded, a look of supreme tenderness, as if the
spirit of the mother, to which the speaker alluded, had actually taken possession of the Trapper's heart, and was
pleading within his bosom in behalf of her unfortunate boy.
For a moment after the youth had done speaking, the Trapper stood gazing at him in silence ; then he said :

"Boy, ye may come with me, and whether ye know little
or much, be quick or slow in larnin' and doin', I will be yer
friend. Ye may not be knowin', and I honestly doubt if the
Lord has favored ye in that respect, for sartin ; but His gifts
are not all in one direction, and the cunningest beaver hasn't
always the deepest fur; and He has sartinly gin ye an
honest face and a sperit as innocent as a faan's, and that
goes furder in His sight, both here and in the world to
come, than a knowin' head and a cunnin' tongue, as I jedge.
So ye may go to yer boat, which I conceit to be in the outlet, and we will fetch our'n over the carry and jine ye as
soon as we may. And Henry," continued the Old Trapper,
as he turned toward his companion, "do ye take the hand
of the lad, for the Lord alone knows the parpose He has
had in bringin' us together in this ambushment, nor where
the trail that leads us from this mash will tarminate."

At the word of the Trapper, Herbert had advanced and took in a frank, hearty way the hand of the youth, who seemed greatly embarrassed at the friendly overture, but who nevertheless extended his hand to Herbert's grasp, but in a timid way that characterizes the act of a bashful and shrinking spirit. " Ye sartinly don't look much alike," remarked the Trapper, as he stood looking from one to the other of the young men, so nearly the same in age, and so totally unlike in other respects. " No, ye sartinly don't look alike, and yer gifts are wider apart than yer looks, and I marvel that the Lord should give to one of his cretur's so much and so little to another; but I dare say he has his reasons and acts with jedgment in the matter, though to a mortal who knows only what he sees, it looks unfair and agin reason. But the Missioners say — and I conceit there may be truth in it, — that things on the arth got twisted by some devilment or other in the beginnin'; but that afore long the Almighty will straighten things out, and he who has leetle shall have much, and the last shall be fust; but it will take a good deal of overhaulin', as I jedge, and I don't see jest how it is to be fetched about though it ought to be, for sartin. Come, lad, ye go yer way to yer boat, and we will jine ye as soon as we can fetch the canoo and the pack over the carry."

Thirty minutes later, Herbert and the Trapper had crossed the carry and stood on the bank of the stream where they had expected to find their new acquaintance, but no one was in sight. They had traversed the carry in that noiseless fashion which a life of caution, natural to those who

depend for their food and safety on the stillness of their
movements, quickly makes habitual, and now they were
standing, the Trapper leaning on his paddle at the end of
the canoe ready to launch it forth on the stream, and Herbert, rifle in hand, on the extreme edge of the bank waiting for the word to embark when the old man should shove
off. For several minutes they stood listening for some
sound that should reveal the coming of their comrade; but
no sound could be heard, save the rustle of the beech leaves
overhead, and the squeaking of some mold-mice in a bog
near at hand.

"I say, Henry," said the Trapper at length, in a low tone
of voice and scarcely above a whisper, "where do yo think
the lad is? Here we be on the outlet where we told him
to meet us, but I see no signs of the boy. What shall we
do, — Hoot! here he comes! The lad has his gifts, but he
isn't parfect at the paddle yit, for I sartinly caught the
sound of it in the sand, where the stream shallows into the
lake. You will see him round the bend in a minit, or the
hole in my ears has growed up."

Sure enough, in a moment the boat came round the
curve, and was laid along side the bank where they stood.
In the boat was a pile of traps of various makes and sizes,
and just from the maker's hand; for they had the new,
fresh look about them which even one season's use would
take away. A pair of oars of uncommon length and admir-
ably modeled, trailed from their row-locks. A rifle of unusual size and weight, with horn and bullet pouch, was lashed
with buckskin thongs to a resting place evidently made

for it, along the right side of the boat, which was itself extraordinarily long and narrow, being fully seventeen feet in length, and not more than three feet in its widest section at the center, and the lines on which it was built was perfection itself, for fast running. A hound, of great-size and beauty, evidently a cross between the Irish and German breed, sat upright on its haunches on the forward thwart. As the boat moved easily up to the bank at his feet, the Trapper said : —

"Well, lad, ye are well furnished for sartin, though yer boat is too long to work easy in the cricks, and would make a good many backs ache on the carry. Yer traps is all right although a leetle too newish for ra'al sarvice, but a few months' usin' will limber them up mightily. The dog is a good un and I marvel where ye found him, for next to Rover here, he is the biggest dog of his cross 1 ever seed in the woods. I think if they consort well together and are friendly we will let them drive one buck this fall in company for the sake of their music, for a hound's mouth has a great many tunes in it that are wurth listenin' to on a frosty mornin', if I am any jedge. Yer rifle looks biggish to one who has larnt that a heavy barrel don't make the lead go any furder, but it has, as I see, a big bore, and chambers a handful of powder, and that's in it's favor when ye want to do long work on a windy day, or ye are on the pint of squarin' accounts with a panther. Ye needn't git out lad, but shove down the crick and we will follow. We are pushin' through to the Saranacs to see the boat race there, and take a hand in it too it may be, and we must

camp to-night thirty mile from here, and the sun is on the
west side of the pines already.   We shall have time to become better acquainted afore we git through." So saying
the Trapper launched his canoe and the two boats disappeared down the crooked stream.

CHAPTER III.

"In Nature there is nothing melancholy." — Coleridge.

IT was nigh sunset when a boat, followed closely by a canoe with a paddler at either end of it, shot out of a bay that indents the western shore-line of Big Tupper, near its southern extremity, and headed toward the falls made by the water that comes tumbling out of Bog River, over the ledge of rocks which impedes its easy entrance into the lake below. Both boat and canoe were being propelled at a rate which showed that the man who bent to the oars, of the boat, and those who wielded the paddles in the canoe behind him, were accustomed to the work they were at and were not disposed to loiter. The lake was as smooth as if no ripple had ever stirred upon its surface, and the clouds which lay in rolls and patches overhead, crimsoned on their western sides by the red rays of the declining sun, and dark on the other with the gloom of the coming night, were perfectly reflected in the still depths. The bay out of which they had come was speckled with the highly colored autumnal leaves which the winds of the day had blown from the maples that lined the upper end of the cove, and lay like great flakes of crimson snow that could not sink nor melt, on the blue-green surface. Through the still air came the roar of the falls in solemn murmurs, now swelling with full volume of sustained sound, and anon sinking and dying away until the ear almost lost the direction of the smothered swell. The mountains to the east stood forth in all their grand proportions, their vast sides from base to summit red with solar flame, and their peaks showing sharply in outline against the dusky blue of the remoter sky. The mountains to the west were already dark with the growing gloom, and their ponderous shadows stretched half across the lake.

"I tell ye, Henry," said the man, who, kneeling in the bow of the canoe, was wielding his paddle with the precise and leisurely but powerful stroke of strength and consummate skill, and who was none other than our old friend, the Trapper, — "I tell ye, Henry," said he addressing, without turning his head or varying his stroke, his companion in the stern, "the lad pulls a strong stroke, if it be rather slow and not so snappy as is jedicious in a light boat. His gather isn't very handsome, for sartin, and his head sort of lops down on his chest, but his boat runs on an even keel and he reaches for a good deal of water. I conceit we had better flirt this birch up to him a leetle and let him know that we mean to git to the pint soon enough to take supper with him any way. Do ye lengthen yer stroke a foot or so, Henry, and give me the beat of a leetle livelier tune, back there, as the fiddlers say, for the paddle in the bow must take its hint from the paddle in the starn, onless ye would have yer boat rockin' like a cradle in the settlements."

To this injunction Herbert yielded a ready assent, and set

the Trapper a stroke that gave him a chance to put his enormous strength into his paddle. For half a minute not a sound was heard, save the dip of the paddle-blades as their thin edges were whipped in and out of the water, and the hiss of its parted surface as the sharp canoe flew through it. Up and down the paddles flashed. They rose and fell with the precision of machinery, and driven by their powerful pressure the canoe fairly flashed through the dusky air. For a moment it gained rapidly on the boat — so rapidly that in an instant its beak was within a dozen feet of the boat's stern, and the Trapper called good naturedly to the man who was working soberly at the oars ahead : —

"Look out, lad, we are comin' for ye. Henry has sartinly tuck the floor in arnest, with his moccasins off, and has sot my paddle agoin' to the motions of a jig that the parsons in the settlements never danced to. We don't want to run ye down, lad, and spill yer traps and yer dog into the water ; but ye sartinly will have to lengthen yer stroke, and put a little more snap into yer gather, or we shall bunt ye in a minit."

"I don't care if you and Henry do bunt me," returned the man at the oars, "for I know you are only in fun ; but I'd just as soon run faster as not, for the sooner we get in the sooner we will have something to eat — and I am real hungry ; — but I don't think you can catch me, for I've got a first-rate boat to run, and my oars are very long, and I'll lengthen out a bit if you say so."

While he had been saying this, in a simple, quiet tone of voice, with not the least vibration of excitement in it, he had been lengthening his stroke and quickening his gather, until by the time he had done speaking he was pulling with a sweep and finish that no one could have believed possible to one so spare of frame and so awkward in his habitual motions.

By this time the two boats were fairly flying, for THE MAN WHO DIDN'T KNOW MUCH had set himself a stroke which an English coach would have called nearly perfect, — long and strong, and evenly pulled from beginning to end. The immense length of his body and arms, taken in connection with the size of his oars, enabled him to get and keep a hold on the water a full yard ahead of where an ordinary stroke would begin, while the blades remained in the water until they had passed nearly to the stern of the boat and were ready to trail. His recovery was certainly not quick, but it did not linger at any point, and was made with the precision of machinery, while the blades dropped into the water of the lake as if it was oil, for not a drop was disturbed on the surface, and the grip they got on the water was as strong as pressure could make it from the start. It was a stroke such as no one that had not the Lad's enormous length could deliver, and which would require far greater strength than his, probably, to sustain; but if it could be kept up, no mortal man of shorter build could live a race out with him.

" I tell ye, lad," said the Trapper, as he put the strength of his powerful frame into the paddle, until the polished staff bent to the strain, as a foil bends when the fencer suddenly drops his weight on to it, — "I tell ye, lad, I have seed

many men pull oars on these lakes and on the great rivers
of the West, too, when death was in full chase astarn and
they had good reason to do their best; but I never seed a
man pull sech a stroke as ye are pullin'. And if ye had a
leetlo more thickness across the chest and around the small
of yer back, I don't believe a man on the arth could
hold even with ye for a mile, onless the devil was arter him,
and the Lord of Marcy gave him a lift. Now, here be Henry
and me, who have our gifts, and among them I sartinly
reckon the jedicious use of the paddle aint the least; and
onless he has forgot himself, I dare say he is doin' his share.
And I know that if I should put another ounce into my
stroke I should break as tough a paddle as second-growth
ash ever made; and that would be a bit of foolishness, as I
jedge. And yit ye hold yer own agin us handsomely, and
it sartinly looks, as I see the swing of yer stroke, and git
the reason of it, that ye might let out another link or two
if sarcumstances raally called on ye for it. I tell ye, Henry," continued the Trapper, as he turned his face a trifle
toward his companion and lowered his voice, " I've always
held that two paddles, used with reason, could beat any
two oars in the univarse. But the lad, here, is sartinly
holdin' us even, and, I do believe, he has actally gained six
good inches in the last twenty strokes; and if yer paddle
will bear it, I sartinly advise ye to put a leetle more force
into yer stroke, as I shall into mine, if the staff in my hands
goes to pieces; for I'll never own up that one man at the
oars can beat two men at the paddle, if I be one of 'em,
and the ash holds together. So, Henry, quicken yer stroke

agin, and drive the stick ye have in yer hands into pieces, as I sartinly will mine, onless we bunt the lad fair and square, so as to start the paint on his starn-board, within the next fifty rods."

The Old Trapper was evidently warming to the work, at the thought that one of his favorite notions was in peril, and the manner in which he flashed his paddle-blade far out ahead, as he finished his summons to Herbert, showed that his next stroke would test the strength of his paddle beyond what ordinary wood could stand; but the stroke was never delivered, for as his body rose into the air and extended itself forward for the full exercise of his immense powers, a sharp, quick quiver ran through the canoe from stem to stern, and, yielding to the tremendous sweep which Herbert gave to his guiding blade, it swooped so suddenly aside from the line of its previous course that any one less accustomed that the old man to the frail thing would have lost his balance and been pitched headlong into the lake.

"What is it, boy, what is it?" exclaimed the Trapper in a hoarse whisper, as he felt the signal run through the canoe, "and where away is he? By the Lord, Henry," continued he, as his eyes caught sight of an object standing out in bold relief on the shore a hundred rods, perhaps, to his right, "a bigger buck never wet his hoofs in the water or made his bed in the moss. Ye have done this thing sarcumspectly, lad, and larnt an old man the foolishness of talkin' and actin' like a person without eyes when his bolt is slack from emptiness, and there's no ven'son in the pack. That's right, Henry, git round into place and take yer rifle and leave the paddlin' to me, for yer eye is keen and yer hands steady, and the buck, there, is an old 'un and has seed man afore, and ye will have to shoot a far shot and put yer bullet where it ought to go, or we'll sup without meat to-night, that's sartin."

The actions of the two men thus suddenly and unexpectedly interrupted in their race, were characteristic, and perfectly illustrated the habits of those who depend on the alertness of their senses for their profits and their food in the woods.

The eyes of Herbert, even amid the excitement of the race, acting in harmony with a law of habit which had in it from constant practice, the force of nature, had never shortened the range of their observation, but searched with occasional glances the gathering gloom of the western shore for some such presence as they had at last — in the extreme end of a little cove heavily bordered with cedar and balsam — discovered. With instinctive sagacity he had shied the canoe to the left, out into the lake and away from the buck, and in such a manner that when it came to a stand, the end in which he was sitting would be pointed toward the game. Thought is scarcely quicker than the motion with which the Old Trapper, the instant his eyes caught sight of the buck, had slid from his kneeling posture into the bottom of the canoe where, now sitting, he was ready for the advance. Herbert had no sooner delivered the stroke with which the canoe had been turned from its course and checked in its career, than, sliding his paddle into it, he changed his position to the reverse of what it

had been, and with a motion of his hand unlashed his rifle
from its fastenings and lifted it to his knees. Thus, in an
instant, the change had been affected, and the difficult job
of paddling up to a wild deer in daylight, was about to be
attempted.

Thus they sat, ready for the start, but before they started
the Trapper delivered himself, thus characteristically : —

"Henry, we have made forty mile sence we've tasted food,
and the meal is scant in the bag, and the pork no bigger
than the text of a parson's sermon; and the pack of the
lad yender — who hasn't larnt what we are up to yit, for
he's pullin' the same stroke he was when we quit, as if he
had no eyes in his head, and etarnity was before him — has
more traps in it than biscuit, and though traps be good
enough in their way, yit they can neither be briled nor
spitted, and I'm as empty as a horn with not a karnal in it.
I sartinly hope ye may be able to sink the lead into him in
a spot where it will weigh most. Now, boy, I will git ye
as nigh as I can, and give ye the favor of all the light there
is, and I have strong hopes of yer gittin' him, for yer gifts
at shootin' are sartinly wonderful. I know ye be jedicious
in kalculatin' distance, and I've never seen ye miss a cretur
ye drawed on yit, but it's mighty dusky for close work, and
I sartinly wont blame ye if ye miss him. Don't lift yer
piece till I signal, for I know the habits ·of the cretur' and
will keep my eyes on him. I shan't give ye the sign till
he's about to jump. So when ye git it, boy, don't be long
in findin' the bottom of yer sights, and remember to allow
for the darkness. I hope, with the feelin' of a hungry man,

that ye'll hit him, Henry, for I am sartinly empty and the cravin' of natur' is strong within me. Now do accordin' to the gifts the Lord has gin ye, or three men will go supper-less to bed."

As the Trapper concluded his speech the canoe began to move toward the buck, but with a motion so easy and true to the line of its progress that, to one looking at it in the direction of its movement, the movement itself could not be perceived. The arms of the Trapper were sunk well over the sides of the canoe, and his paddle played in the water, without revealing its motions, as noiselessly and al-most as invisibly as do the webbed feet of the Northern Diver. His body was so held as to place Herbert's form exactly between the buck and himself, so that neither the motion of the canoe, as it slowly floated forward, nor the body and motions of the paddler, could be seen. Herbert sat in plain view, with his rifle across his knees, and his finger within the guard; but his body was as motionless as if carved out of the air, and the features of his face, even, were stiffened into the rigidity of marble. Thus the canoe glided into the deepening shadows of the western shore and the mouth of the little cove, directly towards the game.

At the farther end of the bay stood the buck, his feet deep in the brown sands, and his antlered head lifted, as if in proud challenge, into the air. His posture was one of haughty interrogation as to what the dim object gliding in upon him might be, and superb defiance of it. Twice he lifted a fore leg and drove his pointed hoof into the sand, with the expression of lordly impatience at the ignorance

or audacity of those who dared disturb, by their bold presence, his royal privacy. And as the canoe floated still
nearer, twice he lifted his brown muzzle into the air and
blew a blast from his resounding nostrils, that tore fiercely
through the stillness, and made the woods behind him ring
again, while the mountain across the lake received the
wrathful sound, and passed it back in diminutive modula-
tions to the spot from whence it came. Once he started,
as if some terrible suspicion had for an instant broken over
the ramparts of his courage and stormed into the very
pavilion of his kingly spirit; but it was only a passing
weakness. He gave one jump, then stopped, planted himself as if incapable of fear; lifted his nose high up, and
blew again a wrathful challenge to the rude intruders, while
the hair on the line of his back ridged in wrath, and his
feet smote the beach like hammers.

In the meanwhile the canoe floated as noiselessly onward
as a feather, and with a steadiness of motion that never
varied a hair's width. Even when the buck jumped, not
a muscle of Herbert's face moved, and the finger which lay
lightly on the trigger, could not have been steadier had the
hand to which it belonged been incapable of feeling. Thus
the man in the bow held his position with rigid fixedness
and the man in the stern worked his paddle with the same
even and steady play of the wrist. But when the buck
blew his second challenge, after he made his bound, and
the progress of the canoe was fast bringing him in line
with a beech, whose silvery white leaves furnished a back-
ground that would serve to bring out his head in partial re-

lief, at least, the paddle of the Trapper stopped its movement, and settled to a trail, and when the onward progress had lifted the antlers to the level of the silver leaves, the least possible quiver ran along the sides of the canoe.

For a second after the signal was given, Herbert moved not a muscle, and then the rifle jumped to his cheek, and before it seemed possible for his eye to have found the line of the sight, the fiery flame leapt into the dusky air and the mountain rang with the rattling echoes of the sharp explosion. The buck never jumped, but dropped in his tracks as if his legs had been cut from under him, and lay in a limp heap; for the bullet had entered between the eyes and torn its passage through the spinal column as it passed out. The Trapper never said a word until he had reached the spot where the dead deer lay, and had examined both the entrance and exit of the bullet; but after he had bled the game and had wiped his knife free of stain, he turned to his comrade and said : —

" I knowed ye could shoot well afore to-day, for I've seed ye do shootin' that would put to shame many who boast of their exploits with the rifle, but what ye have did here on the buck shows the parfection of the wepon ye carry, and that yer gifts lie in the direction of a grooved barrel. I sartinly thought ye was waitin' a leetle too long on the cretur' arter I gin ye the signal, and my inards sort of shrivelled with disappintment at the idee of losin him, but I conceit the reason of yer waitin' now I've seed where ye've drove the bullet, and I confess ye mixed yer brains with yer powder and shot with reason and jedgment, for the body showed dim agin the bank and the white leaves of the beech here made his head yer best chance; but the chance was none of the best and I honestly question if there's another man in the woods that could have did as ye have considerin' the darkness and the distance. Yis, yer gifts in shootin' are sartinly oncommon, and I trust ye feel grateful to the Giver of them. This buck is as big as natur' allows, Henry," continued the Trapper, as he laid hold of his legs to roll him into the canoe, "and his antlers will make the eyes of the folks in the settlements stick out."

In ten minutes they were off the point on which a rousing fire was burning, while the Lad, for so the Old Trapper had named him, was plying his axe vigorously, preparing wood for the night.

"Well, Lad," called the Trapper from the canoe, as it swung in toward the shore where a stretch of sand made the landing safe for the frail and heavily-laden vessel, "so ye stopped rowin' arter awhile did ye? The last I saw of ye, ye was goin' it as if ye had taken the job for the winter, and was puttin' yer best licks into the beginnin'. The sight of yer arnestness sort of warmed me up, and made my eyes see nothin' but the eend of yer boat. And if it hadn't been for Henry here we should have run by as big a buck as ever wore antlers, and gone supperless to bed. Come down, Lad, and take a look at the cre'tur, for he is as big as an ox, and the fat lies as thick on his ribs as if he had fed in the cornfields of the settlements. There will be some strong and arnest movements of teeth on this pint to-night arter the meat has cooled a trifle, or else you and Henry has had better eatin' than I have, sence wo left the pond of beavers."

Two hours later three men might have been seen reclinin' around a huge camp-fire, whose flame rose directly upward in a steady column, illuminating the branches of the great pines overhead and around, and casting its bright reflections far out over the surface of the lake.

"Yis, this is Tomahawk P'int, Henry, of which ye have heerd me speak afore; and right back here in the swale is 'Bloody Spring.' And it is well named, too; for, though its waters are cool and pure as natur' ever brewed, yit I remember the day when its depths was red with mortal blood; for a dreadful scrimmage was fought here years ago, and the dead lay thick around it, as the cones on the ground tonight. Yis, I was young then; but I did my part accordin' to my gifts, and I was one of the few that came out alive; for 'twas a close thing, hand to hand, and the powder gin out on both sides afore 'twas ended. And we took to the knife and the clubbed rifle, for blood was hot that day, and marcy was little thought of by redskin or white, and few of us came out with full veins, I tell ye."

"What did you fight each other for?" said the Lad. "I think it wrong to fight, don't you, John Norton?"

"Sartinly, Lad, sartinly, under ordinary sarcumstances, and in peace time; but there be times when it's necessary to draw blood, especially in self defence; and war, if it be a righteous one, is self defence in a large sort of a way, as I understand it. But it's a dreadful thing to take a mortal life, I'll allow, and I never lined the sights on a man when it didn't seem to me, all things cons dered, that he had lived long enough, and should git a taste of the Jedgment; but I will confess that when things git close, and ye have to take to yer knife, and there is two to one agin ye, a man hasn't much time to arger the question of right and wrong, and I dare say in sech sarcumstances I have used the rifle-stock and the knife a leetle loose and careless-like; and I recollect the awful scrimmage we had here sixty year agone as if it was but yesterday, and it was a most onreasonable and bloody battle, for sartin, for when 'twas ended, I was the only man who could keep his feet, and I had three bullets inside of me, and a knife blade driven into my shoulder here, with the handle broke square off in front, and the p'int stickin' out of my back. But it wasn't our fault, for when their powder gin out, the Huron's came at us with their tomahawks, and they outnumbered us four to one, and we had to show the scamps the borderers' grit, and we did, for I sent the last of the vagabonds into etarnity with marks on his throat and a hole in his side, which told the Lord as plain as writin', I reckon, that John Norton was sarvin' him in arnest on the arth. But, Lad, yer sperit is right, and it is better to live in peace with yer fellow-men, if ye can."

"That's what mother used to say to me," replied the Lad, and the good Book says: 'If – thy – enemy – smite – you – on – the – one – cheek, – turn – to – him – the – other, – also; and – if – a – man – take – away – thy – cloak, – give – him – thy – coat, – also.' Haven't I said it right Henry ?"

"Yes, you have said it right, word for word," replied the other.

"I knew I hadn't forgot it," continued the Lad, with the least possible inflection of pride in his voice, "and I know it is a wise saying, for last fall a bad man got on the line of my traps, and stole my skins as fast as I could trap them. And one day I caught him stealing a mink, and I went up to him so still he never knew I was nigh until I touched him, and he jumped as if he had been shot, and drew his knife on me; but I didn't fear him, for I knew I was right, and he was wrong, and I told him 'twas wicked to steal and that if he wanted skins I would give him some, rather than he should steal them, if he would go to the cabin. And he went, and I made him up a roll of good nice ones, and in the morning, when he was about to go away, I gave the roll to him; but he wouldn't touch it, but said he would never steal another skin as long as he lived; and I don't believe he will, do you, John Norton?"

"I shouldn't think he would, Lad, if he has any inards to him," returned the Trapper, as he looked steadily into the guileless face before him, "it sartiuly worked well in your case, but I don't conceit the rod would fit every bore. Now, I've read the Bible off and on for sixty year, and take it all in all, its a pritty reasonable book, although there be portions of it that I can't make sense of, and now and then ye run agin a sayin' that's sartinly onreasonable, and the varse the Lad has quoted, Henry, is one of 'em. I've thought a good deal over those varses, and I've ruther settled down to the opinion that either the words have got into the book

by mistake, or else that the Lord didn't know much about
the cost of jackets, and sech like garments. For it's sartinly agin reason to tell a man who has had his westcott
stole, to give the vagabond that stole it, his shirt also;
especially if it be late in the fall, and thread is scant in the
cabin. Now I run agin a half-breed on the line of my traps
last winter, and he had a fisher in his thievin' fingers, and I
told him to drop it or there would be trouble. I reasoned
with him about the onrighteousness of the act, not exactly
as the Lad would, perhaps, but I gin him a bit of my mind
which I dare say was equal to Scriptur', under the sarcumstances. Well, two weeks later—and I had lost a dozen
good pelts in the meanwhile, — I caught the scamp fishin'
around for a beaver that had run out into the pond with
one of my chains to him, and I conceited the thing had
gone fur enough, and I put my mark on him so the Lord
shouldn't have any doubts who he was, or who he stole
from when he should come sneakin' into the jedgment, even
if I shouldn't be round to testify in the case. The Lad's
way is a good un' for sartin, if it will work; but bullets is
cheaper than pelts, and I shouldn't offer a roll of good skins
to any thief I catched at my traps, Scriptur' or no Scriptur'.
I tell ye, powder makes a louder sound than pious words,
in the ears of a sneak when fingerin' pelts that don't belong
to him. What say ye, Henry?"

"I say we had better go to sleep, now, and talk some
other time. But before we turn in, what think you of a
hunt in the morning. The hounds take kindly together,
and would run a buck to water in an hour. We could take

his body out and sell it at the Saranacs, or jerk it here before we start; for there's two days yet before the races. What say you both?"

The idea was a pleasing one both to the Lad and the Trapper, and after a few moments further canvassing the matter, they wrapped themselves in their blankets, and with their feet almost in the warm ashes, and with no covering but the sky above their heads, fell asleep.

CHAPTER IV.

*"The bounding elk, whose antlers tear
The branches, falls before my aim." — Bryant.*

MORNING in the wilderness. The east was rosy red, save where a layer of clouds lying athwart the rising light cut it from north to south with its black plane. The mountain summits to the east were crested with reflected fire, while the snow which crowned them with its cold beauty blushed at the kiss of the ardent morning. The lake was one vast valley filled with fog. The impenetrable fleece possessed the intervening space from shore to shore, and even masked the lower mountains from sight. The trees dripped lazily. The gayly tinted leaves of the maples in the coves, without cause, let go their hold upon the stems and floated in indolent, zigzag motions downward. The squirrels in the thickets were waking the tiny echoes with their noisy chatterings. At intervals the harsh shriek of the king-fisher disturbed the air, while now and then a loon sent forth its weird call from amidst the feathery fleece. Soon the sun let loose its energies; the red beams marshalled themselves upon the eastern crests and then charged downward in fiery squadrons upon the fog. Into it and through it they dashed. They trampled it under foot,

opened broad lanes from shore to shore, cut into it right
and left and sent it flying. The warm, vibrant life was too
much for the cold, inert deadness, and in a brief space the
mighty orb of day stood forth in the blue sky in all his
glory. The lake lay plain to the view, but its surface still
smoked. Soon the dead air became a current, and waves
of thinnest vapor rolled along the smooth surface. Here
and there a shortened column of denser mist rose from the
water. In the bays and around the shores of the coves
where were the inlets, a few vagrant patches might be seen
stealing like detected guilt from the sight of day. Thus
morning, bright and clear, with all it brings of light, and
warmth, and renewed life, had triumphed over its gloomy
foe.

Just as the fog began to lift from the surface of the water,
a boat with the Lad in it, shoved out from Tomahawk Point
and started down the lake. As it glided forward the old
Trapper, who was in the act of charging his rifle, paused a
moment with his palm on the top of his ramrod, and
said:—

" Now, Lad, don't ye forgit where ye are to watch; Henry
will lie off the big rock, and ye are to place yerself inside
the island, so ye can see well down the lake. I shan't start
the dogs 'till I find a big un, and he won't run fur if he's
fat, and ' Sport' is as ye say he is in a race; and I warrant
' Rover' won't fool away time, for I can see by the look in
his eye that he's hungry for the scent, and will be crazy
when he gits it warm and strong. Keep yer eyes open,
Lad, for I shall drive in a big un, an' if ye are as good at

shootin' as ye be at rowin' ye'll kill him afore he gits within
a half a mile of the lake;" and the Trapper laughed at his
own conceit. "I tell ye, Henry," he continued, as he drove
the bullet home, still keeping his eye on the receding boat,
"The Lad has his gifts, but it's wonderful that the Lord
should do them up in that sort of a fashion; for he's un-
naterally lengthy to begin with, an' looks as if he was built
in sections, an' as if the sections was not half put together
at that; but his sperit is right, an' he sartinly pulled a
stroke last night that was amazin'. There, Henry," he continued, as he carefully capped the tubes, "I didn't like the
way the bullet in the left barrel felt as I sent it down, for it
went onsteady; but the one I have put into the right was a
beauty, an' it drove even and true from muzzle to chamber
as a bullet should drive. So now if ye are ready, take yer
rifle and the dogs, an' we will start the canoe. The sun
has eat up the mist an' it's high time the pups was out."

In a moment the canoe, containing the Trapper, Herbert,
and the hounds, left the point and in five minutes was
across the bay. The Trapper stood holding the dogs in the
leash on the rock for an instant, and said : —

"If I was in yer place, Henry, I would lie well off here
abreast of the rock, for the runway comes out by that ledge
there, an' more than one deer have I seen take the jump
flyin'; an' if the dogs play fast, as I think they will, — for I
shan't start 'em ontil I start a buck from his nest, — an' if
he should take water here ye will see as pritty a sight as a
hunter ever saw, an' one to make yer eyes brighten, an' the
blood in yer veins to tingle." So saying the Trapper disap-

peared with the dogs in the thicket, and Herbert, acting on the old man's suggestions, paddled sixty rods out into the lake, and lifting his rifle to his knees, waited.

Thus Herbert sat listening. The morning had brought no wind, and the lake stretched in level expanse, unruffled, from shore to shore. Objects were not wanting to amuse the eye. A partridge strutted out on the trunk of a huge pine that projected outward from the shore, ruffed its neck, clucked, spread out its fan-like tail, and raising itself to its highest stretch, drummed with nervous strokes of its wings, loud and long, with evident pride at its brave performance. A family of wood ducks, a mother and six younglings, of full size but lacking the beauty of older birds, led by the lordly drake in full plumage — his crest of purple and bronze alive with color, and his whole body, as the warm rays of the sun smote upon his back, ablaze with brilliance, fairly converting him into a bunch of floating radiance — swam in Indian file around the outer rock and continued on their course, until their tiny wake faded from sight in the inner cove.

A great northern diver, that had dived from some unknown point, rose for air within six rods of Herbert's station, shook the water from its eyes, flattened itself an instant in suspicion as it caught sight of the canoe, and the motionless man sitting in it; then, reassured, rose on its webbed feet, shook its narrow wings, showing the rounded fulness of its snow-white breast, and the spotted beauty of its back; then settled back upon the water, thrust its head playfully beneath the surface, withdrew it, lifted its black bill into the air and laughed its weird, witch-like laughter, till the honest hills mocked wickedly in reply. So Herbert sat, observant of nature's doings, with eyes that lost not a motion on lake or shore, and with ears open to receive the slightest sound. At last it came. One instant, and the hills embodied silence; not a vibration stirred above their motionless pines. The next, and the hollow air rang as if with the notes of a dozen bugles suddenly blown by practiced lips, clear, strong and full, from the signal.

No initial yelp, no whimpering and doubtful prelude, prepared the listener's feelings for the coming peal; but loud, and long, and full, as voice of hound could make it, when the game starts from his nest in close and maddening view, did the clarion peal ascend. It rose above the pines, and filled the upper air, rolled down the ravines an avalanche of softening sound, swelled up above the peaks, and ran in minor ripples of noise along the ridges, and even sent its waves of melody across the level lake, breaking at last, and dying away in melting reverberations on the farther shore. The cheek of Herbert flushed, his eyes lighted, and the blood within him tingled in its every vein, as he heard the glorious cry. Again and again did the sounds swell upward, and roll down the mountain. Peal on peal, torrent, eddies, and cataracts of tuneful noise, did the hounds send rushing and rolling out into the resounding air. Onward in swift career they tore. Now flying along a ridge, now plunging into a deep ravine, where the thick balsam branches half-smothered their clarion cry; now streaming in swiftest race down a steep slope, while above, the air fairly quivered, torn apart and shiveied into tuneful fragments by the imperious summons of the dogs' hot throats, beneath.

Thus went the race. And with feelings which only a hunter knows, did Herbert sit and mark its changeful course,—holding his very breath to listen, when the sounds made ærial angles, and expecting that each turn would bring the dogs' mouths toward the lake. At last, the buck, pressed by the hounds, doubled short upon his course,— which had been upward, as if he would climb the crest, and seek refuge in the western lakes. He turned, and shot with all his speed along the very runway the Old Trapper had mentioned, straight for the lake and the ledge; abreast of which Herbert, intense and ready for his appearance, sat. Down, down he came, and after him the hounds. It was plain to Herbert that the dogs had held their own from the start, and were running in full sight of their game. Onward and downward came the race. Buck and dogs and noise came on together. The mountain flowed with sounds. The steep declivity resounded with the rush of the vocal torrent. To north and south the echoes barked and roared. The owls flew up into the dazzling sun, affrighted by the tempest of noises that swept and eddied underneath their gloomy roosts. The ravens, with wavering wings, fluttered above the trees, harshly croaking. The white gulls, sailing on circling pinions far overhead, screamed their shrill interrogations to each other, and soared yet higher.

Thus, with bay of hounds, with scream and croak of bird, and volleying echoes pouring down straight toward the

shore, like a tornado's flight, came on the hurrying race.
Soon the sound of parting brush was heard, of crackling
stems, of dead wood crashed wildly through, of vault, and
plunge, and all the noises which an impetuous race down a
steep mountain side, on a still morning, makes. Nearer
and nearer the uproar came; until it reached the very limit
of the brush, and breaking through the interlacing shrubbery, with antlers laid well back, eyes on fire, tongue hang-
ing out, froth flying from his open mouth, the buck, with a
hound at either flank, burst out upon the rock, and with a
mighty leap flung himself with all the momentum of his
flight to help, full thirty feet into the waters of the lake:
not unaccompanied; for the two dogs — strong in structure, and brave in their breeding, with courage hot as their
heated blood, — took water as boldly, if not with such
length of leap as had the game, and whimpering as they
swam, still held their swift pursuit.

In the canoe Herbert sat motionless, until the buck, with
plunging and nervous leaps through the level water, had
covered two-thirds the distance that lay betwixt the ledge
and boat. Then the rifle jumped to his cheek, and the
quick explosion ripped the air asunder with its fierce concussion.

The head of the buck dropped, as the hammer fell, and
lay motionless; while the hounds, giving each a sharp,
quick bark, turned back, and swam contentedly towards
the shore.

The race was over, and a brave one had it been. Herbert, having lashed his rifle to its fastenings, paddled to the

game, feeling that the evening and the morning had given him the two best shots he had ever made, and the two largest sets of antlers he had ever seen.

It was a difficult job to ship his game; but the lake was as smooth as glass, and the canoe of large size, and Herbert had taken too many deer from the water not to know the method of proceeding. He careened the canoe well over on its side, and laying hold of the buck by the tail and haunches, lifted him, with a skillful motion, upward. The hams of the buck were already above the surface, and level with the edge of the canoe, when, with a quick and nervous energy that only a deer can exhibit, he delivered a kick with his hoofs against the side, which stove it through, as if it were but paper, and sent Herbert head-foremost over the horns of the animal into the water.

The position of Herbert was now one of extreme peril. The bullet had struck the skull of the deer, but at such an angle that it had not penetrated it, but glanced upward into the air, only stunning the creature for a moment. The instant that the head of Herbert rose to the surface, which it did almost within reach of his horns, and worse yet, of his sharp-edged hoofs, the buck, with a snort of pain and rage, his back curved and bristling, plunged at him. Sudden as had been the catastrophe, and startling as was the peril, the self-possession of Herbert had not left him; for he came to the surface, knife in hand, and ready for the rush he knew would come. As the creature lunged at him, by a dexterous movement he flung himself aside, and lifting himself in the water, drove, with all the strength of his arm, the blade downward, aiming at the root of the neck. But the motion of the buck was swifter than he had calculated for, and the blow falling a foot behind the point aimed at, the knife struck against the shoulder-blade with a directness and force which parted the handle from the hilt and snapped the blade short off at the middle. A sound almost like a groan escaped the young man, as he dashed his wounded hand, lacerated by the broken fragments of the horn-handle, into the water. But no time was left him to consider, for, quick as a flash, the deer turned and again plunged at him. For several minutes the unequal contest raged. The garments of Herbert were pierced and torn in a dozen places; the flesh of his cheek was opened by the sharp-pointed prong of the buck's antlers; and before he could lay hold of his neck, or get along side of him, one of his sharp-edged hoofs had lanced across his chest and torn the flesh to the very bone. The young man hesitated no longer, but lifted his voice with all the force given him by the thought of his peril, and shouted till the startled air rang to the cry: —

"*John Norton ! — John Norton ! — help !* "

The call of Henry was sent forth with all the power of a man from whom it is wrung by the emergency of extreme peril. The cry rose into the air with a volume and energy that filled the hollow atmosphere with waves of sound, rolled far down the lake, and smote against the mountain side with such directness and force, that twenty echoes gave it back with startling distinctness. The Trapper was well down the mountain and within fifty rods of the shore, when

the terrible call of his young companion, — whom he had
grown to love as if he were his own son — smote upon his
ear. Well did he know that nothing but the direst extremity could have extorted a call for assistance from Herbert
— much less such a cry as that. Not knowing what was
the cause of it, nor hesitating an instant, he dashed for the
lake with a recklessness and velocity which would have
been perilous to one of less vigor and agility. Over prostrate trees and boulders he leapt, tore his way through a
wind-fall, as if he embodied the violence which years before had caused it, burst through opposing thickets, and
with a mighty leap over a monstrous pine that blocked his
way, with bared head, and hair streaming behind him, and
with his rifle at a trail, but ready for action, stood upon the
rock. The scene which met his gaze blanched his cheek to
the whiteness of coming death; for there, forty rods from
the rock on which he stood, was Herbert struggling with
the buck in the water, while the canoe was rods away and
full to the brim; and to make it more startling, the Lad,
who was pulling with all his might toward the spot, was a
half mile down the lake.

A single glance revealed to the Trapper the true state of
things, and showed to him the extreme peril of his companion; for well he knew the desperate strength that Herbert was putting forth to avoid the horns and sharp-pointed
hoofs of the wounded and frenzied creature with which,
with desperate efforts, he was contending; and the blood
which streamed down his face, plainly visible from where
the Trapper stood, bore witness that he was not altogether

unhurt. He hesitated not an instant, but lifted his voice
into the air with an · energy of utterance which sent each
word with the momentum of a cannon ball across the level
water, to the fast-coming boat.

" Pull, Lad, for the love of God ! " shouted the Trapper,
" lengthen yer stroke and quicken yer gather, or yer comrade will die afore yer very eyes ! Pull, Lad ! and put yer
soul into yer oars, and may God give ye strength for the
deed ye must do."

The stentorian voice of the Trapper reached the ears of
the Lad, as if he had been but a few rods away. The energy of the appeal, as truly as the revelation of peril to
Herbert that it made, broke into his habitual indifference,
as a bomb exploding unexpectedly in the inner court of a
secluded palace startles those within. For, although he had
been pulling a stroke such as the Trapper had never seen
pulled, even before the cry had reached him, yet no sooner
had the call of the old man sounded, than, as if power had
indeed been given him of God for the moment's need, the
boat actually jumped into the air as he bent to his stroke ;
and fairly flew over the water as he swept it along. The
Trapper's eyes glowed, as he saw the tremendous stroke of
the Lad, for he knew that two minutes would bring his boat
to Herbert's side. And after an instant, with a heart full of
hope, he turned his gaze from the on-coming boat toward
his companion in the water ; but a look of agony swept
into his face, as he saw that Herbert was weakening, and
that he was even then barely able to keep his hold on the
horns of the buck.

"SHOOT THE BUCK." Page 171.

"Hold on, Henry, and hold up a leetle longer, for the love of God," the old man shouted, "the Lad is sartinly pullin' with the strength of Heaven in his stroke, and will be at yer side in a minit. Lie close to the cretur's ribs: keep one hand over his shoulder, and hang to his horns with the other, and the Lad will save ye yit."

For an instant there was no reply. Then feebly and faintly, so unlike the ordinary tone of Herbert's voice that the Trapper started as if an electric current had entered him, as his ears received the thin, wavering sound, — feebly and faintly over the water came the words, steady and even in tone, but low, as if spoken in mortal weakness : —

"JOHN NORTON, SHOOT THE BUCK ! "

" Aye, ·aye, Henry, I've thought of it; but ye are full forty rods from where I stand, and the lead must pass within six inches of yer head. No, no, boy, it isn't best, onless yer blood is oozin' fast, and yer strength eenamost gone. It's a picked bullet I've got in the right barrel of my rifle, — praise the Lord — and I might perhaps do it, but my eyes aint what they was forty years ago, and the odds are agin me; but if ye can't hold on, and yer jedgment says it's yer only chance — as it sartinly is if ye can't, for the buck would kill ye with a single thrust of his foot if ye let go — I say, Henry," repeated the Trapper, as he drew back the hammer of his rifle, and pressed the trigger to the set, " if ye can't hold on, and yer jedgment says it's yer only chance, I'll do my best, and may the Lord in his marcy steady me for the deed. So if ye can't hold on, say the word, and John Norton will shoot for yer life: and his own too," continued the old man, in a lower tone, speaking to himself, "for I wouldn't be a minit behind the boy, if he goes to the jedgment with my bullet in his brain."

A moment the Trapper waited for Herbert's final reply. His face was white as ashes, and the sweat stood in beads on his forehead, while the rifle in his hand trembled like a tamarack in the wind ; and then, from over the water, feebler and fainter even than before, came the same calm, steady tone ; and out of the air as it passed, the old man's listening ear could catch only the words : —

" SHOOT THE BUCK ! "

The Trapper hesitated not an instant. He drew himself to his full height, advanced his left foot, lifted with an easy sweep of his arm his rifle into the air, and as the barrels dropped into his extended palm his cheek settled to the stock, and his eye without a quiver in the lid ranged along the sights. For an instant the rifle lay on his palm as motionless as if fastened in an invisible vise, and then a fiery stream spurted from the muzzle, and the sharp crack rang out on the morning air. He had shot for a life, and so far as skill could do, had saved it, for the bullet, passing so near the head of Herbert as to lift a lock of his hair, buried itself in the buck's brain under the root of the horns.

The Trapper saw Herbert fall away from the deer — saw that he still had strength enough to make the needed motions to keep himself afloat, and then he turned his eyes in the direction of the coming boat. It was within twenty rods, and the Lad was pulling a stroke which seemed to the Trapper to have in it the energy of more than mortal power

but miraculous as it was in its length, sweep, and quickness
of recovery, the body of the oarsman rose and sank to the
motions as if no excitement had stirred his ordinary simple
composure, and the long blades entered and left the level
water with a precision and finish that tossed not a drop of
spray into the air, while the line of the eddying wake astern,
led as straight from the spot from which he had started
far down the lake, to the body of Herbert, as a line could
have been drawn on a level floor by skilled direction. The
Lad gave three more strokes and then dropping his oars to
a trail he lifted himself, in all his ungainly height, in his
boat and turned his eyes forward, searching for the head
and body of his friend; but above the level water was neither body nor head in sight, FOR HERBERT HAD DISAP-
PEARED.

"WHERE IS HENRY?" asked the Lad of the Trapper.

The Trapper made no reply; indeed, it is doubtful if he
could, for his tongue clove to the roof of his mouth, and
his rifle dropped from his hands on to the rock at his feet
as if it had been only useless iron.

"WHERE IS HENRY?" repeated the Lad, as his boat glided
on; but before the words had fairly left his lips a gleam
came into his face, and with a motion quick as an otter
when he lifts for the dive in the midst of the hounds, he
launched his body into the depths of the lake.

The feet of the Lad had scarcely disappeared beneath
the surface, before the Trapper, with a mighty leap from
the rock on which he stood, had also taken the water and
was swimming with tremendous strokes toward the now
empty boat.

CHAPTER V.

THE RESCUE.

"One that I saved from drowning." — Shakespeare.

THE Trapper had covered half the distance between the shore and the boat, and was swimming with the strength and swiftness of one swimming for a life, when the head and shoulders of the Lad came to the surface as a diver emerges from the depths when struggling with a weight. As the old man saw the face of Herbert, as his head lay lifeless on the bosom of the Lad, he jumped half his length out of the water in the eagerness of his joy, and shouted: "Ye have saved him, Lad! Ye have saved him! The Lord of marcy has helped ye, and ye have saved yer comrade! Can ye hold him up a minit, — can ye hold him, I say, till I can reach the boat and bring it to yer side?"

"Of course I can hold Henry up," replied the Lad, in a simple, quiet tone, as if he were only doing an ordinary service. "He had got a good ways down before I caught up with him, but I got hold of him finally and fetched him up. I'm a little short of breath, for you called so loud to me that I knew you wanted me to come right along, and so I pulled real hard; but you needn't worry about my letting Henry go, for I'm a first-rate swimmer, and don't feel tired a bit."

"Pulled hard?" quoted the Trapper, as he laid hold of the stern of the boat, which he had reached, and with a strong skillful movement lifted himself astride of it, when he instantly seized the paddle and started it toward the Lad, "I think ye did pull hard. Ye have did what no other man John Norton ever seed could do; and the Lord, whose eyes has been on this lake this morn, will remember ye, Lad, when he gives his rewards to them who did well on the arth; and I sartinly hope I may be there to give my idees of yer conduct, and put a few words in as to yer stroke. I don't believe the Lord would refuse to hear the jedgment of an old man who seed the thing from beginnin' to eend, either. There, Lad," continued the Trapper, as he swept the boat alongside and checked it with a reverse stroke of his paddle, "give the boy to me, and do ye swim to the other side and steady the boat while I lift him in." So saying, the old man passed his strong arms under the shoulders of Herbert as tenderly as a mother might prepare to lift a sleeping child, while his eyes fixed themselves on the pallid face with an intensity as if they would penetrate the mortal frame to see if the soul still hovered within.

The Lad promptly obeyed the old man's directions, and in an instant the body of Herbert lay stretched in the bottom of the boat, while his head was supported by the lap of the Trapper. In another instant the Lad, with surprising agility, climbed over the bow of the boat, and, sliding into his seat, laid hold of the oars, and with a long, strong stroke, started toward the point which they had left scarcely an hour before, and above which a thin volume of blue smoke from their mouldering camp-fire was still ascending.

The Trapper had, in the meantime, unbuttoned the collar of Herbert's shirt, and laid his hand over the heart, searching for evidence that life still held her uncertain residence within.

"You don't think Henry is going to die, do you?" said the Lad, as he laid to his stroke till the long blades of his oars bent to the pressure.

"No, Lad, no; not if the Lord is mindful of the livin'. The boy is too young to die, and the arth needs him; for his gifts is wonderful, and I have heerd said that thousands love him in the settlements. And I know," he continued, "that there's an Old Trapper here in the woods who loves him, as he hasn't loved man for forty year, and never thought to love agin this side the great Clearin'. No, no; he mustn't die. I've reckoned on the boy's company for many a year yit when he comes to the woods, and conceited that perhaps the Lord of Marcy would let him be nigh when me and the hound start on the trail that leads into the Valley. Take him by the feet, Lad, lift easy, and we will bear him to camp. Yis, yis, I know now, why the Lord brought us three together at the pond of the beavers."

While the Trapper had been thus half talking to himself, the boat had run in on to the beach off the point, and the two men, by a common movement, had lifted Herbert in their arms and borne him to the fire.

For nearly half an hour the two worked over their inanimate companion, striving to bring the departed breath back to his motionless nostrils, and to start the sluggish

current of his chilled blood to its accustomed movement;
but his limbs still remained limp, his eyes closed, his nostrils inactive, and the features set in the quiet, rigid smooth-
ness which marks the countenance of one who has passed
forever from the mortal tenement which his presence had
once made animate and lovely. Still above the heart the
skin was warm, and the palm lightly placed over it could
interpret the faintest of movements within. It was as if
the spirit, called suddenly away, still lingered with one foot
on the threshold to take one more last and tender look at
the loved home it was compelled to leave forever. The
face of the Old Trapper was grave with the gravity of one
who, while determined to hope on, nevertheless feels that
one by one the evidences which warrant hope are failing
him, and that he will soon be standing in the presence of
an overwhelming calamity; while the countenance of the
Lad, as he came and went on his hurried errands, as directed by the Trapper, who, naturally from his age and experience had assumed the management of the case, showed
the agitation of one through whose dull senses the sharp
edge of a dreadful fear was slowly but surely making its
way.

"Lad," said the Trapper, in a voice so hollow and solemn
that the one he addressed started, while his hand that was
holding a cup of warming water over the fire, shook and
trembled; "Lad, I fear that the boy is goin', and that you
and me will be here with the dead afore the shadows of the
mornin' are shortened."

"John Norton," said the Lad, "God won't let Henry die

if we ask him not to; for the Bible says: 'Ask, - and - it -
shall - be - given — seek, - and - ye - shall - find — knock, -
and - it - shall - be - opened;' and, if you say so, I will go
back of the lodge and ask Him to make Henry live. I
know I'm not wise and don't know much, and I suppose a
great many folks would laugh at me if I should try to pray,
but I know what I want God to do to Henry, and I guess
he can understand me, even if I do spell out the words,
and get stuck sometimes on the big ones. Shall I go and
try, John Norton?"

"Yis, yis, Lad," replied the Trapper, while his voice shook,
and the great tears came into his eyes and rolled down his
weather-beaten cheek, "pass me the cup with the brandy
in it, and then do ye go back of the lodge and tell the Lord
the best ye can of yer troubles, and ask him to give us a
lift in our endeavors; and put the case before Him as strong
as ye can, Lad, and don't forgit to spell in all the Scriptur'
ye remember, especially those varses where he has promised to help the children of arth when peril is nigh. An'
while ye pray I will keep rubbin' and pourin' the hot drink
into him, an' it may be, betwixt us both, with the help of
the Lord, an' the drink, an' the rubbin', we'll fetch Henry
back to the land o' the livin'."

The Lad did as the old Trapper had directed. He poured
the last drop of brandy in the flask into the heated water,
passed the cup to the old man and then, with a face to
which absolute trust and undoubted hope lent illumination,
he retired behind the lodge and kneeling down on the stem-
matted sod, he linked his awkward fingers together, and

lifting his guileless face upward he closed his eyes and with many a stammer, but with directness of entreaty and earnestness of faith which kept his speech straight to the line of his wish, prayed: —

" Father - in - heaven, - mother - told - me - to - always - call - you - Father, - I - want - you - to - hear - me - while - I - tell - you - what - I - want. Henry - is - dying - and - we-both - love - Henry, - and - you - can - save - him - as - well - as - not, - for - you - art - able - to - do - anything. The - Saviour - told - us - that - whatsoever - ye - ask - of - the - Father - in - my - name - that - will - he - do - unto - you. I - and - John - Norton - ask - you - to - bring - Henry - back - to - life, - now, - right - off. It - is - written, - according - to - thy - faith - be - it - unto - you - and - I - have - faith, - I don't - doubt - a - bit, - I - know - you - will - bring - Henry to. O - Lord, - thou - hast - been - our - dwelling - place - in - all generations. Thou - art - a - present - help - in - times - of - trouble. Establish - thou - the - works - of - our - hands - establish - thou - it. Help, - Lord - for - our - strength - faileth. Deliver - us - from - evil - and - thine - shall - be - the - glory - forever."

The Lad had got so far, and as he had gone on in his simple, laborious, but accurate and direct way of petition, his face had changed by reason of a glow, and sweet, fine light that had come into it and spread in softest radiance over his upturned countenance until his poor, simple face actually shone as those of old who talked with God. The Spirit which is not of man, and which finds its home in the humblest breast and can give wisdom to the feeble minded, had

entered and filled his soul with its own fine fervors; and to
what passion of entreaty it might have lifted him can be
known only to him who knows to the full its exalted and
sublime energies, which out of the mouth of babes and
sucklings have perfected praise; but at this point the voice
of the Trapper interrupted him.

"Lad, Lad, hold on and come here! The Lord has heerd
ye, for the blood is sartinly stirrin' and the sperit of the
boy has come back to the body, an' life is movin' in his
members. Hurry, Lad, an' see the answer to yer prayer.
Be quick or the Lord will be here ahead of ye."

The words were barely out of the Trapper's mouth before
the Lad, with the beautiful light still shining in his face, was
kneeling at the feet of Herbert and gazing with steady yet
glowing eyes into the pale face, into which the slightest
possible flush had already come.

Thus Herbert, with the Trapper still holding with sup-
porting hands his head, with the Lad kneeling at his feet
and the hounds standing on either side of him in grave attention, lay, while the warmth of renewed life grew within
his breast and sent its reviving fervor through the chilled
currents of his veins.

In a moment a quiver ran through his frame, his chest
rose to a full inspiration, his eyes slowly opened, and fixing
them first on the Lad, and then on the face of the Trapper,
his lips moved slightly and he said in a tone barely above a
whisper: —

"*Old man, where am I?*"

"In the land of the livin', boy, in the land of the livin'

praise God!" responded the Trapper. "In the land of the livin' and here on Tomahawk P'int, with the Lad at yer feet and the pups on either side, and myself here at yer head;. and now take a swallow more of the drink and then we'll tuck ye away in the blankets and pile the hot stuns round ye, for ye have had an onmarciful soakin', and been in a scrimmage which taxed ye like a clinch with a Huron, and ye need rest and warmth, for sleep and heat is the best doctor in the world to one who has been in a tussle and come out weak and sore as ye are. I warrant ye will be frisky as a young pup arter ye have had a good, long sleep."

It was past midday when Herbert awoke, and rolling himself out of the blankets in which he was swathed from head to foot, and shoving aside several of the heated stones which had been placed in a row on either side of his body, rose to a sitting posture, and looked about him as a man just awaking from a vivid dream. His sleep had been such as the strong and healthy experience after complete exhaustion — an oblivious slumber, which had blotted so many hours from his life, — a chasm stretched across the plain of consciousness, deep and wide, whose either side was unconnected with the other by even the filament of a dream. On the other side of the fire, some distance away, the Trapper and the Lad were seated talking in subdued tones and casting an occasional glance toward the spot where their comrade was slumbering. The hounds lay stretched side by side in the sound sleep of dogs resting after a race. The three rifles were leaning against a small pole a few feet from the fire in such a position that the heat might best penetrate the barrels. In a moment Herbert took in the position of things and with a light laugh said : —

"You didn't mean to bake me, did you, friends ?"

"Not egsactly," returned the Trapper, "but we did mean to heat ye up pritty well, Henry; leastwise, we sartinly meant to dry ye out and season ye a bit, for ye was mighty well soaked, I tell ye, and we thought a good sweatin' would open the seams and let the dampness out of ye, for ye was eenamost waterlogged when the Lad fished ye up from the lake, and so we fenced ye in with the heated stuns, and between them and the fire and the warmth of yer body the blankets have been smokin' like a dish-cloth in the sun. Now, boy, how do ye feel, and what more shall we do for ye ?"

"I feel first-rate," Herbert replied, "save that my chest smarts as if a hot gridiron was tied across it, and my right hand here is puffed up like a toad-stool. Have you got the buck from the water, and where is my rifle ?"

"The buck is in the boat, and he's a big un too, and there is yer rifle clean, and dry from muzzle to breech-pin, ready for the powder; for I said to the Lad that I knowed the fust thing ye would ax us about would be the leetle gun, for I know yer love for the piece, and it desarves all the care ye give it, for two truer barrels was never spliced together. My ears could tell the crack of it among a thousand ; and now what shall we do, for ye are captain of this squad, and me and the Lad wait for yer orders?"

"I think," Herbert replied, "you had better skin the buck, and save his hide and head, but the body burn or

bury, for I never wish to see it, much less taste a morsel of
it. Then cook us a rousing dinner, for I am as hungry as a
shark; and after we have eaten our fill, I propose that you
fix me up some kind of a bed in the bottom of the boat,
and we will go on toward the Saranacs, for day after to-
morrow is the boat race, and although I don't think, by the
way I feel that I shall pull an oar in a month, yet you and
the Lad can enter, and I can see the fun as an outsider."

"I think ye talk like a gineral," said the Trapper, as Herbert ended. "I had sot my heart on seeing you and the
Lad pull agin those Saranacers, but ye are in no condition
to handle the ash, for sartin, but the Lad is, and he can
larn them a lesson they wont forgit, or I'm mistaken; and
if I can find a good boat—though my gifts lie more in the
direction of the paddle than the row-locks,—yet, if the
Lad wont pull onless I do—and he says he wont,—I will
try the boastin' chaps a lick, and if I can only git the kink
of the Lad's swing, and the length of his sweep, I will show
'em what an old man can do, who boated in these waters
afore their fathers was born." So saying, the Trapper, with
the Lad, rose from the log, and addressed himself to the
preparation of the meal.

The sun had passed the meridian when the boat, with the
Lad at the oars, the Trapper at the paddle, and Herbert
lying at length on a soft couch of balsam and cedar boughs,
with the two hounds at his feet, shoved out from Tomahawk
Point, and started down the lake. It was such a day as
can be seen nowhere in the world save amid this forest of
the North, and from no point of view to such advantage as

from a boat as it glides easily along on its course through the middle of one of its larger lakes.

The water was as smooth as if no wave had ever rolled across its tranquil surface, save where a loon in diving, or in rising from his dive, sent from himself, as the living center, an undulating circumference outward. On either side the shores lay in deep repose, as if the very trees were sleeping in delicious trance. Over them the mellow haze of autumn was spread wide-cast as the peace of heaven. Above, the mountains rose, with their peaks cutting the cooler air, bathed in the blue atmosphere. The islands looked, from the distance, as if they were floating on the water — huge rafts of invisible timber freighted with moss-covered rocks, evergreen shrubbery, and near their centers with great pines. Around the edges of several, the white birches, with their yellow leaves, stood out in bold relief against the surrounding green. The air was mellow and soft, and scented with the odors of ripened leaves and dying grasses, while now and then the quickened nostril caught the smell of odorous smoke blown from some distant camp-fire. Overhead, the white gulls wheeled in snowy circles lazily. In the upper sky the falcons soared on even wing. And now and then, higher yet, the watchful eye would catch the sight of darker and lengthier pinions, and follow the majestic movement of the bald eagle, as, on stately and motionless vans, he swung around in his aerial circles.

Through such an enchanting scene, and as the living, watchful center of it, our three friends moved along, the Lad pulling a long, easy stroke, and the Trapper keeping

time with his paddle. They had proceeded on their course
a full mile before either spoke a word and then the Old
Trapper in a low tone said : —

"Many be the seasons I have passed in the woods sence
I struck the eastern shore of the Horicon, more than three-
score year agone, and many be the men I have seen fall by
my side, and many be the 'narrer escapes I have had from
death by bullet and water both, but I tell ye, Henry, I never
seed a man delivered from greater peril than you was in
this morn, and the Lad's rowin' and divin' saved ye for
sartin', onless, as it seems reasonable to do, ye set a share
down to his prayin', for arter he had fished ye from the lake
yer sperit was as near gone as it could be and not be actally
in the jedgment. Yis, the Lad sartinly saved ye."

"I hope I did help," said the Lad, "for it would be awful
to have Henry drown with both of us in sight. I don't
know what we could have done had he died; but I don't
think my rowing or diving would have done any good had
it not been for your shooting the buck, John Norton; I
think your shooting saved Henry, and I don't see how you
could have shot so well. I am sure my hand would have
shook dreadfully."

"The sarcumstances was agin me, for sartin, Lad," responded the Trapper, for the distance was too fur for close
work, and the buck was mighty lively, but the bullet was a
good one and the air so clear that I could actally see the
curl in the cretur's hair at the roots of the horns when I
sot my eye into the sights; and Henry, weak as he was,
knowed enough to lop his head aside a leetle to make a

path for the lead, and the Lord used my gifts, and the habit of sixty year of shootin' in cloud and shine, in deadly scrimmage and playful practice when the horn was full and lead plenty, to furder his parposes of marcy, jest as he used my rubbin' and the brandy to help the Lad out in his prayin' and Scriptur sayin', back of the lodge."

"Don't you believe," interrupted the Lad — "Don't you believe, John Norton, that God can do anything he wants to without our helpiug him a bit?"

"Sartinly, Lad, sartinly, if he only had a mind to, for I have seed enough of his power when he put out his strength amid the scenes of natur' to conceit he can do anything. For I have seen the wind cut a swath through the woods as a man in the settlements cuts a path through the grass with his scythe; and I have seed the frost pry up acres of rocks and silo with the trees all standin' in them and slide em down a mountain as if they were on greased skids; and I heerd a man, who was a furiner, say once, that in his country at times the very arth under one's feet got onsteady and shook like a half-breed with the ager, ontil a man couldn't keep his legs; but I have my doubts on that pint, and I told him so to his face, for it don't seem reasonable that the arth, which hasn't any bowels or narves, should have any sech kind of spasms, or git coliky like. Still, if the Lord raaly set about it in earnest it may be he could make the very arth quiver like a human bein' in pain; but the arth is a big thing, and can't be handled round careless by anybody, as I conceit."

"But," again interrupted the Lad, "don't you think that God can do anything without our helping?"

"Well, no, Lad, if ye want my raal idee on the matter, I don't," returned the Trapper. "Leastwise, he seems willin' to jine works with his creturs, I notice, when he has any special job on hand, that needs raal arnest and lively work to git it done in time to answer his purpose. Now, Henry's scrimmage with the buck is a case in p'int. For Henry had sartinly got into a pritty tight fix, if I am any jedge, and if he was to be saved it had got to be done in a jedicious and lively manner. So the Lord jined works with ye and ye gifts, and ye sartinly did yer full share, for ye pulled like all possessed; and how ye got yer feet into the air so quick considerin' the length of yer legs, is wonderful, and can be accounted for only on the ground that divin' is one of yer gifts — and ye yerself has said that the bullet I druv in under the buck's horns, helped matters considerably."

"But, but," exclaimed the Lad, feeling he was being out-reasoned, but none the less steadfast in his simple faith, "don't you think the prayer did any good?"

"Yis, sartinly, Lad," promptly replied the Trapper, "I think ye are gifted in that way, and that the Lord heerd ye, but," continued the old man, as if he feared he had made a fatal concession, and in common with all theologians was inclined to maintain his point, right or wrong — "but ye must remember that yer prayer was well mixed in with my rubbin', not to speak of the stimulant and hot stuns. No, no, Lad, the Lord' couldn't have got along without yer pullin' and divin', and the bullet and the rubbin', anyhow. Could he, Henry?"

The only reply Herbert made was to move his hand

slightly under his cheek; for, lulled by the easy dip of the
oars as they came and went in their measured stroke, and
perhaps by the murmur of the low, earnest voices above
him, yielding to some subtle but unknown law of reception
and impartment by which the slumberous peace of surrounding nature entered into and possessed his senses, the
young man had sunk into a restful sleep.

And thus past the anchored islands, with their walled
rocks; past the mouth of sleeping bays; past beaches of
golden sand; through the yellow autumnal haze, the boat
moved on, until it entered the easy flowing stream of the
beautiful Racquette, then with all its loveliness unmarred
by the devastating hand of human selfishness. Thence upward against the easy current the boat sailed on. Up long
stretches of level water, whose surface was strewn thick
with leaves that flamed with color, while underneath the
depths reflected the fiery hues of the overhanging maples,
— up over the glancing rifts whose first noisy ripples awoke
the sleeper, and sailing in easy curve around the great
bends the boat went forward on its course, until, as the
shadows began to darken on wood and stream, it reached a
spot where the pines came to the water's edge, and stood
like great sentinels, with arms at rest along the bank, as if
within their dark recesses the Genii of the woods had their
pine-guarded home. Here the three men landed, and with
rapid movements made ready for the night whose dark
wings were fast drawing their gloom-bringing flight between the earth and sky.

CHAPTER VI.

THE OVATION.

"His life was gentle, and the elements
So mixed in him, that Nature might s .and up
And say to all the world, *This was a man.*"
Shakespeare.

EVENING in the woods, on a still September night. In front a river, which sends its current deep and dark, with steady pressure, against the base of a hill, as if it would undermine its broad foundation and float it off. A beach of sand where the bend in the bank curves sharpest. Ten feet above, a narrow, level stretch of land — a natural terrace — with great pines growing thereon, whose trunks rise clean of limbs, and straight as the masts of a ship, full eighty feet, then tuft themselves in heaviest foliage. From the inner edge of the level space the hill lifts, steep and far, a thousand feet; but even to the ridge the pines grow thick and strong. On the level bank a camp-fire burning brightly, and with an energy that lifts the flame in a fiery pillar, ten feet upward. The light and shade play ghostly hide-and-seek amid the distant trees and neighboring thickets. Above the river, through the opening in the trees made by its width from shore to shore, a space of sky, dusky and dim, in which large stars burn and glow as diamonds set in jet against a swarthy forehead. Around the fire, our three friends, engaged in conversation, their voices pitched to a low key, but animated and earnest in tone.

" I tell ye, lad," said the Trapper, " ye oughter pull without me ; rowin' comes nateral to ye, and yer stroke is sartinly wonderful. I never seed anything like it. Ye can walk a boat along for half a mile, quicker than any other man livin', if I am any jedge ; but ye don't look to me as if ye was put together for a long race, and I conceit a fourmile stretch would blow ye, for ye are mighty light in the middle, and yer chest is too thin by half. If ye had the shoulders of Henry, here, I would wager my last horn of powder, and my bullet-mould into the bargain, that ye could beat 'em at any distance ; for I have seed Henry fetch his boat, loaded deep at that, for three miles agin a wind that whitened the lake from shore to shore, and never weaken on a stroke. What do ye say, lad, — can ye pull a long course if the rogues set us one ?"

" I don't want to pull at all, John Norton, nor go nigh them, for I know they will laugh at me and call me names, because I aint handsome and smart. The last time I went out with my skins, they bothered me dreadfully about my legs and hands, and hadn't it been for Sport, I don't know but they would have hurt me ; but if they touched me even so much as with a fish-pole, Sport showed his teeth at them. He bit one of them badly because he tried to push me into the water. It hurts me to be laughed at, and called names, and besides — "

" Lad," interrupted the Trapper, " ye are with John Norton this trip, an' though I hope I can take a joke in good natur', as a reasonable man should, and hold that the bullet an' knife should be used carefully, and only agin inimies; yit a noisy mouth and a loose tongue need to be larnt manners occasionally, and if they start any of their foolishness at ye, there'll be a scrimmage, for sartin, that they won't forgit for the tarm of their nateral lives, even if the markins' of the knife has to be put on to some of 'em. No, Lad, ye aint goin' to be imposed on, this trip, I can tell ye. Come, Henry, what do ye think, for yer jedgment is good on sech a p'int, can a man, with the build of the Lad, pull a long course?

"I don't think his 'build,' as you call it," responded Herbert, "is especially against his chances; it is not bulk of frame, but sinews, and stroke, and pluck that win in a long race; and, as you say, the Lad is a natural oarsman and his stroke is simply perfect. You see, it's a saving stroke, as we call it, for he doesn't waste an ounce of strength in pulling it, and however long and sharp it is, I notice he pulls it even from dip to finish, and his boat moves on a level keel and cuts the water like a knife. I dare say there will be several fine oarsmen in the race, but I am confident the Lad can beat them, if he will only try. And, moreover, I doubt if there will be a man of them, old John Norton, who can beat you, either, especially if the course is a long one; for although you don't think much of the oars, yet you pull a very strong stroke indeed, and are cool, and that counts in such matters; for a level head and a stout heart wins many a race, and especially when the course is long and the race a hot one. I think, therefore, the Lad is right, when he

says he wont pull unless you do; for I know that a man
pulls better with a friend by his side, especially if he be
timid and is in a strange and perhaps hostile crowd; and
I think a word from you would be worth the race to him if
the finish should be close and the shores noisy. You understand, John Norton."

"Yis, yis, Henry," returned the Trapper, while a glance
of mutual intelligence passed between them, "Yis, I understand what ye mean, and yer idees are sound, and jedg-
matically spoken, too, for in my young days I used the oar
myself, an' pulled in a good many races, an' I never pulled
a race I didn't win, either. But the paddle is the raal instrument for the hunter an' scout, an' my gifts sartinly lie
that way; but yer words has reason in 'em," said the old
man, as he looked into the face of the Lad, the features of
which were entirely lacking in shrewdness and the positive-
ness of a resolute will. "Yis, yer words sartinly has reason in 'em, an' if ye can find a boat for me with row-locks
and oars that will hold, I'll keep the Lad company. — Yis,
yis, Henry I heerd 'em afore they reached the bend; it's
some boat comin' up the river. We'll hear their hail in a
minit — I'll keep the Lad company, I say, an' I'll do my
best to beat him, too."

"Hallo, the camp there!" shouted a voice from the middle of the river.

"Hallo it is," returned the Trapper, without moving an
inch from his recumbent posture, or scarcely lifting his eyes.
"What do ye want, and what can we do for ye?"

For a minute or more there was no reply to the question

of the Trapper, but a confused murmur of several voices in quick and whispered conversation, and the noise as of several boats huddling together was audible to those on the bank, and then an interrogation came out of the darkness:—

"Aint you John Norton, the Trapper?"

"Well, it may be I am, and it may be I aint; but the chances favor the idee that I am John Norton," returned the Trapper, "leastwise the signs p'int in that direction, and now let me ax you, who be ye that travel at night— and a chilly one at that,—and where ye are going as if the day wasn't long enough for yer business."

"We are bound for the Saranacs," replied the voice, "to see the boat race, and it may be take a hand in it ourselves. Shall you be there yourself?"

"Yis, I shall be there," returned the Trapper; "and ye may tell 'em.so; and ye may say that I mean to pull, myself, if they don't bar a man because he haint pulled a race for forty year, an' has as many white hairs as black in his scalp."

"All right, John Norton, we'll tell them so; but you'll be wiped out, sure; for there's to be some New York professionals there, they say, and a mighty slim chance any of us chaps stand beside them I reckon." And with this discouraging prediction the boat started on up the stream."

Not 'till the last murmuring sound of their rather noisy progress died away did the Trapper speak; then he said: "Ye see, Henry, what's in the wind. There'll be buzzin' in the hive when they hear I am coming out and mean to pull,

too. I thought I'd poke 'em up a leetle, anyhow, and I
warrant I've did it; for there be some old men livin' yit who
remember the times we had on the Horicon waters fifty
year agone, and they'll tell 'em what John Norton was, at
the ash afore these waters was knowed by them in the settlements. I tell ye, Henry, it seems foolish for a man of
my years to say it, but if ye can find a boat for me that
suits yer jedgment, I'll have a lick at them perfessionals, hit
or miss. It'll be an etarnal shame if them city boasters
beat the men born in the woods, and on their own waters
too. What do ye think of it, Henry; is there a chance for
me and the Lad?"

"I certainly think there is a chance for you both, John
Norton," replied Herbert, "and a good one too. In the
first place, you are both in good condition and used to the
boats, which the professionals are not, and that's in your
favor. Then again a four-mile course is a long one to pull
in these Adirondack boats, and wind and grit and sheer
strength count favorably against any extra skill the professionals may have. If the Lad only had your muscular
power and grit, or you had his stroke, I would bet my last
dollar on either of you."

"Aye, aye, Henry, that's jest it. Ye have sartinly struck
the trail right eend to and gin your opinion like a jedge in
a school house. I tell ye what, Lad, I must git yer stroke.
Leastwise, I'll study the reason of it to-morrer as we go up,
if ye'll put in a lick or two occasionally. And if ye see the
perfessionals beatin me, Lad, and them that was born in
the woods about to be shamed afore the men, aye, and the

wimin folks too, and I give ye the word, will ye pull accordin' to the gifts that the Lord has gi'n ye, boy?"

"I don't want to pull at all, John Norton," responded the
Lad, "and I don't know how I shall feel, for I never pulled
a race, and I know that they will all laugh at me; but I
won't see you beat by anybody, and I'll pull as hard as I
can, if they seem likely to do it. But I guess you can beat
them, and I would rather have you beat than to beat myself."

"No doubt, no doubt," returned the Trapper, in a tone
that plainly showed the great relief he felt at the promise
he had succeeded in getting from the Lad. "I tell ye,
Henry, the thing is settled. The perfessionals shant take
the prize out of the woods, if the Lad and me can help it.
Come, let's to bed. What a marcy it is to sleep in sech a
chamber as this, where ye can breathe all the air ye want
to without robbin' anybody, and there's no danger that the
roof will fall in onto ye."

So saying, the Old Trapper stretched himself on the
ground strewn thick with the fragrant pine stems, and
with a small bag of meal for his pillow, sank quickly into a
slumber which many a king on his soldier-guarded couch
would envy. His friends followed his example, and in a few
moments the three were resting in soundest sleep.   But
the river still flowed on, incapable of weariness.   The stars
stil. burned with undiminished fervor, and over the sleepers'
heads the pines continued to make their soothing plaint.
In the cities, men were cursing and fighting, but Nature,
strong and safe in her innocence, rested in holy peace.

It was well on to noon of the next day when our friends entered the waters of the Lower Saranac. The Trapper was at the paddle and the Lad at the oars, and the long, sharp boat, loaded as it was, passed through the water at a rate few boats ever keep for any distance.

"I tell ye, Lad," remarked the Trapper, "ye had the right idee of a boat for straight runnin' in yer head when ye shaped the bottom board for the one we are in; for it sartinly gits through the water in a way that's surprisin'. In a crooked creek it must be a mighty onreasonable thing to handle, and I conceit that none but a prayin' man, and one careful in the use of his tongue, could manage it for any length of time and not git arnest in his speech; but for open waters and a strait run it's parfection itself. I'd give a dozen of my best pelts for another jest like it for to-morrer."

"You are right," said Herbert; "it's just the boat for straightaway work, and I mean to get one as near like it as I can for you to pull in to-morrow. It looks heavy, and most would pick a lighter one; but a long boat is the thing for a long race, and long oars, too, with wide blades, if one has power and grit enough to pull them strongly. Where shall we stay to-night — at the hotel?"

"The Lord forbid!" exclaimed the Trapper, "It's nigh on to fifty year sence I've slept under a shingled roof and smothered within the walls of men's buildin', and natur' and reason are both agin the doin' of sech foolishness; for there be good camps nigh the upper eend of the Lake, where we can eat and sleep in peace, and where the hound and the Lad can have contentment; for the dog is a knowin' in' dog and understands his rights, for his blood is without a cross of low stuff in it, and he can't bear the mongrels and half-breed curs of the settlements, nohow, and the tramp of feet and the buzz of voices distarbs him as much as it does me. And a man who isn't an Indian should think of the comfort of his dog and plan for his happiness, as I conceit. Yis, we'll go into camp, and arter we've eaten our fill and made ready for the night, we will go down to the hive and hear the senseless things buzz awhile. Mayhaps I shall find a few yit livin' who have slept on the trail with me and heerd the crack of my piece in a scrimmage, when powder was powder and every bullet was worth its weight in gold."

It was well on toward the close of the afternoon when the Lad's boat, containing our three friends, came out from behind the "Three Sisters" on its way toward the rendez-vous. At the hotel all was expectation. For a great crowd had gathered in anticipation of the morrow's races, and the thought that they were to see the celebrated Trapper and Scout of whom they had read and heard so much, but whom they had never seen, stirred them with the feeling of intense curiosity. The three guides that had hailed the camp on the Racquette the evening before had brought the word that "Old John Norton" was not only coming, but that he was going to enter the free-for-all race, and pull against the professionals. This raised the excitement to fever heat, and the feeling became intense. Indeed, two parties had already sprung up. In the crowd were several aged men who remembered the great fame which the Trap-

per had as an oarsman fifty years before, when they and he
were young; and, to interested groups during the day, they
had been narrating the stories of his skill, enormous
strength and unrivalled agility, exhibitions of which they,
with their own eyes, had seen, as called forth by the supreme exigencies of deadly conflicts in hand to hand fights,
or in the playful but manly games of peace. And the conviction of these old men — some of whom had not only
been overtaken by age, but also by the vicious habits of
civilized life — was well expressed in the strong assertion
of one of their number, who closed a heated verbal contest
with a gentleman from the cities, with "I tell ye, sir, there
is'nt a man on God's arth can beat John Norton at the
oars."

On the other hand the professionals had their advocates.
Fine, spruce college boys "doing the woods" in jaunty
straw hats with broad bands of blue ribbon round them,
and twirling little rattan canes in their dapper thin fingers;
English tourists, strong-built and burly, in checked suits of
woolen stuffs, several of whom affecting the heavy sportsman's style, lugged about their double English-made rifles,
"such as Gerard used in the jungles, you know, sir;" while
their cartridge belts sagged, heavy with lead, as they
tramped back and forth along the piazza in broad-soled,
broad-toed, gaiter-boots, with spotless leggins reaching from
ankle to knee; quiet city gentlemen, lawyers, bankers, cler-
gymen, whose knowledge of boating extended no further
than seeing or reading a newspaper account of the annual
race between Yale and Harvard in their long, pencil-like

shells. These, with here and there a single exception, all discussed the race as if lying between three professionals that were already entered to pull. Even the guides, over-awed by the high-sounding word, "professional," and by the marvelous stories of their ability at the oars which were passed from group to group, were intimidated to such an extent that of all their number, representing as it did nearly every boat in the wilderness, two brothers alone had entered. And hence, although their sympathies were strongly with the Trapper, they readily admitted that the "professionals" would win. But though his party was in the minority as to numbers, its spirit was self-asserting in the extreme, and not a few sportsmen and guides, who had seen him pull his boat against a wind that scooped the water into the air, as steadily as if the lake lay level to his stroke, or thrust it up a stretch of rapids where the water quivered with the swiftness of its descending flight, took stock in his chances and endorsed the saying of the old chap who in his excitement, born of argument or liquor — perhaps it would not be kind to inquire too closely which — had declared that there wasn't "a man on God's arth could beat Old John Norton at the oars."

Thus stood the feeling and the crowd when the boat, with the Lad at the oars and the Trapper at the paddle and Herbert amidship, came out from behind the "Three Sisters" into plain view of the hundreds that were watching for their appearance.

Nothing could excel the fineness of the tribute which the crowd, composed of several hundreds, were uncon-

sciously paying to the fame of the Old Trapper; for as the
boat came on, the talking ceased; even the giggling of a
knot of young misses who had been flirting with shameful
ostentation with a couple of undergraduates from Harvard,
was checked before they were aware of it, by the sudden
silence which had fallen on the densely packed throng, and
amid a stillness more impressive by far, when associated
with a popular assembly, than the loudest cheering, the
Lad's boat drew on. The Lad was pulling the same nonchalant stroke as was his custom, his head lopped as usual
on one side, and his body doubled up as if shrinking to get
away from its own enormous hight and ungainly appearance.
But the professionals, who, with observant eyes, were watching the approach, noted that the oars were of unusual
length, that the blades were nearly twice the customary
width, and that they entered and left the water with a precision which nothing but long experience can give, while in
their recovery they passed along the level water with an
evenness which bore witness that the wrists that guided
their return were educated by years of practice. As the
boat came on so that the several forms could be recognized,
one of them drew a long breath, nudged his companions
and whispered : " I'm glad it isn't the Trapper that's handling those oars."

The old man was seated in the stern of the boat, and
using his paddle with an unconscious grace; but it is certain that, beyond a slight sense of the ludicrous at the
peculiar reception that he and his companions were meeting, he did not appropriate the fineness of the compliment

that in it was being tendered him. For in his own eyes he
seemed but an ordinary person, and one to whom belonged
the least possible amount of popular applause. He was
bare-headed as usual, and the full exposure of his countenance and forehead, as the bright sun fell on him, made it
possible for the gazer's eye to take in the noble majesty of
a face to which years had brought no weakness, and unto
which they had given a characterization and dignity truly
imposing.

"Aye, aye, the bees have swarmed for sartin, this time,
Henry, and the whole hive is empty. By the Lord, Lad,
they look like a bunch of frightened Hurons huddlin' together in the midst of a sudden ambushment afore they
have had time to think or get to shelter. Hoot! There's
more colors in their garments than the squaw of a chief
would have at the feast of the Succotash, and the toggery
that some of them chaps has on would make a dead moose
bellow, — but why be they so arnest-like in their looks, boy,
and what be the sense of their silence!"

To this interrogation Herbert made no reply, for he understood the pent-up excitement of the crowd they were approaching, and knew that the explosion was sure to come
at the proper moment; and he would not for the world
have robbed himself of the pleasure of seeing the Old Trapper's surprise. He therefore made no reply. The boat by
this was within twenty rods of the landing, and was gliding
rapidly in. The Lad, affected by the silence, and surprised
at it, suddenly trailed his oars, and half turning in his seat
lifted his simple face upward to see what was the cause of

it. The Old Trapper, surprised at the extraordinary conduct of the crowd, and not dreaming of the real reason of
it, also intermitted his stroke and brought his paddle to a
trail, while his eyes went and came from object to object
as if in the presence of an enemy.

Thus the boat slowed its progress and came nearly to a
pause within fifty feet of the landing, when suddenly an old
white-headed man, dressed in humble garb and leaning
heavily on a stout stick, who stood near the outermost
angle of the pier, and who had been shading his eyes for a
moment from the western sun that he might assist his failing sight, and gazing fixedly at the countenance of the
Trapper, whose features he had not seen for thirty years,
flourished his stick in the air, and exclaimed with a voice
that shook with the intensity of his emotion : —

"John Norton ! He saved my life at the battle of the
Salt Licks forty year ago. Three cheers for John Norton !"

And then, as if the cord which held the crowd to silence
had suddenly snapped and yielded to the pressure of the
pent-up excitement, or as if the edged words of the old
veteran had cut it like a knife, a cheer arose which burst
the stillness into fragments, and, thrice repeated, rolled its
roar across the lake and against the distant hills, until their
hollow caverns resounded again, while on the instant a hundred white handkerchiefs, waved by whiter hands, sprung
into sight and filled the air with their snowy flutterings.

It was then, when the mighty .cheer broke forth, and
while the roar of it was around him, that the Old Trapper
realized the honor which by silence and voice alike, was

being shown him. Herbert's eyes were on him with the glad watchfulness of one who knew what was coming, and knew also how totally unprepared the old man was for the reception, and was curious to note his bearing of it. For one instant the color came and went in the Trapper's face as in the face of a girl whose beauty, at her entrance to the parlor, has brought every eye in admiration upon her. The least possible quiver played on the edges of his lips, and a gleam as of a fine light shining from within came into his eyes. And then he rose and stood at his utmost height in the boat, erect as a pine which has come to its fullest girth, ripened its fiber to toughness, but has not as yet felt the weakening of coming decay. So the old man rose and stood for a moment, in acknowledgment of the greeting, with a grace and dignity that a trained courtier might envy, but could not assume, while the eyes of the multitude had time to take in the size of his splendid proportions, and the grave majesty of his countenance; and then he settled to his seat and the boat moved to the landing.

"By heaven!" exclaimed the professional to his companions again, "if the Trapper can handle the oars like that chap in the bow, we are beaten!"

And this was John Norton's reception.

CHAPTER VII.

THE RACE.

" A larger scene of action is displayed."
Virgil, Dryden's Translation.

IT was high noon at the Saranac, and a brighter day was never seen. The sky was so intensely blue that it fairly gleamed, as if, like woods of compact fiber, it was capable of taking polish. In it the sun stood and shone with self-asserting brilliancy. It glistened, it scintillated, it sparkled, as if its rays were actually frosty. The sky above was wintry. The cold of the North was journeying southward, like her feathered couriers on lofty wings. The upper atmosphere was chilly, but on the earth summer still tarried with its hazy warmth and slumberous airs. The heat came from the earth rather than from the sun, and lingered like a happy child near the mother that gave it birth, and from whose bosom it would not fly. The lake had not stirred a ripple. It took its mood from the atmosphere, and matched it perfectly. Perhaps it had said to the wind: "Oh, let me rest to-day! You have blown me about and kept me moving until I am weary. Do give me a little peace. Come, dear, sweet wind, if you love me so, do let me have one day of rest!" And the wind, thus coaxed by the sleepy beauty, had humored her luxurious whim, and stood all day holding his very breath. The air was thickened as with golden-colored smoke. It was not common air; it was incensed, aromatic, pungent. The nose found strange, spicy scents in it, and breathed it in slowly, as a delicate mouth receives cream, not to swallow, but to taste. No one could breathe such an air simply for the purpose of ordinary life, — mere respiration, — but as one breathes perfume; receiving its delicious sensation as a luxury, and drawing each breath, not for life's, but for joy's sake. In front of "Martin's," across the lake, the hillside fairly flamed. The leaves had a ripened glory, rich as that which the old painters, with their ardent colors, painted into the faces and around the heads of their saints. Along the shores, blown by previous winds the bright-colored leaves lay thick; some lying limp and flat, — patches of crimson on the dull water, — some half immersed, while others, curled and curved, floated jauntily on the surface, as if they could scarcely bear to touch the element on which they rested. Nature, on tree and water, and in the air, was lavish of her highest tints; until the gray moss on the rocks, and the gray rocks themselves, looked, with the golden colors on them, almost gorgeous.

On some the beauty of the day was not lost. . But the noise and excitement of the sport had shut the eyes of most to its extraordinary charms, or caused them to look upon it from the purely utilitarian standpoint of a tin peddler from New Hampshire, who, hearing of the great gathering, and having an eye for business, had made a forced drive of fifty miles in the hope of finding a market for his wares, and having sold his last kettle, was now giving his undivided attention to the cause of his good fortune, and

who, after a profound inspection of the surroundings, pronounced it a "blamed good day for a race." Nor was he
wrong in his estimate. It was a good day for a race, and a
long race at that. For of wind there was none. The water
was level as water might be, and the air was of that genial
quality that one could breathe under the necessities of violent exertion, even with gasps, and not have it "cut" windpipe or lungs.

It was nigh noon, and the "free for all" was to be pulled
at one o'clock. The entries were closed the evening before
and stood seven•in all; the three professionals; the brother
guides, known as Fred and Charlie, respectively; the Old
Trapper, and the Lad. When the names were announced
from the front piazza to a highly interested crowd, which
numbered every man and boy, guide and gentleman on the
place, the other names were received with cheers, but the
greeting given to the Lad was peculiar. When the chairman of the committee of arrangements announced it, it was
heard by the throng in dead silence, none knowing to whom
it applied; but when the chairman in response to a question from the crowd explained that "it belongs to the tall
young man that came in with Mr. Herbert and John Norton
yesterday," the most extraordinary explosion, and one characteristic of an American audience, followed. It was not a
cheer, nor a groan, but a monstrous roar of good nature,
astonishment, contempt, and mirthfulness all combined in
equal measure.

Interrogations crossed and re-crossed each other in the
air. The old chap who had started the cheer for John Nor-

ton the previo is day, wanted to know "which section of
the boy was to pull, the upper or lower half, for no Saranac
boat would hold both halves of him at once." Remarks
more or less witty were made as to the length of his legs
and arms, the enormous size of his hands, and the lathe-
like shape of his build. Many of these remarks were directly or indirectly addressed to the Trapper, as the only
one who could give information who and what the Lad was.

The old man bore the badinage of the crowd for several
minutes with immovable good nature ; and it was not until
the hilarity passing downward from the better class to the
coarser and half-drunken hangers-on that can always be
found in a crowd at a country hotel — began to be tinctured
with vulgarity, if not with abuse, and the questions put
with offensive directness to the Lad himself, who was standing timidly behind him, that he made any reply. But then
he stepped suddenly aside, bringing by the motion the Lad
into full view, and laying one hand lightly on his shoulder
and stretching the broad palm of the other out, he said : —

"I sartinly hope I can take a joke, either on my own account or on account of a friend ; but there's a pint beyend
which it's onreasonable to go, and beyond which it's axin a
good deal of human natur' to stand. And a few of ye noisy
chaps in this matter of the Lad's rowin' to-morrer, has gone
about fur enough, and I'd advise ye to fetch up, or ye'll sartinly git yerselves into trouble. And sence I've got a chance
I might as well stop a leetle nonsense that the Lad has told
me ye practised on him when he come out with his pelts
last spring ; and so I'll jest say — and there be a few here

who will tell ye that John Norton is apt to keep his word —
that if this boy by my side, which I call the Lad, but who
calls himself, ' The Man Who Don't Know Much,' ever comes
here agin, and any of ye git careless in yer speech toward
him, I'll come out and settle the matter with them that
does it, and in a way they won't forgit while they live on
the arth."

It was five minutes of one o'clock, and the seven boats
were already in position and the seven oarsmen, excepting
the Trapper and the Lad, had their oars at a rest. The
course ran straight down the lake to a line of seven buoys,
so that each boat had its own buoy to turn, and thence
back again to the line at which they were now stationed for
the start. The length of the course was, therefore, just
four miles; two out and return. A straight-away race it
was to be, and longer by half than was ever before pulled
on those waters. The fact alone increased the interest of
the spectators, and provoked a deal of discussion. Since
the previous evening, divisions had taken place in the opinions of the crowd, and every competitor but the Lad had
his backers. The professionals, of course, had the majority
still, but the Old Trapper was well backed, especially by the
older men among the natives, and by the ladies of the hotel,
upon whom the simplicity of his manners, and perhaps
even more, the greatness of his fame, had made a profound
and most favorable impression. But the two young guides
Fred and Charlie did not lack supporters either, — the
former because of his enormous strength, which had already
given him a brilliant local reputation, and because although

he had never pulled in a public race, he was nevertheless known to have such command at the oars as few attain, and none unless they have a natural aptitude for the work. Herbert believed that Fred. would win the race if any accident should happen to the Trapper, and if the Lad should, through timidity, fail to exert himself; for the young man had been his guide several seasons and he had assisted him with suggestions in mastering a stroke which allowed his enormous strength to expend itself to the best advantage. Indeed, many of the spectators were aware of this and in default of Herbert's pulling, himself, which was the subject of keen and universal regret, Fred. was looked upon as in a certain sense his representative, and was backed accordingly. His brother, although of lighter proportions, had already won in many races, and was known as one of the best, if not the best oarsman among the guides, and his party was strong in numbers and equally strong in hope, including as it did nearly every visitor from an adjoining hotel, and every guide in the St. Regis region. Indeed, as between the two brothers, Fred. and Charlie, and the Trapper; the guides and dwellers in the woods were well represented, and they felt that the chance of their champions winning the prizes over the professionals was as good as it could possibly be, and they backed their men with all the earnestness of their earnest natures and the talkative confidence of local pride now thoroughly aroused. The Lad had not a single backer with the exception, strange to say, of the professionals themselves: for even Herbert did not feel persuaded that he would pull with energy, and therefore said nothing openly of his chances. But the professionals, who had watched his stroke as he came down the lake the day before, and knew nothing of his timid temperament, inwardly feared him more than all the others, and decided among themselves that he was their real antagonist, though of this they said nothing to others, but through a " silent partner " they " hedged " on him in the betting which quietly and without the least publicity had been indulged in to a considerable extent, especially among the guests of the hotel and the city visitors from the adjoining houses. The boats in which the several contestants were to pull were by no means of the same length or shape, for the conditions of the race allowed them to "take their pick," and each had followed his own inclinations. The three professionals had picked the lightest boats they could find, and those in which they sat averaged about sixty pounds and were some thirteen feet long. Charlie selected a light one belonging to a lady, one of the guests of the house, of lapstreak build but narrow and low, made of Spanish cedar, polished till it shone like glass, twelve feet in length and weighing only forty-six pounds. The other guide, Fred, pulled his own boat, over fifteen feet in length, and which weighed eighty pounds and more. For the Trapper, Herbert had selected one of precisely the same length and weight, while the Lad sat in his own that measured seventeen feet and upward and weighed over ninety pounds.

The Trapper had with him his rifle, from which no argument of Herbert — because of the extra weight it added, — could separate him ; and in the stern of the Lad's boat sat

Sport, the hound, with an expression of such gravity as
only a hound's countenance, when in repose, can show; as
if he had been elected to preside as judge over the race,
and felt to the full the grave responsibility of the position
and its accompanying dignity.

The number of the spectators was a wonder to all, and
entirely unanticipated. For although it was expected that
a large crowd would be present, yet the gathering had
grown into unprecedented and enormous proportions.
Where the people came from was a mystery. It seemed as
if not only had the wilderness sent out every guide and
party camping in it, but as if every hotel in the whole region
had emptied its guests upon the waters and shores of the
Lower Saranac, and that even the outlying villages had
poured their entire population into the same receptacle.
The long, wide piazzas of the hotel, the wharf, even the
roof of the boat-house, swarmed with human beings. The
shore on either side of the lake was also lined with spectators for the distance of half a mile, while on the waters of
the lake itself, stretched on either side of the course which
was duly protected from infringement by guard boats stationed at suitable distances by the committee of arrangements, at least five hundred boats lay loaded deep with
eager spectators. From a flag-staff in front of the hotel
the stars and stripes hung pendent in the still air, a drapery
of glorious color in the bright sunshine, while numberless
smaller flags and showy streamers flecked the air with their
rich shades everywhere. Nature and man seemed in rivalry
and striving to outdo each other in contributing most to the
spectacular glory of the scene.

Such was the position of things at five minutes of one
o'clock, — the seven boats in line, and the seven contestants waiting for the word, with every eye among the thousands fastened upon them amid a silence as profound as if
by some supernatural power every man and trace of man
had been suddenly banished from the spot, and nature had
returned to the uninterrupted silence of her primeval solitude.

"Now, boys," said the Trapper, speaking to the two
brothers on his right, "ye must remember that a four-mile
race is a good deal of a pull, and the go-off isn't half as
decidin' as the come-in. I don't conceit we can afford to
fool away any time even in the fust half mile, for them
three perfessionals have come up here to row, and they look
to me as if they had a good deal of that sort of fun in 'em;
but it won't do to git flustered at the start, and if ye see fit
to follow it, I will set ye a jedgmatical sort of a stroke
which will send us out to the bys yender without any raw-
ness in the windpipe or kinks in the legs. Still, if ye don't
think ye are pulling fast enough take yer own lick, — for in
sech matters the best jedgment may prove like a hound off
the scent, and I wouldn't spile yer chances of walloping
them perfessionals, to-day, for all the money on the arth.
And in sech a race as this is likely to be, it's only just and
reasonable that every man should foller his own notions,
and act accordin' to his gifts."

"Do you think we shall win, Old Trapper?" said Fred. in
a low tone.

"I dunno, I dunno, boy; I sartinly dunno," returned the

Trapper in a tone scarcely above a whisper. "I like yer build, for yo are broad in yer chest and thick in yer loins, and yer jaw bone is a big un, and that means yo have got plenty of grit, as I have observed natur'; but I don't like yer oars. No, I can't say I like yer oars, specially that left one, for there's a knerl in the shank of it that oughtn' to be there, and I fear the pesky thing will play a trick on ye at the finish. But, Henry has great confidence in yo and Henry knows what rowin' and oars is, for sartin'. I'd give every skin in the cabin if the boy was atween me and the Lad here, aye, and throw in a dozen or two of my best traps to boot."

"Your oars are big enough to hold, any way," rejoined the young man, "and I hope to heaven you will win."

"Thank ye, boy, thank ye. It is well spoken in yo. Yis, I sartainly shall try, for it would be a mortal shame to have the prize go out of the woods, for the piece is a likely one to look at, and they say it has a long range. And if nothing gives way I'll give 'em a touch of the stuff that's in me, for the last half mile that will make them git down to their work in arnest, yo may depend on it. But if anything happens to us, or we can't do it, I have great hopes of the Lad, here, for his gifts be wonderful at the oars, and if he will only pull as I seed him day afore yesterday he'll —"

"*Ready, there!*" said the sharp, clear voice of the Starter. "*Ready there, for the word!*"

"Aye, aye, ready it is," replied the Trapper, as he advanced his blades well ahead ready for the signal. "Now, Lad," whispered the Trapper hoarsely, "don't yo forgit yer promise, and if anything happens, or ye see I can't win, and I give ye the word, John Norton will never forgive ye if ye don't pull like a sinner running from the jedgment."

"Ready there all of you. *One*, TWO, THREE. GO!"

At the word, "*Go!*" the seven boats started; but not together. The oars of the three professionals dropped into the water as if their blades were controlled by one man, and their stroke was so tense and quick that the light boats fairly jumped ahead like three arrows shot from one quivering string. But lightning-like as was their stroke, it was no quicker than the one that Charlie, the guide, had delivered, nor had they thrown an ounce of vigor into theirs which he had not also put into his; and the little boat in which he sat had the best of the send-off by at least a foot. The other guide and the Trapper had been slower to get away — as in reason they must, being in heavier boats, — and were at least a full length behind, before they had fairly got 'into motion. Nor even then did the Trapper seem to be anxious to make up the lost ground, nor to care if he lost more; for his stroke was long, steady, and to the lookers-on it seemed leisurely pulled. The Lad was the last to get off, and his stroke was even longer, easier, and more deliberately delivered than the Trapper's; and so careless and ungainly was his appearance, and so little snap did he evince, that the crowd, who cheered the passage of the others as they swept past, laughed and groaned and roared their fun out at him as he swung nonchalantly along. For forty rods the race continued, without change in the relative positions of the seven boats. The professionals pulled a quick, sharp stroke of forty-odd to the minute, which was precisely matched by the young guide, and the gain of a foot he had at the send-off he still held almost to an inch. A prettier sight than the four leading boats presented never gladdened a boatman's eye, nor stirred the gazer's blood. The eight oars flashed, dropped, and flashed again as the oarsmen swept their blades ahead, as if their motions were regulated by machinery, while their heads and bodies rose and sank with automatic precision. Some rods behind, the Trapper and Fred. were pulling side by side and stroke for stroke, — long, strong and steady.

"I tell ye, boy," said the old man to the young guide by his side, as he half turned his head and threw a glance forward, "them perfessionals have got their match for quickness in yer brother, if I am any jedge, and if he's got wind and grit they'll like him as leetle as a half-breed likes the pill of the doctor; for the more they chew him the bitterer he'll taste. It does me good to see the boy hang to 'em. Lord-a-massy! how the folks are yellin', and the wimmin' themselves are screechin' like squaws at the maize dance. Yis, yis, boy, I understand ye; but don't ye worry; four miles is four miles; and it's a long oar and strong back that's goin' to win this race, and no clipper-clapper work that's makin' the folks screech so ahead; but if ye are narvous we'll lengthen out a leetle jest to show 'em that we aint more than half asleep." "Come, Lad!" called the Trapper, to his comrade astern, "don't ye mind the foolishness they are saying to ye and the dog, but hist along a leetle faster, for we are goin' to let out a link or two, and I

feel a leetle easier to have ye nigh enough to catch the reason of yer stroke and feel the ease of it in my elbows."

So saying, the old man set his comrade a stroke so long
and sharply pulled that the two boats fairly doubled their
rate of speed, and in a minute were end and end with the
boats ahead, while the exhibition of strength thus made,
taking the spectators, who had begun to look upon the race
as lying between the four contestants in front, by surprise,
brought a roar of astonishment and wild delight from their
mouths that fairly lifted the air as with an explosion. But
here and there a watchful eye, and pre-eminently that of
the "silent" partner of the professionals, noted that, rapid
as had been the movement of the two boats forward, as
impelled by the tremendous spurt of the Trapper and Fred.,
and although the Lad still swung along in his nonchalant
manner, yet when the spurt had ended and six instead of
four boats were now in line, the boat of the Lad was in the
precise position as regards its nearness to the Trapper that
it had been from the beginning of the race. And seeing
this, — a very instructive fact to one of his profession — he
proceeded to "hedge" yet more.

"There!" said the Trapper to the young guide at his side,
as the two boats came up even with the other four, and he
had breathed himself a moment, "I guess we'll ease up a
leetle, for the time to raally pull hasn't come yit. I tell ye,
boy, ye needn't be afeared about the race. That rifle is
goin' to stay here in the woods, and I sartinly hope ye may
git it, too; for ye have got the raal grit in ye, and yer stroke
is so much like Henry's, that when ye let out back there I

almost conceited the boy himself was pullin' yer boat. No, no, boy; don't say a word, but keep yer breath to yerself, for ye'll need it all at the finish. No, no," continued the Trapper, as if talking to himself, "I don't need the piece, and Henry has as good a one already as man ever handled, and a good rifle aint got every day and is better than a fortin' to one of yer years. Yis, boy, you let me set ye the stroke, and I'll bring ye in ahead of them chaps, and of yer brother, too; for it's agin reason that a light boat and a quick stroke should win agin a long boat and a long oar, with sech a back and sech grit as ye have. So save yer breath as much as ye can for the finish, and the rifle shall be in yer cabin to-night, or my name ain't John Norton."

"Now," resumed the Trapper after a moment's pause, "there's the Lad back there that can beat us both, but his sperit is agin it, for he thinks it would tickle an old man like me to win the prize, and so he won't pull. Jest watch his stroke, boy, and observe the reason of it. Did ye ever see a boat run like that with sech leetle effort? Lord bless the Lad! its a marvel, how the Creatur can put so much power into sech an onreasonable body. — Easy, boy, easy, .et 'em git ahead if they want to. The comin' in is what decides a race, and I'll give ye a stroke on the last half mile that'll make 'em feel like an over-fed hound in a hot chase."

Thus the boats rushed on their way, each running as straight towards its appointed buoy as a bullet could fly; while the multitude, now far astern, watched with eager eyes and bated breath the receding race. As the boats passed farther and farther down the lake the murmur of renewed conversation arose; while speculation, guesses, and strong assertions as to who would win were heard on all sides. It was evident that the party of the Trapper was already in the ascendant; for the spurt he had made, and which had carried his boat with such a rush up even to the front, had revealed the tremendous power of the man, and shown that age had not weakened, to any extent, his enormous strength. The old men in the crowd, whose sympathies were naturally enlisted in behalf of their former comrade, were nearly beside themselves with delight, as they saw him rush his boat forward. They swung their hats; they shook each other's hands; they cheered with their thin, tremulous voices; they actually wept, while the old fellow who had repeated it at least twenty times before, again asserted: "I tell ye, there isn't a man on God's arth can beat John Norton at the oars."

At last, a man with stentorian lungs, who stood on the ridge of the boat house, shouted with all the power of his voice: "They have turned the buoys! They have turned the buoys! The professionals and Charlie are ahead!" At this announcement a silence fell on the multitude for a moment, and then the buzz and murmur of mingling voices again arose.

"How far behind is John Norton?" said the old chap on the wharf.

"He and Fred. are four rods astern, at least," bellowed the man in reply.

"Where's the Lad?" asked the "silent" partner, in a clear tenor voice.

"Oh, he's out of the race," said the man on the roof. " He's full ten rods behind the Trapper and Fred." ,

At this the " silent" man with the tenor voice looked puzzled. He took a cigar from his pocket, and, as he coolly struck a match on his boot heel, those standing near him mutter: " Ten rods astern! His stroke is a winning stroke. What's the matter with the fool ? "

By this time the boats were plain to the view, and the stillness which had settled on the crowd which, with eager eyes and shortened breath watched their coming, was so profound as to be absolutely oppressive; for the contestants were barely a mile away, and every boat, and even the action of the several boatmen, was clearly visible.

" There, boy," said the Trapper to the young man at his side, " ye have trusted to an old man's jedgment, who played the game we are at afore ye was born, and I told ye comin' down, the piece should be in yer cabin to-night. The time has sartinly come for us to show the grit that's in us. Are ye ready for the stroke, boy ? "

The guide made no reply, save a quick, sharp nod of his head and a slight tightening of his lips, while his heavy brows fairly lowered over his eyes.

" All right," said the Trapper; " ready for the word; long and quick ; NOW ! "

The swoop of a hawk into the thicket after its prey is scarcely swifter or straighter than was the rush of the two boats, in which the old man and the young guide sat, to the front, until their bows lined exactly with those of the other four.

"Easy, easy now," said the Trapper. "Git yer breath, boy. Yis, Henry was right; ye are grit from yer head to yer toes. The rifle is yours or John Norton is a — "

A groan of pain and rage interrupted the Trapper He threw a glance to the left and the cause was apparent. The oars of Charlie were trailing, while the white shirt that he wore was spattered all over with blood. His tremendous exertions had been too much. He had broken a blood vessel, and from mouth and nose alike jetted with every gasp the sanguine tide.

"Never mind the boy," hoarsely whispered the Trapper; "they'll pick him up. The piece must stay in the woods if yer whole family dies. These chaps pull well. Now, boy, put yer soul onto yer oars, and pull yer arms out of their sockets, or win. Ready for the word? Now!"

The young man obeyed the Trapper to a fraction. He threw the full force of the enormous strength, for which he was noted, on to his oars. The cords of his neck swelled and stood out like ropes; his nostrils dilated; his face fairly sharpened to the effort; but the sudden vigor of his stroke was too much for the wood. The miserable oar, to which the Trapper had alluded, parted with a crash. The guide was thrown upon his side on the edge of the boat; the boat careened, swayed, swooped suddenly aside, and the young man, unable to recover his balance, rolled headlong into the lake.

The Trapper was now thoroughly aroused. The boats were within a hundred rods of the home line, and the Lad was fully fifteen astern. The roar of the crowd was deaf-

"GO IT LAD!" Page 221.

ening. The professionals pulled like mad. The old man's eyes fairly glowed; through the roar of the multitude who were literally frantic with excitement, his ear caught the voice of Herbert calling clear and strong: —

"John Norton, now is your chance! PULL!"

The old man gathered himself for a supreme effort. His blood was up and the lion in him fairly aroused. Never before was such a stroke pulled, and never before was such a catastrophe. The blades were too broad to yield; the boat too heavy to get away quick enough; the oars too strong to part at the stroke; his tremendous effort tore the row-locks from the gunwales as if they had been paper, and the Trapper measured his length in the bottom of the boat.

The catastrophe was of such an unexpected and over-whelming character that it hushed the roar of the crowd as if an awful visitation had terrified them to silence. Even the professionals intermitted a stroke and the Lad turned his face ahead. The old man had risen and was standing erect in his boat, still holding the oars in his mighty hands. His eyes flamed; his face was bloodless in the whiteness of an unutterable rage; he shook the heavy oars in the air as if they had been reeds, and shouted with a voice that sounded awful in its intensity: —

"Lad, now pull for the sake of John Norton and save his grey hairs from shame! Pull with every ounce of strength the Almighty has given ye, or my curse shall follow ye to yer grave!"

It were worth a thousand miles of travel and a year of life to see what followed. It seemed as if the strength of

the Trapper, by the medium of the awful appeal, had actually been imparted to the Lad and put at the disposal of
his skill. His head suddenly sat erect on his shoulders.
His body straightened as if fashioned in perfect symmetry.
His stroke lengthened to the full reach of oar and arm.
The oars bent like whip-sticks. The flash of the blades on
the recovery was so quick that the eye caught only the
gleam. His boat sprang, flew, flashed, and as it jumped
past the Trapper, the old man again wildly shook the oars
he clutched in his hands, and shouted : —

"Go it, Lad ! The honor of the woods be on ye ! Give it
to 'em ! Ye'll beat 'em yet, sure as Judgment Day ! "

Except the voice of the Trapper not a sound was heard.
The feeling was too intense. Men clinched their fists until
their nails cut the skin of their palms. They never felt the
pain. Women fainted where they stood or sat. No one
noticed them. One of the professionals threw up his oars,
crazed by the excitement. The other two pulled in grim
desperation, their faces white as chalk, but grit to the last.
They pulled, but pulled in vain. The boat of the lad caught
them within fifty feet of the line, and shot across it half a
length to the front.

THE RACE WAS OVER AND THE RIFLE WOULD STAY IN THE
WOODS !

For an instant not a sound was heard. Then such a shout
went up as was never heard before from human throats.
The noise tore and stormed through the still air, rolled and
reeled this way and that ; exploded again and again, until
the very heavens quivered and shook ; while amid the up-

roar the sonorous voice of the Lad's hound sent forth its gladsome challenge as if he shared the joy of the crowd and appreciated the honor it was paying to his simple-minded master.

The "silent partner" on the wharf spat out of his mouth the stump of the cigar which, without knowing it, he had bitten in two in his excitement, took a fresh one from his pocket, lighted it, and muttered to himself, —

" I'M GLAD I HEDGED ! "

CHAPTER VIII.

THE LAD'S TRIUMPH.

" Your grace has laid the odds on the weaker side."
Shakespeare.

THE scene which followed is indescribable. Hats and caps went into the air in clouds, handkerchiefs fairly whitened the shores, the wharf, and the front of the hotel, men yelled and women clapped their hands, dogs barked and guns exploded, while amid the uproar, confusion and babel of indistinguishable noises, in some way — no one could tell precisely how — the boats of the contestants reached the landing, and the oarsmen, every one of them save the Old Trapper, white and tremulous from their tremendous effort, stepped or were helped ashore.

The crowd, like all American crowds, when greatly and happily excited, was generous to an excess, and gave to each a reception whose warmth and enthusiasm were sufficient to have broken down the barrier of professional pride, and remove from vanity itself the sting of defeat. Even the professional who had lost his head in the awful excitement of the last moment, and thrown up his oars in mental bewilderment, was not excluded from the ovation, for it was felt that the circumstances had been so extraordinary that it furnished an ample excuse for his aberration. Indeed, the crowd felt that every man had done his best, and given an exhibition of skill and pluck seldom witnessed, and were determined to slight no one in the award of their praise.

But it was evident that if the Lad had won the prize the Trapper, in the latent thought of the spectators, still carried the honors of the race; for the ease with which he had pulled the race up to the moment of the catastrophe, and the astonishing exhibition of strength which had caused it, had made such an impression on every one, that all were unanimous in the feeling that but for the mishap, the old man would surely have won the prize himself. As to the exhibition of the skill and energy of the Lad, there was but one opinion ; nothing like it had ever been seen. The distance he was behind when the Trapper yelled for him to pull; the weight of his boat, increased as it was by the weight of his hound; the vim and grit with which the two professionals fought it out; all these points and others were mentioned by the crowd in swift succession, and the more they thought of it the more astonishing did the performance seem. Had they not seen it, they would not have believed it. The professionals themselves said that they did not understand it. That he came in ahead they admitted, but how he did it they could not tell. The "silent" partner, when questioned by his panting companions themselves, took the "Victoria" he was coolly smoking, from his mouth, drew them quietly aside, and while a gleam came into his eyes, said : —

"The fool has the champion stroke of the world. I saw it as he went down the Lake." And then he looked steadily

for a moment into the anxious faces of his friends, knocked
the ashes from his cigar and said in the calmest of tones :
"Don't worry. *I hedged !*"

At the landing the tumult was uproarious. Above the
heads of the jam the countenance and shoulders of the
Trapper could be seen, while his arm was stretched to its
fullest length to reach the extended hand of Herbert, who
was vainly struggling to get to his side.

"Yis, yis, boy!" shouted the Trapper, "I know what ye
would say, but luck was agin me. It was the Lad's day for
sartin. Did ye see him pull, Henry, arter I yelled at him ?
Was there ever sech a stroke and sech a gather on the arth
afore! Didn't I tell ye we'd have some fun on this trip ?
And the pond of the beavers, do you remember the pond of
the beavers, boy ? " And the old man laughed with extended mouth, while, in the ecstasy of his happiness, he
continued to wring the hand of his companion, whose face
was as radiant as his own, and whose grasp was nearly as
strong.

In the meanwhile the Lad was sitting in his boat, with
his face still white from the effects of his recent effort, and
shrinking timidly back from the extended hands that would
fain have lifted him bodily upon their shoulders and borne
him into the hotel in triumph.

"Stand aside, stand aside!" shouted the Trapper, as he
pushed his way through the jam as if they who composed
it had been only reeds on a marsh, "stand aside for a minit
and let the arms of the man he saved from bitter thoughts,
lift the boy from the boat. Come, boy," continued the Trap-

per, "let the man who lost the prize by his foolishness, carry ye ashore, and bear ye to the jedges, who are waitin' to give ye the prize."

So saying, the old man with no more effort than if he had been lifting a babe, swung the Lad up to his shoulders, and facing the crowd he shouted: —

" Here be the one who calls himself ' The Man Who Don't Know Much,' but that he knows enough to pull a four mile race is mortally sartin. And when he comes out agin with his pelts I know ye will remember his deed this day, and treat him as he desarves; for he has made good the honor of the woods agin strangers, and kept us who be of the wilderness, whether trappers or guides, from shame."

The answering cheer of the men who were around him, rising loud and long, satisfied the Trapper, and as he started up the bank and pushed on to the front of the hotel where the judges were he said, " Ye hear 'em, Lad, ye hear 'em ! There'll be no more laughin' at ye when ye bring out yer pelts, for ye be a man among men arter this, for mortals git fame by an act, and a single deed can keep their memory better than the hewed stuns in the grave-yards of the settlements. Here I be, and here's the Lad," said the old Trapper as he planted the boy by his side in front of the judges. " Here's the Lad who won the race, and it may be ye have somethin' to say to him."

" Young man," said the chairman, who stood holding a beautiful rifle in his hand, of the breech-loading pattern whose fame for accuracy and range had just begun to challenge the admiration of the world, as it has since retained it, " young man, who are you ? "

The Lad lifted his eyes from the ground on which they
had been steadfastly fixed, and looking timidly into the face
of the speaker, said in a deprecating voice, "I be The Man
Who Don't Know Much."

The gentleman regarded him for a moment amid a stillness which enabled each word to be plainly heard by every
person in the immense throng, and then said : —

"Where were you born, my boy, and where are your
parents ? "

"I was born by the sea in the state of Connecticut," responded the Lad in his peculiar, quiet, halting manner of
speech, "where father lives still, I guess, but mother has
gone away to heaven."

A slight tremble of agitation rustled through the crowd
at the answer of the Lad, and one old chap standing in the
inner circle, and whose highly colored visage gave unmistakable evidence of his habits, jammed his thumb and fore-
finger into his eyes, and, passing them downward, blew a
clarion blast from his nose muttering something about
the "blasted sun shining inter a feller's eyes so he can't see
anything."

"Where did you learn to row, and who taught you your
stroke ? " said the gentleman.

"I never learnt to row, as I know of," replied the Lad ;
"and no one ever told me anything about a stroke ; but I
always loved to be on the water, for the water never laughs
at me, nor calls me names, and I guess it come sort of natural for me to pull a boat."

"That's it, jedge, that's it," interrupted the Trapper.   "It comes nateral for the Lad to pull, and the Lord has sartinly gin him gifts at rowin', as he has the otter at divin', and a beaver in steerin'; for there's an old dog beaver on a leetle pond, nigh the Dreary Lake, that manages to steer himself without a tail, for he left it in my trap two year ago; and a beaver must sartinly be gifted in steerin' if he can navigate himself, especially in a current, without his tail. Yis, specially in a current," reiterated the Trapper, and he laughed to himself in his own noiseless fashion.

"Well, young man," continued the gentleman, "you have certainly won the race, and in a most wonderful manner; for you have won it against men who make the art of rowing a study, and follow it as a profession. And you are entitled to this beautiful rifle which was offered as the prize to him who should win the race. Can you shoot any, young man ?"

"I can't shoot as well as Henry, or John Norton," said the Lad; "and I suppose there are many men here who can shoot better than I can; but I like to shoot, and I shoot a great deal better than I did a year ago."

"Well, well, my boy, I'm glad to hear that you love to shoot, for this rifle has been thoroughly tested by the maker, and he says it will shoot a mile and kill. And in presenting it to you, in the name of the donors, allow me, in their name, to express the hope that you will find it a noble piece, and learn to shoot as well as you can row." And the gentleman advanced and placed the rifle in the hands of the Lad, and then stepping back, stood as if expecting some reply.

The Lad stood a moment holding the prize in his hands as if he could not realize that it was his, and then, as if his mind had slowly taken in the meaning of what had been said to him, and more yet, of the silence, he looked timidly up at the crowd, and then he turned his eyes appealingly to the Trapper. The old man understood the entreaty of the look and said : —

" Ye see, jedge, the Lad isn't much at talkin', for his gifts don't lie in that direction; but ye may take the word of an old man that he thanks ye all the same and will sartinly use the piece as a man should who arns his livin' by the use of his wepon and his traps. And now if ye haven't more to say to the Lad we'll go to our camp, for it's too crowded and noisy here to suit one of my gifts, and besides the sun is settin', and the wood for the night must be got in, and supper cooked. Come, Henry ; come, Lad ; let's git to the boat."

So saying, the Trapper and his two companions entered their boat, the Lad at the oars, and the Trapper at the paddle, as usual, while Herbert and the hound occupied the middle. The boat turned the angle of the wharf and headed up the Lake, the Trapper wielding his paddle with a natural grace that no art could imitate, and the Lad pulling the same long, leisurely stroke that had drawn the eyes of the professionals to it the day before. Not until the boat had disappeared behind the Three Sisters did the crowd cease to watch its receding form, but when it had passed behind the islands and disappeared from view, the throng broke up into knots, and until late in the evening continued to canvass the day's proceedings.

It was evening, and on an island that lay half way down the Lake our three friends had made their camp and were now seated around their cheerful fire conversing upon the great event of the day. The strong blaze brought out their faces in clear relief, revealing the features of each, and even the changing expressions of their countenances as they came and went, as the conversation proceeded. Now and then the countenance of the sturdy Old Trapper would yield to the pressure of his inward mirth, and his mouth would open to its widest stretch, while his body swayed to and fro, showing that he was fairly convulsed with laughter although his mouth emitted scarcely a sound. His two companions yielded with all the abandon of woodmen to the moods of their companion, and the roars of Herbert and the shorter and quicker cachinnations of the Lad, revealed how entirely they were surrendering themselves to the hilarity of the occasion.

"I tell ye, Lad," exclaimed the Old Man, "ye gin it to them in a way they'll never forgit till their dyin' day. I sartinly thought etarnity had come when I went into the bottom of the boat, for I'd sot onto them oars in a business sort of a way, and the thump I got riled me tremendously. I was madder nor a hornet punched out of his nest by a pole, when I ris up, and I jest hopped round in that boat and yelled like a Huron at a war dance. They actually say that I flourished them oars as a Dutch woman does her broom-stick when a neighbor's cow is rummaging among the bean-pods in her garden. Did I do it, Henry? tell me, boy, did I actually do it?"

"You did, for certain," answered Herbert, laughing until he fairly choked; yes, you did flourish them over your head like whip sticks, and you fairly hopped up and down in the boat as if you were crazy, John Norton, although at the time no one noticed it; for you see we were all mightily wrought up, and what seems funny to think of now that it is all over, seemed only natural and fitting at the moment it occurred. I never saw such excitement, and doubt if I ever do again. I was cool enough until your rowlocks gave way, but then I became as wild as the rest. My own ribs seemed to crack when you went into the bottom of your boat."

"Did they! did they!" ejaculated the Trapper, "you see, I had reckoned for sartin on yer guide's winnin', Henry, for the boy has a stroke eenamost as good as yourn, and he's a ripper to pull, and I thought the race was in our own hands. I had determined the young man should win, as he sartinly would, hadn't it been for that pesky oar; but when I seed him roll into the Lake, and I heerd the sound of yer voice, Henry, callin' on me to let out, it stirred every drop of blood in my skin, and I pulled an onreasonable stroke. When I called on the Lad my grit was up as if I was in the smoke of a scrimmage, with the odds agin me. Lord-a-massy! how strange it is that mortal man, and a man whose head is whitenin', too, should git so arnest over sech a playful matter."

"I think," said the Lad, "I ought to give the rifle to Fred. I know he wanted it badly, and he would have won the race if it hadn't been for his oar's breaking. Don't you think I had better give it to him, John Norton?"

"Not by a long shot!" returned the Trapper, "ye won the race, and won it when none of the rest of us could win it, and the rifle is yourn by right, and yourn it shall be till yer dyin' day. And may the Lord of marcy keep that day far from ye, Lad, till yer face is as wrinkled and yer head as white as mine."

"But," responded the Lad, whose face became almost beautiful as the light of the sweet thought within him flashed into it, fairly illuminating its ordinarily simple listlessness, "the Bible says it's-' more-blessed-to-give-than-to-receive,' and I'm sure it's an easy way to be blessed to give away a gun that only cost me a few strokes to win."

"I tell ye, Lad," exclaimed the Trapper — "the Lord forgive me for sayin' it, if it be wrong, — but the Bible don't say any thing about boat racin', and yer Scriptur' will be the death of ye yit. No, no, ye don't git the true trail of the varses Lad. It's downright foolishness, and I conceit that it's actally sin for a young man like ye, to give away a rifle that's worth forty mink skins and can send a bullet a mile and kill. I tell ye, Lad, the Scriptur' is all right if ye understand it and be strong headed enough to hold it steady, but if ye aint, it's like a overloaded rifle to a weak shoulder; it hurts the man who uses it more than it does the feller at the other eend. Good common sense is better than Scriptur' in matters of rifles and rowin'."

"But," returned the Lad, "it will do Fred. more good than it will me, besides —"

"How do ye know? How do ye know?" interrupted the Trapper, "how do ye know that the boy has any gifts in handlin' the piece, and what right has any man with a grooved barrel if the Lord hasn't given him the right idee of the wepon."

"But how do you know I can shoot any better than Fred. can? You never saw me shoot."

"Hoot, hoot," retorted the Trapper, "Didn't you show me a roll of skins ye had hid in the holler pine on Toma hawk Pint, and didn't I note that them which didn't show marks of the trap had three holes in the head, instead of the two the Creatur had put in 'em. A man must have gifts to put his bullet through the head of a mink, in the shade and shine of actual shootin'; and when ye emptied yer piece at Pine Ridge, day afore yesterday, to freshen yer loadin', didn't I see the knot ye shot at, and that ye drove yer bullet into the very hole where the stem once stood. I sartinly don't conceit that ye can shoot as well as Henry here, whose gift is onusual, and whose piece is parfect; nor as well as myself, whose eye has knowed leetle but the sights for sixty year, and whose narves has been steadied on the scout, and in the scrimmage; but ye sartinly have the gift in ye, and while I don't expect ye will ever handle the rifle as ye can the oars — still, be governed, Lad, by the jedgment of an old man and don't fool away a promisin' piece for the sake of a few varses of Scriptur'. For although it don't load at the right eend to suit my notions, yit Henry says the barrel is a good un, and ye remember that the jedge said it would carry the lead furder than man could see."

"What about the match to-morrow?" queried Herbert.

" Didn't I hear you half promise the judges you would come down and shoot for the purse, and if you do why shouldn't the Lad shoot with the rifle he has won to-day ? "

" Yis, yis, Henry," replied the old man, " I did sort of promise, — that is, I said we would come down and *see* the shootin', but I didn't say we would shoot, and I told 'em why. For I didn't think it fair that you and me should shoot agin the boys and the city folks, for ye know they couldn't git a thing if we was onreasonable enough to shoot agin 'em. — Lord-a-massy, how careless they do handle their paddles on the Saranac ! That bungler has grazed the rim of his boat three times in as many minits, or my ears have growed up. A bell on the end of his paddle-staff wouldn't make more noise. Do the fools think we be asleep like a Frencher in a drunken fit, that they must make such a racket comin' into our camp."

" Camp ahoy ! " cried a voice from the darkness.

" What of it, what of it ? " returned the Trapper. " Don't stay there callin' with a voice ye might hear to the Upper Carry. We heerd ye comin' afore ye started, and the noise ye made as ye came up the Lake eenamost drowned our talkin'. Come in, come in, and tell us what ye want ! "

" You don't compliment the paddling of my guide much, John Norton," said a man, as he sprang ashore and joined the group at the fire, " we didn't expect you knew of our appearance until I hailed, for I'm sure we came in very still — "

" Still ! " interrupted the old man, " I heerd the gratin' of his paddle shaft agin the boat when ye passed the Three

Sisters, and that's a mile away if it's a rod. And ye've spit a dozen times sence then, if ye have once, not to speak of the noise ye make when ye hitched on yer seat, and the crack of yer match when ye lit yer cigar. I've seed the time on this lake when a dozen Huron canoes would have been hangin' round yer wake had ye so much as rubbed yer hands on the legs of yer breeches or moved yer foot on the bottom of yer boat on a night like this; but what do ye want, and what can we do for ye?"

"I have come," said the man, "by the request of the judges of the matches to-morrow, to urge you and your two companions to enter the list and shoot for the prizes. The shooting will be at all distances, from fifty to a thousand yards, and there's twenty prizes in all, from a flask of powder to a purse of a hundred dollars in gold, and everybody says you must come or the affair will be a failure. All of us have heard of your skill, old Trapper, and hundreds of people, some of them foreigners, have staid over just because you are to shoot, and the judges say you must come."

For a minute or two the Trapper made no reply, but sat gazing into the fire, then lifting his eyes to the face of the messenger he said, "Now, friend, John Norton never lost a chance to shoot in his life if it was just and reasonable for him to do it, and many be the matches I have shot, and many be the pounds of powder and bars of lead I have won, not to speak of money and other things which stir the pride and vanity of man, but I ax ye, if it would be fair to the rest, for Henry, here, whose piece is parfect and gifts on

usual, and me, who have used a rifle for nigh on seventy
year, to shoot agin boys and city folks who can't be expected to know how to bring out the fine pints of a rifle,
and who have sot their hearts on the prizes ? "

"But, John Norton," returned the man earnestly, "you
mistake — some of the best shots in the woods, and a half
a dozen gentlemen from the cities with great reputation for
skill, are entered. And better yet, two Englishmen, who
have won prizes in their own land and have never been
beaten, have entered also. Indeed the betting is two to
one in their favor. And the ladies are crazy to see you
shoot, and charged me to say that you must come down and
contend for their prizes, at least, a hundred golden dollars
in a silken purse and a horn of solid silver with a deer and
hound in full chase engraved on it. If you don't come down
they declare they will come up in a body and bring you
down in the morning."

"Well, well," returned the Trapper laughing, "if the
wimmen folks are raally in arnest in the matter, and if
'twill make them happier to see an old man shoot, they
shall have their way for sartin; so tell them that we will
come down and jine in the fun, me and Henry and the Lad,
all three of us. The gold is nothin', but the Englishers
shant git the horn if a man who has spent his life in the
woods can win it. But I give ye notice — and ye may tell
'em so — that the raal trial will be atween Henry and me."

"They want the Lad to bring the rifle he won to-day and
shoot too," said the messenger as he turned toward his
boat.

"Aye, aye," said the Trapper. "The Lad will be there, and they'll hear the voice of the piece when the talkin' begins."

THE MAN WHO DIDN'T KNOW MUCH.

PART II.

CHAPTER I.

THE SHOOTING MATCH.

" And still as each repeated pleasure tired,
Succeeding sports the mirthful band inspired."

Goldsmith.

THE morning opened bright and clear, and every indication pointed to an eventful day. The best marksmen of the woods were there, guides and sportsmen alike, and among them not a few were known to be extraordinary shots and good at all distances. The prizes were numerous and so divided among different classes, that nearly every one who had skill in shooting might enter for some one of them, with a fair expectation of success. Local pride and personal favoritism were warmly enlisted in connection with many of the contestants, and each group of heated partisans warmly backed their man. The two great prizes were to be shot for after the minor ones had been allotted. The former was named the "Long Range" prize, because the distances to be shot by the contestants for it, were five hundred and one thousand yards. This was a distance far greater than any of the guides, or sportsmen either, had ever seen shot, and the majority of them unhesitatingly declared that "there wasn't a rifle made that could throw a bullet a thousand yards."

One old fellow known as "Old Bill," whose reputation for

close shooting and hard drinking was universal, declared
that "a feller would have to climb a tree to see the mark
at such a distance." And when pressed by a young man
with the assertion that the Englishmen would certainly
shoot the distance, admitted that "them darned Englishers
might possibly do it, if they had fetched in cannon, but no
regular rifle, sech as a decent man wanted to lift, could
throw lead any sech distance, nohow."

Indeed, it was universally understood by the crowd that
ths long range prize was especially gotten up for the "fur-
riners," as the guides called them, and that no one would
enter against them. This had been the feeling up to the
time the messenger returned from the Trapper's camp ; but
when he had got in, and standing on the front steps of the
hotel announced to the hundreds who had been eagerly
awaiting his coming, what John Norton had told him to say
— which he did, like a true herald, word for word — the
state of opinion underwent a sudden change, and a great
excitement sprang up. If the announcement had simply
been that the Trapper himself was to shoot, it would have
entirely changed the aspect of things, but when it was proclaimed that Herbert was to join in the shooting, and that
even the Lad would compete, with his new rifle, it was felt
by all that new, unknown, but potent elements had been
introduced into the problem. As to the abilities of the Lad,
all were in entire ignorance ; but after a thorough canvassing of the possibilities the prospects were pronounced as
against him : for his physical shape, his youth and timidity
were all considered as precluding the possibility of success

against such men as he must contend with. Still, every one felt kindly toward him and wished him luck.

Of Herbert more was known, and what was known was all in his favor. Gentlemen there were who had seen him shoot in target practice on the club ground, and some of them in prize matches, and they declared he had never yet lost a match, and, barring accidents, could not be beaten by anybody at long range shooting, they didn't care who the man might be. Guides there were who had seen him shoot in actual hunting, by day and night, in heat and cold, on land and when tossing about in his light boat on uneven waters; and with these there was but one opinion, and that was, that shooting his own rifle he was the quickest and surest shot that ever came into the woods, and that old John Norton himself couldn't beat him. These views they backed to the full extent of their means.

On the other hand, many — and these represented the majority, — believed that the Englishmen would certainly win the long range prize, and that the Trapper would as surely take the silver horn. But whatever might be the views of the individuals that composed the crowd, all were agreed in the opinion that the morrow would prove a great event, and the shooting be the best ever seen in the wilderness.

The professionals who had pulled in the race the day before had, with their companion, remained over to see the shooting, and for the "excitement of the thing," as the imperturbable gambler affirmed. But, for once in his life, he was actually in doubt how to proceed, and his disgust was

correspondingly profound; but his ears were open to every
remark made by those who knew anything of the principal
parties in the match, and a close observer might have
noticed that leisurely as were his movements, nevertheless,
his quiet, placid face could be seen on the edge of every
group as soon as it was formed. At last he drew his companions aside and said oracularly, but with the quietest of
tones : —

"Herbert wins the Long Range, but hedge on the Trapper. The Old Trapper will probably win the horn, but hedge
heavy on Herbert." So saying he took the cigar from his
mouth, flung it into the grass, and mounted the stairway
leading to his room.

There was one matter which quickened intensely the interest of the crowd : for while the conditions of the shooting for every other prize were duly advertised in the pro-
grammes which had been posted up by the Committee of
Arrangements in every convenient locality, the conditions
of the contest for the Silver Horn were not announced, save
that it was stated "that the shooting for this prize, given by
the fair ladies of the hotel," as the announcement gallantly
read, "would be at distances not exceeding forty rods, and
must be done off-hand." And then the poster significantly
added : "If the shooting be close there will be several contests of an unusual character, which will not be announced
until the emergencies of the competition elicit them." It is
impossible to say whether the extraordinary vagueness of
the announcement, or the language in which it was written,
caused the most comment among those whose education

had been of too limited a character to make their tongues familiar with polysyllabic words. The probability is that the feelings of the largest part of the native population were expressed by a young guide from Brown's Tract, who, after deliberately and rather painfully spelling out the "Announcement," turned to a companion, a little less cultured than himself, with the startling interrogation: "I *say*, Bill, who is this feller they call *Emergencies*, anyway? I haint never heerd of him, has you?"

It was ten o'clock of the morning, and the shooting was to begin at half past ten. The several distances had all been measured, the targets prepared, the markers and judges appointed, and everything was ready. The thousand-yard range had been measured — approximately, — and it stretched from the lawn in front of the hotel to a large rock on the opposite side of and some distance up the lake. From the wharf to the target-rock, buoys had been anchored, at the distance of five rods apart, into which little flag staffs, some five feet high, were set, while to the top of each was attached a crimson colored streamer. This had been done at the request of the Englishmen, who feared the wind might arise and they should need the flags to show them the direction and force of it.

It was ten o'clock to the minute, and the crowd, which was only a trifle smaller in point of numbers than on the preceding day, were all grouped in front of the hotel, crowded on the piazzas, clustered on the roof, or located in whatever position offered the best opportunity to watch the firing, and to note the results of it. They were evidently waiting the appearance of the Trapper and his companions, for the buzz of conversation was constant but not loud, while nearly every face was turned toward the point at which the coming boat would first show itself.

All at once from the roof of the hotel a voice sounded sharp and clear : —

" There they come ! all three of 'em ; there they come ! "

And on the instant the murmur of conversation ceased, and every eye strained itself to catch the first glimpse of the coming boat. An instant more and it came sweeping out from behind the island in full view, the Lad pulling a stroke longer and quicker than was his wont, as if those in the boat knew not the precise time and feared they might be late ; while the Trapper was wielding his paddle with a freedom and energy of motion that matched the earnestness of the Lad. Under the combined pressure of the oars and paddle the boat was being driven through the water at an astonishing rate, and came racing onward with a velocity which stirred a hundred exclamations from the mouths of the crowd.

The three professionals and their companions were standing on the outer angle of the wharf, watching, with eyes that never winked, the approach. For a full minute they said not a word and then the gambler, without taking his eyes from the boat, said : —

" There ! see the fool row ! Where does he keep, in his slab-sided body, the strength to pull that stroke so easily ? and where did he get the hint of it ? I tell ye, Bill," he exclaimed, with the least tremor of excitement in his voice,

I've seen the best scullers of both countries, and I've never seen a stroke I'd put up so much money on as that one he pulled yesterday, and which you can get the hint of now. What a joke 'twould be if the fool can shoot, too! Bill, I'll go you two to one he beats the Englishmen for the purse!"

"Bob," returned the one he had addressed, "you are crazy. The stroke is a winning stroke, for he proved it yesterday; but it doesn't stand to reason that such a lathe-like, long-legged, awkward cuss can shoot; and so you may regard that little matter you propose, of two to one, as *done.*"

"Done it is!" retorted the other, and turning away on his heel, carelessly, he glanced at a little blue covered book he held in his hand and muttered: "Well, I can't lose much whoever wins, for I've hedged on them all." And then he laughed at — from his point of view — the extraordinary oddity of the precaution.

In the meantime our three friends in the boat were holding a very important consultation, and one which decided, as the event proved, one of the two grand results of the day.

"Easy, Lad, easy," said the Trapper, ye are pullin' as a pigeon flies when he sees the hunter's smoke and hears the whistling of the lead in the air. Ye have got to do yer best to-day, and ye'll need a steady narve and a even pulse when the work begins; for them Englishers have got guns eenamost as big as cannon, they say, and can hit the size of a man's head furder than they can see. Do ye raally conceit, Henry, that we had better all three shoot for the purse agin the Britishers?"

"I certainly do," responded Herbert. "The more we are the better our chances; for it is in shooting as it is in rowing, accidents will happen, and who knows that there may not be as many to-day as there were yesterday; and where would the Lad's rifle be now if the two hadn't been made three? Yes, I certainly think we should all enter; for the English gentlemen are noted shots and have never been beaten, and the messenger said last night that the betting was two to one in their favor."

"Who cares! who cares!" exclaimed the Trapper; "I tell ye, Henry, there isn't a Britisher livin' can beat a American shootin', if the weepon has a grooved barrel; but still I like the jedgmatical way ye talk, for it shows ye are cautious, and caution is a good thing afore a scrimmage, and a mighty mean thing in it. But what can we shoot with, boy? for though the pieces you and me carry be as parfect as man ever made, yit they can't send lead the whole length of the Saranac for sartin, and a thousand yards is a bigger distance than I ever sighted for, onless it be now and then in fun, or on a ventur.'"

"We will use the Lad's rifle, all three of us," responded Herbert. "The conditions give each contestant his choice in respect to the rifle he uses; and all we have to do is to name his gun as our choice, when we enter for the thousand yards prize."

"But do ye think the Lad's gun will hold up to that distance? It won't weigh an ounce more than ten pounds."

"It isn't the weight of a rifle, John Norton, that decides its range, but the way it is made, and the quantity of powder and amount of lead it can bear. I have a gun of the same make at home that weighs only eight pounds, and I have shot it twelve hundred yards, and put every bullet of the string into the size of a beaver's hide."

"Well, well," exclaimed the trapper, "I s'pose I must believe ye, Henry, but it sartinly seems wonderful to me that lead can be throwed so fur with any sartinty. But what about the sightin' of the piece, boy? — for it's no better nor a smooth bore if it beant sighted fust."

"I thought of that," returned the young man, "but we can manage it. You see, each contestant is allowed three 'sighting shots' and that gives us nine, all told, and it will go hard with us if we can't know where we are shooting before the ninth shot, especially as the range is across the water."

"Aye, aye, that it will. I warrant ye will find the center with yer three bullets alone. But look, boy, and tell me what be the meanin' of them leetle flags fastened to the logs yender?"

"Those are what long range shooters call 'wind flags,'" replied Herbert, "and they are very useful, too, when the wind blows. I shot a match last fall when I had to allow five feet for the 'drift' of my bullet, and I won the match simply because I studied the flags better than the others."

"It's reasonable, yis, it's sartinly reasonable, what ye say, Henry," said the Trapper after he had pondered the matter for a moment; "and still as it is now, ye are likely to need them afore the day eends, for yesterday was a weather-breeder for sartin, and the wind will be liftin' by spells by and by, or natur forgits her promises over night. But if the wind does rise, Henry, ye must intarpret the motions of the flags to me and the Lad, for we are ignorant as babes of their language. Lord-a-massy!" continued the old man, "it will be strange for John Norton to shoot by the words of another and not by what his own eyes tell him!"

By this time the boat had nearly reached the wharf, and amid the cheery and multitudinous greetings of the throng, prominent over all being the greeting which the ladies from window, doorway, and piazza, with fluttering handkerchief and clapping of hands, gave the Old Trapper whom they had, with that enthusiasm for which, in cases where their feelings are moved by strong preference, their sex are noted, named "Our Champion."

In the midst of this pleasant recognition the Old Trapper, Herbert and the Lad stepped ashore, and with their rifles in their hands proceeded to the front of the hotel where stood the committee.

"Well," said the Trapper as he and his companions swung into line in front of the judges, "here be me and the boys, armed and equipped as ye see for sarvice. I didn't mean to burn a karnal of powder to-day, but last night yer messenger said that there was to be a puss of money and a silver horn shot for, and that the women folks want to see an old man, whose head has whitened in the woods, use the weepon a leetle, which he's handled for sixty year. And so I said to him that me Henry here and the Lad would come down and jine in the fun, not enough to spile the sport of the others, but jest enough to make things lively a leetle — especially for the Britishers, which he told us was goin' to have everything their own way."

"What do you want to shoot for, John Norton," said the chairman of the committee of arrangements, "or do you wish to compete for all the prizes?"

"Lord bless you, Squire, exclaimed the Trapper, "we wouldn't spile the boys' sport for nothing. No, no! let the people shoot and git the prizes as they can. Henry and me wouldn't hinder 'em; but the Lad, here, wants a leetle change to support his rifle with; — for a new rifle in the woods is a good deal like a new wife in the settlements, it takes a good deal of money to keep it goin', and me and Henry sort of thought we'd jest jine in with him to steady his narves a bit and make a sure thing of it. So ye may put us three down for that puss of money. Then, about that silver horn, ye see me and Henry both wants it bad, and its goin' to be nip and tuck atween us which shall git it when the raal shootin' begins, and I sartinly hope ye wont set up any barn door to shoot at like that on the rock there, but give us something small enough to try our gifts, that the ladies, here, may see us bring out the fine pints of the rifle. So ye may put us all three down for the puss and the horn, and ye'll see shootin' worth seein' afore the Englishers tote them both off."

It was one o'clock, and eighteen of the twenty prizes had been shot for, won, and distributed. The contest in several cases had been sharp, the result close, and not a little extraordinary shooting had been done. Indeed, the average had been very high, so high that it won from the Old Trap per, who, with Herbert and the Lad had closely watched the several contests, his warmest commendation.

" I tell ye, Henry," said he as the firing ceased, " I have seed more good shootin' to-day than I ever seed in the settlements afore. Some of them pieces must be nigh on to parfect, and some of them city boys need nothin' but edica·tion to make them raally larned and useful men. But, Lord bless me, what can ye expect from a boy born in the city and edicated by the school teachers of the settlements, who know nothin' but letters, and figures, and parsin'. Lord-a-massy, Henry, I've seed them perfessers that couldn't tell a mink from a fisher, or the difference atween a hound's foot and wolf's track. It sartinly seems sinful for a man to live in the world and be so ignorant of its signs and its ways. Yo are the only one, Henry, I have ever met that had the knowledge of books and of natur', too, and I should eena·most doubt"—

"The contests for the Long Range prize will now begin. The several contestants will take their places and listen to the rules that govern the shooting," shouted the Chairman of the Committee of Arrangements.

In a moment the five contestants were standing in front of the Judges, and the rules were read as follows :—

" 1. The shooting to be at two distances—five hundred and one thousand yards.

2. Each contestant has his choice of rifles.

3. Shoot any way they please, except with a table rest.

4. Order of shooting to be decided by lot.

5. Three shots allowed at each range for sighting.

6. A snap or miss fire to count as a shot.

7. A string to consist of ten shots, — measurement of each string to be from the inner edge of each bullet hole to the tack.

8. To miss the target altogether rules the shooter out of the match.

9. The prize to be awarded to the man with the lowest total in the measurement of the twenty shots."

Such were the rules as read by the Chairman. After reading them amid a profound silence, he proceeded to insert several slips of paper between the leaves of a book, and, holding it out to the five men in front of him, he said : "Gentlemen, you will now draw lots for the order in which you will shoot."

The slips were drawn, and it was found that the two Englishmen had drawn numbers one and two; the Lad had drawn three; Herbert, four; the Old Trapper, five.

At this point the Judge announced that the "sighting" shots would now be made. The Englishmen fired each one shot, and the white disk of the marker showed them within eight inches of the tack, — seeing which the crowd sent up a roar of astonishment, and the marksmen announced that they didn't care to shoot the other two shots allowed by the rules. The noise had scarcely subsided before Herbert, stretching himself at full length upon the ground, and resting the barrel of the Lad's rifle over a log some eight inches in diameter, on which he had previously laid his hunting jacket, and resting with his elbows braced in the form of a V, exploded the piece. The marker's disk showed the shot directly in line two feet below the tack.

"Good enough!" said the Trapper, "put in another cart-ridge, and hist the sight a leetle, Henry. The piece has sartinly got the trail, but is runnin' with her nose a leetle low. Give her a lift, boy, and try her agin."

While the Old Trapper had been talking, Herbert had been elevating the sight, and the last word was hardly out of the old man's mouth before the piece again exploded, and the "tick" of the striking bullet came sharply back through the still air. The disk again went up, and this time rested exactly over the center of the target.

"By the Lord, Henry!" exclaimed the old man, while a smile lit up his wrinkled face, "the gun's a good un, if she does load at the wrong eend. She minds the sights as a canoe does the paddle, and she's got a voice like a Dutch woman when she's angered. Wipe her out, boy, wipe her out; for a smutty bar'l bothers the bullet, and we'll show the Englishers that a gun in the hands of a woodsman can throw lead as straight as a cannon."

This was said in reference to the strangers' rifles, that were of heavy English make, weighing sixteen or eighteen pounds.

"What rifle are you to shoot, John Norton?" said the Judge.

"Well, squire," said the Trapper, "ye see, although the pieces that Henry and me use are parfect to a certain dis-tance, yit they wasn't made to shoot round the world, and yer ranges here are beyend the power of their bar'ls to cover; and as ye want to see the Lad's rifle here put into sarvice, we conceited we'd all three use her, and see if she was worth takin' into the woods. And as Henry, here seems to have got the p'intin' of the piece about right, and there isn't any time to spare, ye may begin to call off as soon as ye please, and let the talkin' begin. I feel as if I'd like to git my eye into the sights pretty soon, myself."

"The shooting for the five hundred yards range will now begin," said the Judge. "All the spectators are requested not to indulge in loud talking lest they disturb the marksmen. I shall call each in his order, and no one will shoot until I call his number. Number One!"

One of the Englishmen, a noble looking man of about forty, deliberately laid himself down on his back, rested the muzzle of his rifle between his feet, that were crossed, passed his left arm under his head, grasped the stock of his rifle with his hand, and taking a deliberate sight fired. His companion, when called, took the same position, and the marker's disk showed that both bullets had been lodged within the eight-inch diameter ring which surrounded the tack. The exhibition of skill was too fine to be received in silence, and the crowd broke into a cheer at the result.

"The Englishers call that shootin', do they?" said the Trapper in a low voice. "Yer way of shootin', Henry, is bad enough, for sartin; although I allow there is reason in yer elbow-rest, as ye call it; but I never expected to see a man shoot in that kinked-up fashion. They look more like a turtle lyin' on its back than human bein's. Why —"

"Number Three!" called the Judge.

Amid a silence as profound as if each spectator had been suddenly turned to stone, the Lad stretched himself beside

Herbert on the grass, and imitating his position, set his eye to the sights. One instant, and then the explosion came. The next and the marker's disk settled to the target within four inches of the tack. The yell that succeeded was simply tremendous.

"Well done, Lad!" shouted the Trapper, as he brought his hand with a mighty slap against his thigh, while his mouth opened to its widest stretch. "Ye'll give them Britishers the cramp in the small of their backs, if ye can stick 'em in in that style. Now, Henry, hist her nose a leetle and show 'em the fine pints of the piece."

"Number Four!" called the Judge, as soon as his voice could be heard. Herbert had already his eye at the sight when the word was given, and before the sound of the caller's voice had died away, the gun exploded. Again the disk settled to the target, showing that the bullet had divided the distance between the hole made by the Lad's ball and the tack.

It was a full minute before the Judge could make his voice heard, for the tumult of a thousand open mouths was in the air, and the noise was overwhelming. Amid the uproar the Old Trapper's voice was the loudest, for he was wise enough to know that the gun was working well and could be relied on, and that his two companions had the match in their hands. Indeed, so strongly was this fact impressed on his mind that he bent down to Herbert, who was still lying on the grass, and said : —

"I tell ye, boy, yo've got 'em. The bar'l is a true one and ye and the Lad don't need my help. I aint goin' to shoot."

"John Norton," said Herbert, "you talk nonsense. The Lad isn't certain, for he never shot a match in his life, and this is the short range. At the long range the gun may not work so well, and some accident may happen. Remember your own fame. A thousand people are looking to see you prove your skill. Besides, I want to see you shoot, myself. Above all, I want these Englishmen to see what an American gun can do."

"Well, well, Henry," interrupted the Trapper, "ye shall have yer way. Clean the piece and shove in yer cartridge. I never thought John Norton would shoot a rifle that was loaded at the breech pin."

"Number Five!" shouted the caller. "Silence. John Norton is to shoot."

The old man took the piece, and turning to the caller, he said : —

"Ye see, squire, I've never handled the piece, and if ye have no objection I would like to run my eye through the sights, for new sights to the eye are a good deal like a new knife in the mouth, ye· have to use it awhile afore ye git used to it."

"No objection ; you can look through the sights as long as you wish."

The old man lifted the rifle to his cheek and lowered it again. This he did several times; at last he said : —

"I can't say, squire, that the piece balances jest right, for it's a leetle too heavy at the breech and too straight in the stock, and the bar'l is colored a leetle too high, and it sartinly loads at the wrong eend; but the sights be right

and the air is clean as the Lord ever makes it. A man
ought to do eenamost anything with a true bar'l, to-day.
Now a hundred rods is a good range, for sartin, but the
board yender is well placed, and the white shows as clear
as a white gull in the air. Now Henry says the gun shoots
full three inches under, and advises me to hold up, and the
boy's jedgment is onusually good in sech things. And I
shall be governed by him in the matter, and if he is right
the lead ought to be found pretty near the tack, if the powder burns quick, and nothin' onnateral happens; but the
credit of the shot will half belong to Henry, if his advice
is correct. Now, yo may git yer eyes onto the board as
soon as ye please or the bullet will git there ahead of ye."

In spite of the Trapper's advice not an eye in all the
throng turned toward the target, but remained steadfastly
fixed on the marksman. Nothing could be finer than the
old man's appearance as he straightened his form to its full
height, advanced his left foot and lifted the barrel into the
air. Slowly and easily it settled down into the broad hand
extended to receive it, stood fixed for an instant, as if it
was a part of the atmosphere itself, then burst out its explosion. Before an eye in all the crowd had turned to the
target, the gun, with its muzzle still smoking, lay resting in
the hollow of the old man's arm, while his hand, from long
habit, was involuntarily feeling for the powder-horn to re-
charge the barrel.

CHAPTER II.

"On thee the fortunes of our house depend." — *Virgil.*

BUT recollecting themselves in an instant the spectators, as with one movement, turned their gaze at the target. The marker stood in front of it for a moment and then he waved the disk upward and downward, ending with a flourish into the air over his head.

"John Norton!" exclaimed the Judge, "you have missed the target entirely, and I regret to say you are ruled out from farther shooting."

"Missed the target!" said the old man, while the silence of the crowd was absolutely oppressive, and every word could be heard by the listeners. "Missed the target!" repeated the Trapper, "that would be a good 'un, and something the Saranacs wouldn't forgit in a day. No, no, jedge; its a big distance I'll allow, but the air is clear, the sights showed plain, the powder burnt quick; and the piece, considerin' it loads at the wrong eend, is a good 'un. Henry told me to allow three inches, and if the boy was right, as he is likely to be in sech a matter, yer marker there oughter find the lead in the black around the tack.".

At that instant a shout came booming over the water. For a moment the marker was seen swinging his hat over his head and then the white disk was placed squarely over the center of the target.

The roar that the crowd sent upward into the air was positively deafening. It lifted the atmosphere like an explosion, and swelled as it rose until the upper air was filled with the enlarging sound. Again and again did the crowd explode. Cheer upon cheer chased each other across the lake, and rolled their aerial waves against the distant hills. Amid the tumult the Old Trapper, whose hand Herbert had grasped, and was shaking with unconscious vigor and energy, exclaimed : —

"Lord ! Henry, did the folks think that a man who has used the weepon all his life, till his head is whitenin', could miss a board as big as a door on a day like this? I tell ye, boy, if the wind wont lift, and the piece works well, I'll drive every bullet of the ten inside the size of a sasser. Lord-a-massy, Henry, what a grip ye have! The Lad and me has seen ye when yer fingers hadu't pinch enough in them to break an egg-shell." And the Old Man laughed heartily at his own thought.

Presently the crowd regained their composure, and the shooting proceeded with regularity and precision. In less than an hour the string was shot, the judge had measured the distance of each of the marksmen's bullets from the tack, and announced that he would declare the score : —

"Ladies and gentlemen," said he, " the score of the shooting at five hundred yards stands as follows : Total distance of the ten shots from the tack for Number One, is 60 inches; Number Two, is 58½ inches; Number Three, is 55 inches;

Number Four, is 47 inches; Number Five, is 47½ inches.
Mr. Herbert leads the score at the five hundred yards range,
beating Number One, 13 inches; Number Two, 11½ inches;
Number Three, 8 inches; Number Five, ½ inch." And then
he added: "We will now adjourn the shooting for twenty
minutes, at the end of which time the shooting at one thousand yards will begin."

During the intermission speculation raged, and the discussion as to the chances of the several contestants was
warm. All agreed that the Trapper's shooting — firing
as he had " off hand" — was never equalled. Such steadiness of nerve all admitted was never seen before, and that
his string would stand forever unrivalled. But still, it was
claimed that no human being could shoot one thousand
yards " off hand" and stand any chance beside men accustomed to the distance, and shooting from a rest. On the
other hand the partisans of the Trapper asserted that so
clear was his eye, so steady his nerves, and so perfect his
control of the piece, that he could shoot, and would shoot
at the longer as well as he had at the shorter distance;
and they backed him at any odds against everybody but
Herbert.

In respect to Herbert, the backers of the Trapper admitted that he might win; indeed, they went so far as to
own that he probably would. Like the Trapper, he had
shot with great steadiness; his bullets being " bunched" a
little under, as the Trapper's were a little over, the center;
and the manner in which the Old Man treated him, as truly
as the words of praise he had spoken in his behalf, had

made a profound impression on the throng. So that as be
tween the two no bets were made, all admitting that it was,
as the Trapper said it would be, "nip and tuck" between
them.

The Lad rose in popular favor, with every shot he made.
Indeed, his shooting had improved from the start, and his
last three bullets had been driven within three inches of
the tack and so close together that their edges touched.
This had not escaped the notice of our "silent" friend, who
had watched the Lad as the contest proceeded and the excitement grew, and noticed that whether the crowd was
noisy or still the look of placid simplicity never left his face,
and when he sighted the last shot, not a muscle in his face
even tightened, nor the least particle of stiffness came to
the long, awkward finger as it rested on the delicate trigger. Profoundly impressed by these facts he was "laying
heavy on the fool," as he expressed it.

Still, the Englishmen had strong backing. They freely
admitted that the American gun shot "beyond all prece-
dent," but they as stoutly held that "no breech loading
arm, and especially of so light a character, could possibly
compete at a thousand yards with such guns as they were
firing." And this judgment was endorsed by many among
the spectators. Indeed, the majority, for the reason above
mentioned, still stood with the strangers and confidently
asserted that "they would surely and easily win at the thousand yard range."

While the crowd were thus discussing the chances of the
several contestants, Nature was busy in introducing new

and potential features into the problem. The sky that had been cloudless suddenly darkened, and great black patches began to float through the firmament. The winds were unloosed and gusts began to spin themselves in eddying courses across the level lake. The flags on the staffs, that had hung all the morning pendent, or clung in coils around the slender sticks, began to flap and flutter, one instant streaming free, the next sinking again into utter repose. What made it still worse the winds were changeful. One instant a breeze would blow straight up the lake, the next a gust would spin squarely athwart the range. The Englishmen hailed this with unconcealed delight, thinking that their long experience on windy ranges would tell strongly in their favor. Even the Old Trapper, as he watched the rising wind, got uneasy, and calling his two companions to him said : —

"Now, Henry, ye see the wind is risin' as I felt sartin it would afore long, and the Englishers are tickled, for they think they can beat us, as they sartiuly can me and the Lad, in calculatin' the force of the squalls. What say ye, Henry, can ye match 'em in watchin' the flags ? "

"You needn't worry, John Norton," replied Herbert, "I've had as much experience with flags and windy ranges as they have, and I doubt if they can beat me at the business. But I warn you both to remember that the wind exercises a great influence on the flight of a bullet at a distance of one thousand yards — greater than one would suppose unless he has had experience of it, and that you must shoot when and where I tell you, no matter how strange the direction may seem to you. Of course it's a little awkward, but if you will obey me I think we can beat them at their own game, wind or no wind."

"Don't ye fear about that, Henry," responded the Trapper, " I'll shoot where ye say if ye tell me to shoot into one of the winders of the tavern here. So ye jest give us the word and the lead shall go where ye say, if I have to send the bullet over to the Upper Saranac."

" The shooting at the Long Range will now begin," shouted the Judge. " Each man is allowed three sighting shots and they can shoot them when they please, taking advantage of the lulls between the gusts of the wind."

The marksmen were already in their places, and in a few moments the Englishmen had made their trial, and with success. Herbert watched his chance and shot each of his three shots when the flags hung unmoved on their staffs. His last two bullets had struck within two inches of each other, eight inches under the center. He was delighted at his good luck, for he knew that the least trifle of elevation would give the piece the center range, and he announced to the Judge that the Trapper, the Lad and himself were ready.

In a few moments the firing began. Number One put his bullet within ten inches of the tack, directly to the right, and was cheered. Number Two nearly duplicated the shot, only his bullet "drifted" to the left. He, too, was cheered. Indeed, the crowd was in excellent humor and ready to be pleased with anything. Besides, the range was so much beyond the capacity of ordinary guns that even to hit the target seemed to most of the spectators a wonderful exploit, and to plant a bullet within a foot of the tack was enough to set them yelling. It was now the Lad's turn, and the wind was blowing up the lake with decided violence.

"Hold on, Lad; hold on," said the Trapper. "Wait till Henry gives ye the word and then fire where he tells ye, if yer bullet has to go round the Three Sisters to git at the target. This shootin' by flags and orders, and with a gun that loads at the wrong eend, is squaw's work anyhow; but the Englishers must be beaten if we have to shoot in platoons — "

"Ready, Lad!" said Herbert, sharply. "Aim two feet under — in direct line, — *fire*."

The astonishment of the crowd was intense, and their consequent noise deafening, when the marker's disk showed the Lad's bullet but five inches from the tack — directly below it.

The Old Trapper said not a word. Indeed, he had no opportunity; for Herbert had instantly inserted another cartridge, and before the marker had fairly sunk from sight, his piece exploded. Quick as a flash the marker lifted his disk and set it to the target *in the identical spot he had laid it* for the Lad's shot. Indeed the two shots — by one of those strange occurrences which occasionally happen in shooting — had penetrated the target so near the same point that their edges actually cut into each other.

The exhibition of skill on the part of the marksmen, and of the extraordinary accuracy of the rifle itself, and the intelligence which Herbert brought to watching the flags,

made a profound impression on the throng. The English
men themselves came over, and looked curiously at the
gun which had proved itself able to project its bullets with
such force and precision. It was several minutes before
anything like order prevailed, and then the judges called
out: —

"*Number Five!*"

"Now, Henry," said the Old Trapper, as he lifted the
piece, "ye give me the true p'ints of the case, as the lawyers say, or I wouldn't give a cent for the vardict. It's a
big distance, for sartin," continued he, as he ranged his eyes
over the water to where the target stood. "Yis, it's a big
distance, and I marvel that so small a gun can bear the
chargin' she does. Didn't ye say, boy, she barnt a hundred
grains, and fine karneled at that? A hundred grains! Why,
Henry, I've toted a piece nigh on to twice the heft of this,
that didn't chamber a thimbleful, and carried a bullet no
bigger than a pea. Yis, yis, I begin to see the reason of it.
A hundred grains! why it's enough to carry a bullet half
way to Tophet, if the muzzle of the piece had the right lift
to it. Aye, aye, Henry, I understand. Don't be oneasy,
boy; when ye give the word, ye'll find me ready; but when
a man has nothing else to do it doesn't hurt him any to talk
a leetle, as I conceit, especially if he talks to himself and
in a jedicious manner — "

"*Ready!*" said Herbert. "Level with the tack, — three
feet to the right, — *fire!*"

The piece exploded with the word. Indeed, the explosion actually drowned the voice that pronounced it. It was

all done so quickly that it seemed incredible that the Trapper could have sighted.

"Aye, aye, Henry," said the old man laughing, as Herbert glanced interrogatively up at him; "level it was, and three feet to the right, jest as ye told me to do it. The piece was held as ye said it should be, though where the bullet has gone the Lord only knows. For the range ye gave sartinly brought the sights full three inches off the board, and I had all of West Bay to sight at."

What more the Old Trapper would have said, had he not been interrupted, will never be known; for he was interrupted in the midst of his sentence by a· yell so wild and strong that it fairly startled him. His eye glanced quick as a lightning flash toward the target, and beheld, as he did so, a perfect explanation of the enthusiasm of the crowd. The bullet, driven with terrible velocity through the air, had traversed its thousand yards of flight, and, so nicely had Herbert calculated the influence of the wind and the resultant drift, and so exactly had the Trapper obeyed him in his aim, that it had penetrated the target almost at its central point; for the disk of the marker lay directly over the tack.

It is but truth to say that of all those in the crowd, not one was more astonished than the Old Trapper himself. The idea that so small a barrel should be able to project its bullet the distance of such a range and enter it so accurately at the point aimed at, was a revelation to the old rifleman's mind. He looked at the piece, as it lay balanced in his mighty hand, and then measured with observant eye the length of the range, with features whose expression revealed the thought that was within.

"I'd never believed it, Henry. No, boy, I'd never believed it, onless my own eyes had seed it done. I'd never
believed that a bar'l not twice as big as a soldier's ramrod,
and but a leetle heavier, could have throwed an ounce of
lead across that distance. They say strange things have
been found out, and many inventions diskivered in the settlements senco I fust struck the trail. But among them all,
there can't be a greater, no, there can't be a greater, than
this leetle gun that has set a man, who has used the rifle
for sixty year, and thought he knowed all the strong p'ints
of the weepon, to marvelin'. No, I'd never believed it if I
hadn't seed it with my own eyes."

In this manner the match proceeded up to the sixth shot.
The shooting had continued in favor of the Old Trapper and
his companions as opposed to the Englishmen. The American gun was proving its superiority over the English ones
with each successive discharge. But as to the three that
shot it the closest observer was in doubt as to which was
leading his companions. The shooting of the three as directed by Herbert had been remarkably even; for so skilled
was he in watching the flags, so exact was his judgment,
and so promptly did his companions respond to his directions, that their shooting had been distinguished by all the
accuracy that would have attended their practice on a parfectly calm day. The Englishmen had shot well, but they
had been unable to gain any advantage over the Americans
by reason of any superior knowledge touching the atmospheric influences on the flight of their projectiles, while in
point of skill and capacity of their guns they were evidently

inferior to their rivals. The Old Trapper, as the shooting proceeded, was in his element, and appeared to the best possible advantage. Noble and generous as his nature was, there was nevertheless in it that quality of ambition which gives to rivalry the keenish relish, and he enjoyed with intense delight the idea that he was "beatin' them Englishers." Indeed, he was full of jokes and comments as the match proceeded, and shot after shot revealed the accuracy of the gun he was using, and the fine discrimination with which Herbert was directing the bullets.

"I tell ye, Henry," he exclaimed, as the marker's disk revealed the fact that his sixth ball had struck within four inches of the tack, "I tell ye, Henry, ye are sartinly gifted in readin' them flags, and yer jedgment in the matter of squalls is as good as a Dutch woman's with a dozen children. I eenamost think ye have got an understandin' with the clark of the weather techin' the way he is to blow. Now, ye told me to hold a foot over the target, and I obeyed ye like a Hessian privit, that knows nothin' but the orders he gits from his sargeant, but I was mortally sartin that that bullet wouldn't fetch up this side of Upper Saranac; and there it is, as the boy yender says, stickin' close to the tack. I say, jedge," exclaimed the old man, as he turned to the gentleman who had charge of the match, "suppose ye send down to the barn-door yender, and have a leetle measurin' made that we may have some idee of how the thing is gittin' along. It aint necessary, ye see, to strain the gun, because enough is enough. And as we can't all three beat, we would like to know how the thing stands, or we may all come out alike; and ye can no more divide a puss of money than ye can a beaver's hide. While it is fust rate for one, it won't split up wuth a cent for three. So I sartinly advise that ye let us know where we be, or we may have to shoot this whole thing over again."

This request met with universal approbation; and in a few moments the several strings had been measured, and the scores put into the hand of the judge, who announced the following results : —

"Number One, six shots, total, 58 inches; Number Two, 64 inches; Number Three, 50 inches; Number Four, 48½ inches; Number Five, 49 inches.

"Ye see, Henry," said the Trapper, laughing, "the Lad has got the raal gift in him, and he is arter us in 'arnest. I conceit we shall beat him if he don't grow any in the next four shots; but if he gets a leetle more length he'll head us, sartin as fate. It would be the queerest thing I ever seed if we three should go out abreast. It would take considerable figurin' — yis, it would sartinly take a good deal countin' of fingers to divide that puss out there, so that all of us could have as much as we want. We shall have to squint a leetle closer, boy, or the Lad will beat us at our own game.

"I hope he will," said Herbert, "for I never saw a man of his age and inexperience at long-range shooting take to the work so handily. But there are four more shots to come, and while the Englishmen are a good ways behind us, still it is any one's match as yet. They have shot well, and the least mistake on our part in estimating the force of the wind, or the least unsteadiness in our aim, may give them the prize."

"The shooting will begin," called the judge, — "Number One!"

The rifle of Number One cracked at the word, and the marker's disk showed it a *center shot.*

"Well," said the Trapper, grimly, "he's found the mouth of the tunnel at last, anyway."

"Yes," replied Herbert, "and he may find it again."

"Number Two!" cried the judge.

And the bullet followed so closely the flight of his companion's that the white disk settled again squarely over the center.

"Good enough," said the Trapper. "Those two augers fit the same hole."

"Number Three!" shouted the judge.

"Wait" said Herbert to the Lad. "A foot to the left; level with the tack. Fire!"

The lad obeyed to the letter. The result justified the judgment of Herbert. Again the disk settled over the center.

"There'll be a winder through that barn-door," said the Trapper, "afore we're through. Now Henry, make a leetle more room for the daylight atween the sash."

"Number Four!" called the judge, somewhat excitedly.

For a moment Herbert waited. The flaw passed and the long line of crimson flags hung pendent on their staffs. The crowd stood breathless. The Old Trapper bent forward with his eyes on the distant target as if with unassisted

vision ho would fain mark the entrance of tho bullet. And
then, the sharp, clear click of tho hammer as it struck the
rim of tho cartridge, sounded on tho air.

THE GUN HAD FAILED TO EXPLODE !

The excitement was so intense that a cry that sounded
like a groan rose from the throng.

"DEATH AND JEDGMENT!" said tho Trapper. It was all
he said, but into the expression he had put the emphasis of
such disgust that the crowd from a sudden revulsion of feeling laughed and roared.

"There, I am out of tho match," said Herbert calmly, as
he rose to his feet and extended the rifle to tho Trapper.
"I trust that you and the Lad will have better luck, but
shooting is full of chances, and you never know until tho
score is counted who has won."

"Give me the bearin' of tho wind, Henry," said the old
man grimly. "This is what comes of usin' a piece that
loads at the wrong eend. I sartinly expect tho breech pin
will blow out this lick. Now, an honest gun — "

"Ready," said Herbert. "Don't fool now, John Norton.
Steady — cover the tack — FIRE."

At the word the old man pulled the trigger, but no explosion followed, but instead, only a sputtering sound; for
the cartridge was a false one, there not being a grain of
powder in it. The percussion alone ignited, and driven by
its feeble force tho bullet went barely a rod and then
dropped idly into tho water.

The look of disgust which swept into tho Trapper's face as
he dropped tho gun on to the ground perfectly reflected the

state of his feelings. The cords of his neck ridged, his countenance flushed with vexation, and the muscles of his face twitched. For a moment he stood glaring down at the gun as if he would stamp upon it in his rage, while the great crowd, hushed to silence at the double misfortune, watched him, half frightened at the exhibition of repressed passion they beheld. At last the humor of the man prevailed, his tense muscles relaxed, and an indescribable look of fun softened the rigid lines of his face and beamed in his eyes.

" Well, Henry," he said, " the pesky thing managed to git the victals out of its mouth without wrenchin' itself, anyhow, and that's a good deal for a gun that is loaded in the settlements and shot in the woods to do." And the Trapper, who had now regained his habitual balance, laughed in his silent fashion, good naturedly, as he picked up the piece and handed it to Herbert.

" Yis, jedge," he continued, as he turned his face toward the hotel, " Henry and me be out of the match, ye needn't tell us that. And I am sorry for the sake of the ladies that I couldn't shoot the match out, but I've lived too long amid the unsartanties of life to be soured at disappintment, and if they'll be patient they shall see some shootin' yit atween Henry and me that'll make 'em clap their pritty hands and remember the difference atween a rifle a hunter can trust his life to and a miserable invention that loads at the wrong eend. And I take ye all to witness," continued the old man earnestly, " that the boy and me shot this thing out like men who understand the vartues of a grooved bar'l, ontil

the gun failed us. But the Lad still has a chance, and I sartinly hope the gun will act like a rational piece for the rest
of the match, for the boy needs the money." So saying the
Trapper folded his arms and turned his face toward the distant target.

The Lad rose to his feet and coming to his side said: —

"John Norton, I'm real sorry the rifle has acted so to you
and Henry. Shall I shoot the match out or stop now ? I
don't feel like shooting when you and Henry can't."

"Lord bless ye, Lad," said the Trapper, "of course ye
must shoot the match out. Ye aint to blame for the gun
actin' so. Henry," said the old man, "come here. What
do ye think, can the Lad win the puss yit ?"   •

For a moment Herbert made no reply. He looked steadily at the Lad, and seeing that his face revealed not the
slightest trace, either of fear or excitement, he answered:—

"The thing is likely to be very close, close enough to try
the nerves of the steadiest man living, but the Lad is ahead
and if I make no mistake in directing him, and he shoots
as I tell him, the chances are certainly good for his winning.

"Lad," said the Trapper, and a gleam of repressed feeling shot from his eyes, "I can't bear to have them Englishers beat. Can ye shoot as well as ye have been shootin' ? "

"I don't know why I cant," said the Lad. "I feel well,
and if you will only set down beside me, and Henry will tell
me where to aim, I think I shall shoot as well as I ever shot
in my life."

"Sit down beside ye ?" said the Trapper laughing. "Lord

bless ye, Lad, I'll sit on top of ye if ye want me to, and it will help ye any. Come, Henry, git yer eyes onto them flags, for the shootin' must begin."

"I know," said the judge, "that I express the sentiments of all this large company when I say that I profoundly regret the misfortune that has befallen two of the contestants, but by the rules of the match they are ruled out, and the three that remain must complete their strings. They will therefore prepare themselves."

"Number One!"

The wind was now blowing almost a gale, and the shot struck fully ten inches from the center.

"Number Two!" called the Judge.

The second Englishman shot with no better result.

"Number Three!"

"Wait!" said Herbert; "now, ready, — three feet to the right — six inches above the center — fire!"

"Well, Henry, ye didn't git that quite right, for sartin," said the Trapper, "but the Lad did as well as the Englishers, anyway."

"The wind was a twisting one," answered Herbert, "and I couldn't tell exactly where the strength of it lay."

"Was I to blame?" said the Lad.

"Not a bit, not a bit," answered the Trapper; "ye shot as well as a mortal could, and ye haven't spil't yer chances a bit. I think the puss will go down to the camp yit if yer gun doesn't bust."

Again the marksmen were called off in order, and the result was nearly the same. It was still "anybody's match."

Only one shot remained, and the excitement back of and around the marksmen was intense.

The Englishmen arose and walked about a minute. They talked a little with their friends. Their faces were a trifle pale. Herbert stopped in swabbing the piece to wipe the sweat from his forehead. The Old Trapper looked steadily at him, and said, in his ordinary tones, while his features tightened, " I'd give twenty beavers' skins if I had the load-in' of the next cartridge."

The Lad, still stretched in all his awkward length on the ground, fixed his mild eyes on Herbert as he was wiping his face, and said : "What makes you so hot, Henry ? Do you feel sick, anywhere ?"

"I suspect he does," said the Trapper. "The fact is, Lad, I don't feel quite right myself. Not that I've got any great pain, anywhere, exactly, but I feel sort of hollow-like at the pit of the stomach."

" Mr. Herbert," said the gambler, as he struck a match and pulled a cigar from his pocket, unconscious that he had one already in his mouth : " I hope you won't make a mistake about them little flags. I've gone my last dollar on the Lad and I'd like to leave to-morrow."

" Gentlemen," said the judge, and his voice was far from steady, " Gentlemen, will you please stand back from the . marksmen ? The decisive shots must now be made, and I can see you are greatly excited. The marker reports that the strings are very close, and a centre shot will decide it. I shall now call : — "

" Number One ! "

Even as the call came the wind suddenly died out. The flags clung to their staffs; and, seizing the opportunity, Number One fired.

It was signalled as only seven inches from the tack.

"Number Two!" shouted the judge.

Still the flags hung downward; the rifle cracked, and the white disk was set four inches from the center.

Still the flags were motionless; but the trees on the western shore of the Lake swayed and bent, while the roar of the coming wind was plainly heard by the crowd who, in front of the hotel, stood holding their very breath. The Old Trapper, knowing that the gale would cross the range in an instant, and indignant at the tardiness in giving the call, turned half over on the grass and shook his gigantic fist at the judge, while his face fairly flamed. It is only justice to say that the man was too excited to speak.

"Why don't he give me the word?" said the Lad, in his quiet, simple voice.

"Cover the tack!" said Herbert, in a steady voice, though the lips that pronounced the words were white as ashes. "Cover the tack — wait for the word — Ready!"

"Number Three!" shouted the judge, with a voice that fairly broke into a scream, from the tremendous effort he was making to articulate.

The Lad never stirred. His body stretched to its full length was as limp as if it contained not a muscle; his eye was at the sight; his long finger against the trigger. The gale had struck the Lake and was careering onward toward the flags. The air was full of dried stems and flying leaves.

The Old Trapper's eyes were fixed on the whirlwind and his fingers half-buried in the sod.

"READY!" said Herbert. '"Fi—"

The full sound of the word was never heard. The crash of the rifle drowned it. Not a lip moved until the marker lifted the disk, and after looking a moment placed it exactly on the center.

"Glory to God!" yelled the Trapper, as he jumped to his feet, and seizing the gambler, who happened to be standing within reach, lifted him into the air and held him at arm's length with a single hand while he swung the other over his head. "The MAN WHO DON'T KNOW MUCH, and the gun that loads at the wrong eend, and the puss of money, will go to John Norton's camp together! HURRAH!"

CHAPTER III.

"When Greek joins Greek
Then comes the tug of war."
Nathaniel Lee.

THE tumult which attended the close of the long range match at last subsided. The Lad was pronounced the winner of the ladies' purse, and the poor shrinking fellow was overwhelmed with congratulations. He kept close by the side of the Trapper as a timid boy does by the side of his father on his first experience in a city crowd. And in truth it must be said that the old backwoodsman was an ample protection. Indeed, it was touching to see how utterly child-like was the attitude of the Lad toward the Trapper, and how fatherly was the bearing of the old man toward the simple-minded youth. In the one was timidity, entire unacquaintance with men, and the painful sense of his own awkwardness and lack of ability. In the other was the bold front, perfect self-reliance and superb balance of a man of extraordinary physique endowed by nature with shrewdness and wit and furnished with the discipline of faculty, which a long life spent in reflection and mingling with men in serious undertakings alone can give. Because of this contrast, perhaps, the evident affection of the younger for

the older was the more touching, and the crowd was not
slow to perceive and be impressed by the unusual and inter
esting connection existing between the two. It is hard to
say which was the stronger feeling in the bosoms of the
spectators who had watched the contest and the two men:
admiration for the Trapper, or pity for the youth who, while
lacking in all those attributes of body and mind which command applause, had nevertheless given such unmistakable
evidence of skill, generosity and genuine power. Even the
gambler, who, under the hard, smooth complacency of cunning selfishness, fostered by his professional practice, had a
noble, if a cynical nature, came to the Lad and insisted on
" dividing the little pile with him," as he expressed it; and
strove in vain to make the Lad take an enormous roll of
greenbacks which he extended to him.

"Look here, friend," said the Trapper, as he pushed the
money back to the gambler, "ye better put that roll of rags
into yer own wicked pocket, for, though I don't wish to say
anything oncivil to ye or hurt yer feelin's, yit I sartinly conceit that ye don't git yer skins by honest trappin', but by
stealin' 'em out of traps that ye never set; and though yer
practices may be accordin' to the ways of the settlements,
yit ye should know that they don't square with the idees
that honest men have in the woods. And if ye will take
an old man's advice, whose head has whitened in gittin' an
honest livin accordin' to his gifts, ye had better quit yer
tricky habits and arn yer money in a straighter fashion, or
it will be likely to go hard with ye in the Jedgment, when
ye are questioned about the way ye got yer pelts and yer

profits on the arth. And I hope ye will take the advice in the sperit it's sartinly given ye."

"Old man," said the gambler, as he coolly stuffed the bills into one of his capacious pockets, "your advice is certainly worthy of consideration, and I have sometimes thought I had better take a new deal and play a straight game; but there's one or two points to be considered first, and I don't feel that I shall be in quite the right position to go it alone until you and Mr. Herbert have got through with the little business you are coming to; and if you can give me a point or two as to how the thing will come out, you will encourage me to reach a right conclusion in the matter, and put me in a condition of mind to give due weight to your judgment."

"It strikes me, friend, returned the Trapper, "that ye are haltin' atween two opinions, as the missioners say, and are likely to go to the devil arter all, if ye don't fetch up with a sharp turn afore long. And as to this matter atween Henry and me, I won't tell ye a word, for it's nip and tuck, and neither the boy or me know which will win; for the pieces be parfect, and all that can be done with grooved bar'ls both of us can do. And whether the horn will go to the settlements, or stay in the woods, no mortal can tell, and what is better, neither of us care; for I dare say if the boy wins it he will give it to me, and if I win it the Lord knows I'll give it to him."

"All right," said the gambler, "I'm much obliged to you for your advice, and I guess I'll play cautiously and follow the chances."

It is hard to say which feeling predominated in the Trapper's mind, — vexation at the thought that the gambler had outwitted him and actually got the " chances " out of him, or a sense of humor at the shrewdness of the man, for his countenance showed both feelings in equal proportion. He was about to reply, when the call of the judge summoned him to the front of the hotel where the shooting was to be done. The old man left the spot, and, finding Herbert, the two proceeded to the lawn, where the committee of arrangements had already roped off a space from which the marksmen were to shoot.

"Well, Squire," said the Trapper, as he and Herbert reached the judges' stand, "me and Henry have put in our appearance accordin' to orders; and are ready to do whatever ye ax us to do if it be in the line of our gifts. And as the sun isn't apt to fetch up when it's fairly got started down hill, ye might as well set us agoin' as soon as ye can; for the light will be dim afore long and ye can't bring out the fine p'ints of a rifle onless ye have plenty of sunshine; so if ye've got anything to tell us our ears are open, as the Hurons say, to yer words."

"Ladies and gentlemen," said the chairman of the committee of arrangements, "we have now come to the last match of the day; and we think we may safely say, without disparagement of the shooting which we have already witnessed, the most interesting match of the day. The prize is a horn of pure silver that will hold a pound of powder, and is beautifully engraved, as you see, with an elegant sketch of a deer and a hound in full chase. It is the most valuable prize which has been given; and one of the most beautiful results of artistic skill that I have ever seen. The shooting for this prize must be off-hand and at such distances as the committee shall announce. The contestants, — no one else having entered, — are these gentlemen whose presence has done so much to enliven and make memorable the sports both of yesterday and to-day. The object of the committee in this match is to show to all the spectators, especially to those gentlemen who have visited us from abroad, what the American rifle, in the hands of skilled men, can do. In other words we desire to tax the skill of the contestants, both in respect to accuracy and quickness of aim. We are fortunate in having been able to secure the presence of two men, one of whom has been noted for half a century as one of the best if not the best rifle shot in America, and the other of whom is known to many of us as being an extraordinary marksman, in reference to whose skill no higher endorsement can be given than his companion and rival in the match has freely bestowed. The two contestants, I need not say in this allusion, are Mr. Herbert and the Old Trapper, John Norton. And it is safe to say that we shall see a very fine and exciting contest, — the strong friendship existing between the competitors making it all the more novel and delightful. The shooting will be of a character that cannot be decided by measurement in inches and fractions of inches, but must be left for decision to the judgment of the committee; and even of the two marksmen themselves."

"That's it, jedge, that's it, — me and Henry knows what

shootin' is, and either of us be parfectly willin' to own up
beat if the p'ints of the case be plain. Ye see he and me
understand each other; and though the boy might be too
modest to say it, yit in his innermost feelin's he knows jest
as well as I do that it's nip and tuck atween us; and that a
slow burnin' cap or a hollow bullet that'll bust in the air or
go onsteady, is more likely to decide the matter than any
difference atween us as to quickness of eye and touch. And
I want ye all to understand that while we shall shoot honest
and true, each doin' his best, and leavin' his chances to fortin, yit we don't care the tail of a beaver which wins, and
look upon it more as a cheerful divarsion or a leetle camp
practice on a lazy day, than any fight atween us."

"Yes, yes," said the judge, "we all understand it, John
Norton. We all understand how it is between you and Mr.
Herbert, although he will not feel offended if I say that we
do not credit him with such skill as your reputation has
secured to you. But whichever way it goes we will look
upon it as a bit of friendly sport between you and not as
an antagonistic contest. For, whichever wins, we know
that we shall have an exhibition that will show us whatever
is possible in rifle practice; and it is proper for me to announce to the company, and to say to you, that as the object is to bring out, in the best light, your skill, we shall feel
permitted to consult you as the match proceeds, if circumstances make it necessary."

"Sartinly, sartinly," said the Trapper, "ye may ax us anythin' ye are a mind to, and ye'll find our heads as clear as a
quill on the p'ints of the case. Only git to work as soon as

ye can, for natur' has got the sun goin' down hill, and he's histin' along like a thievin' half-breed with an honest trapper at his heels."

"The shooting for the silver horn will now begin," said the judge, "and the first trial will be at fifty yards. Two shots from each marksmen. The target is a four inch diameter ring of white, centered by a tack with the head the size of a bullet." And as he spoke the target was placed at the distance mentioned in such a way that the sun lighted it perfectly. The two men stood side by side, each holding in his hands his favorite gun, a double rifle with both "open" and "globe and bead" sights, both made by Lewis, of Troy, and so nearly alike that were it not for the slight difference in the ornamentation of the stocks they could scarcely have been distinguished one from the other. The lock of either could be worked with or without the "set."

"I hope," said the Trapper, "ye have got more than one tack in that keerd-board, or ye had better start a boy for the carpenter shop." And as he spoke the muzzle of his rifle was lifted into the air, dropped suddenly into the palm of his outstretched hand, and exploded. The target, as the Trapper had predicted, fell at the explosion to the ground.

A murmur of delight rustled through the crowd.

"No, no!" said the Trapper. "No, no, jedge, ye needn't send the boy for the tack, for the hole that the lead made shows daylight through it, and I warrant that Henry has a key that'll fit it." And even as he spoke the rifle of Henry rose to its aim, with a motion but a little less careless apparently, than had been the movement of the Trapper's, and

exploded, and the bullet passed so neatly through the ori-
fice made by the former that scarcely a splinter was stirred
around the ragged edges of the hole.

"That's a true piece of your'n," said the Trapper, "and
many a scrimmage with the red skins have I had when its
crack would have been better than a psalm tune in my ear.
Yis, the two pieces be pitched on one key, as the fiddlers
say, when they are tuning for a jig." And while he had
been talking, the rifle had again been lifted, settled into his
hand, and at the closing word cracked strong and clear.
The smoke had not vanished in the air before the piece of
Herbert responded, and the first trial was over.

"There, jedge," said the Trapper, "ye'll find that hole
bored by a sharp auger and cut in a business-like way. I
shall sartinly be surprised if, when ye put yer eye to the
hole and turn it up to the sky, ye can see any shape in it
but what three bullets ought to make when they foller each
other as straight as young otters swimmin' a crick."

The board was inspected by the judges, and then it
started on its mission among the crowd. And as the Old
Trapper had predicted, no eye could detect that more than
one bullet had passed through the opening, unless, perhaps,
it were slightly enlarged and freer of splinters than would
have been the case had but one bullet penetrated it.

The Trapper and Herbert cleaned their rifles and re-
charged them with the painstaking carefulness of men who
thoroughly understand how delicate are the causes which
command success in such work as they were now being
called upon to do; and how the slightest neglect in the

treatment of their guns would endanger success. Indeèd, if the two pieces had been animate and sensitive to their touch they could not have handled them with greater care, nor treated them with more tender regard.

" All right, Squire," said the Trapper, as he lifted the piece into the hollow of his palm, " Henry and me be ready for any other leetle playfulness ye may p'int out to us."

" Has any one a pack of cards," said the judge. " Perhaps our friend here, has some," — and he turned to the gambler, who chanced to be standing near him.

" It is very singular," said our silent friend, as he drew a pack out of his pocket, " that I happen to have such an article about me. I don't remember how they happened to get into my pocket. I presume that my wife made a mistake and put them in instead of something else about the same size, which she has a fondness for advising me to carry around with me. If these aren't colored just right," said he, as he pulled out another pack, " it may be these will suit better. Or, if the Old Trapper, whom I owe something for good advice he has given me to-day, would fancy a more neutral tint, I'll just step up to my chamber and see what there may be in the bottom of the trunk."

" Lord, Lord ! " said the Trapper, " ye haven't a cart-load of the pesky pictur's have ye ? Them leetle keerds will sartinly be the death of ye yit; and I dare say this is the only honest use they was ever put to. As for the color, it don't make any difference, jedge, if Henry and me can only see the spots through the sights."

In a moment the deuce of spades was fastened to the target, by a tack driven at an equal distance between the spots, and the crowd stood expectant.

"I want to have ye understand," said the Trapper, "and I want the wimmen folks to understand, that me and Herbert don't call this anything more than common shootin', for the markin' shows plain and the light is good, and the distance is no greater than the eye can manage. But it's good enough, perhaps, to start with, and it may be"—and here his piece exploded—"we'll git down to some raal fine work arter a while. No, no," continued he, as the target tender was about to inspect the target, "ye needn't look at the leetle keerd, for the bullet is in the upper spot, and the reason it don't show is because the patch of ink is bigger than the hole that the lead made. Come, Henry, git the lead out of yer gun, for we don't want to fool away any time in gittin' ready to do some raal shootin'. There, jedge," continued the old man, whose words had been scarcely divided in their utterance by the crack of Herbert's piece— "now there is two bullets that is eenamost as big as the markin's on the keerd, and yit ye'll find that ye can't see even the grease stain that the lead made when it passed through, beyond the black. It may be handier for the boy to bring the keerd in if he has that tack drawed for him, and so to save time we'll start it a leetle." And even with the words the smoke burst from the muzzle of his rifle, and the card fluttered downward to the earth.

It is impossible to describe the feelings of the spectators. The shooting had been so accurate as to astonish them; and yet the aim of the marksmen had been so quick that it bordered apparently on carelessness — the carelessness of studied art, or else of men who, in doing what they had done, had not felt themselves called upon to bring into exercise the resources of that ability which had given to one a fame beyond question, and had made for the other the reputation of being the only man who could compete with him.

The committee conferred apart for a moment, and then they produced a bottle, and, turning to the Trapper, the judge said : —

" We have heard, John Norton, that you have been seen to uncork a bottle like this with your bullet at fifty paces."

"Sartinly, sartinly," said the Trapper. "It is no great thing to do, and I dare say Henry, here, has done the same hundreds of times; and it is the only way in which a rifleman can use the bottle and keep the sartinty of his aim. For there's nothin' that upsets a man's narves more than drinkin', and I never seed a man, who was a rum-drinker, have eyes wuth a cent when ye come down to fine work — 'specially on a windy day. But Henry and me will uncork as many bottles as yo want us to, and we'll never start a flake from the nozzle, and we won't upset a bottle nuther."

The Englishmen who were standing by, and who were getting intensely interested in the shooting they had already seen, plainly stated to those standing nigh, their utter incredulity that such a feat could be performed. And in courteous phrase they plainly stated the same to the committee, and even to the Trapper himself.

" Look here, jedge," said the old man, "talkin' about it

won't do it, and the thing can be done, you can depend on't. But if ye want to see Henry and me git right down to the work, and if ye want to see what bar'ls we've got to squint over, ye had better bring out some of them bottles whose corks are wired down; for while eenamost anybody, who has the gift of handlin' the rifle, can uncork the common bottles, yit it takes an oncommon bar'l, and a sharp eye, and a finger that knows how to work with it, to draw one of them wired kind. But it can be did, and here be the men and here be the guns that can do it."

The murmurs and ejaculations which rose from the crowd revealed the fact that the incredulity was felt not only by the Englishmen, but by the spectators, also. Indeed, discussions started on the instant. Here and there a voice was heard declaring the certainty of its being done. Here and there a guide positively declared that he had seen Herbert do it. And the gambler, acting true to the instinct of his profession, boldly declared, with mock seriousness, that he " had no faith in the bottle, and would back the Trapper against it two to one."

While all this had been going on, the clerk of the hotel had produced four champagne bottles, whose corks were quite prominent, but most thoroughly wired down ; and having been inspected by the Englishman and the Committee, they were placed on the railing that ran round the lake side of the wharf.

" Now," said the Old Trapper, as he tapped the stock of his rifle, " there aint but two guns in the woods that a man could depend on to do sech a job, and they be twins. And there sartinly aint but two men who can draw them. corks in the way the boy and me will sartinly do; onless something onusual happens. Henry," said the Old Trapper, "ye take the one to the left, and be keerful of the glint of the sun on the nozzle, for its likely to divart the aim. Now, jedge, ye put yer eyes onto that cork, and I'll give ye tho silver horn if ye can tell where it goes to."

If there had been any carelessness in the action of the Trapper and Herbert in their previous efforts, there certainly was none now in the movements of tho young man as he prepared to perform the extraordinary feat that he was called upon to do.

The crowd became breathless. The silence was as profound as it could possibly be. He straightened himself to his full height, advanced his left foot, pressed the trigger to the set, and, lifting the rifle to his shoulder, passed his eye into the sight, and, with a motion as true and precise as if the muzzle was being moved in steel grooves, the barrels began to pass from right to left toward the cork. And even when it exploded, the rifle was still in motion, and so little had the discharge disturbed the marksman that the motion, with the same precision, continued an instant after the bullet had been sped. The bottle waved a trifle on its base, spun half round and stopped, and the eyes of the spectators saw, no longer restrained, the froth of the spirited contents foaming out of the mouth.

"I am sorry ye started the bottle, Henry. Yis, I am sartinly sorry ye started the bottle; and I don't understand the reason of it, boy. I should eenamost think that ye

wasn't quite parfect in yer narves, to-day, onless I had
watched ye in yer aim. What was the reason of the jug-
gle, Henry? Did the tumbler creep a leetle, or wasn't the
tube quite free?"

"The wires over the corks are unusually strong," said
Herbert.

"It may be so," said the Trapper. "If ye say it's so, it
must be so, and we'll see if it is so in a minit, for the same
thing don't happen twice onless there is reason in it."

The old man paused. He looked an instant at the minute
mark ahead of him, drew himself up, advanced his left foot
lightly, and as his huge frame came to its perfect balance —
in a pose that an artist would have loved to sketch, — he
swept his rifle upward, and dropping it into his extended
hand, it rested there for an instant, while his eye settled into
the sight, and then burst out its flame.

So intense was the nervous tension on the part of the
spectators, that nearly every individual member of the
crowd actually jumped as the rifle cracked. The bottle
swayed, spun round, tottled for an instant, then stopped,
while the froth spurted sharply a foot or more into the air.

"That's enough," said the judge. "That's enough," he
repeated; and the Englishmen nodded as he looked at
them, "I have seen what I never would have believed had
I not seen it."

"Yis, yis," said the Trapper, "it is enough; and ye see
the boy was right. The wire is strong, as he said, and the
corks set deep in and the thing can't be did without jostlin'
the bottle. But ye give me a common bottle and a common

cork, and Henry and me will snap 'em out for ye without startin' a ripple on the liquor inside."

"Now," said the judge, " we will give you a flying shot. And the man that stands the test will get the silver horn."

" Ye'll have to split it, then," said the Trapper; "for I can see that Henry's warmin' to the work, and his piece is workin' to parfection. What be the trial, jedge?"

" It is this," was the reply, and he took a couple of potatoes from his pocket and handed them to the Lad.

"All right," said the Trapper. " Yer language is as plain as the pictur' talk of the redskins. Now, Lad, toss 'em straight and toss 'em high. Henry, you take the fust one, and I'll take the second. Now, Lad, wait for the word. Ready with yer piece, Henry. One, two, three, HEAVE!"

The Lad pitched the potato at the word. It mounted upward into the air, and as it came to the apex of its flight, Herbert's rifle cracked, and the potato disappeared.

"Heave agin!" said the Trapper, and while the potato which the lad pitched earnestly into the air was still going up, the bullet of the Trapper caught it and drove it into a thousand pieces!

" There," said the Trapper to the judge, " Henry showed ye the science of the thing, for he waited as a man should, when life or honor depend on his shot, and took it at the proper p'int. And I showed ye the trick of the thing, and shot as a man who is over-sure of his game, and don't wait till his jedgment tells him to act. Yis, the boy's shot was a jedgmatical one, and shows that he mixes his brains with his powder when he shoots; and that will sartinly win agin haste if there be chances enough. I don't think that ye know for sartin, who has got that horn, yit, jedge!" and the Old Trapper laughed till his great strong face fairly beamed with good nature.

"Come, jedge, what have ye got next? The pieces be ready, and the horn don't know whether it's goin' to the settlements or stay in the woods yit."

"We've got but one more," responded the judge, and the committee did not dream that they would have to resort to it. Nor do we suppose now that it will be of any avail, for we firmly believe, as do all to whom we have mentioned it, that it is beyond the possibility of human skill to accomplish. The target will be a flying one, and it will not be revealed to you until it is in swiftest motion; for we shall place your backs to us and deliver it over your heads. You may take positions; and we trust you will not blame us if the trial should seem unreasonable.

"Lord-a-massy, jedge, Henry and me don't care what ye start agoin' over our heads, for there be nothin that goes so fast that a bullet can't overtake it, onless it be another bullet; and ye may heave anything ye are a mind to and set it travellin' as fast as ye please, and I warrant that we'll stop it for ye afore it gits a hundred feet from the muzzle of our guns. Come, boy, back up; the Lord only knows whether it is a stun or a panther that the jedge has got in his hands, and the sooner the thing gets in motion, the quicker we'll git our eyes onto it."

The two men stationed themselves in front of the judge with their backs towards him — each in position, and each rifle at a poise. In a moment the crowd actually shook and swayed with tumult. Laughter, and roars, and exclamations such as "That isn't fair!" "Yes, it is too," "Let them try it anyhow. There isn't much danger that they'll hit it."

"Are you ready, gentlemen?" said the judge?

"Sartinly, sartinly," responded the Trapper, "let her come, jedge; panther or stun, or whatever it is, the pieces will bust if they wait much longer."

"Ready 'tis," said the judge. "Now!"

He opened his hands, stretched over the heads of the two men. A whirr, a buzz, a roar of wings, and a brown object glanced through the air straight from the two men as a bullet could spin.

A flash of lightning is not quicker than was the motion of the two guns, as they were swept to their level. The explosion of one of the pieces, at least, did not wait. The partridge had not gone a hundred feet before the bullet of Herbert's gun overtook it, and actually blew it into fragments!

The Trapper had not fired. He had checked himself in the very act of pulling the trigger — his rifle dropped into the hollow of his arm, and turning to Henry he said : —

"The life that the Maker gives them is sweet to his creetur's, Henry, and may the Lord forgive ye for takin', without cause, the life that ye cannot give back to the bird. No, no, boy, I don't blame ye; ye was taken onawares, and it was quick work, and I come near jinin' in the murder myself. I tell ye, Squire," said the old man, as he turned to the judge, "ye have did an onwise thing, and in yer mer-

riment made an innocent man do a deed he would not naterally do. No, no, the horn isn't worth a life to John Norton, even if that life be the life of the smallest of God's
creeturs; onless the takin' of it can be of sarvice to man."

The Old Trapper had said this with all the solemn gravity
of a man who was speaking from the conviction not only of
principle, but of a life-long practice, and as one who had
forgotten in the larger and graver thought, the smaller and
lighter one of the sports around him. And as he closed,
he turned to Henry in the act of speaking; but Herbert —
who, while he sympathized with the old man's sentiments,
and deeply regretted that, betrayed by the suddenness of
the event, he had unnecessarily taken a life — was nevertheless anxious, lest, in the mind of some of the crowd, not
to say in the mind of the judge himself, the Old Trapper's
fame might suffer, checked him by the motion of his hand,
and pointed his finger out over the lake.

The old man's face lighted, for he saw not only what Herbert had pointed at, — a large fleecy plume, that, torn from
the skin of the bird, was still drifting in the golden air, —
but also the generous thought of his companion's heart for
him. He turned to the judge, and said: —

"Do ye see, jedge, what the boy means? Do ye see that
bit of down floatin' out there across the sun, that came from
the back of the bird? The boy wants me to shoot at it;
for he fears lest the man whose head has whitened in the
woods should lose his fame here, to-day; and I'm glad he
has done what he has done, for while it's nothin' he can't
do himself, yit it is enough to show these ladies, here, and

yerself, too, that John Norton's finger did not quit the trigger when he lined the sights on the bird because he feared his lead would go wild."

"Now, Henry," he continued, "yer heart is right toward an old man, and he'll remember yer thought in his behalf when the miles be atween us, and ye be in the settlements amid many and I be by the fire in the cabin alone. Yis, boy, it's nothing ye can't do, for ye have mastered the weepon, and if I could live my life over, I would ask no better way of spendin' it than of spendin' it together with ye in the woods, for yer piece and yer heart is both true. Yis, ye sartinly could do it, but ye sartinly couldn't do it quicker than this!"—and with a motion so quick that those who stood nighest to him started back, the old man jerked his rifle into the air, and before it would seem it were possible for hand and eye to have come into conjunction the smoke belched out from the muzzle, and the golden colored plume that had come from the poor bird's back, lying swathed as it was in the warm red rays of the declining sun, darted forward through the air as if a minute jet of wind had struck it in the center, and when it stopped, the two halves floated off and stood inches apart.

The shooting was ended. The voice of the judge only expressed the unanimous feeling of the crowd when he proclaimed "that no further trial could with propriety be made, and that the silver horn would be given to the two contestants; leaving it in their hands as their joint property."

A happier conclusion, or one more gratifying to Herbert and the Trapper, or to the spectators, could not have ter-

minated the day's sports. In connection with the announcement the committee of arrangements further proclaimed
that in honor of the occasion, the proprietor of the hotel
would furnish an entertainment to the guests of the house
and the visitors from the adjoining houses, who could make
it convenient to remain, and that the evening would be
spent in merry-making— of which music and dancing would
form an attractive and prominent feature. In short, they
proposed to have a ball !

CHAPTER IV.

THE BALL.

"And his the music to whose tone
The common pulse of man keeps time,
In cot or castle, mirth or moan,
· In cold or sunny clime." — *Halleck.*

IT was evening — dark, cool and starry. The earth and water lay hidden in the dusky gloom. Above, the stars were at their brightest. They gleamed and glowed, flashed and scintillated, like jewels fresh from the case. Their fires were many-colored — orange, yellow and red ; and here and there a great diamond fastened into the zone of night, sent out its intense, colorless brilliancy. Through all the air silence reigned. The winds had died away, and the waters had settled to repose. No gurgle along the shore; no splash against the great logs that made the wharf; no bird of night calling to its mate. Outside all was still. Nature had drawn the curtains around her couch, and, screened from sight, lay in profound repose.

Within all was light, and bustle, and gayety. From every window lights streamed and flashed. The large parlors were alive with moving forms. The piano, whose white keys were swept by whiter hands, tinkled and rang in liveliest measure. The dance was at its height; and the very

floor seemed vibrant with the pressure of lively feet. The
dancers advanced, retired, wheeled and swayed in easy circles, swept up and down, and across the floor in graceful
lines.

Amid the happy scene the Old Trapper stood, his stalwart
frame erect as in his prime; while his great strong face
fairly beamed in benediction upon the dancers. For his nature had within its depths that fine capacity which enabled
it to receive the brightness of surrounding happiness and
reflect it again.

It was a study to watch his face, and mark the passage
of his changeful moods : surprise, delight, and broad, warm-
hearted humor, as they came to and played across the responsive features. The man of the woods, of the lonely
shore, and of silence, seemed perfectly at home amid the
noise and commotion of human merry-making.

At last the music died away. The dancers checked their
feet. The lady who had been playing the piano rose weari-
ly from the instrument and joined a group of friends. The
music was not adequate. The notes were too sharp; too
isolate; they did not flow together. There was no sweep
and swing, nor suavity of connected progress in the strains.
The instrument could not lift the dancers up and swing them
onward through the mazy motions.

"I tell ye, Henry," said the Old Trapper, as he turned to
Herbert who was standing by his side, "the pianer isn't the
thing to dance by, for sartin. It tinkles and chippers too
much; it rattles and clicks. It don't git hold of the feelin's, Henry; — it don't start the blood in yer veins, nor set

yer skin tinglin', nor make the feet dance agin yer will. It's good enough in it's way, no doubt; but it sartinly isn't the thing to lift the young folks up and swing 'em round. The fiddle is the thing; — yis, the fiddle is sartinly the thing. I would give a good deal if we had a fiddle here to-night, for I see the boys and girls miss it. Lord-a-massy! how it would set 'em agoin' if we only had a fiddle here."

"John Norton," said the Lad, who was sitting on a chair hidden away behind the Trapper, "John Norton," and the Lad took hold of the sleeve of his jacket and pulled the Trapper's head down towards him, " would you like to hear a violin to-night?"

"Like to hear a fiddle? Lord bless ye Lad, I guess I would like to hear a fiddle. I never seed a time I wouldn't give the best beaver hide in the lodge to hear the squeak of the bow on the strings. What's the matter with ye, Lad! What makes ye look so, boy?"

Well might he ask the question, for the Lad's face was absolutely radiant. His eyes were glowing and his lips fairly apart as if with suppressed eagerness, the eagerness of restrained excitement.

"John Norton!" said the Lad, and he drew the old man's head still closer to him until his ear was within a few inches of his mouth, "I love to play the violin better than I love anything in the world, and I've got one of the best ones, you ever heard, out there in the bow of the boat."

"Heavens and 'arth, Lad!" ejaculated the Trapper, " did ye say ye could play the fiddle, and that ye had a good one out there in the boat? Lord-a-massy! how the young folks

will hop. Scoot out there and git it, boy, and Henry and
me will let the folks know what ye've got and what ye can
do."

The Lad fairly flashed out of the room. He was gone in
an instant; and in a few minutes he had returned, bearing
in his hands a bundle which he carried as carefully as a
mother would carry her babe; but brief as had been his
absence it had allowed sufficient time for Herbert to com-
municate with the master of ceremonies and for him to announce to the company present that the great lack of the
occasion had fortunately and unexpectedly been supplied;
for the young man who was with Mr. Herbert and John Norton not only knew how to play the violin but actually had
one in his boat and had just gone to get it, and would be
back in a moment. The announcement was received with
applause. White hands clapped, and a hundred ejaculations
of wonderment sounded forth the surprise and pleasure of
the eager throng. And when the Lad came stealing in,
bearing his precious burden, he was received with a posi-
tive ovation.

It was amusing to see the change which had come over
the looks and actions of the company at the mention and
appearance of the violin. The faces that had shown indifference and the look of languid weariness freshened and
became tense in all their lines; and on their heads again
animation sat crowned. Those who were seated jumped to
their feet. The conversationalists broke their circle and
swung suddenly into line. Eyes sparkled. Little happy
screams and miniature war-whoops from the boisterous

youngsters rang through the parlor. In eye, and look, and voice, the popular tribute spoke in honor of the popular instrument, — an instrument whose strings can sound almost every passion forth : The quip and quirk of merriment, the mourner's wail, the measured praise of solemn psalms, the lively beat of joy, the subtle charm of indolent moods, and the sweet ecstasy of youthful pleasure, when with flying feet and in the abandon of delight she swings, circles, and floats through the measures of the voluptuous waltz.

In one corner of the parlor there was a raised platform, from which charades and private theatricals had been acted on some previous evening, and to this the Lad was escorted; and strange to say his awkwardness had departed from him. His form was straight. His head raised. His shambling gait steadied itself with firmer confidence. His long arms sought no longer feebly to hide themselves, but held the package that he carried in fond authority of gesture, as a proud mother, whose pride had banished bashfulness, might carry a beautiful child — a child that was her own. So the Lad went towards the raised dais, and seating himself in the chair, proceed with deliberate tenderness to uncover the instrument.

An old, dark-looking one it was. The gloom of centuries darkened it. Their dusk had penetrated the very fibres of the wood. Its look suggested ancient times; far climes; and hands long mouldering in dust. It was an instrument to quicken curiosity and elicit mental interrogation. What was its story? Where was it made? By whom, and when?

The Lad did not know. It was his mother's gift, he said
And an old sea-captain had given it to his mother. The old
sea-captain had found it on a wreck in the far-off Indian
Ocean. He found it in a trunk — a great sea chest made of
scented wood and banded with brazen ribs. And in the
chest, with it, it was rumored were silks, and costly fabrics,
and gold and eastern gems, — gems that never had been
cut; but lay in all their barbaric beauty, dull and swarth as
Cleopatra's face. Thus the violin had been found on the far
seas — at the end of the world, as it were, and in companionship of gems and fabrics rich and rare; and in a chest
whose mouth breathed odors. This was all the Lad knew.

"Henry," said the Old Trapper, "the Lad says the fiddle
is so old that no one knows how old it is; and I conceit the
boy speaks the truth. It sartinly looks as old as a squaw
whose teeth has dropped out and whose eyes are half shet,
and her face the color of tanned buckskin. I tell ye, Henry,
I believe it will bust if the Lad draws the bow with any 'arnestness across it, for there never was a glue made that
would hold wood together for a thousand year. And if that
fiddle isn't a thousand year old, then John Norton is no
jedge of appearances; and can't count the prongs on the
horns of a buck."

At this instant the Lad dropped the bow on to the strings.
Strong and round, mellow and sweet, the note swelled forth;
starting with the least filament of sound, it wove itself into
a compact chord of sonorous resonance; filled the great
parlors; passed through the doorway into the receptive
stillness outside; charged it with throbbings — thus held

the air a moment; reigned in it — then, called its powers
back to itself; drew in its vibrating tones; checked its undulating force; and leaving the air by easy retirement came
back like a bird to its nest and died away within the recesses of the dark, melodious shell from whence it started.

When the bow first began its course across the strings
the Old Trapper's eyes were on it; and as the note grew
and swelled he seemed to grow with it. His great fingers
shut into their palms as if an unseen power were pulling at
the cords. His breast heaved full. His mouth actually
opened. It was as if the rising, swelling, pulsating sounds
lifted him from off the floor on which he stood; and when
the magnificent note ebbed and finally died away within the
violin, not only he, but all the company stood breathless:
charmed, surprised, astonished into silence at the wondrous
strain they had heard.

The Old Trapper was the first to move. He brought his
brawny hand down heavily on to Herbert's shoulder and
with a face actually on fire with the fervor stirred within
him, exclaimed : —

"Lord-a-massy! Henry, did ye ever hear a noise like
that? I say, boy, did ye ever hear a noise like that? Where
on 'arth did it all come from? Why, boy, 'twas as long and
as solemn as a funeral, as arnest as the cry of a panther;
and roared like the nest of hornets when ye poke 'em up
with a stick. If that's a fiddle I wonder what the other
things be that I have heerd the half-breeds and the Frenchers play in the clearin's."

Well might the Old Trapper be astonished. The violin of

unknown age and make was one among ten thousand. It
was a concert to hear the Lad tune it; which he did with a
bold and skillful touch, and the exactness of an ear which
nature had made exquisitely true to time and chord. His
bashfulness was gone. His timidity had departed. His
awkwardness, even, went out of body and arm and fingers,
with the initial note. His soul had found its life with his
mother's gift; and he who was so weak and hesitating in
ordinary moments, found courage and strength, and the
dignity of a master, when he touched the strings. At last
the instrument was ready. And with a flourish bold and
free he struck into the measures of a waltz that filled the
parlor with a circling noise, and made the air throb and
beat — swing and swell, as if it were liquid, and unseen
hands were moving it with measured undulations.

There was no resisting an influence so sweet, subtle, and
pervasive, as flowed from that easy-going bow, as it came
and went over the resounding strings. Couple after couple
swung off into the open space until the entire company
were swinging and floating through the dreamy and be-
witching measures. The god of music was actually in the
room, and his strong, passionate touch was on the souls of
those who were floated hither and thither as if blown by
his invisible breath. The music actually took possession of
the dancers. It banished the mortal heaviness from their
frames, and made them buoyant so that their feet scarce
touched the floor. Up and down and across, from side to
side and end to end they whirled and floated. They moved
as if a power which took the place of wings was in them.

They did not seem to know that they were dancing. They did not dance; they floated; flowing like a current moved by easy undulations. Their hands were clasped. Their faces nearly touched. Their eyes were closed or glowing. And still the long bow came and went, and still the music rose and sank, and swelled and ebbed as easy waves advance, retreat and flood again, breaking in white and lazy murmurs at twilight on the dusky beach.

Herbert stood still; but his eyes were lifted, the gaze in them was far away, and one foot beat the measure. Beside him stood the Trapper. His arms were crossed; his eyes were on the bow that the Lad was drawing, and his body swayed, lifted and sank in perfect harmony with the motions and the accompanying sound, with a grace which nature only reaches when the will is utterly surrendered to a power that has charmed the stiffness and tension out of the frame and made it yielding and responsive.

At last the music stopped; and with it stopped each form. Each foot was arrested at the point to which the sound had carried it when it paused. Each couple stood in perfect pose. The motive power which moved them was withdrawn, and the limbs stood motionless as if the soul that gave them animation had retired. They had been lifted to another world — a world of impulse and movement more airy and spirit-like than the gross earth, — and it took a moment for them to struggle back to ordinary life. But in a moment thought recalled them to themselves, and they realized the mastery of the power that had held them at its will, and the applause broke out in showers of happy tu-

mult. They crowded around the Lad — strong men and
beautiful women, — gazing at him in wonder; then broke
up into knots, talking and marveling. In the Old Trapper's
face, as he gazed at the Lad, a strange look came, — the
look of a man to whose soul has come a revelation so pure
and sweet and clear that he is unable at first to compass it
with his understanding. He came close to the Lad, and sitting down on the edge of the platform, put his hand on the
knee of the youth, and said: —

"I have heerd most of the sweet and terrible noises that
natur' makes, boy; I have heerd the thunder among the
hills, when the Lord was knockin' agin the 'arth until it
jarred; and I have heerd the wind in the pines and the
waves on the beaches when the darkness of night was on
the woods, and Natur' was singin' her evenin' psalm; and
there be no bird or beast the Lord has made whose cry, be
it lively or solemn, I have not heerd; and I have said that
man had never made an insterment that could make so
sweet a noise as Natur' makes when the Sperit of the univarse speaks through the stillness: but ye have made
sounds to-night, Lad, sweeter than my ears have ever heerd
on hill or lake-shore, at noon or in the night season, and I
sartinly believe that the Sperit of the Lord has been with
ye, boy, and gi'n ye the power to bring out sech music as
the Book says the angels make in their happiness in the
world above. I trust ye are grateful, Lad, for the gift the
Lord has gi'n ye; for, though yer tongue knows leetle of
speech, yit yer fingers can bring sech sounds out of that
fiddle as a man might wish to have in his ears when his

body lies in his cabin, and his sperit is standin' on the edge of the Great Clearin'. Yis, Lad, ye must sartinly play for me when my eyes grow dim, and my feet strike the trail that no man strikes but once, nor travels both ways."

At this point the announcement of supper was made; and the company streamed towards the tables. The repast was of that bounteous character customary to the houses located in the woods, in which the hearty provisions of the forest were brought into conjunction with and reinforced by the more light and fanciful *cuisine* of the cities. Among the substantials fish and venison predominated. There was venison roast and venison spitted and venison broiled, venison steak and venison pie. Trout broiled, and baked, and boiled; pancakes and rolls; ices and cream; pies and puddings; pickles and sauces of every conceivable character and make; ducks and partridges; coffee and tea whose nature, we regret to say, was discernible only to the eye of faith. In the midst of this abundance the Old Trapper was entirely at home. He ate with the relish and heartiness of a man whose appetite was of the highest order; and whose courage mounted to the occasion.

"I tell ye, Henry," said the old man, as he transferred a duck to his plate, and proceeded to carve it with the aptness of one who had practical knowledge of its anatomy, "I tell ye, Henry, the birds are gittin' fat; and I sartinly hope the flight this Fall will be a good 'un. Don't be bashful, Lad, in yer eatin'," he continued, as he transferred half of his bird to his companion's plate, "ye haven't got the size of some about the waist, but yer length is in yer favor and if ye will only straighten up, and Henry don't give out, there'll be leetle left on this eend of the table when we have satisfied our hunger. I don't know when the cravin' of na- tur' has been stronger within me than it is this minit; and if nothin' happens, and ye stand by me, the Saranacers will remember our visit for days arter we are gone. It isn't often that I feed in the settlements, or get a taste of their cookin', but the man who basted these birds knowed what he was doin', and the fire has given them jest the right tech; for the morsels actally melt in yer mouth."

The Trapper's feelings were evidently not peculiar to him- self. For the spirit of feasting was abroad, and the eat- ing was such as would astonish the dwellers in cities. Wit flashed across the table in answer to wit. Mirth rippled from end to end of the room. Laughter roared and rol- licked adown the hall. Jokes were cracked. Fun exploded. Plates rattled. Cups and glasses touched and rang. Even the waiters as they came and went in their happy service caught the infection of the surrounding happiness and their laughter mingled with that of the guests.

The great pine branches and the evergreen nailed against the corner posts and wreathed into festoons along the walls shook and trembled in the uproar as to the passage of winds along their native hills. And the huge bucks' heads, whose antlers were tied with rosettes and streaming ribbons, lost the staring look of their great artificial eyes and seemed as they looked out through the interlacing boughs of cedar and balsam as if life had returned to them, and they once more were animate.

In about an hour the company streamed back into the parlor, with a mood even livelier than that which had characterized the early hours of the occasion. Their minds were in the state of highest action, and their bodies needed but the opportunity for rapid motion. Even the Lad had caught the infection of the surrounding liveliness, for his eyes and face glowed with the light of quickened animation.

"Have ye got any jigs in that fiddle, Lad," said the Trapper, "can ye twist anything out of yer instrument that will set the feet travelin'? It seems to me that the young folks here want shakin up a leetle; and a leetle of the old-fashioned dancin' will help 'em settle the victuals. Can ye liven up Lad, and give 'em a tune that will set 'em whirlin'.

The only reply of the Lad was a motion of the bow; but the motion was effective; for it sent a torrent of notes into the air, which thrilled through the body and tingled along the nerves like an electric shock. The Old Trapper fairly bounded into the air; and when he struck the floor his feet were flying. Nor was he alone; the jig had started a dozen on the instant; and the floor rattled and rang with the tap of toe and heel.

"Henry," said the Old Trapper, "hold on to me or I shall sartinly make a fool of myself. The Lad is ticklin' me from head to foot, and my toes are snappin' inside of the moccasins. Lord, who'd a thought that the blood in the veins of a man whose head is whitenin' could be sot leapin' as mine is doin' at this minit' by the scrapin' of a fiddle."

The Lad was a picture to see. His bow flew like lightning. His long fingers drummed and slid along the strings of the violin with bewildering swiftness. The little instrument jetted and effervesced its melody. The continuous and resounding noise poured out of it in tuneful bubbles. The air was full of tinkling fragments of sound. The Lad's body swayed to and fro. His face glowed. · His eyes flashed. The sweat stood in drops on his forehead, but still the bow snapped and crinkled, and the instrument continued to burst in musical explosion, while the floor shook; the windows rattled; the lamps flared and fluttered, as the dancers chased the music on.

"Heavens and arth !" said the Trapper. "I can't stand this," and breaking from the hold that Herbert had on him he whirled himself out to the center of the floor, and with his face aflame with excitement, and his white hair flying abroad, he led the jig men off with the lightness of foot and rapidity of stroke that forced the music by half a beat. The effect was electric. The room burst with applause, and the Lad fetched a stroke that seemed to rip the violin asunder. It was now a race between the violin and the dancers. One after another fell out of the circle as the moments passed, until the Trapper was left alone and was cutting it down in a fashion that both astonished and convulsed the company. More than one of the spectators went on to the floor in paroxysms of laughter. Herbert, bent over with his hands on his knees, was watching the Trapper with mouth stretched to its utmost, and streaming eyes. The gambler was jumping up and down, utterly beside himself, calling for "odds."

It is impossible to say which would have triumphed, had not an accident decided the contest and brought the jig to an abrupt termination. For even while the Lad was in the midst of the swiftest execution, the hind legs of the chair in which he was sitting were whipped from their fastenings, his heels went into the air, and he turned half a somersault backward, and the music stopped with a snap.

It was minutes before a word could be heard. Roars and shrieks, and screams of irrepressible and uncontrolable merriment shook the house from foundation to garret. The Lad picked himself up, and for the first time since they met Herbert saw his placid countenance wrinkled and seamed with the contortions of uproarous mirth. The sluggishness of his temperament for once was thoroughly agitated, and the manhood which never before had come to the surface found in hilarity a visible and adequate expression. The Trapper had spun to his side and the two had joined their hands, and looking into each other's faces were laughing with a boisterousness that fairly shook their frames and exploded in resounding peals.

Gradually the uproar subsided, and the company settled by easy transition to a quieter mood. The hours of the night were passing, and the moment drawing nigh when those who had mingled their merriment must part. The Old Trapper had regained his gravity and his countenance had settled to its customary repose. It seemed the general wish that the Lad should favor them with a farewell piece, and, in compliance with the request of many, the old man turned to him and said : —

" The hours be drawing on, Lad, and it's reasonable that
we should break up ; but afore we go the folks wish to hear
ye play a quiet sort of a piece that may be cheerful and
pleasant-like for them to remember ye by when we be gone.
So Lad if ye have got anything in yer head that's soft and
teching, somethin' that will sort o' stay in the heart as the
seasons come and go, I sartinly hope ye will play it for them.
And as ye say ye was born by the sea, and as ye say the insterment ye hold in yer hand was gi'n ye by yer mother,
it may be ye can play us something out of yer memory that
shall tell us of her goodness to ye. Somethin', I mean, that
shall tell us of the shore where ye was born and the love
that ye had afore ye laid her to rest and came to the woods.
Can ye play us somethin' like that, Lad ? "

"I can play you anything that has mother in it," said he,
and a wistful, yearning, hungry look came into his eyes, and
the edges of his simple lips quivered.

The company seated themselves, and the boy drew his
bow across the instrument. The brush of a painter could
not have made the picture more perfect, than the vision
the Lad brought forth as the bow played on the strings.
The picture of a sea, sunlighted and level, and stretching
far out; the picture of a curved shore : the shore of a quiet
bay, rimmed with its beach of shining sand and noisy with
the gurgle and splash of lapsing waves; the picture of a
home quiet and orderly, and filled with the tenderness of a
gentle spirit; and then a heavier chord told of the coming
of a darker hour when the mother lay dying. The violin
fairly sobbed and groaned and wailed, as if the spirit of

inconsolable grief were tugging heavily at the strings.
Anon, a bell tolled solemnly out of it, and its heavy knoll
clanged through the room. And then the music rested for
a minute, and in the silence a grave came into sight as
plainly as if the eyes of all were actually looking at its open
mouth. Again the music sounded, and the sods, one after
another, fell on the coffin dull and heavy, changing to a
smothered sound as the grave filled. Once more it paused,
and then a clear, sweet strain arose, sad, but pure, and fine,
and hopeful, as voice of angels could have sung it, trustful
and resigned. The bow stopped again; for a moment the
violin was silent. And then the Lad lifted his face, and, laying the bow softly upon the strings, he began to play what
all instinctively felt was a hymn to the spirit of his mother.
Slowly, softly, sweetly as the strains which the dying sometimes hear, the pure, clear, smooth notes, stole out into the
hushed air. It was playing, not such as mortal plays to
mortal, but such as spirit might play to spirit, and soul to
soul, across the street of heaven. The Lad still used an
earthly instrument and touched its strings with mortal fingers; but never, while they live, will those who heard that
hymn believe that anything less than the spirit of the boy;
— as it shall be in mood when, in the spirit world, he first
beholds his angel mother, — drew from the instrument the
notes that filled that room with their divine sweetness. Indeed, the Lad did not act as if he were conscious of his
body, or of bodily presences around him. His face was
lifted, and his eyes, from which the tears were streaming,
were gazing upward, not as if into vacancy, but as if they

saw the bright being that had passed within the vail, but which now, for a moment, stood in all the beauty of her transfiguration before them. For a smile was on the boy's lips, even while the tears were rolling down his cheeks; and when, at last, the arm suspended its motion; when the sweet notes ceased to sound, and the last chord had died away, the Lad still kept his uplifted posture and his features held the same rapt expression.

The company sat motionless, their gaze fastened on the Lad. Not an eye was without its tear. The cheeks of the Old Trapper were wet; and Herbert, touched by some memory, or overcome by the pathos of the music, was actually sobbing. The old man, with a tread as light as a moccasined foot could make, stepped softly to the side of the Lad and taking him by the arm, while the company rose as one man, he motioned to Henry with his hand, and then, without a word, the Trapper, and Herbert, and "The Man Who Didn't Know Much," passed out of the room, and taking boat, shoved off and glided from sight in the blue darkness of the overhanging night, amid whose eastern gloom the great, luminous mellow-hearted stars of the morning were already aflame.

CHAPTER V.

THE PARTING.

" Once more ye woods, adieu."—Virgil.

An island : small in size, lifted but a few feet above the water, and wooded heavily with pines. A camp-fire near the centre, whose flames were fed by logs of beech and birch intermixed with resinous woods. Underneath the logs, a great bed of coals and brands vividly on fire and hot as the mouth of a furnace. Above, flames sent illuminations everywhere ; bringing the trunks of the great trees out in bold relief and brightening the gloomy foliage so that the withered cones stood out to view. A current of cool air ; the breath of an ice-king which had been blown a thousand leagues, nor lost its chill. Between it and the fire was mutual hate ; for when it blew a stronger puff the flame in hot resentment flared hoarsely up and roared wrathfully. Amid the rocks that lined the shores the waves washed noisily. Above the pines a great gloomy dome, whose vault was traversed by a broad belt of snowy appearance, and studded with millions of dazzling stars.´ In front of the coals two giant dogs lay curled, back to back, basking in the heat. Farther away, their faces lighted by the fire, three men sat or reclined in easy posture, their backs supported by a great log. This was the scene.

"I'm sorry, Henry, that ye must leave us to-morrer," said the Trapper, breaking the long silence that had preceded the remark, "but ye say ye must go, and I suppose we must give ye up. There be many in the settlements, I dare say, that love ye and long to see ye; and it's but right for ye to go. But ye won't quite forgit us, boy, when ye're livin' in the great city, and the han'some and the rich be round ye?"

"I shall never forget you, John Norton, nor the Lad either," responded the young man; "I owe my life to both of you, and while I live I shall remember it. My life was saved here in the woods, and here would I live were I not bound to civilization by ties I cannot in conscience break. But I mean to have you both visit me this winter. Do you know it is only two days' travel from this island to my city home?"

"It isn't distance, Henry," said the Trapper, after a moment's pause, "that makes a visit likely or onlikely atween friends. I footed it from the shore of the Horicon to the shore of Ontario once, jest to call on a comrade I heerd was campin' on the Big Water. No, it sartinly isn't distance, Henry, but difference in ways of livin' that keeps friends apart. Lord bless ye, boy, if miles was all that lay atween us, me and the Lad, and the pups there, could make ye a visit cenamost any time arter the snow has crusted; for the trappin' is onsartin then, and the snow-shoes be famous things to travel on. But ye see ye live one way and we another; and though ye be a nateral woodsman, and take to our way of living as easily as a young otter takes to the

crick, yit I conceit it be different with me in the settlements, and that yer way of livin' wouldn't suit an old man
whose days have been passed in the woods, and whose ears
hate the noise of the clearin's."

"I don't know about that, John Norton," replied the
young man, "you should live as you wished to with me,
and I would do everything I could to make your stay pleasant."

"Aye, aye, Henry," responded the Trapper; "I understand the goodness of yer heart and the openness of yer
hand; and if anything could make me contented with the
ways of the settlements ye sartinly could do it. But natur'
and habits be stronger than wishes; and my natur, and habits be agin it. Why, Henry, I should smother in the city;
for I've heerd that the cabins be made of brick and stun,
and stand so nigh together that they actally tech; and that
the smoke of the fires be so thick that ye can't tell when
the sun rises or sets; and that the carries from p'int to p'int
be covered with folks; and that the trails be thicker with
people than the trunk of a bee-tree when the bees be
swarmin'. Is it raally so, boy?"

"Yes, the houses do stand side by side," replied Herbert,
"and the streets are full of people from morning till late at
night, and the noise and jar of cars and carts are continuous."

"That's it," interrupted the Trapper, "that's it. The
noises would eenamost kill me; for beyend the crack of a
rifle, or the sound of an axe cuttin' wood for the camp, my
ears hate noises; onless it be sech as natur' makes. For

when the ears be full of noise the eyes can't obsarve, nor
the heart meditate on the things around. It isn't what
folks tells us that makes us knowin'; but it's what we find
out for ourselves. It's the blaze on the tree that the
hunter sarches for and finds with his own eyes, that he
never forgits; and I have never seed a city man yit that
knowed anything, of his own self; for his edication was
what he had been larnt by others, or had read in books.
And ye know Henry, that the raal wisdom of Natur' has
never been printed in books yit."

"I think you are right there, John Norton," returned the
young man, "the best wisdom has never been printed; for
scholars, as a class, never study for the new, but for the
old; and the present generation only recites the same lessons that the fathers had recited."

"Yis Henry, that's it; and queer enough it seems to a
man of the woods. Lord! I guided a man a year or two
ago that knowed everything that books could tell a mortal.
He was as full of figgers and facts as a hedgehog is of quills.
And if ye poked him up a leetle with a question or two
he'd shed 'em faster than ye could pick 'em up. But when
ye got him right down to it he didn't know nothin' Henry.
He couldn't tell the p'ints of the compass on a cloudy day;
nor keep the trail on a carry; nor tell a doe's track from a
buck's. He didn't even know how to dress out his venison
nor cook a pancake. And I do believe the creetur' would
have starved to death when the Lord had made plenty
around him. And it made me thankful for my gifts and
my larnin' as I observed his ignorance."

"And yet," replied Herbert, "he was very likely a wise man in his way."

"Sartinly, sartinly," admitted the trapper. "But the way wasn't a good un, Henry, for what's the use of bein' knowin' if ye can't make it sarve ye. The larnin' that don't help a man find his way when he is fetchin' his trail through the woods, and don't tell him where to find the spring holes or the spawnin' beds or the places on the mash where the bucks feed, or how to cook his venison arter he has got it to his camp, isn't wuth much to a mortal for sartin. For larnin' is given to us, as I conceit, as the scent is given to the nose of the hound, for the parposes of life; and larnin' that don't tell a man when he is in danger how to git out of it, or when he is hungry how to satisfy the cravin's of his natur', is of no raal use to a man as I jedge."

"The Bible says," interrupted the Lad "'Take-no-thought-of-what-ye-shall-eat-or-what-ye-shall-drink,-or-what-ye-shall-put-on-for-after-all-these-things-the-Gentiles--seek.'"

"Yis, yis," said the Trapper, "them Gentiles always seemed to me to have the right idees of it. And I never could understand how the Lord could think they was off the trail, if they was honestly sarchin' for victals and clothin' to kiver their nakedness. No, I never could see quite how they was wrong in doin' jest what every man has to do to keep body and soul together. What did he mean, Henry, when he told them not to think about their victals and their garments? He didn't mean to have them go naked did he, or trust to luck in the matter?

"No, by no means," responded Herbert, "the phrase 'take no heed' means not to be *anxious*; not to *worry* about it."

"Well, well," said the Trapper, "now I git the direction of the trail. Lord-a-massy! how different the Scriptur' looks from one p'int than it does from another. It sartinly don't do any good to worry over a thing. Many be the nights when I used to be out scoutin' that I've gone to bed in the leaves hollow as a horn without a karnal in it, wonderin' where I'd find breakfast in the mornin'; but worryin' never brought a partridge to the snare yit, or a trout to the hook. And there's but one way for a mortal to act when he's in a pinch, and that is to do the best he knows how and trust to the Lord for the rest. But the doin' must be put under the trustin' as the powder is under the bullet, as I conceit."

It was with such converse that our friends beguiled the evening, as the hours sped along. Now and then the Old Trapper was prevailed upon to tell the story of his life, or narrate passages of it as it had occurred on the trail and in battle, or in times of peace when he lived quietly amid the solitudes of nature. These narrations of experience were told with a vividness of imagery and energy of utterance that made the scenes he described stand out in startling clearness to the minds of the listeners; for he told them with the voice and action of one who was not only speaking of deeds, in whose performance he had been the prominent actor, but also with the uncon-

scious grace and power of a man whose blood kindles with
heat at the reminiscence; and who, without knowing it,
lent to the narration the charm of a superb, because a
natural, elocution. To-night Herbert had purposely drawn
him out in this direction, for he and his companion liked
nothing better than such an entertainment as the stories of
the Old Trapper afforded. In this way the hours had come
and gone until the evening was far advanced, and the noon
of night was actually nigh. But neither of the three had
noted the passage of time, nor would they even then had
not the Old Trapper's eye caught the gleam of a star above
the mountain which revealed to him the fact that he had
been talking for hours.

"Lord-a-massy, Henry!" ejaculated the old man as he
caught the gleam of the distant orb. "It's arter ten o'clock
and ye've kept me talkin' like a dozen Frenchers when lost
in the fog. But it's the last night ye'll be with us, Henry,
and mayhaps it's well as it is. Come, Lad, git yer fiddle out.
Don't let it be said that the boy went to the settlements
without takin' yer music in his ears. Ye needn't play anything lively to-night for we sartinly don't feel like dancin',
but somethin' pleasant and cheerful like, and a leetle easy
in its motions, as a friend would say 'good-bye' to friend
when standin' at the p'int where their trails parted.

The Lad did as he was requested; and involuntarily gave
in exhibition of his command of the instrument which astonished Herbert; familiar as he was with the playing of
the masters of his time. The moment that the Lad's fingers touched the strings, and the bow began to move over

them, the violin seemed no longer a foreign substance but a
portion of himself. And of that self, too, within his body
which stood not for his personality alone, but for that greater
one who, while limiting him in the average human faculties,
had endowed him with compensating liberality with a faculty
of reception and impartment which could not be called less
than divine. There was no mood of nature that the poor boy
with the violin in his hand could not reflect. It laughed —
it wept — it rollicked — it joked — it sobbed. The fluttering leaf — the sighing wind — the roaring hurricane — the
laughing splash of happy waters — the loon's weird cry —
the robin's flute — all the sounds his ear could catch, his
fingers could draw forth.

It was certainly, a scene that Herbert would not be likely
to forget. The great fire flared and flamed upward. The cool,
pine-scented air blew steadily across the lake, and the waves
fell with measured splash on the beach. The great pines
overhead swayed by the wind, sent out their softened mono-
tones. The Lad sat with his back to the fire gazing out
into the star-lighted darkness. The Trapper and Herbert
reclined in easy posture, gazing steadily at the upward-go-
ing flame; and all the while the violin sent out its tuneful
strain. Not light and airy, nor grave and sad; but pure,
cheerful and sweet, as is the mood of friend parting with
friend when love has made the parting tender, but hope
forbids it to be sad.

At last the music ceased, and the Lad turned his simple
face toward the fire with a light on it finer than the reflection that an earthly flame could give to human countenance.

"Yis, Lad, ye've said it well," said the Trapper, "ye've sartinly said it well; and Herbert and me have understood it as ye have gone on. Ye sartinly aint over-knowin' with yer tongue but yer sperit is right; and the Lord has gin ye a gift that the great ones of the 'arth might envy. I sartinly wish ye could play to the folks in the settlements; it would set them wonderin'."

"I don't think I could play in the cities," said the Lad. "I never could play to anyone but mother in the house, and I never played but a few times to her there; for when she was tired and wanted comforting she used to go down with me to the shore and have me play for her there. And she used to kiss me when I finished playing, and say I was the best boy she had, and a great comfort to her, even if I didn't learn so fast as the other children did."

"I understand it, Lad," said the Trapper, "yis, I understand it, and yer mother was right; and ye comforted her in the days of her trouble beyend what ye know, and ye'll sartinly find her ag'in, and I dare say waitin' for ye when ye come to the Great Clearin'. Come, let's go to bed," continued the old man. The night is passin', and the mornin' is drawin' on, and we three shall start on a long trail to-morrer, and it's best that we strike it well rested."

It was morning; and the Old Trapper was up with the earliest dawn, busy in preparing the morning meal. It was evident by the amount and variety of the dishes, that he was anxious that it should be more than ordinary; for it required every plate and dish in the camp to hold the result of his labors. He worked at his self-imposed task as

one whose mind is pre-occupied, and who would fain seek
in activity, relief from what would otherwise oppress him.
An observer would have noticed that as he came and went
in his motions around the fire, his eyes frequently turned
toward the spot where Herbert was sleeping, and at every
look the shadow on his face grew deeper. It would have
been evident to such a spectator that the old man had become strongly attached to his young companion, and could
with difficulty bring himself to think with equanimity of
the coming separation.

At last his preparations were all made. The meal was
ready. Then lifting the corner of the blanket beneath which
the Lad and Herbert lay stretched, he said :

"Come Henry; come Lad; breakfast is ready, and the
sun will soon be on the mountains. The venison is done to
a turn, and the trout be ready for the teeth. It be the last
meal we shall eat together for many a day, and it isn't
cheerful-like for friends to be hurried in their eatin' when
the hour of partin' is nigh. So dip yer heads in the lake a
minit, and we'll have a meal that'll be pleasant to remember when the miles be atween us."

In a few minutes the young men were ready for the repast, and the three seated themselves at a table loaded
with food of a quality, and cooked with a skill, that the
cities cannot provide, and were soon eating with appetites
which no ordinary circumstance could affect; nor was the
humor which was wont to enliven their companionship
lacking.

"It strikes me, Henry," said the Trapper, as he shoved a

plate loaded heavily with broiled venison from which the red juices were actually dripping toward him, with a motion whose invitation Herbert was not slow to accept; "it strikes me, Henry, that yer appetite is gittin' dangerous; and it may be that yer goin' home is providential, as the missioners say. There sartinly has been a good deal of cookin' on this trip; and considerin' that we be but three, it's puzzlin' to think where the meat has all gone to. Ease out another hole in yer belt, Lad," said the old man, laughing, "and clean the plate. If ye'd had this feedin' when ye was a boy ye'd been bigger waisted than ye be; for its a • thin s'ile where the trees grow spindlin'. Ye'll thicken up, afore Henry sees ye agin, or John Norton don't know the habits of natur'."

The two young men laughed heartily, and renewed their attack on the edibles in a manner which threatened to speedily clear the table.

" Now, Henry," said the old man, as he arose, and taking a frying-pan from near the fire, where he had carefully placed it at the beginning of the meal, "if the Lad will bring the honey that he found on the carry the other day, I'll give ye some pancakes that'll make ye hate the cookin' of the settlements when ye be away from us. Lord! I thought I should die laughin' when I seed the Lad peelin' it through the scrub oak with the bees peltin' him in his back arter the plug come out of the hole, and the leetle chaps had diskivered who was pillaging their winter's store. His legs couldn't have played livelier if they'd been keepin' tune to one of his jigs. If there's anything that'll make

a man nimble, it's when he's emptied a hive round his ears
and the water is forty rod away. Did ye feel any oneas-
iness Lad as ye struck for the lake? Ye sartinly wasn't
mindful where ye stepped, for ye made a trail as wide as a
harrer!" and the old man actually had to pause a moment
to wipe the tears from his eyes; while his two young companions roared and screamed in the merriment of the recol-
lection.

"Look here, Henry!" exclaimed the Trapper, in a moment, "did ye ever see a nicer brown than that?" and with
a skilful upward turn of his wrist he sent the five pancakes
into the air in such a way as caused them to turn a complete somersault, and skilfully them caught in the pan as
they descended. "Did ye ever see a better brown than
that, Henry?" Ye'll find it eenamost the color of the honey
itself when it drips from the comb onto it. A strip of
pork, good flour, a leetle Indian meal, the right kind of a
pan, and a heap of beech coals like these — is sartinly what
makes the cakes look right. And then, if the butter be
sweet, and the honey pure, and the appetite keen, I can't
conceit of any better eatin' in the world. Now, ye eat and
I'll cook ; for a cake aint wuth a cent when it's cold. It
gits soggy, and lays on the stomach like a lie on the conscience. And though I know ye be lively with yer teeth,
yit if the coals hold hot I sartinly think I can keep up with
ye."

It might have been ten minutes that the cooking and the
eating continued ; and, to borrow a commercial phrase, "the
supply was just equal to the demand." A happier face than

the Old Trapper's, as he stood, pan in hand, with the heat
of the coals brightening his countenance, was never seen.
Benevolence and humor united themselves in its expression. A wise, strong face it was, without a coarse line in
it; without a trace of weakness; and on whose front, in-
firmity as yet had worn no prophetic mark. The face of
a man who had done no evil, had yielded to no vice, but
lived in the innocence of a nature to which the exercise of
virtue supplied all the stimulation that it craved. The face
of a man thus gifted in birth, and thus educated by life, in
happy mood: the mood of one who feels that he is ministering to the happiness of those whom he loves.

"Come," said Herbert as he rose from the table and approached the fire, "give me the pan, John Norton, and as
you have cooked for me so I will cook for you, and I think
I'll give them a brown as rich and warm as you have been
doing."

"I don't doubt it, Henry, I don't doubt it; for sartinly ye
have the gift of cookin'. Ye haven't forgotten the time I
met ye, boy, on the lonely lake, have ye, nor the steak and
the cakes ye cooked for me, and the tea that ye steeped?
Lord-a-massy! what tea that was. Do ye think ye could
git any more of the yarb like that in the settlement?"

"I'll send you a chest, John Norton; and I'll start it the
first day I get back."

"A chest! Lord, boy, what be ye takin' about? What
does an old man like me want of a chest of tea? Ye don't
think I'll turn into a Dutch woman, do ye?—that does
nothing but drink from mornin' till night! No, no; if ye

would send me a pound, say, and do it up in strong wrap-
pin's, and put my name on it, I warrant it'd come through
all right. And it would be a great comfort to me to steep a
leetle of it arter I'd got in from the line of my·traps, wet
and hungry, some nights. Yis, it would sartinly be cheerful
to steep a leetle of yer gift, Henry; for it would sorter bring
ye back into the cabin, and the sound of yer voice and the
sight of yer face would brighten up the place a leetle, —
especially if the night was stormy and the Lad should chance
to be away."

"Well, never mind about the amount," said Herbert.
"You shall have the tea; and enough so you needn't be
sparing of it." ·

While they had been talking, Herbert had dipped the batter into his pan, and the first dish of cakes was now ready
for the plate. He approached the old man as he sat at the
table, and taking a couple up with his flat turner, he placed
them before him. They were amber-colored about the
edges, and rich chestnut brown at the center, and so light
that the upper scarce seemed to touch the lower one as it
lay on it. The old man looked at them critically a moment,
and then he took a spoonful of the honey and let the contents drip in great golden globules on to the cake beneath ;
then taking his knife he spread the transparent liquid
smoothly over the cakes. All this was done with the delicacy of touch of a true artist in eating ; of one who feeds heartily, but not grossly, and eats with his eyes as well as his
mouth.

"Henry," said the old man, "them cakes be jediciously

cooked. I actally think that ye've beaten mine in the color,
— 'specially in the color round the edges; but ye'll allow
that my cookin' warmed the pan up, and ye can't color a
cake jest right onless the pan is properly heated. And now
that the iron is jest right, I hope ye'll keep it a-goin' for a
few minits till I have eaten my fill."

The sun had scarcely risen when the three were ready to
leave the island. The Lad was already in his seat, holding
his oars for the start; and the Old Trapper was steadying
the stern on the beach. The two hounds were standing on
the sands, and Herbert had paused on his way to the boat
to caress them a moment. Both of them were lifted erect
on their hind legs, with their paws on the young man's
shoulder, while with either hand he was stroking their
heads.

"That's right, Henry," said the Trapper. "The pups
know ye be goin', and in their way they be wishin' ye good-
bye. They've been oneasy all the mornin' for they know'd
that something onusal was goin' on. It'll be many a year
afore they see ye ag'in, perhaps, but they'll not forget ye;
and when ye come back, if they be livin' ye'll be sure of a
welcome that'll make yer face shine. Ah, me! It seems
a long time sence we met at the pond of the beavers; and
it'll make many a long evenin' shorter to think of the frolics
that we have had together."

While the old man had been speaking Herbert had parted
from the dogs, and stepped into the boat. The old man
lifted it from the sand, and with a strong shove pushed it
suddenly out into the lake, springing with the agility of

youth into his seat as he did it. The Lad swept his oars
into the water, and the Trapper joined the stroke with the
motion of his paddle. The two hounds sat down side by
side on the sand, and, with the gravity of their species,
gazed silently at the receding forms. Nor had they moved
from their position when the boat glided round the northern
point of the island, and the intervening rocks shut them
from view.

"I'm glad the pups didn't give mouth at yer goin', Henry," said the Trapper; "for though I know a dog can't shorten the days of a man, yit the Maker has given a curious
sense to some of his cretur's; and I never yit know'd a dog
to howl at the goin' of his master, and something not happen afore he returned. Yis, I sartinly take it as a cheerful
sign that we three shall come together in health and happiness ag'in in the day that the Lord app'ints."

It took but a few minutes for the boat to cover the distance it had to go; for the air was sharp and keen; the
water level as a floor, and the Lad pulled a stroke which,
assisted as it was by the paddle of the Trapper, shot the
sharp vessel along at an astonishing pace.

At the hotel no one was stirring, save here and there a
guide was washing out his boat preparatory for an early
start.

A moment after the boat touched the landing Herbert's
pack had been transferred to the shore, and the three men
were standing side by side. Things had occurred since they
met which made the parting unusually tender. Herbert was
thinking of the death he had narrowly escaped, and that it

was solely owing to the skill and affection of the two men from whom he was now to part, that he was still alive.

"I shan't forgit the spot nor the hour, Henry;" said the Trapper, referring to some previous conversation, "and if the Lad and me be livin' ye'll find us at the time app'inted on the big ledge at the mouth of Cold River when the early shadders be darkenin' the stream. And ye needn't worry if ye be late by a day or two, for the boy and me will camp there till ye come, even if ye be a week behind yer time."

"If I don't come by the second day," returned Herbert, "you may know that something has happened to keep me from coming in, and you needn't wait longer; but if I am alive and well you'll see my boat heading for that rock, when the sun is an hour above its setting on the date I gave you, next summer or the first summer I can come."

"I have ben thinkin' about the horn, Henry," said the old man, as he took a bundle from under his jacket and handed it to Herbert; "yis, I've ben thinkin' about the horn, boy, and it'll sartinly make my heart lighter if ye'll take it home with ye, and hang it to the hammers of yer rifle where yer eyes can often see it. For I be older than ye, and though I conceit the Lord will spare me many a year, yit a man whose head is whitenin' can't look with sech sartinty ahead, as the young; and if anything should happen it would be better that the horn was with ye. I don't give it to ye, because it's yourn as much as mine, and accordin' to the laws of the shootin' it's yourn altogether; but it's the only thing I have to give, ouless it be the rifle, and if ye'll take the horn and anything happens, the Lad will see that the gun

gits to ye, also, for ye be the only man I ever seed whose
eye and finger could bring out the vartues of the piece.
The two would help ye remember an old man that shot for
yer life once, when the chances was agin him, and that loved
ye as if ye was his own boy. We shall camp on the head-
waters of the Racquette this winter, and if ye felt like
writin' the Lad and me a letter some time, it may be some
trapper might fetch it through ; but it's by no means sartin,
and ye needn't trouble yerself with the matter. Now, boy,
as the folks will soon be stirrin' it may be jest as well that
the Lad and me be off; for the sun be fairly up, and afore
it sets we must be sixty mile to the south. Come, Lad,
take the hand of the man ye saved by yer divin', and then
we'll go. The Lord brought us together at the pond of the
beavers, and the Lord will bring us together ag'in on the
ledge at Cold River if his will shall app'int."

The lad took the hand of Herbert, looked for a moment
into the face of the man he had saved from death, and then
without a word, but with a face slightly paler than was its
wont, stepped into the boat and seated himself at the oar.
The Trapper took the hand that the Lad had dropped, and
for a moment the two men gazed into each other's faces.
Once the old man essayed to speak ; but as if he had
checked the rising thought while his tongue was striving to
form it into sound, or from some other cause, the sentence
remained unspoken. For his hand released its hold on Herbert's, and without uttering a word he turned, and lifting
his paddle he shoved the boat from the landing and leapt
lightly to his seat. The boat moved round the angle of the

wharf and headed down the lake. Herbert stepped to the piazza of the hotel, and leaning against a pillar, watched it steadfastly as it receded from view. In a few moments it had reached the first of the islands, and as it swung round, Herbert fancied that he saw the hand of the Trapper lifted into the air; but in this he might have been mistaken. The next instant it shot beyond the huge bowlder that made the point of the island, and vanished from sight.

For a moment the young man stood with his eyes fixed upon the spot where the boat had last been seen; and then he turned, and lifting his pack passed into the house. Many things transpired of which they little dreamed; and years, bringing their changes, came and went before the three met again.

THE STORY OF

THE MAN WHO DIDN'T KNOW MUCH.

Part III.

CHAPTER I.

"Far from gay cities and the ways of men." — *The Odyssey.*

IT was July; and a hot summer's day was drawing to a close. A torrid wave, born of the intense heat of the tropics, had moved northward; and the northern mountains had not cooled it a degree. The heated wave had rolled across the lake, and up the valleys, and over the crests of the great hills, until the very atmosphere, ordinarily deliciously cool, seemed blistered, as if it were being burned through and through by invisible fire. The tall pines, tasseled with their needle-like stems, fairly glistened in the hot scintillating light. The winds kept their caves, as if afraid to move beyond their dripping mouths. The water stood with a dull gleam on it, like molten metal. The reeds on the marshes drooped and hung their heads, as with fatigue. Even the cool, dark balsams for once looked hot; and under the intense heat hung damp with gummy sweat. The wild roses shrivelled and disappeared. The white lilies contracted, and hid their beauty and perfume within the cool protection of their green, almond-shaped lobes. Above, the sky was brazen. In it the sun stood red and blood-like; its orb quivering with intense fervors, and clearly rimmed as if it had lost the power to emit its dazzling rays. The wilderness was silent. The heat had acted like a drug on bird and beast and fish; and even on water and air. Only one sound survived: the mouth of Cold River, where it poured its current over the shining sand and the smooth beaming pebbles into the Racquette, still sang its rippling song. But beside the musical gurgle and tuneful lapse of the easy-flowing current, there was no sound in all the air.

On the great ledge which thrusts itself sternly out into the Racquette, just below the mouth of Cold River, two men were standing. It needed but a glance for one to recognize in the two forms the Old Trapper and the Lad. The Lad was leaning on his paddle; and the Old Trapper was standing erect, with his rifle resting in the hollow of his arm, gazing steadfastly down the stream.

"Three years have come and gone sence he told us to wait for him here. And twice afore this have you and me waited on this rock till the sun darkened the stream; but the boy did not come. And here we be ag'in accordin' to promise. And the hour has sartinly come for his appearin', for he said, 'If I be alive and well ye'll see my boat headin' for that rock when the sun is an hour above its settin', on the date I give ye, next summer, or the fust summer I can come in.' Yis, them be the very words, Lad, he said on the landin' at Lower Saranac, the morn when we parted. And I know if he be livin' he'll keep his promise which he gave to an old man who shot for his life when the chances was ag'in him. But the hour has sartinly come and the boy is not here. I fear, Lad, yis I sartinly fear that somethin' is wrong; and that I shall never hear the crack of his piece ag'in, or see his face by the light of the camp-fire."

" It may be that he has forgotten us, John Norton; for the folks that live in the city, I have heard, have a great deal to do, and forget things easily."

"Lad," said the Trapper, "I've lived on the 'arth eighty year, and have knowed many men; and have seed them that be true and them that be false: and I larnt fifty year ago to know the difference atween 'em. And I tell ye that Henry be one of the kind that never forgits. Ye can see it in his eye and ye can hear it in his voice. The boy is true as the barrels of his rifle, and that is sayin' all that can be said in praise of any man; for the barrels be actally parfect. No, no, Lad, the boy hasn't forgot, and he'll sartinly come this year or some other year if he's in the land of the livin'."

At this point the Lad, who was standing within reach, slowly stretched out his moccasined foot and softly touched with his toe the ankle of the trapper.

"Aye, aye, Lad, I know what ye mean," said the old man, without lowering his voice, "for I see what ye see, and I seed her afore she put her head through the branches of the balsam. But she's a mother doe and her faan is not far away, and she's come down to drink of the water that the Lord has made for her comfort as he has made it for ourn. And never yit did lead of mine tech the life of a creetur when Natur' made its life sacred. She may drink of the water to her fill, and go back to her faan and the bed she left in the mosses. I know we be without meat, Lad, and we'll go without meat afore we'll eat the body of a doe when her faan still claims her."

"But what shall we do for supper, John Norton," responded the Lad; "there is flour enough and pork enough, but we have no meat, and I am pretty hungry to-night."

"I dare say ye be empty, Lad, and I am not over full myself; and it's only right that the flour and pork be used sparin', but when the Lord can't feed a man one way he feeds him another, and I sartinly think there is a trout or two lying round here in this pool that the Lord has appinted for the safety of the faan to-night. Step to the boat, Lad, and untie the rod, for the sun be almost down, and the smoke on the water shows that its coolin', and we'll make a cast or two that mayhaps will fill our emptiness arter the fire be kindled."

In a moment the rod was unlashed, and the Lad stood holding it in his hand, ready for a cast. It was plain that it had seen service, for the varnish had been worn from the wood, while the butt and hand-piece had the peculiar, dark appearance which comes to wood only after long handling. The reel was of brass, but through carelessness or design, rust had been allowed to gather on its once polished surface, as also on the brass ferrules at the joints. The line was of silk, closely woven, while the nine foot leader to which three flies were attached, looked chafed and ragged, and the flies themselves scarcely retained half their original plumage. The whole appearance of the rod suggested that it was the victor in many a tussle with the finny foe.

"Will you take the rod, John Norton?" said the Lad.

"No, not fust," returned the old man; "ye shall sartinly have the fust cast yerself, for it's wicked for an old man to rob a young man of a chance to larn the right way to do a thing that he needs for his stomach's sake to know how to do well. No, Lad, ye shall have the fust cast, and I'll take the second."

"But I don't know how to fish as well as you do, and I'm awful hungry, and I should feel dreadfully if I missed a good one."

"Don't ye worry, Lad, don't ye worry. I don't suppose it's now as it used to be, but I've stood on this rock and skittered a piece of pork across the stream, and seen them go for it like a Frencher for his garlic. Yis, I've stood on this rock and seen the water bile as they riz from the bottom and shot this way and that, so crazy was every one to git at the bait fust. But years have come and gone sence then, and many be the fish that have been taken here, for this pool has its fame, and no city man passes it— nor guide neither, —for that matter, without givin' it a try. But they can't catch 'em all, for trouts be like men, some be wise and some foolish; and the foolish die young and die fast, but the wise shun danger and live out their days. And I shouldn't be surprised if there was a four pound trout some where in the bottom of this pool yit, and it may be a dozen of 'em, for Cold River is a famous breedin' ground, and Cold River empties all its big fish into this bend; for a big fish hates shaller water; and I shouldn't marvel if ye lifted a big un if ye do the thing jediciously. So try yer skill, and remember ye are fishing for a supper."

The Lad did as he was directed. With a motion by no means awkward, he swept the point of the rod upward. The leader straightened itself in the air, and then the flies shot forward and fell with gradual inclination upon the water. They had not trailed a foot before a trout broke the surface with such energy, that he shot his body full three feet into the air and fell with a splash into the tide. The size of the fish, the suddenness with which he had appeared, the energy of his rush and the noise of it, had taken the Lad so by surprise, that he fairly jumped from the rock and an exclamation escaped him. So startled was he that he actually forgot to strike, and the fish, having held the feather in his mouth and tasted the deceit, ejected it and went to the bottom unharmed. The Trapper laughed in hearty amusement at the Lad's expense.

"Did ye think he was a whale, Lad?" exclaimed the Trapper, "did ye think he was a whale, and he was goin' to swaller ye? Ye jumped as if ye thought he had come up arter ye. Lord, Lad, what a thing narves be! Now, here ye be, that can pull the strongest oar I ever seed pulled, and I've seen ye shoot in sarcumstances which would try most men, and ye stood the test, and now ye be jumpin' a foot; yis, ye sartinly jumped a foot, Lad, from that rock, when the fish broke water. What a thing narves be!"

"Shall I try again, John Norton?" said the Lad, who was laughing himself, at his own foolishness, in spite of his evident mortification. "Shall I try again?"

"Sartinly, sartinly," said the old man, "he's a good un, and he'll rise ag'in if ye'll give him a chance. Shall I hold on to ye, Lad? It sartinly isn't safe for ye to be jumpin' in that way standin' where ye be on the pint of the rock;" and the old man laughed.

"I don't think I shall jump again, John Norton. I mean to hook him this time, sure."

"I guess ye will, Lad, I guess ye will. There's nothin' so sudden as a thing we don't expect, and ye didn't expect him and it started ye; but I think ye'll be too quick for him this time if he gives ye a chance. Cast at the same spot, Lad, for a trout is like a man, he resks his life at the same spot and by the same peril, and larns no caution by escapes."

Even as he spoke the flies again settled to the water, and true to the prediction of the Trapper the trout rose the second time with the same quickness and energy; but the eye and the wrist of the Lad were alike ready for him, and the rod doubled up to the strain which the Lad's sudden stroke put upon it. The fish was fairly hooked, and the Lad played him with dexterity, and in a minute he lay within the meshes of the landing-net upon the rock.

"He's a good un, Lad; yis, he's sartinly a good un," said the old man. "He'll weigh two pound and a half if he weighs an ounce. He's eenamost enough to make a supper; that is, he would be if he wasn't a fish. But a man can eat jest as much fish as he wants to, for there is no eend to his eatin' till he comes to the eend of the fish. Fish aint solid: they don't brace a man out like venison or bear meat. Now a piece of bear meat as big as that fish would make

ye feel like a flour bag when it comes from the mill; yis, as
if ye weighed a ton. But one fish aint enough for two
men, if they be long and empty. Come, I'll try a cast myself, and it may be the Lord has a bigger one than this
waitin' for us in the bottom of the pool." So saying the
Trapper loosened some twenty feet of line from the reel
and made ready for the cast.

"How I wish the boy was here," he said, "how I wish
the boy was here," he repeated, "for I never seed a man
cast a fly quite as well as he can do it; and this rod was his
favorite. He said he had used it twelve year afore he gin it
to me; and that is three year agone, and I can't see that it's
weakened a bit with all the usin' it's had. Many be the time
I've seen the tip brought eenamost down to the butt when
a big fish sot his heft onto it, but I never seed a fish git the
better of it yit. Lord, Lad, what a whirl that was! I didn't
think there was as big a fish in the river. I wish the boy
was here to make the cast, but as he isn't, here goes!"

As he spoke the Old Trapper lifted his hand into the air
and swept the point of the rod upward and back. Thirty
feet of line followed the movement and straightened taut,
while the flies hung in air far up the stream, midway between the trees. A quick turn of the wrist, and the flies
leapt forward, shot through the air past the rock, until the
line straightened in the reverse direction, and then the feath-
ers floated, wavering, downward until they flecked the tide.
They lit upon the water as lightly as if they were not
weighted with the hooks, and without pausing an instant
began to trail across the stream. They had not gone a yard

before a yellow gleam flashed past the point of the ledge on which the Trapper stood, and a monstrous trout broke, with a headlong rush, out of the water, and shot upward into the air, as if projected by an unseen force. Its very eagerness thwarted his purpose, for he missed the gaudy bait altogether. An instant he hung in air, at the point to which his upward movement had carried him, and then fell, with a splash, into the stream.

An ejaculation of astonished delight broke from the Lad's mouth as he saw the monstrous fish above the stream. The Old Trapper said not a word, but a light like the flash of a sudden flame came to his countenance, and quick as lightning he snatched the flies from the water and swept them backward for another cast. Again they darted forward to the full length of the line and again settled slowly upon the tide. They had barely touched the surface before the head of the fish showed itself, and his monstrous jaws closed on the feather. The old man struck so sharp and quick that the rod fairly doubled with the stroke and the line quivered with the tension thus suddenly put upon it, till the water flew from the compressed braids.

"You've got him, John Norton, you've got him!" cried the Lad, fairly startled out of his ordinary composure in his excitement.

"Yis — I — have — got — him," said the Trapper, "and if the gut don't part, and the old rod holds together, we'll bake the biggest fish to-night I've seen for years."

The scene which followed was one which only a fisherman can realize, and which only a fisherman can enjoy a dozen times in his life. The fish was the biggest of his species; strong, thoroughly aroused, and game in every bone of his body. The action of the fish and the play of the man who held the rod, made a picture such as is seldom seen. No sooner had he felt the sting of the barbed hook than the fish leapt wildly into the air, flinging himself out with the energy of a black bass; but he fell on a line slackened to receive him, and when he struck the water it was as if he had struck it in full motion, for he tore his progress up against the current with a velocity that caused the line to cut the water with an angry hiss. He might have passed the point of the rock by fifty feet, when, with a quickness that only a trout can exhibit, he doubled short upon his course and launched himself down the stream, with an energy which only the largest fish, when thoroughly aroused, can show. So quick was the manœuvre and so tremendous was the velocity with which he passed the point of the rock, that he was seventy feet below the ledge before the old man could get the needed pressure on him. Only the eye and the finger of an expert could have done it as it was done. The strain was not put suddenly on the rod, but with such steadiness that the pressure on the tackle was gradual. But skillful as was the management, the fish was under such headway, and his momentum was so great, and he fought the tackle with such determination, that for an instant even the Old Trapper doubted if he could stop him. The rod doubled itself up until the tip was almost even with the butt. It quivered and swayed as a stubborn rod will when tasked to the utmost, and all that the Trapper could do to ease it seemed to bring it no assistance. It fairly creaked, as if its fibers were about to part.

The Lad was too anxious to say a word. His eyes were fastened on the rod, and his mouth half opened in suspense. The Old Trapper was the picture of determined coolness. His face tightened in its lines, and his teeth set themselves. He had done all he could do. This he knew; and the rod and fish were fairly pitted against each other. For a few seconds the struggle lasted. The fish tugged and shook himself, determined not to yield, but the wood could not be overcome. The pliancy of perfect nature and of scientific workmanship in its construction, at last prevailed. The trout flung himself into the air, and when he fell the snap was out of him. He sank to the bottom, and began to fin himself easily up against the current. The Trapper improved the opportunity, and stowed the line upon the reel with the dexterity of long practice, quickened into swiftest action by the emergency. Like a true fisherman, he gave the fish no rest, but when the line was packed and ready to render, he stirred the trout to action by a sharp upward jerk that sent him flying. Round and round he went. He circled the pool from bank to bank; swimming so nigh the surface that his curvatures marked the tide with whirls and eddies. Now and then he left the water, but the eye of one that could not blunder, was on his movements; a hand that could not mistake, governed the action of reel and rod; and in one-fifth of the time that it would take some club men, who measure the skill of fishing by the length of time to which they can prolong such an exercise, the Old

Trapper had the trout lying on his side, panting with great gasps, and had drawn him into the landing-net that the Lad had scooped beneath him.

In another minute the great trout lay upon the rock, and the two men were kneeling over him admiring his huge proportions and the gorgeous beauty of his tintings; but even as they thus knelt, and before either had a chance to say a word, the sharp crack of a rifle ripped through the silent air, and frightened a dozen echoes from the neighboring hillsides.

If the bullet had cut its way through the garments of the Trapper, he could not have leapt to his feet with a quicker motion. He fairly snapped himself into the air, and as he struck the perpendicular he dashed a hand upward, and exclaimed : —

"*Henry* ! "

CHAPTER II.

THE AMBUSH.

"Like guests that meet and come from far,
By cordial love invited." — *Wordsworth.*

IT was all that he said, but he said it with an intensity that made the exclamation as sharp as the crack of the piece which had caused it.

"What do you mean, John Norton ?" said the Lad, who still kept the kneeling posture, as he looked up into the face of the old man, that showed white through the dusk of the darkening shadows, "what do you mean, John Norton ?"

"Mean !" exclaimed the old man, "Lord of marcy, Lad, Henry is within a mile of us ! Didn't ye hear his piece ?"

"I heard a rifle," said the Lad, in reply, "but there are a great many rifles in the woods, and I don't know why you should think it was Henry's."

"Lad," said the old man, "ye are good at rowin' and divin', and ye fiddle as naterally as a rabbit runs ; and ye sartinly can set a trap that even a fox wouldn't suspect — and that's sayin' a good deal, — for a fox is the cunningest creetur the Lord has made. But ye haven't the hunter's gift, and yer ear is lackin'. I tell ye, Lad, that was the boy's rifle

that sounded. I should know it if I was dyin', and heerd
it amid a hundred, when the ambushment was onkivered
and the scrimmage was hot. The boy is within a mile of
us. And the trout won't be needed, onless it be to make a
show."

"Why won't we need the trout? It's all we have got,
but the pork and the flour; and if Henry is coming he must
have pulled fifty miles since morning, and be as hungry as
I am."

"Lord! Lad," said the Trapper laughing, "don't ye suppose I know how the boy feels? He's empty enough, beyend doubt, and the air of the woods has sharpened his
hunger; but he's sparin' of his lead, and he shoots too well
to act like a boy from the settlements, who explodes his
piece for the sake of hearin' it's noise. Yis, he's sparin' of
his lead, and that bullet didn't go fur afore it found somethin' to stop it. Lord-a-massy! how I wish I'd been lyin'
in the mash grass when he sunk his eyes into the sights.
It's almost as good to see the boy go through the motions,
when the buck stands lookin' at him, as it is to hear ye fiddle; for the bow comes nateral to the one and the rifle
comes nateral to the other. I tell ye, Lad, there'll be venison in the camp when the boat teches this rock. Come,
let's draw the boat up into the bush, and let's make an ambushment. Ah, me! it's wuth waitin' three years, to come
to the time when I can lie down in the grass and watch
him paddle his boat up sech a stretch of water as this.
How well I remember the night I ambushed him on the
Lonely Lake! Yis, yis, let's make an ambushment for the

boy, and see how he acts when he thinks that we've forgotten what we pledged him, and that nobody's here." And the old man laughed heartily to himself, out of sheer delight, and the pleasure that had come to his heart at the thought that he would soon have Herbert by the hand.

In a moment the boat was carried up the ledge, and sufficiently back from the river to be hidden, and then the two men crawled back to the edge of the stream and drew the grass over themselves in such a way that even in broad daylight no eye could have detected them.

In the mean time night had settled darkly over the woods. The sky was too hazy to reveal its stars, and the lingering sunlight in the far west had been suddenly extinguished behind a great black bank of clouds that portended storm. The darkness had come with unusual suddenness, and was growing denser with the passing of every minute. The pines seemed to emit gloom; the balsams to breathe out blackness with their odors. The very water of the river flowed on, as if it were ink. In twenty minutes from the time they had dragged their boat over the bank, and gathered the grasses over their backs and heads, the darkness was oppressive. The blackness actually burdened the air. Like the darkness of old, it could be felt.

"I kalkerlate," whispered the Trapper, as he put his lips to the ear of the Lad, "I kalkerlate the boy must be pritty near the bend; and if we have made an ambush for him, he'll sartinly try to ambush us, for he's great at the paddle and full of his tricks."

"Do you think, John Norton, that Henry knows we are here?"

"Knows it! of course he knows it," whispered the old man in reply. "Didn't I tell him we'd be at this pint on the day and the hour? And aint the day and the hour come? And don't he know that if I be livin' on the 'arth I'd be here? Sartinly the boy knows we'd be here, and he'll act on the knowledge. See if he don't."

"Do you think he can get his boat into this pool without our seeing him?"

"*Without seein'* him, Lad; of course he can. Do you think he'll carry a bonfire on the eend of his nose to tell us he is comin'? And unless he luminates ye couldn't see him if his boat lay in the pool within length of his paddle from our eyes. No, we won't see him, for it's ag'in natur'; but I do kalkerlate to hear him; for the stream shallers below the pool, and he has got to pole his boat up ag'iu the current; and I don't believe a man can sink the eend of his paddle into the sand, on a night as still as this, when my ear is within four feet of the stream, and I not hear the sands move. No, I sartinly don't believe Henry can do it. And if he does git his boat into this pool without my hearin' him, he'll do what John Norton don't mean to have him do. Now, Lad, if ye've got any more questions to ask ye'd better put 'em off till arter somethin' has happened; for Henry has got an ear like a lynx, and we can't be convarsin' here in the grass, much, without the boy hearin' us; and as he's got to the bend by this time, we'd better let our tongues rest a while and keep our ears and eyes as open as natur' will permit."

All this had been said in the softest possible of whispers,

and with the concluding word the two men became silent and profoundly attentive.

Forty rods below, in the midst of the impenetrable darkness, was a boat. In the bow of the boat was a buck; at the stern was a man, — his paddle moving in the water as easily as the tail of a fish, when with lazy motion, which yields sufficient force, he holds himself steadily against an easy-going current. His position was such as to command the stretch of water, and the ledge in the pool at the head of the stretch. The absence of any light or signal, did not cause him to doubt for an instant the presence of his friends. He knew them too well to suspect even for a moment that they had either forgotten the date or their pledge, fixed and given years before. He knew that if John Norton was living, the old man was standing in the darkness on the ledge, or nigh it. And he more than half suspected, in the absence of any signal, the trick that the old woodsman was trying to play on him. He felt that the old scout, whose paddle might be said to have been made from silence itself, so noiseless could he make it when stealing on to game or up to an ambushment, had in this quaint and perfectly natural manner, challenged him to an exercise of his skill. He knew as well as the Trapper how delicate was the undertaking, and how fine would be the exploit if he could accomplish it. For out of the pool the water ran with rippling swiftness, and with barely a foot of depth over a stretch of sand, which, for a dozen rods, forbade paddling, and brought the boatman to the necessity of poleing his boat up against the current. To do this on so dark

a night, in so strong a current, and in such shallow water,
in a way that the ripple of the flowing tide against the
curved prow of the boat, or the grating of the sand against
the paddle blade, as it was sunk into it, should not be detected by the skilled ear that he felt lay almost level with
the water, listening for the sound, the young man knew
would tax his skill to the utmost. But difficult as was the
task, he determined to attempt it; and knowing the waters
well — having pushed his boat over the same stretch, on
many a night, when hunting in years past, — he felt that
if he were careful, the chances were in his favor.

The reader can scarcely appreciate how strongly the
young man desired to place his boat, under the cover of
intense darkness, within twenty feet of John Norton's eyes
before the old man should know of his presence. With a
determination not to lose his opportunity by any carelessness on his part, the young man put a little stronger
pressure on his paddle, yielding to which, the boat began
to steal its way up against the stream. Slowly he forced it
along with a motion that had for its guiding impulse the
patience of a man who knows that to do well the thing he
intends to do, he must do it slowly. Inch by inch the little
vessel glided up, until the young man knew by the increas-
ing pressure of the current that the bow had almost if not
quite come to the shallows. Easier yet he pressed it forward, feeling with his paddle for the sand that he knew he
must soon touch. At last he found it, and the really difficult part of the undertaking was now upon him. With the
utmost steadiness of motion and pressure; with a dex-

terity of wrist that few could equal; with the sense of feeling performing the office of sight, he gauged the varying
pressure of the current as it eddied up, — now against this
and now against that side of the boat,— the strength of
the opposing current, and the quality of the sand into which
he passed and from which he withdrew his paddle-blade;
slowly, steadily, noiselessly, he thus worked his way upward.

There is a faith among boatmen that boats have their
moods; that there are days when they mis-behave and days
when they do their best. Engineers have the same feeling
for their engines. Some days they make steam, some days
they won't. One trip they act " beautifully," and the very
next trip they act viciously. Whether the theory is true or
false, the facts are undeniable, and the faith of boatmen and
of engineers touching the matter is too firmly established to
be shaken. Whatever be the truth of the case, we say,
Henry felt this night, as he was working his way against the
current through the darkness, that his boat was acting
" beautifully."

Perhaps spirit is superior to matter, and can assert its
superiority unconsciously. Perhaps the inert wood can become, as it were, partly conscious, and have charged into it
something of the vital quality that directs it. Be this as it
may, as we have said, Henry felt and said to himself, as he
manœuvered in the darkness, that the boat was behaving
finely. It faced the current with the calm, easy determination of the man whose strength was pressing it upward. It
swayed this way and that in obedience to the slightest

pressure from behind. If the water shallowed, it seemed
to dread the possibility of touching sand, and eased away,
as if in search of deeper water.

The young man was in his finest mood; the subtle forces
of body and mind seemed to concentrate in union of endeav-
or to accomplish the deed. His senses were sublimated.
Ear and feeling made good the lack of sight. Aye, more
than made it good, for he found a swifter, more accurate
interpretation of surrounding conditions in deprivation, than
could have been his in supply. The spirit of success was
in him. He knew he should accomplish the deed. He did.
His boat stole into the still pool so gradually, that had it
been in broad daylight, even John Norton's eyes must have
looked twice and closely to see that the boat had actual
movement, so slowly did it pass its length into the pool.

It entered the pool; fairly entered it; on that side of the
current which carried it gradually to the right as it passed
in; entered it, and floated idly into the elbow made by the
ledge and the bank, so that when it stopped, Henry, with
the point of his paddle, could have parted the grass from
over the heads of the old man and the Lad, where they lay
listening, with every sense alert for his coming. And thus,
in the dense murk and the heavy gloom, the three men sat
almost within hand's reach; the two listening for the one,
and the one listening for the two.

How long the position would have remained thus, or
what Herbert would have done had there been no interruption, cannot be told; for an interruption came, and of a character which made the revelation instantaneous. Through

the gloom of night the forces of Nature had been martialing for display. The great bank of clouds which had enveloped the sun at its setting, had moved up through the darkness and enlarged its borders until its upper point had been pushed half way to the zenith, and its extremities almost touched either pole of the horizon. Nature had made her ambush as truly as man, and uncovered it with startling energy. For suddenly, out of the invisible clouds a shaft of condensed fire leapt, that lanced through the gloom from west to east—cut it in twain, and set the black halves of the divided atmosphere aflame. If the darkness had been one vast body of percussion, and the god of fire had smote it with his hammer, it could not have exploded in fiercer light. The hazy sky; the tremendous clouds piled in vast convolutions in the firmament; the forest, the river, the ledge, the boatman and the boat, all on the instant stood revealed vividly distinct. The prolonged flash and flame had not faded away, when the Old Trapper leapt from the grass on the bank in which he lay hidden.

"Ye've did it, Henry! Yis, ye sartinly have did it! Ye have fetched yer boat through the ripples and over the sands, while the ear of a man whose life has been saved more'n once by his hearin', was within four feet of the water. And ye've drifted yer boat within two yards of his ears and he never knowed ye'd come. Ye was born too late, boy; for yer gifts piut to the trail and the scrimmage, and the ambushment; and if ye'd lived in the old war time ye'd had somethin' to bring out the stuff that's in ye. And a good comrade ye would have been to consort with. No, don't come ashore, boy, but shove up the stream and put yer best licks into the paddle, for the storm be comin', and we must be gittin' home. I sartinly long to take ye by the hand, but it's comfort enough to know that ye be in the land of the livin' — which I eenamost doubted, — and that ye be here in the woods ag'in. Ye'll find the lodge on the big bank to the right as ye enter the lake, and the pups will be glad to see ye. So push on, boy, and be lively, and me and the Lad will foller on. I doubt if ye git there much afore us."

The sound of Henry's stroke showed that his boat was rods away before the Trapper's sentence was concluded, and in a few minutes the Trapper and the Lad had launched their boat; and lashing the rod to its place, and putting the fish in the bottom, they entered it and started up the stream.

It took but a few moments for Henry to reach the lake, and in a minute more he ran the boat ashore on the soft sand that made a little beach at the water's edge of the bank, and lifted itself sharply some forty feet upwards. This he mounted, and seizing an armful of brush and dried boughs that lay by the fire-place, in which the coals still glowed, he threw them on to the bed of embers, and in an instant a flame leapt up.

Even before the flame rose into the air the two hounds were tugging at their chains at the mouth of their kennel in the wildest ecstasy of delight. By eye and nose alike they had recognized the comer; and as Henry approached them — which he did on the instant, with such hearty words of greeting as a hunter, after long absence, gives on return to his favorites, — the hounds poured into the silent air of night their rejoicing notes. They jumped, they stood erect, they put their paws upon his shoulders, they kissed his face and hands, they bayed their gladsome welcome out so loud and strong that the shores resounded with the cry; and even the mountains, with a hundred imitative echoes, hailed Henry's return.

Having received the hounds' happy salutation, Henry turned toward the fire; and as he came to it on one side, the Old Trapper, having clomb the bank from the beach, approached it on the other. Without a word the two men joined their hands, and for a moment each looked into the face of the other, with that affectionate curiosity with which friends that have been parted gaze at each other when they meet, studying the changes which the intervening years have wrought. Nothing is more touching than such a greeting. The gaze means so much and suggests so much. The eyes have their own language then, and many an interrogation is asked and answered by their glance.

Thus the two men stood gazing at each other in the light of the blazing fire, so intently that neither noticed the approach of the Lad. "Henry," at last said the old man, "I be glad to see ye ag'in in the land of the livin'. Twice afore have we waited yer comin' at the rock, and twice have we camped on this bank a week waitin' ye, and ye didn't come. And when the sun went down to-night and ye didn't come, I eenamost thought I should see ye no more; and the crack of yer piece lifted a heavy load from my feelin's, and made my sperits frisky. Yis, the years have changed ye, boy, for they've sartinly added some lines to yer face, and mixed the gray in yer hair, and gin ye a kind of sober look that shows that they were filled with labor, and that the Lord didn't altogether keep sufferin' out of 'em. But barrin' this ye are the same, onless ye be fatter by a trifle. But the city, I have heerd, is a famous place to make fat, and a month at the oars will sweat ye down to the size that natur' ordered for ye."

"I can truly say," said Herbert, speaking in reply, "that I am as glad to be with you again as you are to have me. And you, John Norton, have changed next to nothing since we parted. Your eye is as bright, your grip as strong as ever, and I doubt if your head has added a gray hair to it."

"I dunno about that, Henry; no I dunno about that," returned the old man, while a look of humor smoothed in part the carved lines of his countenance and sharpened the gleam of his eye, "the grip is all right yit, for sartin, and the sights look open and clean as they orter when I put my eye into 'em, with a buck or a bit of fur that I want, or a duck or a partridge for that matter, at the other end of 'em. But the white hairs be comin' for sartin, for a man is like a tree, and the frost teches the top of him fust; and a mortal that's lived as long as I have on the 'arth has lived through the spring and summer of his days, and has come to that season whose days be short, and whose nights be long, and whose frosts be many and cold. But the Lord is sartinly gracious to me, and it looks as if my days would be lengthened out beyond the ordinary life of my kind.

But bless my soul! here stands the Lad, and we haven't given him a chance to greet ye."

It was with but little less feeling than that which characterized the meeting of Herbert and the Trapper, that the two young men greeted each other. Long and heartily they shook each other's hand, and a goodly sight they presented as they stood in their youth and manly vigor facing each other; their countenances lighted up with friendship and with smiles.

"Do ye see, Henry," said the Trapper, "how the Lad has thickened up sence ye seed him? I can't say that he's actally pussy yit, but he's bigger 'n he was round the waist, and, as I tell him, he's only jest begun to grow. He looks a leetle lank to-night, for he and me come through from the Racquette sence ten in the mornin', and we haven't eaten a morsel sence breakfast. But arter he's had supper, if the buck down there in yer boat is a good sized un, so he can feel he can eat enough without robbin' us, if ye'll inspect him ye'll see that his feedin' has been of the right sort sence ye left; and, if nothing happens, I'll have him in good condition in a year or two more."

"I don't care," said the Lad, "if you do make fun of my eating, for I know you love to see me eat; and I think the best thing we can do is to get some tenderloin steak out of that buck in Henry's boat, and get supper soon as we can; for the storm will be here by and by, and I don't like to eat in the storm."

"I agree with the Lad," said Herbert. "I ate breakfast at seven, and I have taken nothing but a biscuit and a lemon since, and I doubt if I was ever hungrier in my life."

"Well, well," said the old Trapper, laughing, "you and the Lad tend to the buck, and I'll get the fish and flapjacks ready, and if there be a tater left in the bag we'll have it biled; for if there ever was a time, Lad, for you and me to celebrate, it's to-night, for Henry is here; and if there be a tater, he shall have it, for sartin."

The quickness with which a meal can be prepared in the woods by three men, when provisions are plenty, the fire well a-going, especially if the men are hungry, would be a revelation to most of the cooks at our aristocratic hotels. Not more than thirty minutes, at the most, had passed before the three men were seated round their bark table, which was moved up within the circle of the clear firelight, and discussing the viands with appetites whose sharpness forbade, for several minutes at least, conversation.

"One thing is sartin," said the Trapper, as he put the second steak on Henry's plate, and followed it with the remaining potatoe, "one thing is sartin, ye have changed somethin' in yer looks, but ye haven't changed a bit in yer appetite. If ye do manage to git round that plateful, and then dip into the cakes, hearty like, and fill in the chinks with some of the fish, ye'll have a feelin' of fullness in ye that'll be comfortin'. It'll be nip and tuck atween you and the Lad arter this, and I'm mighty glad ye can run together, as we say of the dogs, for yer mouths are jest alike, and the way they open and shet as the victuals go in is enough to make an old man wish he was younger; for the years that add to the head take from the stomach, and the aged, whether it be dog or mortal, eats sparin';" and the old man moved his rude stool back a foot or two from the table, and gazed at his young companions with a look in which gravity and humor were equally mingled, as if the spectacle of their heartiness, while it stirred the sense of the ludicrous in him, called up at the same time reminiscences of his own earlier days.

It is only in the interest of accurate statement to say, that when the young men moved their stools back from the board, steak, fish, and cakes had alike disappeared, even to the last scrap.

"Well," said the Trapper, "I'm raaly thankful that the plates be left, for the dishes be handy, and I don't think they would have set wuth a cent on yer stomachs if ye'd eaten 'em. Lord, what appetites the young have! The sight of yer eaten' takes me back fifty year, and brings up many a feastin' I had in the years that be gone, both alone and with comrades that slept and eat on the trail with me. The comrades be scattered now, and the greater part of them be gone forever, but natur' is the same to-day as it was then, and the sight of yer eatin' has called up a hundred faces that I knowed when I was a young man myself. Come, let's clear away the table, and pile on the hard wood, for the thunder is rollin' in the mountains, and the rain will be comin' afore long. I never knowed a hotter day than this, and the 'arth will shake under the lodge afore mornin'."

In a few moments the dishes were washed, the table removed, and the greenwood logs so placed that, while the lower edges lay in contact with the glowing coals underneath, the upper sides made a protection like a roof for the fire. The three men stretched themselves in easy recumbent postures at the entrance of the lodge, and awaited the coming of the storm. The conversation was of a character naturally suggested to the mind by the grand and indeed sublime surroundings.

CHAPTER III.

THE THUNDER STORM.

"I have called forth the mutinous winds,
  And 'twixt the green sea and the azured vault
  Set roaring war : to the dread rattling thunder
  Have I given fire, and rifted Jove's stout oak,
  With his own bolt." — *Shakespeare.*

THE forces of the storm were now so far developed as to have fairly come into action. The earth and sky were alike electric, — the air and ground thoroughly charged with the subtle fluids. The atmosphere was ready to ignite at every point, and the explosions followed each other in volleys. The lightning was incessant; it ran in fiery rivers down the declivities of the firmament, emptying itself in the far distance. It cut its fiery zigzags hither and yon, so lurid and fiercely hot that the eyes ached as they beheld. It shot its bolts horizontally through the air, which exploded ever and anon like powerful rockets; the very water burnt with a blue light, as if the electric fluid floated like oil upon its surface. There were flashes of darkness, but the illumination was almost instant, as if the body of the air itself were combustible, and incendiary imps were flinging blazing brands through it.

As the old Trapper had predicted, the earth was tremu-

lous. Its solidity was assaulted with such violence that its
subterranean pillars trembled through all their mighty
shafts, and shook on their broad basis. The crust of the
globe was jarred in its every particle. Whatever substance,
earth, rock, or log, the spectator occupied, he felt the grains
and fibers jump as the concussions ripped above him. The
cloud, or clouds, for the whole firmament was now possessed, brought out by the lightning's blaze to plainest
vision, were awful to look upon. The heaven was in tumult;
embodied violences tore through it; huge convoluted masses
of rolling darkness hung overhead; cumuli were rolled upon
cumuli; white scuds sped, like vapory ghosts in terror, in
all directions; the winds chased them at random; the
atmosphere was in anarchy; ungovernable forces rioted
overhead; the world trembled as with fright, and one
might almost imagine that the stars would be shaken from
their orbits, and consummate the universal disorder with
universal ruin. The mountains bellowed; the ravines
belched noises; reverberations from either side of the lake
met in mid career and swallowed each other up; the minor
echoes were struck dumb in their leafy doorways, and now
and then, for a single instant, an awful silence reigned,
which, in an instant more, burst at its very center with
tremendous explosions. The face of the Lad showed white
in the glare of the lightning. Herbert watched the exhibition with an eye educated by science to note cause and
effect. The dogs cowered, trembling, in their kennel.
They shook with the ague of fright. The countenance of
the Trapper was grave, with the gravity of a man devoid

of fear, but profoundly impressed with the majesty of the scene.

Up to this point the storm had been a "dry storm." Not a drop of rain had fallen, nor had the atmospheric convulsions reached the earth. The winds were "running high," as the Old Trapper said ; they were at war with the clouds, and amid the clouds they rioted. But signs were not lacking which revealed to a woodsman's eye that the commotion was descending, and that ere long the earth would be the scene of the same confusion which thus far had prevailed only overhead.

"I've lived," said the Old Trapper, "more'n threescore year in the woods, and amid the scenes of Natur', and I have seed and heerd most of the sights and sounds that larn mortals their weakness, but I've never seed lightnin' that fixed itself on the eyeballs hotter than this does tonight, nor heerd thunder jar the 'arth under me more arnest-like than these claps do. I should think, Henry, that the very underpinin' was givin' out under me, and that the Lord was eenamost shakin' his own buildin' to pieces by the way that the ground quivers as the peals roll overhead."

"I never heard such thunder myself," said Henry, "but once before, and that was eight years ago on the Racquette, and I am sure I never saw lightning so fierce and hot, even then."

"I doubt if ye ever did, boy," returned the Trapper, "for the air seems to burn as if it was tinder. Lord! what a flash that was. It made my eyes fairly shrivel; and there's

sartinly one pine less on you hill, for I saw the bolt strike
it; and when lightnin' hits a pine it's apt to make kindlin'
wood out of it from top to bottom. I've sometimes thought
that even the Lord got careless and wasteful-like at times,
when I've seed the pines and the spruces that he had ripped
open without cause. I never sunk an axe myself into the
stump of a tree yit that didn't show signs of dyin', or else
was too crooked to have any right to live; and I've wondered that the Lord didn't exercise more jedgment in his
choppin', for I never seed a dead tree or a crooked un that
his lightnin' struck yit, and it sartinly don't seem jedicious
to rip open the best trees for sport, when the bad uns do
jest as well. But I s'pose he has reason on his side if we
mortals could see it, or else he gits playful-like now and
then, and things happen that wouldn't happen if he was in
sober 'arnest."

"You don't think that the Lord is really playful, do you,
John Norton?" said the Lad, moving his seat up nearer to
the old man, as if he thought a greater degree of safety
could be found in close personal contact, than in the edge
of the firelight where he had been sitting.

"I sartinly do, Lad; yis, I sartinly think there must be a
good deal of playfulness in the Maker, for I don't see how
he could git the idee of makin' his creeturs so playful and
frisky like if there wasn't plenty of fun in him somewhere.
Now when I have laid in the grass and watched the beavers
and seen the cunnin' of the creeturs, and when I've stretched
myself over a ledge and seed the little wolf whelps caper
and cut up their antics at the mouth of the der, laughin'

till my eyes watered at the tricks of the leetle woolly scamps, and recollected that the Lord made 'em and put everything in them that is in 'em except their bite—yis, except their bite—I've sartinly felt that there must be a good deal of playfulness in himself or he never would have thought of makin' sech playful creeturs."

"What do you think about the panthers?" said Herbert.

"Henry," said the old man, as he rose to a sitting posture with deliberate earnestness, "I've thought a good deal about them panthers, and wondered how they come to be made anyway, for they sartinly be the most cowardly, sneakin', savage animils that runs in the woods. And I never seed a good thing in one of 'em, and I don't believe that the Lord ever made a single one of the pesky things."

"Why how do you think they were made, then?" retorted Herbert.

"Made!" said the old man, "I think the devil made 'em! Yis, they be the devil's own children, them panthers, for they be jest like him. They won't look ye in the eye and they won't fight ye if ye have a *wee*pon; and they are always watchin' to take ye onawares; and there's no marcy in 'em, and they kill for the love of killin'. I was trailin' last year near the head waters of Cold River, yender, and I heerd a great bleatin', and I scooted up on my snow-shoes toward the sound, till I run acrost a yard with a dozen deer in it, and I found what I thought I should find : an old panther at work there, and he had killed five of the innercent creeturs, and his teeth was in the throat of another—a two year old buck, — and I drawed on him, and I larnt him

a lesson of marcy quick as powder could burn. Yis, I
pulled both triggers at once, and the bullets took him
square over the eyes, and they lifted the scalp of the varmint; and I never felt better than when I tore the skin off
from his carcass and flung it out on the snow for the ravens
to pick. No, no, Henry, the Lord never made a panther,
I'm sartin on that."

"What is that?" said the Lad, suddenly.

"Ye'll know what it is afore long, Lad," said the old man,
after a moment's listening. "It be the might of the storm
on the other side of the mountain. It's nigh on to twenty
mile away, but ye can hear it comin' as if the Lord's own
feet was tramplin' down the trees. Yis, the winds have
settled to the 'arth and the trees are bein' tested as mortals
be tested in the jedgment. The rotten hearted uns and
them whose roots be weak, must go down when the breath
of His power and His wrath blow ag'in 'em. Hark! and ye'll
hear how small is the strength of the 'arth when the wrath
of its Maker be stirred."

The three men became silent. Their senses turned toward and concentrated on the approaching storm. Dull,
heavy, monotonous, the dreadful sound came on. The far-
off, portentious murmur grew and swelled, until it became
a roar. It moved up the western slope of the mountain
range until it reached the crest, and without pausing for a
moment, came tearing downward with accelerated speed.
The lightnings lit its path as if to make more dreadful its
approach by the revelation of its power. The eyes of the
three men were lifted toward the western ridge. The air,

for miles along the front of its advance, was thick with the evidences of its violence. Leaves, moss, tufts of branches, and even great boughs, wrenched from swaying tree-tops and hurled upward, were flying overhead. Soon individual noises broke the monotony of the terrible uproar. The crack of mighty trunks snapped shortly off, fifty feet from their roots; the crash of rending wood as the fierce suction wrenched giant branches from their fastenings; the rush of descending tree-tops as they swept through the air in act of falling; the heavy thud as they struck the earth with reverberating thump; the shriek and fierce whistling of winds tearing onward in mad career — thus came the storm. It was as if the king of tumult himself had harnessed his steeds and mounted his chariot, whose wheels in revolution drowned even the thunder's peal.

As the storm came on and the evidences of its terrific violence accumulated, the Lad, perhaps unconsciously, had crept nearer and nearer to the Trapper, until his frightened countenance was within a foot of the old man's calm, uplifted face, and his hands were actually clutching his garments. Henry, in his excitement, had risen, and unable to restrain himself longer, exclaimed: —

"John Norton, I never saw anything like that!"

The old man never moved a muscle; his eyes never wandered from the line of the storm's approach. His expression was one in which curiosity, awe and calculation were equally mingled. The terrific violence was within a half mile of the spot where he sat, and the air above his head was already thickening with the fragments which the upper

winds were bearing forward in the advance, when he rose
suddenly to his feet. He seized the Lad by the arm, and
swinging round he laid the other hand on Herbert's shoulder and shouted — for the uproar had now fairly reached
them, and ordinary utterance could not be heard : —

"The strength of the storm be beyond mortal measurement, and this spot is not safe. We must take to the bank
and burrow into the sand under the ledge. Cut the dogs
loose, Henry, that the pups may find safety. Git yer fiddle,
Lad, while I git the guns and the powder. The lodge may
stand, for I built it myself, and the withes round the timbers
be strong, but if the wind gits under it, it won't tech the
'arth this side the head waters of the Hudson. Be lively,
boys, for the Lord is in 'arnest, and it behooves mortals to
be active."

In an instant, as it were, his command had been obeyed,
and the three men, with the dogs, the gun, the violin, and
the boats — which Henry had seized, one with either hand,
and dragged with him, as he struck the beach at the foot of
the bank — were collected under the ledge.

It was well that they had bestirred themselves, for they
were barely at the spot which the Trapper had designated
as the point of safety, when the line of the storm swept
over them. The ledge was of such a nature that it inclined
outward from the base at an angle sufficient to protect
them both from the plunging rain, which suddenly descended in torrents, and from the falling fragments which
were hurtling through the air. The huge bank out of which
it jutted, gave abundant protection from the tornado itself

And thus kneeling on the sand with the ledge projecting above them, and the huge bank rising behind, they were able to observe the movement of the tempest from a point of observation perfectly secure. The violence of the wind was astonishing. It tore its way through the beach grove that nestled in the swale at the foot of the mountain with such fierceness as to virtually destroy it. In the morning half the trees were found prostrate, and the branches of those that remained were sadly wrenched and disfigured. It struck the water with the force of an actual concussion. It cut grooves through it, scooped depressions along its surface, and blew the edges away in flying froth. Whirlwinds darted downward and spun themselves along the water with a revolution so swift that the suction fairly lifted it in spirals. The sands on the beach jumped upward and were sent hissing through the air; the marsh-grass and reeds along the shore flattened and lay prone. The wind was too fierce for waves — the crests of the growing undulations were sheered off as if the wind had an edge keen as a knife; the under halves were pressed downward and the upper portions blown upward through the air in mist. For ten minutes, perhaps, the tempest kept the full proportions of its fury, and then the winds sank perceptibly, although they still blew with the velocity of a gale. The lake began to roll in great waves, their crests white as if edged with dry snow; and the hollow intervals, deep and dark, were streaked with frothy lines. The billows swelled, curved, and roared. They splashed and hissed as they seethed along. They rolled tumultuously one after the other, as if

in mad pursuit and madder flight, pursuer and pursued. At
times the rain fell in torrents. It burst out of the clouds
as if the reservoirs of the upper air had broken their bounds
and poured their deluge bodily downward. At other times
it ceased and for minutes not a drop would fall. The storm
was passing eastward. The thunder, though incessant, was
less concussive; and the lightning, though vivid and fierce,
flashed on the lake from a farther distance. The uproar
had now so far subsided that with a little extra effort conversation could be carried on.

"It is a dreadful blow for sartin," said the old man, "and
mighty leetle choppin' will me and the Lad have to do for
the lodge fire this winter, for I heerd the wind comin'
through the beech grove in the swale as I dove down the
bank, and I know by the sound that it did a good deal of
cuttin'. I sartinly hope the lodge has stood, for it's been
my home off and on for twelve year. And a man gits used
to a shanty as he does to his garments, and it takes some
time afore he can git used to the change. I hope no man is
on the lake to-night, for there's nothing but a canoe that
could live in that sea, and there aint many paddles in the
woods that could manage one jediciously in sech wild water.
A man must be a fool or crazy to ventur' out"—

"What's that!" screamed the Lad.

The voice of his exclamation was so sharp and piercing,
and so suddenly ejaculated, that Herbert and the Trapper
fairly started.

"Where is it, Lad? where is it?" exclaimed the Trapper,
as he peered into the darkness. "Wait for a flash and pint
it out when it comes."

For a moment the three men stood waiting, while through the darkness the white crests of the billows alone showed themselves, and out of the gloom the thunder of their roar harshly ascended, and then the flash came.

It needed not the finger of the Lad to point out the object, the sight of which had opened his mouth with the startling cry, for there in full view, a mile from the shore, in the midst of the rolling waves, and lifted on the very crest of a billow was a boat, and in it, vividly outlined, was seen standing the form of a man with his arms outstretched and his hands and face lifted to the heavens.

" Crazy John ! "

The words were heaved from the very depths of the Trapper's chest, and as he spoke them the flash died away, and the vision disappeared in the darkness, and again through the gloom only the white flash of the waves could be seen, while out of the darkness sounded heavy and solemn the roar of their dirge-like roll.

"I will save him ! " said the Lad, and he laid hold of the bow of his boat to drag it into the water.

"Stop where ye be ! " exclaimed the Trapper, as he seized the other side of the boat and held it with so strong a grip that the Lad could not move it an inch. "Stop where ye be, Lad, and leave this job to the plannin' of an older head than yourn. The man must be saved for sartin, if it be within mortal power; for though the fit be on him and he has leetle sense, it musn't be said by a man on the 'arth, or by the Lord in the heaven, when we come to His presence, that three men stood on this beach and seed one of his

crceturs in peril, even if he sought it in his foolishness, and
made no effort to save him. Yis, he must sartinly be saved
if it be within mortal power; but a boat can't live in that
sea, and the canoe and the paddle must do it. Henry, I've
seed ye fetch a canoe through water wild enough to be fearful to most men, and ye have follered me down rapids that
even a Huron would falter to shoot; and ye must take the
starn and I will take the bow, and the Lad shall stay on the
beach here while you and me make the ventur'."

"But I want to go, too, John Norton. What can I do if
I stay here on the beach?"

"Lad," said the Trapper, as he seized his paddle, and
lifted the bow of the canoe, while Henry lifted the stern,
"there be times when one mortal must act while another
must wait; and I know that the waitin' be harder than the
doin'; and I know ye have the harder work, but ye must
do it. But ye needn't stand idle, for ye can gather some
sticks and start a fire under the ledge here, and make the
flame go high, for it will give Henry and me the bearin's,
and mayhaps it will help us greatly."

"I will, I will," said the Lad. "I will make the blaze go
high, John Norton, and I will ask God to help you save
the poor man, and bring you and Henry safe back to the
shore."

"That's right, Lad, that's right," said the Trapper. I
remember yer prayin' on Tomahawk Pint, and I raaly think
it was an actaal help, and it may be the Lord will hear ye
agin. But be sure and don't forgit to put in some 'arnest
words for crazy John, for me and Henry can take care of

ourselves. But if the fool keeps standin' up in his boat as he was when the flash showed him, he'll need some help to steady him, or he'll lose his balance for sartin." And, even as he spoke, the Trapper waded out into the lake till the proper depth had been reached, and then, with practised agility, he leapt upward and lighted on his knees in the bow of the canoe, giving, at the instant he landed, a powerful sweep with his paddle, which, assisted as it was by the push and spring of Herbert, as he jumped to his place in the stern, sent the light vessel far out amid the agitated water. And so the boat disappeared in the gloom.

It was, indeed, a perilous venture. Even the old Trapper had not realized the height and velocity of the billows until the canoe had fairly entered into them. The water foamed and hissed around the vessel; it heaved it up as with the power of mighty hands, and then let it down with a splash into the hollow troughs, with a suddenness that made the frail thing quiver through all its slender frame. It flung its spray into the eyes of those struggling at either end until they were almost blinded. It strove to wrench it from its course, and turn it round and roll it over, but the skill and strength of those who knelt at either end still held it to its course, and forced it up against the pressure of the gale and the sweeping force of the waves, at an astonishing speed. Half the distance had been traversed before a flash of lightning came, and when it came again the boat and the man standing in it flashed into sight.

"The Lad must be prayin' in 'arnest," the Trapper shouted back to Herbert, "and the Lord must be sartinly helpin'

Crazy John, or he never could keep his footin' in a rollin'
boat, jumping and pitchin' as his is doin'. Heave her staarn
up, boy! quick! heave her up. There's a big un comin',
and she'd never lift to it if we struck it head on. Heave
her up and take her a little sidlin', or the Lad will sartinly
have three to pray for instead of one."

Herbert could just make out the words of the Trapper
as they were borne to him on the rush of the wind, and he
obeyed to the letter. He put every ounce of strength in
his frame into his stroke, and the little vessel responded to
its pressure. It met the wave a little quartering, and balanced at precisely the proper angle as it was by the Trapper, it clomb up the side of the huge billow laboriously
but safely, and shot down into the farther recess with a velocity as if it were conscious of the danger from which it was
flying.

" Ye did that well, boy, ye did that well. It was as big a
wave as I ever seed a canoe lifted over, and ye did it handsome. We must be cenamost to the boat and another
flash will show us if Crazy John be in the boat or—"

He was interrupted by a vivid and prolonged blaze. The
whole heaven kindled, and the lake stood forth to view as
clear as at noonday. The boat in which Crazy John had
been so recklessly standing, was not thirty feet away, and
was being blown forward by the winds at the speed of an
arrow. But no man was in it; and the quick eye of the
Trapper, with lightning glance, was searching the hollow of
the waves and running along their crests, seeking the head
of a man. He saw it! For out of the lake, as if rising

from a depth, shot the head and shoulders of crazy John. His face was still upturned and his hands still lifted high.

"Sheer to the left!" yelled the Trapper. "Sharp to the left, and sweep her round!"

It was done. The canoe swooped to the left, glancing upward on the swell of the wave and shot into the opposite trough with a leap. As it fell, the blaze of the lightning died out, but the eye of the Trapper had measured the distance, and as the canoe dropped into the hollow of the sea he bowed himself till his broad breast rested on the prow, and stooping far over, drove his hand into the water.

The deed was done! The man was saved!

The fingers of the Trapper closed on the long hair of Crazy John, and in an instant his other hand had fastened its grasp on the collar of his coat.

"Tip her over to the left, boy!" called the Trapper, "tip her over to the left. He isn't as big as a buck, but it'll take a good deal of purchase to hist him over. Down with her, boy! for here goes!"

The feat was accomplished handsomely. The Old Trapper, with the exercise of gigantic strength and the dexterity of a practiced canoeman, lifted the poor man out of the water and landed him full length at his feet; and in such a way, too, as to scarcely disturb the proper balance of the light shell, which was now heavily loaded, considering the violence of the water it had to traverse on its way to the shore.

CHAPTER IV.

CRAZY JOHN.

"Now see that noble and most sovereign reason,
Like sweet bells jangled, out of tune and harsh."
— *Shakespeare.*

WHETHER the shock with which he struck the bottom of the canoe had stunned him, or whether he had fainted from exhaustion incident to his struggles in the water, our friends could not tell; but they rejoiced in the fact that the man whom they had saved continued to lie stretched in the bottom of the canoe perfectly motionless. For, had he indulged in any "antics," as the Old Trapper expressed it, it would have made their position one of extreme peril, and as it was, it required all their strength and skill to bring their boat to shore.

In the direction they were now going the wind was dead astern, and it was necessary to keep the canoe in rapid motion, racing along on the top of a wave even with its own velocity lest it should drop into the trough, and, heavily loaded as it was, be overwhelmed by the succeeding billows before it could lift. The two men, therefore, worked for their lives. The forethought of the Old Trapper in his directions to the Lad was now fully vindicated. The flame at the foot of the ledge was burning strong and clear and through the spray and the driving mists blown there-from the Trapper could see the Lad now feeding the fire, and anon kneeling on the sands. The poor boy, acting in harmony with, and under the impulse of, his simple but sublime faith and yet obedient to the directions of the Trapper, was thus giving, unconsciously, a practical illustration of the true Christian conception of the relation which works and faith mutually hold to each other. And well would it be for many of us, who deem ourselves learned and wise, if we could thus unite in our conduct the two great co-ordinate doctrines of the Christian scheme.

"The Lad has the right idee of it," said the Trapper, soliloquizing, "yis, the Lad may not be overknowin', but he has the right idee of it. The fire alone don't seem quite enough, and the prayin' alone wouldn't help me and Henry a bit, but ye jine the two and make the wood support the prayin' and the prayin' sort o' help out the wood, and it sartinly comes nigh the Lord's idee of it, as I conceit."

In a moment the canoe had drawn nigh the shore, and the Lad, running out into the water, assisted eagerly to lift it to the beach.

"We've saved him, Lad!" said the old man.

"I knew you would save him, John Norton, for I asked God to save him; and he has said, 'Ask-and-ye-shall-receive,' and I asked him to give us Crazy John in safety, and I never asked God to do anything yet, that he didn't do."

"I guess ye be more reasonable in yer askin', then, than some of the missioners be in their prayin', Lad; for the last time I heerd one in the settlements he spent more'n twenty

minutes in prayin', and he asked more than a hundred things
of the Lord, and half of 'em at least, to my sartin knowledge, wasn't any way reasonable, for he didn't confine himself to the pints of the case. And there's nothin' like stickin' to the main pints of the case when ye are talkin' to the
Lord, as I conceit."

While he had been saying this he had lifted Crazy John
in his arms and borne him to the fire, and at once proceeded with his efforts to restore him to consciousness. In
this he was soon successful, and in a short time the unfortunate being who had been so nigh death, was sitting with
his back propped against the ledge gazing, with eyes in
whose look consciousness was revealed, it is true, but whose
consciousness was that of one whose reason had been over-
turned, and whose faculties were exposed to the deceptions
which insanity practices on its wretched victims.

A strange and remarkable looking being he was, as he
sat with his back against the ledge in the bright glow of
the firelight. His countenance was cast in a noble mould,
and his features were almost faultless, in the clean outline
of their nearly classic beauty. Age of course had cut its
history in wrinkles and withered the fullness of his appearance, but his forehead was broad and high, the front ample
in its curvature, providing residence for a brain of unusual
size, his nose was straight and thin, with round, curved
nostrils. His mouth generous but not excessive, while a
beard of snowy whiteness covered all the lower part of his
face and lay in waving folds upon his breast. His hair was
long; the growth of years; — none knew how many, — and

whiter if possible than his beard. His eyebrows were as
white as snow, abundant, and straight in their lines. The
brow itself beetled outward. The sockets of the eye were
large, and the orbs themselves which glowed within
the recess, were deep, black and lustrous. The first impression that these strange eyes made upon one was of their
mildness ; a mildness born of suffering, perhaps, as if the sad-
ness of years and loss had softened, if it had not utterly
extinguished the gleam of their original fire. But a close
observer could not fail to note that within and behind their
clear, steady gaze was a wavering light that came and
flitted, and came again, as if nature would thus express
the unsteadiness and insecurity of the disturbed reason,
which formerly held fixed possession of her throne.

"Well, Crazy John," said the Trapper, "how do you
feel ? "

"I am not crazy," he returned, "you are crazy, and
everybody else is crazy. I am the only man that isn't crazy
in the world."

"I shouldn't wonder if ye was about half right in yer
idees on that pint," returned the Trapper, "for I sartinly
think most men be a leetle cracked; and it may be I have
a kink or two in me somewhere, and if everybody was just
like you, I conceit there wouldn't be a crazy man in the
world. But what was ye out on the water to-night for?
And why didn't ye stay in yer shanty or find a safe spot as
we did when the storm came down? It was a bit of sheer
foolishness, Crazy John, for a mortal man to resk his life as
ye did on the lake to-night."

"*She* called me," returned the other, while his eyes dark-ened their glow, "*she* told me to come, and I went, and I found her, too. Found her in the air and the wave and the wind."

"Found who?" said the Lad, "whom did you find in the air and the wind and the wave, Crazy John?"

"*Whom* did I find!" exclaimed the other, "I found the woman I loved, and the spirit I worship; the spirit of white-ness and sweetness and beautiful grace that I loved long ago — long ago — long ago. The spirit that's *mine,* and will be mine when the waves cease to roll and winds cease to blow, and the air is unbreathed by the nostrils of men."

And as he said this the paleness of his face flushed and his eyes glowed like coals, as if they were indeed but the windows of his soul, and his soul was aglow with the fervor of a deathless hope and ardent desire.

"Why did she call you out into the lake," said the Lad, "when the waves were so high and the winds so strong? I don't think she ought to do that."

"Young man!" exclaimed the other, "what cares a spirit for wind ,and waves, the movements of air and of water? Spirits have power in the air, and the sea and the winds do their bidding. I have seen her in the sun when he rose over the mountain, and in the moon when she deepened the blue of the sky with her beams; and the winds have borne me her songs from away, — far away, — far away, and the waves turn to white at the touch of her feet when she walks on their crests. My spirit is queen of the sea, and the waves are her slaves. Old Trapper!" he shouted, as he rose to his

feet, took a step forward, and stretched out his hand with
a gesture as grand as Paul must have used in his appeal to Agrippa, while his face flamed with excitement and
his form trembled, "Old Trapper, you have lived till your
head is whitening and wisdom abides on your lips,—believ-
est thou there are spirits?"

"Sartinly, sartinly I do," returned the Old Trapper, "even
the Hurons believe that, and it would be a shame for a
white man to believe less than an Injun, 'specially a miserable dog of a Huron. Yis, I sartinly believe there be
sperits."

"Have you ever seen them, John Norton?" exclaimed
the other.

"I can't say for sartin I ever did, Crazy John. I can't
say for sartin I ever did actally *see* a sperit, but I'll confess
that more'n once, when standin' by the grave of a comrade,
or on the mound of the trenches where we buried the dead
arter a scrimmage, I have *felt* that the sperits of the dead
was around me."

"They were there! they were there!" exclaimed the
other, in a voice lifted almost to a scream. "They were
there, but you were blinded. You have eyes and see not,
ears and hear not. But my eyes see, and my ears hear, for
I am not of the earth. I died when she died, but I am condemned to stay on the earth for my sins! — *for my sins!* —
FOR MY SINS! — condemned to stay till my sins be washed
away, and I am made white, then I shall go — *then I shall
go* — THEN —"

A clap of thunder, heavy and prolonged, here suddenly

broke in on his speech. The beach trembled under their feet as the peal rolled in awful detonations through the sky. The look of wild excitement faded out of the countenance of the singular being. He bowed his head as with solemn reverence, and when the last heavy reverberation died away, he lifted his face, every line of which was settled in awe, toward the cloud, and said: —

"*Thunder away, Almighty God!* I love to hear thy voice shake the world. Thy power is above all powers, and the spirits themselves veil their faces in front of the glory of thy throne! Almighty God, I love the roll of thy thunder, for *she* has told me of thy love and thy power."

The solemn earnestness with which he pronounced these words; the suggestiveness of his gesture as he stood with outstretched hands; and face lifted toward the clouds; the roar of waves, rising from amid the gloom; the grand and awful surroundings made by the night and the storm, — combined to produce an impression on the three men, two of whom were looking at him with wonder, and the third with curious interest, that would have been difficult for they themselves to explain.

"Come, come, Crazy John," said the Trapper, at leng'h, "Ye are sartinly a good deal stirred up, to-night, and ye'd better sort o' settle down. Ye won't be any wiser for lookin' at that cloud so 'arnestly, for there's nothin' in it for a mortal to see."

"See!" he exclaimed, as he wheeled suddenly around, till he stood face to face with the Trapper, "my eyes have the vision of sight that sees the end from the beginning.

I see back and ahead, below and above, and far off. I am a prophet of God. I am the angel whose head is as wool and whose eyes are a flame; and nothing that has been, and nothing that is, and nothing that shall be, is hidden from me. For I look, and I see, and I know what the years will bring — will bring — will bring."

"It may be as ye say, Crazy John," said the Trapper, "but I sartinly doubt if ye know what ye are talkin' about, for ye be but a man, and I've heerd that the ways of the Lord be past findin' out. But if ye can see ahead, and know, as ye say, what is to come, ye may be able to tell us what is to happen to us 'twixt this and the time when we come to the edge of the great clearin'."

"John Norton," said the other, "as he turned his blazing orbs upon him with a steadiness and intensity of gaze from which a man of less nerve and coolness would have shrunk, "John Norton, you have lived in the woods and you will die in the woods. I see a grave under the pines, and but one man at the grave, and a dog."

"I'm glad it's under the pines, Crazy John. Yis, I'm glad it's under the pines, if the grave be for me. Ye may be right as to the dog, for dogs be short lived, and "Rover" is aged, and it's reasonable to think that I'll outlive him; but "Sport" be a little more than a pup yit, and it's nateral to think that he'll outlive me, for the days of a mortal be fixed, and I conceit that I've come nigh the eend of my days on the 'arth. But ye are sartinly wrong if ye see but one man, for Henry and the Lad be both young, and I know that both the boys will be at the grave when they make it for me under the pines."

" The youth you call Henry is the one that stands here," responded the other, as he turned his glowing eyes towards Herbert, " and he it is I see by the grave; but the Lad is not there, for he has a grave of his own that I see, and his mound will be flat when your mound is fashioned, John Norton."

"Where is my grave, Crazy John ?" said the Lad, " where is my grave ? "

"Your grave is by the sea, young man. By the deep, deep sea; the shining, the rolling, the far-reaching sea. It is a grave among many. It's a grave with a grave: the grave of one gone on before. Young man, I see your grave amid many, and 'tis made with a grave, by the long-reaching, far-rolling, deep-sounding sea."

"Where is my grave, Crazy John ?" asked Herbert, who, leaning on his paddle, had been curiously watching the singular being, " where is my grave ? and who is there by it ? and where is it to be made ? "

" Your grave is not a grave," was the answer. And instead of looking at Herbert he turned himself toward the lake; and, with his back to the young man, and lifted head gazing steadfastly out into the gloom, he continued; " your grave is not a grave. It is not under pines. It is not amid graves. It is not in the earth. Men will not find it; women will not weep o'er it. It rises and sinks. It moves and it rolls. It's a grave without stone, without name, without spot — " and the strange being started along the beach, walking ankle-deep in the froth and the water, muttering to himself, "It rises and sinks. It moves and it rolls. A grave without name, without stone, without spot."

"Will he come back?" asked Herbert, speaking to the Trapper.

"Sartinly, sartinly," returned the old man, "the fit will leave him pritty soon. I've knowed Crazy John for forty year off and on, and usually he's quiet enough; but a storm seems to rouse him, and thunder makes him wild; but the storm is dyin' out, and in half an hour he'll be as calm as the lake. It's no use to foller him, for when the fit is on him ye can't manage him, but when he's cooled down a leetle he'll come back as quiet as a child and be nateral-like."

CHAPTER V.

A PROPHECY.

"The voice sounds like a prophet's word." — Halleck.

Portia. "Why, know'st thou any harm's intended?
Soothsayer. None that I know will be, much that I fear may chance."
Shakespeare.

A S the Trapper had predicted, the storm was passing
away. The body of it had already got beyond the
eastern mountains, and the thunder had sunk away into
murmurs. The lightning blazed dimly, and cast only tran-
sient illuminations through the farther darkness. Where
the clouds had been was now but a thin vapory film, and
even this grew thinner and thinner until the great stars
broke through it with their luminance, and glowed with
ample splendor in a sky which the tempest had washed.
The waves sank with the winds. They died together like
cause and effect, and in a brief time the lake, which, but so
recently had been tossing with violent agitations, stretched
from the beach at their feet to its southern extremity with
a surface so level that scarcely a ripple stirred its smooth
expanse with its motion. In it the sky found a mirror, and
the stars overhead multiplied themselves in its depths.

"It's sartinly a marvel," said the Trapper, speaking to
his two companions, "how quick Natur' can change her
look. Her moods be like the moods of a man. Come, Lad,"

he continued, as he threw some fresh branches into the fire,
" the morn will soon be here, and the sauds under the ledge
be dry; come, onkiver yer fiddle and play us a tune. I
conceit that Crazy John will jine us when he hears ye playin', for I've heerd him play himself, and the music will calm
him."

So saying, the old man seated himself under the projection of the ledge by the side of Herbert, who had already
stretched himself in a reclining attitude.

The Lad took the violin from its case, and after carefully
examining it to see that it had received no injury, he placed
the bow upon the strings and began to move it lightly and
waveringly, as if feeling for the true initial note. In a moment his mind reached the decision. Perhaps some tuneful suggestion or melodious memory had been communicated to, or stirred within his mind by the stray fugitive
chords, for his face suddenly lighted, his hand steadied itself, and the bow, with the proper pressure upon it, began its
progress over the strings, true and even as hand of man
might make it. The note rose clear and high. It rose into
the air, rolled out above the lake, and stole along the listening shore. It was followed in soft and measured succession
by others equally sweet, clear, and fine. The sounds were
as pure as the cleansed air into which they rose. The stars,
shining with steady, self-contained luminance, were no more
mild and soothing to the eye than were the easy, full-
rounded notes that the instrument yielded forth, to the ear.

It was a hymn of peace. A hymn such as angels might
sing to a soul that had passed through stormy passages,

been rudely buffeted, and borne much during its earthly, life, when it had been lifted above the earth, and with its warfare ended was being ministered unto by those who long had known the infinite peace. No words can describe the exceeding softness of the strains. Limited as the poor boy was in the powers that make the average man potential and efficient, his one great gift stood out resplendent. Within his soul the gift or genius of music found its home. His tongue might falter in its attempt to master the form of verbal speech, but music had bestowed upon him a divine expression. No one that heard him play could ever doubt it. In quality it was a revelation of what inarticulate expression might be. To-night his mood was of the finest.

Sitting under the projection of the ledge, with the lake, in which the stars were mirrored, before him, the blue vault bright with its golden splendor overhead, the somber woods around, and the great, solemn, and as it were expectant silence soliciting the presence of his pure soul, through the one medium that God had given him to pour forth the innocence, the longing and the faith of his beautiful spirit, he played with a delicacy of touch and an evenness of pressure that were marvelous. The Trapper lay leaning against the rock with his eyes closed. Herbert sat watching the Lad's lighted countenance with eyes that searched in vain for some explanation of the boy's wonderful gift. He had heard the masters of the world play, and his own ear did not lack culture; but inwardly he was constrained to confess, that never had he heard an instrument yield forth such melody as his simple-minded, awkwardly-formed companion, with long and easy-going motions of the bow, was sending forth into the receptive air.

He might have been playing five minutes when Herbert's quick ear caught the sound of a slow, soft step stealing along the sand ; and in a moment, out of the star-lighted dusk, the form of Crazy John appeared. He stole into the circle of the light so quietly that the Lad did not know of his approach, but Herbert watched him closely and noted the change that had come over him. The wildness had left his countenance, the gleam had faded from his eye, his muscles had relaxed their tension, and his whole face had settled to repose. He sank softly down into the sand, and gazed upon the Lad with a look such as a mortal at his entrance into heaven, might contemplate the first angelic being he chanced to meet. And as the Lad played on, as the sweet consoling notes flowed forth, they carried peace and consolation to the bosom of the unfortunate creature. His eyes overflowed ; the great tears stole down his cheeks and fell into the white volume of his beard, but his gaze remained steadfastly fixed upon the boy's face and the look of worshiping awe remained as steadfastly on his own. At last the Lad paused ; he laid the violin upon his lap with his bow across it.

"Well, John," said the Trapper, as he opened his eyes, "what do you think of that ? "

" Boy ! " he exclaimed, without answering the question of the Trapper and addressing himself to the Lad, " boy, thou art a spirit ! Thy soul is not of this earth. The gift of God is in you. Thou art one of the chosen ones sent out to minister unto the saints. The Lord hath lent thee to the earth; but only for a year, a day, and an hour. Thou shalt not stay among men; thou shalt go hence, but not till thou hast done a great deed; and those that laughed at thee shall know that with thy weakness God hath mingled strength, and made thy lacking to be greater than their full-ness. They call me 'Crazy John,' and they call me so be-cause my ways are not their ways, and my thoughts are not their thoughts. I am not crazy save when the body vexes me and the forces of the earth that are demoniacal possess me. But I do not stay in my body always; I leave it and come back to it. I have left it for hours; yes, for a day and a night, and a night and a day; left and come back to it. And I see things when my eyes are stony; I feel when my body is stiff; I go where there is no time, and all things that have been, and all things that are, and all things that shall be, stand out. And I have seen thee, boy, before we met, and one with thee that is not with thee now."

" Who was it, Crazy John?" said the Lad, " who was it that was with me?" and the poor boy actually panted with excitement, as through his comprehension dimly stole a startling thought.

" It was one thou hast seen and shalt see; but not yet. I shall see her first. You shall come after, and I see the way of your coming and the hour!"

" Come, come, Crazy John, the storm has gone by, and why don't ye settle back to yer nateral sense? Ye'll skeer the Lad out of his wits with yer nonsensical talkin'."

"John Norton!" exclaimed the other, "thou wast born for the body and the earth. Thou dwellest in the body and art earthy. Thou canst not understand the converse of spirits."

"I'm glad to see ye come down to facts, Crazy John; yis, I'm glad to see ye come down to facts. Of course I dwell in my body, and a mighty pleasant place it's been to dwell in for these three-score year. And I can't say that I ever expect to git into a better one; for the Lord made it for me, and I must say he put it together jediciously, as the time it has stood and the sarvices it has done, proves. And as for sperits, I don't know nothin' about 'em; that is, I'm not sartin enough about anything to sight on it. And Henry will tell ye I'm always ready to draw at a ventur' when meat is scarce or there is the least chance of fur. And if ye are raaly sot on talkin' any more about sperits, Crazy John, you and me will jest go one side out of hearin' of the boys, and if I can find a comfortable spot where the sand isn't too wet and the seat has a back-piece to it, you and me will have a great time talkin' about sperits. That is, I'll listen and you shall talk, and that is the best way, as I conceit, for a sensible man to talk with another about sperits. For if he don't say anything wise, he sartinly won't say anything foolish, and that's a raal vartue in a counsel. But don't skeer the Lad any more with talk of his goin'."

"Scared! why should the Lad be scared at thought of his going? I will not talk more, John Norton, for you are ignorant and unbelieving; but you are wise in your order, only you belong to another order and are fixed in another sphere. But the Lad shall go — he shall go! — he shall go! on a stormy night and amid fire; and you and Henry shall see him, and many shall see; — see the fire! see the flame! and you shall feel the touch of the fire, John Norton, and Henry shall be scorched with the flame. For you shall be with the Lad 'mid the fire, and you would go with him, but your time is not yet, for you must sleep 'neath the pines — 'neath the pines — 'neath the pines, Old Trapper; and Henry's grave must be a grave without stone, without name, without spot. But why should I tell you these things? Shall not the Lord reveal them in his time? Let's to sleep! let's to sleep! You sleep while I leave my body."

"That's sartinly good counsel," said the Trapper, "for the morn is comin' and we sartinly have been stirred up a good deal to-night; and nothin' settles a man arter he's been riled, like sleep. Ye'd better not git yer feet quite so near them brands, Crazy John, if yer spirit is raaly goin' out of yer body for a little tantrum in the air; if ye do ye aint likely to find more'n half of yerself when ye come back, and the most valuable half at that, for I count that the legs and feet be the best half of a man if he live in the woods. So crook up yer knees a leetle, Crazy John, or ye'll git singed for sartin."

With this parting admonition the Old Trapper stretched his huge frame upon the sand along-side of his companion and in a few moments the long, heavy breathing of the four gave evidence that sleep had locked their senses in profound repose.

   *   *   *   *   *

The summer was past and autumn had come. The adventures with which our three friends had met we do not purpose to narrate in this volume. It chanced that the man whose story we are telling was not the most prominent actor in the sad and startling experiences the summer brought to them. At another time we may give to our readers the history of an even more singular and unfortunate being than "The Man Who Didn't Know Much" — but of the latter we must write now, and the story that has detained us so long draws to its close.

Herbert, on the eve of his departure from the woods, had succeeded in persuading the Old Trapper to accompany him to his city home. With high anticipations they had struck eastward from the Racquette until they came to the upper branches of the Hudson, down which they proceeded until they came to Albany. There they left their light boat and continued their journey in one of the river steamers. Arriving at New York they crossed the city without delay, and took passage eastward on one of the steamboats that traversed the Sound. At this critical point of their journey our pen resumes its narration.

CHAPTER VI.

THE CATASTROPHE.

"With clashing wheel, and lifting keel,
　　And smoking torch on high,
When winds are loud, and billows reel,
　　She thunders, foaming, by.
　　　　　— *Oliver Wendell Holmes.*

IT was a stormy night. The wind was blowing a gale; and not a star was visible. The wind came from the south-east; raw and damp with briny dampness. The force of a thousand leagues of unimpeded violence was in it. It was full of lusty strength, of unchecked might, rageful and fierce. The center of the storm movement was in the far Atlantic; but, as it swept round on its invisible axis in fearful revolutions, Long Island split the periphery of its power like a wedge, and sheared off a mighty column, which poured itself into and down the Sound, sweeping it from end to end. The waves ran high; they rose out of the darkness, vast volumes of on-rolling water, and white-crested with rage, like mad things showing their teeth, they rushed against the steamer's prow, as if they would keel her over and drive her downward to destruction.

Only a few of her full complement of passengers were on deck. Some were in the main saloon, gathered in knots for comfort. Others sat moodily apart, communing with their fears; while not a few were in their state-rooms, or down below in their berths, sick, or thoroughly frightened. The air was full of foreboding. The prevalent feeling was that of alarm. The plunge of the vessel as she dived down-ward into the hollow of the sea; the tremendous shocks that shook her from stem to stern; the quivering that con-vulsed her huge frame, and tried her timbers in all their joints as the great sea struck her; the groaning of the machinery, and now and then the rush of waters overhead as some sea swept over her bulwarks, — revealed to those that were within the saloon, or lay stretched in their berths, that the gale was at its height.

A few of the passengers were on deck; some were sailors, and from habit kept an exposed position; others, while not seamen, were sufficiently familiar with voyaging, and of such a temperament, that a position on deck and the sight of a storm were more congenial to them than the protected parlors. Among these latter our three friends could be numbered. It was not in accordance with the tempera-ments or habits of Herbert and the Trapper to stay be-tween decks when such a storm was raging, and the Lad could not remain separate from his companions. Indeed, his behavior and remarks revealed the fact that he was familiar with the different portions of the vessel, and with the proper management of such a craft in a storm. He evidently had knowledge of the machinery, knew the name and use of all the equipments, and showed no inconsiderable acquaintance with the force and action of wind and waves, and even with the reefs and islands of the coast along which the course of the vessel was now directed.

Herbert, surprised at this knowledge, had questioned him . in conversation, concerning the origin of it, and elicited from him many facts of his early life ; among others, that he was born on the shore of the Sound, and had often sailed the very waters through which the steamer was plunging. He knew the name and position of the beacon lights they passed, of the various headlands ; and, with his finger pointed out the location and the name of this or that island which was hidden in the gloom; estimating in a manner that showed the accuracy of his memory and his familiarity with the coast, the probable distance these islands were from them, as the boat careered along.

"I tell ye," said the Trapper, as the three stood close to the starboard rail, holding on to an iron rod for support, "I tell ye, Henry," he shouted, "this is a wild un. I was on a government transport in the center of old Ontario once, when it looked mighty squally for all of us; but it sartinly didn't blow harder than it does to-night. I remember how the skipper looked and acted, and what he did, as if it was but yesterday."

"What did he do?" asked the Lad.

"He put his ship about, Lad," responded the Trapper, "afore the waves got half as high as this, or the wind half as strong. He put his ship about, and I remember the drenchin' we all got while she was swingin' round; but when he got her starn on how she did go!"

"Where did she fetch up?" asked Herbert.

"Fetch up?" replied the old man. "We didn't fetch up. There was no fetch up to her that night. She went like a young buck in his fust chase; and when the sun riz and the winds settled a leetle he scooted her in atween two big islands; and the skipper said, — I conceit he may have stretched it a leetle, — the skipper said that the old tub had gone two hundred mile that night. And I was jest thinkin' that if I was skipper of this craft I'd 'bout ship, shut off steam as you call it, and let her drive to'ard York."

"It's not a very easy thing to 'bout ship in a sea like this, John Norton," said Herbert. "Could it be done, Lad?"

"I think perhaps it might be done," said the Lad; "for the engines work well, and she is a good boat to mind her helm; but it don't blow hard enough yet for the captain to risk running on to the coast this side of New London. That's a famous harbor, and if it blows any harder I guess the captain will run in there."

"Lord-o'-massy, Lad!" exclaimed the Old Trapper, excitedly, "ye talk downright foolishness. It can't blow any harder. The air would bust if it did."

"Yes, it can blow harder, John Norton," returned the Lad. "I have seen it blow harder than this; and I don't think it blows as hard as it will by and by."

"If it blows any harder," screamed the Trapper, "we'll all go to the bottom, for any man knows that them leetle boats strung up there couldn't live out in them waves a minute. Lord! What a thump that was! It shook her up as a maul does a wedge. I don't marvel that the wimmen folks be a leetle screechy. I hope the poor creeturs will git safe to shore."

"I have had a feeling," said the Lad, half speaking to

himself, " ever since we got aboard that something was going to happen to-night. I don't know why it should be so;
but I keep seeing the face of Crazy John out there in the
darkness."

" Come, come, Lad, don't ye git skeery," said the Old
Trapper, " Crazy John's face isn't anywhere nigh us; for
Henry and you know jest where it lies; and you know that
we put five good feet of sile on top of him, to say nothin' of
the boughs and grasses, and the wild rose-bushes ye
throwed in."

For several minutes nothing was said, then Herbert continued : —

"I don't see how anything can happen, although it is a
very severe gale; for the ship is a strong one and she is being well handled; and the Lad says that there's a good harbor twenty miles ahead, into which the captain can run if
he is compelled to. I don't see how anything can happen,
— do you, John Norton ? "

" Not as I can see," returned the Trapper, " but I can't
say that I'm used to jest this kind of boatin', and I conceit
my jedgment isn't wuth much. Now if I was on the Racquette in a squall with a good birch under me, and a good
paddle, and wasn't too heavily loaded, I could tell ye jest
about what the prospect was; but this kind of boatin'
makes a man of my natur' and habits but leetle better than
a squaw, for all there is to do is to jest hang on. No, I sartinly don't know much about this kind of boatin', and my
jedgment isn't wuth a cent."

" I don't know what we should do if anything should

happen," said Herbert. " The clerk told me there were. six
hundred passengers aboard, and at the tables to-night I
thought I never had seen so many women and children in
one boat at a time. I don't know what would become of
them, or any of us for that matter, in a sea like this if anything "—

" *Fire!* "

No one could say whence the cry came, nor, at the moment, whether it was the voice of man or woman that sent
it out; but from whatever throat it came, it came projected
with all the energy of terror. It filled the great saloon,—
sank to the lower deck,— penetrated the state-rooms and
berths,— rose into the pilot-house,— and was blown by the
gusts into the farther darkness in quivering fragments as if
the winds in their fierce gladness had seized it, torn it in
pieces, and flung it aside to be ready for its successor. Nor
had they long to wait: it came upon the instant, rising wild
and high — piercingly shrill as mortal fear could make it:

" *Fire!* Fire! F-i-r-e ! "

The effect of such a cry on shipboard at night, in the
midst of such a gale, on a crowded steamer, can never be
known to those who have not heard it; nor communicated
to those who quietly sit in safety and at ease reading its description on the printed page. In the great saloon, when
the awful sound swept through it, men engaged in conversation stopped — looked with startled interrogation into
each other's eyes, with faces that on the instant turned
white as ashes. Women, with a sudden gesture, placed
their hands above their hearts as if they had received an

unseen stab. Some continued sitting as they had been as if
stiffened to the position. Others, with their hands still on
their hearts, sank back in a dead swoon. Children stopped
their play and stood staring at their elders. The sick in
their berths stilled their groans and lay straight on their
cots as if dead, listening with pent breath.

On deck the effect was the same. The sound had the
power in it to drown all other sounds. Those that heard it
rise, heard nothing else. It captured their senses and held
them concentrated to itself. The roar and splash of the
mighty waves —the whistling, screaming wind—made for an
instant no impression on the senses. The one terrible sound
dominated all other noises; and those who heard the dreadful scream were, for the moment, conscious of nothing else.

This was the first effect; but when the cry was repeated,
when the awful scream rose the second time, was reiterated
and prolonged as mortal fear only can prolong a cry, fright
took possession of all. Men tumbled from their berths,
striking the floor with a bound, shouting. The state-room
doors burst open and women ran out screaming. Those
who were below rushed wildly into the main saloon, tramp-
ling on each other in their headlong course. The uproar
was fearful. Men called for their wives. Women screamed
for their husbands. Mothers clutched their children to their
breasts. Calls and shouts, the rush of hurrying feet, and
shrieks, filled the air.

On deck all was hurry and confusion incident to such an
emergency. Hose were being fitted, pumps got in motion,
the crew was being told off into companies, and the proper

officers put over them. The captain was a brave man, and skillful; the officers supported him nobly, and most of the crew obeyed the voice of discipline. The places of those who faltered were more than made good by volunteers, amid whom the Trapper, Herbert, and the Lad were efficiently prominent. Brave men and braver women were among the passengers, who exerted themselves to still the tumult. The captain himself went into the main saloon on his way to the engineer's room, and addressed the passengers in brave and hopeful words.

He said they were in danger, — that he did not deny; but that he had been in great danger before, and came out all right; that the ship was on fire he admitted; but he stated that the pumps were working well, and if they could not subdue the flames, he hoped to keep them under until he could make harbor.

He told them much depended on themselves. He said, "If you people will only remain quiet; if you will only keep order; if you will only stay where you are, and not risk your lives and overwhelm the crew by rushing on deck; I sincerely believe that with the help of God we shall bring you through; and land every man woman and child in safety."

These words had great effect. The uproar subsided. A remarkable calmness fell on the great throng. Most remained standing, but kept their places. Some seated themselves, and assumed a calmness they did not inwardly feel. Many knelt in prayer, and breathed in silence their petition to the great Being whose hand controls wave and flame alike.

The captain passed on, and entered the engineer's room; counseled a moment with the chief, and then, with three carpenters, began to explore the forward hold of the vessel, to find the location and the extent of the fire. It took but a brief search to discover that the whole forward part of the ship beneath was a mass of flames. The freight was of combustible material, and thoroughly ignited. The captain looked at the dreadful spectacle for an instant, while the lines of his face grew absolutely rigid, and said: —

"My God! The ship is a furnace!"

He stood another instant in profound thought, during which his quick and fearless mind had considered all the contingencies, and without a word to the three men that were with him, he started for the deck and the pilot-house. He summoned the chief engineer and his officers around him, and stated what he had discovered, — laid the whole subject in a few terse words before them, and said: —

"Gentlemen, in five minutes the saloons will be like an oven, and the windows of this pilot-house will be cracking. Have you anything to suggest?"

The first officer, a sailor from boyhood, whose head and beard were already gray, said promptly: —

"Captain, we must beach her." The others looked their assent.

"It's our only course," said the captain. "Pilot," said he, turning to the man whose eye was on the look-out, "can you beach her?" The other deliberated a moment, and said: —

"Captain, I am ready to take any responsibility that a

man in my position should take. I am ready to execute any order you give, but I will not take the responsibility of running this steamer, with six hundred passengers aboard, on to a coast that I know nothing of beyond the knowledge I have of the lights, the reefs, and the harbors. It would be mere chance if I got her within half a mile of the shore."

The captain actually groaned. He saw and admitted the force of the pilot's assertion. For a moment not a word was spoken, while the ship went tearing on through the water, and the premonitions of rising tumult came to their ears from below, showing that the passengers were already on the move. He looked an instant into each face before him, lifted his hand and wiped the great drops of sweat from his forehead, and said : —

"Gentlemen, what shall we do? I feel the floor under my feet heating! The passengers are moving out of the saloon! What we do must be done quickly! We are overloaded! Our boats wouldn't accommodate half, and besides a boat couldn't live in that sea. *What shall we do?*"

Not a man spoke. They felt as if the horror of death were shutting down around them. They were brave, they were calm. They showed no evidence of fear. They could meet death as men should meet it; but they could not tell how to escape it. Suddenly the captain's face lighted, with a light which was the reflection of a hope, of a conjecture, of a possibility. He darted out of the pilot-house, swung himself down among the crew, who were busy with the pumps and the hose, and shouted, with a concentration of voice that penetrated the roar of the storm like a knife : —

"*Is there a man here who knows this coast ?*"

When the captain dropped among them the men stopped their work and stood staring at him. Only the Old Trapper and Herbert, each of whom stood above the forward hatch, hose in hand, directing the streams that the pumps sent through the swelling tubes downward, kept their position. The captain waited a moment, while the light faded from his countenance as no response came, and then, as if in very despair, he shouted : —

"*Is there a man here who knows this coast ?*"

Again no reply came, and he was upon the point of turning away, when the Lad, who had been kneeling under the protection of the bulwark, trying to stop a rent which the pressure had made in the hose that the Old Trapper was tending, rose out of the shadow and approaching the captain, said : —

" Yes sir. I know the coast."

" Who are you," said the captain, " that claim such knowledge ? Are you not the youth I saw with the old hunter at the table to-night ? How should you, born in the interior, know anything about this coast ? "

" I was not born in the woods," responded the Lad, " I was born within ten miles of where we are, and I know every rock and reef and point, for I have fished on them all; and I know every beach, for I used to play on them when a boy."

The captain looked incredulous. He had associated him with the hunter and the wilderness, and it seemed incredi-

ble that he should have been born where he said he was
born, and that he should be on that boat that night, and be
discovered by the merest accident at the very instant of
supreme peril.

"Cap'n," said the Old Trapper, who had drawn nigh,
"cap'n, whatever the Lad says ye can sartinly take for gos-
pel truth. And if he says he was born here, he was born
here; and if he says he knows this shore, he does know it;
and ye can rely on him to do what he says he can do; for
his words be truth, and his acts be like his words."

"Young man," said the captain, "have you any other
friend on board beside this hunter?"

"Sartin he has," said the old man, answering the question for the Lad, "there be Henry there, who has boated
with him and camped with him off and on, and the Lad
saved his life once, and that's a sarvice that a man isn't apt
to forgit. Yis, you may set it down, cap'n, that Henry and
me be the Lad's friends."

"Call him here," said the captain, hoarsely, "and then follow me to the pilot-house."

It was with the greatest effort that the four were able to
reach the point designated, for the gale was blowing with
increased violence, and the iron rod, and the ropes they
grasped to steady themselves, were already hot; and even
as they reached the upper deck the flames broke fiercely
out from the hatchways and the fire began to run in wavering lines along the inner timbers of the bulwarks and the
ornamental edgings of the upper deck.

"I have called you here," said the captain, "to ask you

in the presence of my officers if there is any safe spot, any
cove or bay into which the steamer can be run along the
coast abreast of us."

" Do you mean to beach her, captain ? " asked the Lad.

"Yes," he responded, " it is our only chance. We must
beach her. Can you do it ?"

" I can," said the Lad, simply.

" *You can !* " exclaimed the captain, "do you mean to say,
young man, that you can beach this steamer ? Gentlemen,"
he continued, as he turned to his officers, "if this young
man can do what he says, every soul can be saved."

" I can do just what I tell you I can do," said the Lad,
" that is if the engines work, and we can fetch her around
in this sea, and the flames don't get ahead of us ; for there is
a little bay, nearly abreast of us, and the water is deep in
it, and the beach is free from rocks and stones, and I can
tell the pilot just where to steer to get into it."

" But," said the captain, and he spoke with hurried utterance, as one who feels there isn't a moment to lose, "you
ought to know, and your friends here ought to know, the
danger you run, for the flames will break out in a few moments. You can hear them roaring under deck already.
The flames will break out in a moment, I say ; this pilot-
house will be on fire, and he who stands beside it will stand
in the center of flames, and it will be through God's mercy
if he comes out with his life. I feel it to be my solemn
duty to state these things to you, young man, and in the
presence of your friends who are interested in your life.
Now, knowing your danger, knowing that you will probably

lose your life, I ask you again, will you pilot this steamer to that beach? There are six hundred souls on board, and if you do it you will be their saviour. Will you do it?"

The Lad's face never changed a muscle. The light in his eyes may possibly have darkened a little, and the Old Trapper noted that his long, awkward fingers shut into their palms with a slightly tightened grip, but his voice was quiet as ever, as he said: —

"I will help you beach her, captain."

The captain hesitated yet a moment. He knew himself that the Lad was going to his death, — going with a quietness that could have only ignorance or finest heroism for its cause. It was not to be wondered at, that, accepting as he was the sacrifice of a life, he was touched. He gazed at the singular being before him, observed the simple guilelessness of his countenance, and, dashing a tear from his eye, he turned to the Trapper and said: —

"Old man, this boy is your companion, and you love him?"

"Yis, the Lad and me have slept together, and we've eaten from the same bark, and he and me has done leetle services for each other that men in the woods don't forgit, and I guess ye're about right, cap'n, when ye say that I love the Lad."

"God forbid!" exclaimed the captain, "God forbid that I take the responsibility of the sacrifice, — for that's just what it is, old man. Ought the boy to stay?"

"Sartin, sartin," said the Trapper; "if the Lad can save the wimmen-folks and the leetle uns, not to speak of the men, by stayin' here, then he sartinly ought to stay even if he starts on his last trail from the deck of a vessel instead of from the shadow of the pine; for death never comes too quick to one who meets it at the post of duty, and it never comes slow enough to one who shirks. Yis, let the lad stay where he is, and an old man who has faced death on many a field where bullets was thick, will stand by his side, and the Lord of Marcy shall do with us as he will. I should liked to have seed the pups agin; but the Lord will take care of the dogs."

While this conversation had been carried on, the officers of the steamer had made the arrangements necessary to steer the craft from the stern; for the pilot-house was already so hot as to make it unsafe for the four men stationed at the wheel to remain in it longer. The ropes and blocks had been adjusted, the purchase tested, and the steamer was already being directed from behind. The captain still stood by the side of the Lad, trumpet in hand, ready to give the orders to veer her round.

"Young man," said the captain, "you are pilot now. When shall we swing her about? It's a rough sea; but the flames give us no choice."

The Lad looked steadfastly a moment at the beacon they had passed, asked the captain a question as to her course, and then said: —

"We are passing the cove! We mustn't go a rod farther! Quick! Swing her round!"

The captain lifted the trumpet to his lips, and in tones that rang strong and clear above the roar of the storm and of the flame, shouted, "Hard a-port with your helm! Hard a-port, I tell you! Jam her down for your lives!"

The men in control of the helm obeyed with an energy born of the peril of the moment. The mighty fabric swayed for a moment, but tore on as if unwilling to yield. But the next instant the immense pressure of the helm hard a-port began to tell, and the monstrous bulk swung slowly about, rolled downward into the trough of the sea as if she would never rise, reeled over as she met the mighty wave square amid-ship till her larboard rail lay deep in the hissing water, struggled up, righted herself laboriously; and as she straightened her course with the gale square astern, and with her steam gauge standing at seventy-five, shot toward the shore like an arrow from the bow.

"Cap'n," said the Trapper, as he lowered the trumpet from his lips, "give us the instrerment, and do ye run back there and keep the poor creeturs from throwin' themselves overboard, — for they be gittin' wild. I can talk through the horn as well as ye can, — and the Lad will tell me the words."

"I can't leave you, old man; it shall never be said that Charles Stearns left two brave men to die while he saved his own life."

"Cap'n," returned the Trapper, "I know yer feelin's; for I see the stuff ye be made of; but the Lord appints duty unto man, and it's not of his choosin'; and it's yer duty to go, and ourn to stay. Don't ye worry about us, for I be old and a few days more or less on the arth don't matter, and I can see by the look in the Lad's face that he be ready. So give mo the horn and you go where you oughter go, and we'll stay where wo oughter stay."

The old man had uttered these words with such solemn majesty, and tho truth they expressed was so evident, that tho captain did as commanded. Ho passed the trumpet to the Trapper and started aft, where his presence and words soon communicated new hope to tho terrified throng. In a few moments tho shouting and screaming ceased, and not a sound was heard save tho roar of tho wind and tho waves and the flames.

"Henry," said the Trapper, "it's time ye be goin', for tho fire is gittin' hot. It's not likely that me and tho Lad will come out of this; and there sartinly isn't much time for leave-takin'. Ye'll go, I know, and get tho pups, and tho rifle, and tho fiddle. Ye know where they be. And if there be any other things in tho shanty ye would like, remember they aro yourn. This sartinly isn't tho way I thought things would eend; but tho Lord knows when to call, and I daresay it's best as it is. So, boy, jest take my hand a minit'. Ye needn't disturb tho Lad, for ho is busy. No, jest give me yer hand for a minit', and then go. Ye be faithful and true, and may yer days be happy and yer life long on the 'arth.

"I am not going, John Norton," said tho young man.

"It bo well said, boy," returned tho Trapper. "Yis, it bo well said; or would be if things was different. But things bo as they be, and ye must go."

"I shall not go," said Herbert.

"Henry!" exclaimed tho old man earnestly, "this is downright foolishness. Ye can't help us by stayin'; and two'll bo enough if wust comes to wust."

"John Norton," returned the young man solemnly, "say no more. I shall stay with you and the Lad. If we live, all will live. If we die, we will die together, for I will not leave you."

"Be it as ye say then, boy; yis, let it be as ye say. This is no time for words; and I can understand yer feelin's; and it may be ye be right. The Lad and we met at the pond of the beavers, and it may be best we both go with him to the eend of the trail."

In a moment the old man said, suddenly: "Henry, if ye could git one of them water-pipes, and the pumps are still a-goin', it may be ye could save our lives. But be careful where ye go, boy, for it's hot there ahead."

Lightning is scarce quicker than was the motion of Herbert, as he darted forward into the smoke, which was rolling up in great volumes from the front part of the boat.

By this time the forward half of the vessel was almost one sheet of flame.

A column of fire rose out of the forward hatch fifty feet into the air, but was mercifully blown onward by the force of the gale. From this the Trapper and the Lad were at least safe, but the flames were now breaking over all restraint. The deck itself was being burnt through and sections were falling into the hold. The stanchions and timbers of the bulwarks were already in full blaze. The outer edges of the upper deck were girdled with fire. The roof of the pilot-house had begun to kindle. The flames were already eating their way toward the stern and would soon be in the rear of the two men who were standing half hid-

den in smoke at a point which would then be the very center of the conflagration. But they never flinched. They
stood in the exact position where they were when Henry
left them; the Trapper still holding the trumpet in his hand,
and the Lad still gazing steadfastly ahead.

"Tell them to port two points," said the Lad quietly.

The old man placed the trumpet to his lips and through
the brazen tube his voice poured steady and strong : —

"The boy says 'Tell 'em to port two p'ints."

The vessel swayed suddenly to port; and as she leapt
away the Lad said : —

"Tell them to hold her steady as she is."

Again the old man lifted the trumpet and called : —

"The boy says 'tell them to hold her steady as she is.'"

For a minute not a word was spoken. The steamer tore
on through the gloom, lighting her path with her flames.
The roof of the pilot-house dropped in, and the smoke and
cinders hid the two men from the sight of those who, with
prayers on their lips and agonized faces, were gazing at them
from behind.

Suddenly out of the smoke and the fire came the tones
of the trumpet : —

"The Lad says ' *tell 'em I hear the surf on the beach.'* "

Then the smoke suddenly lifted, split by a gust that tore
through the air, and those behind saw three men instead oi
two standing on the deck. The Trapper and the Lad still
at their station, and thirty feet farther aft, Herbert, hose in
hand flooding with water the blazing deck on which they
stood. But what could the power of man do against the,

rush of such flames? The young man did his best. With hands blistered by the awful heat he stood heroically at his post; but the garments of the Lad were on fire, and the hair of the Trapper was burnt to the scalp.

Suddenly the starboard half of the upper deck fell with a crash. As it fell those behind saw the Lad turn to the Trapper,— saw him totter — saw him steady himself — saw his companion catch him by the arm — saw the old hero, with the sleeve of his coat, that was itself smoking, wipe the cinders from his lips as he lifted the trumpet to his mouth; and out of the black, eddying smoke as it swept over the three and hid them from sight, bellowed the words strong as trumpet could send them : —

"The Lad says 'tell them *I see the surf on the beach ! Hold her steady as she is ! God*" —

The sentence was never completed. The flat bottom of the vessel touched the sand — slid along it — and was driven by the momentum of her movement half her length up the beach. Then she rolled over with a great lurch; her smoke-stacks went down with a crash, carrying the upper deck on which they stood with them, and the three men sank from sight in the smoke and fire.

CHAPTER VII.

THE LAD GOES HOME.

"With mast, and helm, and pennon fair,
  That well had borne their part —
But the noblest thing that perished there
  Was that young, faithful heart!"

— *Mrs. Hemans.*

IT was evening of the second day after the catastrophe. Only a few of the passengers had been lost, and the majority of those who were saved had gone on their several ways; but nearly a hundred still tarried, finding accommodation in the farm houses along the shore and in the adjoining village. The noblest of motives held them to the neighborhood, for he who had saved them was dying.

In a house that stood fifty rods from the wreck, lay the Lad stretched on a bed. His body was in a pitiable condition; for the flesh of it in spots was burnt to the bone. With him was the Trapper and Herbert. The head of the former was bandaged, and the hands of the latter were packed. They had been saved by the merest accident; if that which gives or takes life can be so called. As the smoke-stacks fell when the vessel struck the beach, the section of the upper deck on which they were standing had been thrown upward and outward; and the three had been actually cast with the burning fragments upon the sand.

The Trapper and Herbert, although at first stunned, had been able to drag themselves and the Lad, who was insensible, from the neighborhood of the flames. They speedily recovered their strength; but the Lad did not revive. He still breathed; but the life within his poor body held but a feeble hold, and at every breath it drew seemed on the point of taking its final departure. His senses wandered, as if the faculties of his mind shared the misfortune of his mortal frame. All that skill could do had been done. But human skill was powerless to arrest the flight of his spirit from a tenement which had been so rudely assaulted that it could no longer furnish the life that had tabernacled in it with the accommodation it needed. The most that the attendant physician could offer in the way of comfort to the two men, who with stricken hearts watched by the bedside, was contained in the assurance that he was wholly free from suffering; and would probably revive, and enjoy the use of his senses for a brief period before he passed away. In hope of this, rather than from any expectation that he would recover, his two companions kept their steady vigil by his bed.

It was evening, and outside the house nature displayed the quiet and solemn splendor of an autumnal night. The full-orbed moon hung in the eastern sky, and her mellow radiance bathed the rippling surface of the shining sea in floods of glistening sheen. The light waves broke in measured murmurs on the silent shore. In the blue sky were the pale stars, and the moon's splendor lay softly on the white sands, and the rocks, the trees, the fences, and the aftermath of the frosty fields. Surely nature is unconscious of human suffering; or else has in her frame something of that universal consciousness which knows that out of the troubles of life the anxious and the suffering pass at length into eternal peace.

Inside the house lay the Lad, — his head, which fortunately had not been touched by the fire, supported by a pillow scarce whiter than his face, his limbs straightened as if in repose, and his long, awkward-looking hands crossed restfully on his breast, in which the pulse of life beat faintly. Herbert stood at the foot of the bed, and the Trapper sat at its side. Further away stood the physician, and the captain of the steamer, who had shared with an equal constancy the watch of those whose eyes scarcely wandered from the face of the unfortunate boy. Thus in silence the four stood, waiting for the change which they hoped and prayed might come; that out of it they might receive strength to speak with calmness the last farewell.

Suddenly the Lad's lips opened, though his eyes still remained closed, and he murmured, " Crazy John said my grave should be with a grave." And a look almost like that of smiles came to his features as he repeated, " My grave should be *with* a grave."

It was the first time he had spoken, even in his wanderings, for hours; and the Old Trapper and Herbert exchanged glances, while the physician and the captain drew nearer to the bed. In a moment his lips parted again, and he said — while the smile on his features gave place to a look of pain : —

"Why do they all laugh at me? Everybody laughs at me but mother and John Norton and Herbert. Father used to laugh at me; but John Norton never laughed at me. He and Herbert only laughed at me once. They laughed at me at the pond of the beavers. Where is the pond of the beavers? Let me see,—let me see,—it is so thick with smoke that I can't see the pond of the beavers. Mother, did you tell them, when they laughed at me at the pond of the beavers, that they musn't laugh any more at me?"

Here he stopped, while the men looking on held their breath, and not a sound was heard but the tick, tick, tick of the little clock that stood on the mantle. It may have been five minutes that the silence lasted; and then he murmured again:—

"The captain said that there are six hundred souls to be saved. Let me see—how many are six hundred souls?— Mother, can't you tell me how many six hundred souls are? — Are they so many as that! — I think I ought to be willing to die if I can save six hundred souls,—don't you, mother?" And then his speech sank until it became inarticulate, only now and then as they watched his moving lips they caught the words, "six hundred — six hundred — *souls.*"

Again a long silence ensued; but after a while he said, while a look of firmness came into his face, "How hot it is! — I didn't think fire could burn so;—but I musn't show it—no, I mustn't show it." And his fingers tightened on the coverlid as if he were making an heroic effort at self control.

And so his mind wandered,—wandered back to his boyhood; wandered back to the life he lived with his mother. And then he talked of the woods; talked about his traps; talked of the life he had lived with the Trapper; talked about Herbert, and wondered if he would ever come. And so in a wild, senseless, touching way his mind wandered over the past, and his tongue, unconscious of its speech, rehearsed the fragments of his experiences. Then he fell into a sleep deep and heavy. His breathings were regular and strong. He slept for an hour as a weary man sleeps after toil. And the physician said : —

" When he wakes he will wake with his senses, if he wake at all."

And thus they stood and watched him with faces that showed their anxiety. Watched and waited ; — watched and had their reward. For suddenly he moved uneasily; drew a long breath ; opened his eyes; looked at the Trapper and at Herbert. And as his eyes came back to the countenance of the old man who sat by his side, he smiled, and said : —

" John Norton ! Henry ! "

" Yis," said the Trapper ; " yis, Lad, me and Henry be here." He said no more, for as he said it he choked ; and the sentence ended with a sob.

For a minute the Lad made no reply. He gazed into the faces of the Trapper and Henry with a look of unutterable love, — a look that took the place of speech, and did what words could not do ; for it expressed to the two men that saw it the depth of his affection for them.

"How many were saved?" said the Lad.

The captain took a step forward, and said : "Nearly all, boy; nearly all. You saved them nearly all." And the features of the great, strong man convulsed, and the tears broke from his eyes.

"Lad," said the Trapper, after a moment's pause, during which he had regained his composure, "there be something that must be said, and it may be best that I say it now, for the minits be passin' and perhaps ye may have somthin' to tell us. Lad," and here he faltered a moment, "Lad, ye have come to the eend of the trail and yer feet be on the edge of the Great Clearin'."

"Do you mean I am dying, John Norton?" said the Lad.

"That's what men call it, boy,—that's sartinly what men call it. Yis, the doctor here says ye be dyin'."

For a moment the youth fixed his gaze on the ceiling as one might who is lost in reflection, and then his eyes fell until they rested on the countenance of the Trapper, and he said, in his own simple manner : —

"I am not afraid to die, John Norton."

"I know no reason why ye should be, Lad. I've thought the matter over from beginnin' to eend sence I sot by the bed here, and I sartinly know no reason why ye should be, for ye have done no evil on the 'arth and yer sperit is innocent; and if ye had been faulty the Lord would remember the deed ye have did and jedge ye in marcy."

Again he paused a moment and then the old man said, tenderly : —

"Is there anythin' ye would tell us, Lad? — anything ye

would like done, ye know, for it be the duty of the livin' to
sarve the dead, and Henry and me be here, and our ears be
open to yer words."

"Are any of my folks living here now, John Norton?"
asked the Lad.

"No, yer folks be not here, boy; they moved away years
ago, and no one knows where they went. No, boy, not one
of yer kindred be here."

"'Tis well," said the Lad, "mother's grave is here, that is
enough. You will find it to the left of the big pine that
stands in the south-east corner of the graveyard. I told you
the name, you know. You will lay my body there, John
Norton."

"It shall be done as ye say," returned the Trapper.

The Lad remained silent a moment, engaged in thought,
and then he said, "I want you to take the rifle, John Norton, and Sport, for they will be of some service to you."

"Yis, the dog will be of sarvice, for sartin, for he's stanch
and his nose is a good 'un, and Rover is gittin' on in years,
and can't, in the natur' of things, hold out much longer.
I've noted that he lagged this fall in the races. Yis, I would
like the dog, and he will be a great comfort to me, boy,
after ye are gone, for the cabin will seem empty next winter. The thoughts of the old be apt to be lonely, and the
presence of the dog will shorten the evenings and make
the shanty more homelike. But as for the rifle, which is
but leetle better than a miser'ble gun, sence it loads at the
wrong eend, and has a mind of its own about goin' off,—so
that while I'll allow it has a long range and shoots where

ye hold it, yit it can't be depended on, as ye know, boy, and is of no use to a hunter like me whose ranges be short and and will git shorter as my eyes grow dim. But on the target ground of the settlements, which Henry has told us about, where they shoot furder than a man can see, the gun is a good un; Henry thinks one of the best, if not the best, ever made. And so, Lad, while I don't want to argue agin yer wishes or seem ongrateful, yit in the natur' of things it sartinly looks as if I had better have the dog and Henry the gun."

"I think you are right, John Norton," said the Lad, in a feeble but pleased tone, "you are always right. Yes, Henry, you take the rifle I won at the match, and I know you will win many prizes with it, and when you use it on the match-ground, and the people are all standing round, and the rich and the great looking on, as you told us, you must think of me, for you will never know how much I love you. Mother first, John Norton next, and then you. Yes, that's the way it has been. Mother first, John Norton next, and then you."

"I will take the rifle and keep it, Lad, as your gift to me," Herbert said; "the gift of a man who saved my life, and who has taught me the beauty of innocence and the wisdom of a pure mind, as man never taught me before." And he looked at the Lad's sweet face with eyes blinded with tears.

"I don't think that you could ever have learned anything from me, Henry," responded the Lad; "for you are learned and I am ignorant. John Norton is wise and I am foolish.

And they all used to tell me I didn't know much; and I know they were right, for I never was cunning as the other boys; and I had a hard time to learn even to read. But mother told me I could learn if I tried hard enough, and I did try real hard. And in two years I could read the Testament through without making a single mistake; and I remember how pleased mother was when I did it."

"Lad," said the Trapper, gravely, "I've lived beyond the limits of man's days, and I've seed many of the wise and the great of the 'arth, and many that was foolish, and my eyes have been open to what they have seed; and I've noted that some larn from books, and some larn from natur', and some know without larnin'. Yis, some make themselves wise by readin' and seein' and thinkin'. And others be born wise; for they know good from evil, and they strike the trail right every time, and from cradle to grave never lose the line of the blazin'. But there aint many of this kind; no, there be but few that are born wise; but ye was one of 'em. Yis, Lad, ye was sartinly one of 'em; for the Lord gin ye somethin' better than the knowin' head and the cunnin' tongue; for he gave ye a heart to love right and to hate wrong, and he made ye marciful to them that do evil and treated ye onkindly; and he gin ye courage to die like a chief without tremblin' or talkin' when the time he had sot for yer death-hour had come. And more than all of the wise and the great I have known, Lad, I think ye was favored by yer Maker."

The Old Trapper had said this with the decision and majesty of a man who speaks from deliberation, and is expressing the judgment of a mind which, naturally able, had received and been profited by the lessons of a long and varied experience. A moment after he had paused the Lad said:

"There is something else I want to speak about, John Norton."

"Yis," returned the Trapper, "I know there be somethin' else. What do you wish done with it? Speak the word boy, and it shall be done as ye say, whatever be the orders or however fur yer arrand takes me."

The Lad looked at the Trapper and made a slight motion of his wrist toward him; and then he looked at Henry and made the same motion.

"Which?" said the Trapper.

"Both," replied the Lad, softly.

Both knew what he meant. Both knew how he loved it. Both knew what a testimony he was giving them of the depth of his affection, in thus making them joint heirs and custodians of that which had been to him what the harp was to the dumb angel: the source of joy inexpressible, the one precious medium through which that in him in which he was superior to others might pour itself forth with such volume of evidence that none could dispute, and which being admitted gave him at once rank and precedence among men.

"It is well settled, Lad," slowly and solemnly answered the Trapper, after his mind had canvassed the matter a moment. "Yis, it is well settled. It shall stay in the cabin till I go; then Henry shall take it; and when he comes on and jines us, he shall do with it what seems best in his jedgment. Is that as it should be, Lad? Is that what ye mean?"

"Yes," said the Lad, feebly; "that is the way I wish it to be. That is what I mean."

Here the conversation ended, for the Lad had grown feebler as it progressed, and the last words had been spoken scarcely above a whisper. He had disposed of his earthly possessions. The things that he loved he had given to the two men he loved, and as if he was conscious that he had done with the earth his mind retired within itself, and he lay with a look on his face that showed he still had the use of his faculties but through them was communing only with the invisible.

The medical attendant looked significantly at Herbert, and moving within reach of the Trapper, touched him softly on the arm. The old man, whose eyes had not moved from the countenance of the Lad, nodded his head as evidence that he understood the communication. The life that had been peaceful—that had been filled with the peace of innocence—was drawing to a peaceful close. The departure of so simple a spirit from its mortal frame, the rising of so sweet a soul as it left the earth to appear in the presence of its Maker, could not be attended with any sudden or startling manifestation. He opened his eyes only once more; looked for a moment into the face of Herbert, turned them upon the countenance of the Trapper, held them there for an instant as if taking in every feature of the face he had loved so well,—as though he would fix the loved lineaments indelibly on his memory for the long parting, and then he lifted them upward, and while the light of a deep joy darkened in their depths, — the joy of a recognition of some one he had expected to see with too sincere a faith to be surprised at meeting, said, as naturally as a child might say it on the earth : —

"Mother!"

And then the gray film that gathers sooner or later over all mortal orbs formed suddenly over his. And thus without pang or motion his spirit passed away. And there in the farm-house by the sea, near the beach where he played when a boy, and the grave of his mother, "The Man Who Didn't Know Much" lay dead.

SKETCHES.

ADIRONDACK LETTERS.

I.

EN ROUTE.

"Let Hercules himself do what he may,
The cat will mew, and dog will have his day."

Shakespeare.

HERE I am at the half-way house, between Keesville and Martin's, on Lake Saranac, waiting for dinner. You can imagine my feelings, for I am all emptiness, and don't know what has become of myself. Indeed, I feel as if I am only the case in which I once was, but am no more,—I myself having slipped out like a razor from his shell, and been left along the road in little bits at a time for the last fifteen or twenty miles. I am actually hollow. I am like a tin canister with nothing in it, or a pepper box from which the pepper has all been sifted. Outwardly I look just as I did after breakfast at the Van Ness House, in Burlington, at six o'clock this morning; but inwardly I am not the same. I know that I should look as I feel, but I can't. If I did—. Dinner! Hurrah!

It's done. I have eaten! I am full! I feel natural-like I am actually heavier on my legs, perceptibly so, than I was twenty minutes ago. I can turn round and keep my bal-

ance like a top that isn't all point and shank. I can put my
hands on either side of my body and press myself without
fear that they will meet in the middle of me. What a glorious thing corporosity is! I understand now what Hamlet
had in mind when he said to his Father's shade: "Poor
ghost." He pitied it because it hadn't any body. It was
thin, unsubstantial, hollow, as a man who has ridden in a
stage-coach twenty miles over a plank road before dinner.
I know how a ghost feels when he is floating about, light as
a feather, and I feel the fine discrimination shown in Hamlet's remark.

But how glorious is man's estate after he has eaten a good
dinner! What solid dignity he has attained; what a satisfactory sense of substantialness is his; how the blessed feeling of fulness adds to his self-respect; and with what an
unctuous complacency he can regard his fellow men. A full
stomach is the very mother of sweetest charity.

But the dinner, — let me tell you about that; for there is
a great difference in dinners. Some are lean, others are fat.
Some are only tormenting suggestions of what a meal should
be, while others are real, solid, satisfactory. Now, this dinner was a dinner that *was* a dinner. It was not a prophetic
affair, but an actual realization — a fruition of the appetite
— heaven to the stomach. The bell rung, not with a little,
thin, dyspeptic tintillation, but with a hearty, full-toned
sound, as if it appreciated our hunger and was gladly conscious of the benevolence of its summons. It was not a
mere ring. It had a language in its call, and said: "Come
on and eat your fill! come on and eat your fill!" in a deep,

jovial tone, that made you feel that the house was full of food from cellar to attic. Such a summons always starts me. To me it sounds like the voice of duty, which admits of no refusal. I was at the table in an instant.

I slid into my chair as quick as an otter slides into a creek. The serving girl was at my elbow in a wink. She said: —

" Roast-beef-roast-mutton-ham-and-eggs and-trout ! "

I looked at her with my face all beaming, and said: —

" Yes."

She stared at me. I beamed again, and she vanished toward the kitchen with a strange look on her face. But she understood, that girl did. She felt the emphasis of my expression, and began to bring on the food. The roast beef was good, the roast mutton better, the ham and eggs simply delicious. The trout looked a little suspicious — they seemed rather thin and old, as if they had been kept a long time for company, like the politicians' reform principles; — but I took them in — the trout I mean. Then she said: —

" Coffee or tea ? "

I said: —

" Both."

Two cups were brought full of — something. The color of the liquids was identical. It didn't taste like coffee. I tasted the other. It didn't taste like tea or coffee either. I did not like to show my ignorance, but I was compelled to do it. I was for once fairly cornered, and said, looking her mildly in the face: —

" My dear girl, can you tell me which is the tea and which is the cofffce ? "

She looked at the two cups. She lifted one to her nose and smelt of it. Then she lifted the other and smelt of that. Then she lifted both and inspected them critically. Then she put them both down on the table and started to call her mother. She was evidently puzzled. She had probably never had such a question propounded to her before. I felt as I looked at her that it was a question beyond her years. I said : —

"Never mind, don't feel badly over it. When you get older you will know more, or perhaps you can have the cups marked, so there can be no mistake." She smiled — a smile that began at the corner of her mouth, crept round the curve of her lips, clomb up a stairway of laughing lines into her eyes, and finally broke in light all over her face. She was happy again, and coming close up to my chair, said interrogatively : —

" Pies ? "

I fairly jumped. She had touched an hereditary weakness. When was there ever a time when one of my name would not eat pie ? I turned around in my chair and exclaimed : —

" Have you *pies* in this house ? "

Her answer electrified me. It came out of her mouth like walnuts out of their shells, when the bough is shaken : —

" Raspberry, blackberry, apple, custard and mince pie." !

I looked at her as at one who should bring news of the millennium, —

" Bring them on ! " I shouted, " bring them all on ! "

Five kinds of pie all before me at once, and each better than the other — when have I seen such a sight? Those pies came but they never returned. Oh! the pleasure of eating one piece and then seeing four more pieces left untouched! Never have I had such a feast since, when a youngster, I used to steal a whole mince pie from mother's cupboard and go out back of the barn and eat it alone, washing it down with plenty of watermelon. Things taste differently now-a-days.

At the close of the meal there was a novel entertainment introduced, gratis. I had finished the fourth piece of pie, and was just engaged with the fifth, when I heard a hoarse rasping noise, as if a heavy bag was being drawn across the floor, and looking up discovered the cause. In the middle of the doorway stood a cat, — a maternal cat, — who had spied my black pointer, "Jet," who stood at my elbow watching me eat and expectantly awaiting her turn, with no murderous designs on cat or kittens at all. But the feline temperament is suspicious and wrathful; and this cat was a termagent anyhow, born under some evil star, and bent on having a row. Now, to my mind there is always a terrible fascination in the process of preparation which a cat goes through preliminary to a combat. There is such a deliberate spitefulness about it; such a murderous malignity of design as it passes from one phase of expression to another, that it is impossible to withdraw your eyes from the creature as she passes through her spasms. Now, this cat was no exception to her tribe. Her mannerism was perfect after its kind. When I first looked up she stood in the doorway with a suggestive curve in her back and a slightly swollen appearance about her tail. She stood and swelled. The curve in her back grew and grew. Her tail bulged until it was enormous. Her eyes blazed hotter and hotter. Her mouth opened wider and wider, and out of it came a succession of noises that were simply frightful. How that cat could keep anything inside of her and spit in that way was a marvel.

Of course Jet had not been an unmindful spectator of the scene. She had been interviewed before in this style, and knew what was coming. Her hair ridged up on her back; her tail stiffened straight as an iron ramrod; and her lips tightened over her white teeth. Any cat that was at all sensible would have left such a dog alone. But this feline had no caution at all. And when she left the doorway, and began to sidle across the floor toward Jet, I knew if things kept on much longer, the " peace of Europe would be disturbed." I was just lifting myself from my chair, or getting my legs out from under the table so I could lift myself from the chair, when that cat went into the air like a flash, and exploded in a series of the most unearthly noises over Jet's back. Of course, no decent dog would stand any such conduct as that, and Jet didn't. Now you understand this was a suddenly improvised affair; I had no programme to go by, and didn't understand at all where the different parts came in; and besides the actors did not seem to require any special prompting, and evidently needed all the room to themselves. So, feeling that I wasn't needed, and might actually be in the way if I remained, I retired out through the window to the piazza, where I could contemplate the development of the action from a back seat, as it were. Of one thing I am certain: I have never, in city or country, seen a more intense performance. It was the very climax of high tragedy. The actors were up to their best key, and going it strong. I saw that the thing was drawing to a fine point. Either I shouldn't have any dog in a few minutes, or the man wouldn't have any cat to speak of. One of the two things was certain. At that instant the door burst open, and the man himself, with a broom in his hand, burst into the room, and began to lay about him right and left. But this only stirred Jet up tremendously. The cat and the broom together brought out her best points. The way she went after that cat, under the table, between the man's legs, back of the stove, was indescribable. But the actors were not all on the stage yet. For again the door burst open, and a woman, without hoops on, and with a washboard in her hand, shot into the apartment with a look of interrogation on her countenance frightful to see. She didn't stand still more than a second, for Jet came against her in a way that sent her spinning. This was too much. I dropped on the piazza, rolled off upon the ground, dug my fingers into the turf, and laughed!

In less than four seconds, I saw a cat come out through the front door, about half way up from the door-sill to the ceiling, followed by a dog in full bolt, with a big broom and a washboard close behind. The cat lit on her feet, of course, and went up a tree in the door-yard faster than any cat has ever done that thing since the beginning of the world. I clucked to Jet, and sloped around the corner of the house, and streaked it through the garden down back of the barn, where I laid myself down on the grass again, and rolled over and over, wiping the tears from my eyes.

This is all, this time. My pencil is worn down to the last inch, and I must stop. If I ever get to "Martin's," I will tell you what I see. But I think I shall spend this vacation traveling round with Jet, and stopping at country hotels, where there are plenty of cats. I have an idea that such a course would yield me a great deal of innocent fun such as even a deacon couldn't object to.

"IT WAS THE VERY CLIMAX OF HIGH TRAGEDY."   Page 442.

CROSSING A CARRY IN THE DARK.

"Sport, that wrinkled care derides,
  And laughter, holding both his sides." — *Milton.*

" WELL," said I to my companion, "shall we go up or go down ?"

We were at the mouth of Bog River, where it pours noisily into the outlet of Little Tupper, — wet, hungry, and tired. The sun had disappeared behind the pines that crested the mountains to the west, and a bluish dusk was darkening in the air. The rapids back of us were fretting hoarsely in the growing gloom of balsam-bearing banks, while below the water lay level and motionless, save where some tiny fish broke the smooth surface, or a king-fisher stilled his harsh chattering by a noisy plunge after his prey. If we went "down," two miles of easy boating would bring us to Big Tupper, and to the delightful camp-ground on Breezy Point, where we had slept the night before, and where we knew the droning pines would give our weary bodies drowsy welcome. If we went "up," there were eight miles of river and lake boating, and two miles of "carrying," before we could reach "Robbins," on Little Tupper. The one camp-ground was within thirty minutes of us, the other four hours of good sharp work away, and it was sunset, and we were dripping; but, in spite of this, the vote was unanimous to go " up." The work would keep us warm, and the moon was at the full, and Little Tupper for quiet, peaceful beauty and happy memories, to us is next door to heaven. And so we started " up."

We reached the first " carry " before the daylight had wholly faded out; crossed it with hurrying steps, and launched again upon the easy flowing stream. By this time the red in the west had faded into gray. The sky above was a dusky blue, lit into splendor here and there by a small, diamond-like star, that shone with quick, pointed brilliancy. A wavy fleece lay on the still stretches of the river, and the drip of the balsam thickets as their gummy stems yielded forth their liquid odors, could be heard on either bank. To say that it was still, is no description. Even the silence seemed to listen. Night, robed only in thinnest darkness, stood on the mountains, — shy, timid, breathless, as if she feared the Day would suddenly rush back and devour her with his fierce rays. The air was sweet with her breathings. Cedar and pine, balsam and meadow-grass, lily and wild rose, mingled their fragrance in the damp air.

Up through that paradise of odor we slowly passed. Up through the fragrant darkness, with careful paddles at bow and stern, we felt our way, until, half by sight and half by instinct, we recognized the second carry, and ran our boat with easy motion shoreward. The carry is a mile and a half wide, and heavily timbered, but well cut out, and although very uneven, not difficult to traverse in the day.

Now, crossing a carry by daylight is one thing, and crossing it in the night-time altogether another. We had some

fun in crossing this carry that night of which the world will
never know, — fun all to ourselves, and of such a kind as
makes a man sit down and laugh three or four minutes in
one spot. We walked up against two or three trees that
night, and put our arms around them in the most affectionate manner. We found that our nose was in front of our
face twice, — an unnecessary distance in front of our face,
as it seemed to us. We stepped into several holes that
made us cross our legs with a snap, and lurch backward
and forward, as if we had been cut half in two above the
hips, and had lost all our " connections." Once we stopped
suddenly on a slippery stick, in a mudhole, and began to
bow to an imaginary person in the most silly fashion. The
salutations we gave that invisible presence were as profound
as the salaams of a desert Arab. We bowed with emphasis.
We bowed with determination. We bowed with a snap in
the recovery that nearly broke our neck. Oh, we had fun
on the carry that night! — fun that converted our eyes into
springs of happy water, and made our very ribs ache in
laughter. The fact is, the funniest laughter is the laughter
that one has alone. It is very well to laugh in company,
for custom and benevolence alike demand it; but, for the
most part, company laughter is forced. It is a made-up,
artificial thing, or else too slight and decorous to be hearty
and adequate. But when the spirit of fun gets into one
when all alone by himself to such an extent as to fairly possess him, and he sits down and puts his hands against his
sides, and opens his mouth, and begins to sway backward
and forward, until his eyes rain with mirth, and he fairly

wrestles inwardly with his hilarity, then his laughter is the genuine thing. Well, we laughed after this Adamite fashion several times on that carry; laughed so that the solemn old pines fairly danced before us; and Silence, tickled out of her gravity, shouted, "Ha-ha!" and roared, "Ho-ho-o-o-oh!" The fairies, that the legend says sleep in the pines, and from amid their sombre branches moan in sympathy for human woe, must have puckered their tiny faces for once, and screwed their little lips into decorum only by the greatest effort, as they saw the great big human underneath laughing the great, roaring, rollicking laughter of the "natural man."

At last we reached the farther end of the carry, and passing from under the dark archway of the gloomy trees, emerged into the glorious light of the newly risen moon. Upon the white beach of Round Lake we stood a moment to contemplate the scene. The winds were asleep. Not a stray puff skirted the shore, or put the imprint of its tran-sient pressure on the water; the lake lay level and smooth, while the moon poured its beams in even radiance upon its surface, which glinted them back as if it were a great glass mirror. Along the shores, and in the recesses of the bays, Night lay in ambush, watching with lowering brow and gloomy eyes the triumph of the skies. The very firmament seemed to be endued with sense, and to be tranquilly happy as it beheld the peacefulness of the earth. From out its lofty and unvexed composure it looked with sweet complacence down at the heaven of peace which lay defined by its own light tranquilly beneath it. Whatever severance may have come between God and man, I said to myself, the harmony of the old connection between Heaven and Nature, at least, has never been lost.

We pushed our boat out into the yielding water and easily, as those who would not hurry from what is rarely found, passed, with a motion that opened a wedge-like wake through the smooth water into the white light, heading straight toward the field of snow-white lilies, which, by their fragrance, bar the entrance of evil spirits into Little Tupper. In the city, we buy a single lily and rejoice, or if in strolling on a lake shore we find a dozen grouped, we cry out with delight. But here, before me, as I floated through the moonlight, were acres of lilies, in full bloom: yea, miles of them, making the white moonlight still whiter, and yielding forth their perfume to the air, as love yields to love, lavishly. In a few moments we came to them and our boat cleft its way through the clustering globes, that grew only the sweeter at the disturbance. We did not hurry — who would, in such a place and at such an hour? Many a time, in passed years, had we floated across that perfumed field, and as between the fragrance of the lilies to the senses, and the memories of the years to the soul, it was hard to say which were the sweeter. For there is nothing finer in nature than men can make to their souls, if they but love right things and do right deeds. Love is more fragrant and innocence whiter than even the lily may be.

As we swung around the sharp curve that marks the entrance into Little Tupper, a breeze, that had been startled out of its slumber by some vagrant echo, wandering care-

lessly in the air, came bustling down the lake, and striking
coldly against our wet garments, chilled us to the bone. It
is astonishing how loose a man's teeth will get on these
northern lakes, when a current of cold air strikes against
him when his clothes are as wet as his paddle staff, and the
vital force has been drained out of him by fourteen hours
of backing and boating. I had not been two minutes in
that cold current before I had more teeth in my mouth, and
more mouth around the teeth, too, than I knew what to do
with. My upper jaw lost its permanency and my lower jaw
its steadfastness of adjustment, and they hammered against
each other in the most alarming fashion, while the poor
teeth rattled and shook like dried peas in a pod.

There was "Music in the air," and of such a sort as angels
never heard, as we hurried along into that rising current of
cold air; and when we crawled out of the boat at "Robbins," and shook the kinks out of our chilled legs, their stiffened joints fairly snapped, and the cords ridged out as if
the imps of rheumatism had put their fiendish leverage upon
them. We had no "change" with us — we didn't take a
very large wardrobe along on this trip — and when we had
aroused our host our first and most emphatic request was
for "old clothes." Now the resources of the house in this
direction were abundant in quantity, but terribly deficient
in proportion. The garments which fell to my share were
good enough for their proprietor, probably, but they were
evidently cut for a man several years younger than I am.
The pantaloons were two or three stories too short, and the
shirt would have made the Egyptians bow down and wor-

ship. But perseverance conquers all obstacles; and having got myself into the top of those trousers, with the help of my companion, I shook myself down to the bottom of them, and some ways below the bottom of them, too. Indeed, when I fairly got through those breeches I found they were of a Continental cut, and precisely of the fashion our fathers wore a century ago. But the shirt was a mystery. Off from me it looked as a shirt should look, but when I had got it on it looked as no shirt has ever looked for six thousand years. My arms went into and went through the sleeves as a tin peddler goes through a toll-gate, when he is too much hurried by pressure of business to stop and pay the assessment. I never knew what long arms I had until I got into that shirt. There was room for a dozen bracelets below the cuff-buttons, and when I got to bed I felt as if I wanted one bed for my body and another for my arms. But the warmth of those dry, coarse garments! How. the chilled skin glowed under them, and how the shrunken veins swelled again and the cold current flowed with a genial glow. Ah, me! no wonder the old poets sang that "Death is cold but life is warm;" or, that the fire worshippers, amid the Persian roses, dreamed that life came out of the sun, and that the spirit of man was but a spark from a mighty flame, for true it is that the dead are cold and the warm alone are alive. It was after midnight, when, warm and happy, we stretched six feet of comfortable weariness on an easy bed, and with visions of Bog River rapids, dark carries, a moon-lit lake, and a field of white lilies floating dreamingly in our mind, we passed from the world of sense and feeling into that dim land of which we know nothing save that we enter it weary, stay awhile, and come forth refreshed.

III.

CLIMBING WHITE FACE.

"That's a perilous shot." — *Shakespeare.*

"Night's candles are burnt out, and jocund day
Stands tiptoe on the misty mountain tops."

Shakespeare.

WHO ever ascended a mountain, worthy of the name, and did not meet with some laughable experiences? Above all, who ever attempted to cheat nature out of her just dues by riding up a mountain on horseback and was not made to feel her revenge? Now this was precisely what, as a party, we purposed to do. It was five miles from the hotel to the summit of White Face, up two of which the the path or trail, — for it was then a mere trail — was so steep as to compel the pedestrian to crawl at times literally on his hands and knees. The man who cut the trail out had evidently never heard of the beauty of a curved line, for he turned neither to the right hand nor to the left, but having set his nose in a mathematically straight line with the top, conscientiously followed it. Across gulches and over bowlders; down the sides of chasms and up precipitous ledges, steep as a French roof — wherever that inflexible nose pointed, he "went for it." I have often thought what an invaluable piece of property that nose would be-

come should the owner chance to be lost on a western prai-
rie. No danger of his walking in circles with that wonderful projection in front of him. Now, tramping is something
I never admired. I can get along very well tramping down
hill, but when the path begins to run upward, I always get
in and ride. This peculiarity runs all through our family.
When I married I fortunately found a wife of the same dis-
position, only a little more so. The other lady of the party
shared our feelings. So when we were asked whether we
preferred to ride or walk, the decision was charmingly unanimous, — as all family decisions should be. We all voted
one way — to ride.

So we mounted : one lady on a side-saddle, the other *a la*
common sense, which is the way I always ride. I cannot
describe the horses. Mine was not large enough to describe. It might have been different with a shorter man,
but it took me some time after I was mounted to discover
that I was mounted. I finally concluded, on the whole, that
I was, at least as much as I should ever be on that horse.
It was the only time in my life that I could ride or walk at
the same time. I asked the landlord, as I started off, which
pair of legs I was expected to attend to. He pointed out a
very likely pair, and I used them. I got on so well with
them that I brought them home with me, and have kept
them ever since.

For the first half mile I ran. Then I rested, and the
horse ran. Then I let down and took another turn at it.
Then the horse tried it again, and so we kept it up between
us, until we came to a ravine from which the mountain

sloped upward like a roof. By this time I was in good
practice, and ready for almost anything. Up, up we went;
the ladies ahead and nearly out of sight. It was impossible
for the horse and me to spell each other here and so we
both walked — holding each other up by turns. At last we
came to a long, sloping ledge, that rose at a fearful inclination. Directly over this the trail led. A wall of rock, like
the sides of a water-spout, on either hand, made turning
aside impossible. I summoned up all my energies, got the
six feet under me in as good position as I could, and with a
yell calculated to start the carcass of death itself, dashed at
it. Up, up we scrambled. We were twenty feet from the
bottom when the pony, either from exhaustion or pure wil-
fulness, stopped. Of course I stopped too. It was an awkward position. I realized it. Safety lay in the pony's pluck
and power. Never did my affection go out so strongly toward any animal. Never before did I know how much I
could love a horse. I embraced him — putting my arms
entirely around his neck. I exhorted him energetically
with my voice, and a little otherwise. But no argument, no
entreaty, could prevail on that animal to go ahead. On the
other hand, he began to go behind. First one foot gave
way, then another. When he slipped, I slipped. At last
the movement backward began to get lively. If he kept
improving his gait he would land me, as nearly as I could
calculate, at the foot of the mountain in about ten minutes.
The motion had already become so considerable that the
tails of my coat began to stream the wrong way; when, by
a slight deviation from the true line of descent, we came in

contact with a tree. It was a large hemlock of twelve inches in diameter, with a ledge of about ten tons weight back of it. We struck it fair. It held. I involuntarily put my hand to my neck to ascertain if my head had been snapped off. My head was still there. The discovery relieved me. I do not, it is true, know how a man would feel with his head off, but I do know how he feels when he unexpectedly discovers that it is still on.

As I sat meditating on what I should do next, I heard the sound as of some heavy body coming rapidly down the mountain. The next instant it came in sight. It was a horse! Its manner of descent was identical with mine, only considerably more rapid. Being higher up when it started it had had a chance to improve on its gait, and was now making, as I judged, pretty nearly its best time. I can never describe my feelings as I sat and saw that horse coming toward me. It is possible for a brave man to stand and face rifle bullets and cannon balls. There is glory in it if you should get killed, and that thought helps some; but to have a whole horse shot at you at short range is absolutely appalling. But fortune favored me. The animal kept the straight line of descent, and went past without hitting me.

Thankful for my deliverance, and inwardly vowing that I would never attempt to ride up a mountain again, I walked off my horse and toiled my way upward until I reached the Lodge just under the crest, where, in the gathering darkness, I found the ladies safe and sound, and where we passed the night.

Now, if there is a person who has any intention of writing me a letter, begging me to tell him if this *is* a literal, truthful, and orthodox account of our ascent up White Face, I assure him now beforehand that I shall never answer that note, but advise him to go and "ask John!"

Morning dawned. Our feet were on the summit while yet the eastern sky was gray and cold. Anon a warmer hue spread over it. Three gleams of purple shot upward, wavered and waved an instant, then stood in fixed formation. Around their bases a line of carnation appeared, and widened, until it became an arc of rose. The stars above us paled. As if stricken with envy, they sickened and died. Venus alone resisted, and gave up her hold on life as a dolphin, whose colors deepen in death. The fog beneath lay heavy on the valleys, covering with its white folds the lesser mountains. At length the uppermost point of the red orb appeared. A shaft of yellow light ploughed through the upper stratum of the fog as a cannon-ball ploughs through a swarded field, and rent it in twain. It was only the first shaft from a bow that in an instant shot forth a score of flaming arrows. The fog was thick and stubborn; but what might resist the orb appointed of God to lighten the world! The fleece relaxed its hold upon the hills. It surrendered its empire over the valleys. It fled from the still waters of a thousand lakes. It untwined its fingers from the misty pine tops; and, ushered in with glory, God's sweetest gift to man — the holy day of rest came to the world.

To us it was indeed a sabbath in the heavens. The sky was cloudless. Not a scud or patch of fleece in the entire

firmament, — a perfect vault of deepest blue, filled with a
pure, white light. The air was cool, moving in steady current past us. Not a sound was heard, save when an eagle,
swooping upward on his dark pinions, startled at the sight
of human faces a thousand feet above his eyrie, challenged
us with his wild cry, then sailed away. And there for hours
we three sat on the gray rocks, in the deep silence and the
white light, worshiping. Near midday a change occurred.
Beneath us clouds began to form. Over Big Tupper's Lake,
fifty miles to the west, a dark bank gathered. We watched
it rise. We saw a flash cleave it from top to bottom; and,
after a long interval, a heavy boom shook the thin air around
us into vibrations, and the huge bulk beneath us trembled
to the deep jar. It was the signal-gun, ordering an advance. Straight on the cloud came. It marched across the
wilderness as a battery sweeps to the front, in some pinch
of battle, halting ever and anon to deliver a volley. We
saw the shadow on the forest. We saw the flash and blaze.
We heard each successive boom, and felt beneath us the
answering jar. Near and more near it came. It swept
against the mountain on whose crest we stood, as an army
charges a citadel, struck it, and recoiled. But the wild
forces of the wind urged it from behind, seeming to cheer
it on. It pressed to the attack, swept over the outlying
spurs, and wrapped the mountains about on all sides. It
had triumphed. Then did our eyes behold a spectacle rarely
witnessed, even by mountaineers. Five hundred feet below
us hung the cloud. We could look into its black center,
and see the lightnings play. We could hear the crash of

thunder in the gorges far beneath, the dull roar of the gathering torrents, the crush of falling trees as they went down with thump and boom, while above us the sun was shining brightly, and the heavens were cloudless. At last the cloud broke; half swayed to the north, and half to the south: but a black fragment torn off from the main body, and lifted by some rising column of air, rose slowly up, following the gorge on whose brink we stood, until it folded us in its dark vapor. Still rising, until it stood some hundred feet above our heads, the rarefied current died out beneath it, and pausing a moment in the still air, it poured out its myriad drops. The sun smote against the crystal globes, until they gleamed and glowed, and a gorgeous arc grew in the air so nigh that we could put our hands into the crimson tints. "See, see!" said one, "we hold the rainbow in our hands, and we will call this Rainbow Gorge." And the old guide said, "Let it be so called forever."

The hours rolled on; and a Sabbath such as we had never before passed, drew to its close. The sun stooped to its setting; and, standing on the topmost pinnacle, we watched to see the day die out. Never before had our eyes seen, and never again, doubtless, will they behold such a sight. The old guide, whose axe had first blazed a path up its steep side; who, thirty years before, had built him a stone lodge upon its crest, that he might pass his nights upon this mountain, so dearly did he love the charm of its solitude; whose face was as rough and seamed as the gray granite on which he stood, said, as he crouched at our feet, wrapped in his blanket, that never but thrice before had he seen such a sunset. The air was cool and crisp, bearing against us with a steady current from the west. It did not vary. There was no eddy, nor ripple, nor undulation in it. It seemed as if the whole atmosphere had become loosened, and was moving bodily eastward. With what words shall I be able to make you see what we saw? The air was pure and clear as a newly-cut diamond, white and colorless as mountain air always is, — a perfect lens through which with unimpeded eye we saw the marvelous transfiguration from day to night go on. Five thousand feet beneath us, Lake Placid slept, verifying its name. In the south, a hundred mountain peaks were ablaze with the peculiar red sunset light. For a hundred miles the wilderness stretched away, — a deep green sea, across whose surface the sun was casting great fields of crimson. Amid the darker portions eighty patches of gold flashed, representing as many lakes. Eastward the valley of Champlain lay in deep shadow. To the north, bounding the vision like a thread of silver, gleamed the St. Lawrence. In the valley to the south, lay the martyred dust of him who died on a Virginia gallows, that American manhood and American liberty might not perish. The closing moment now had come. The heavens to the west were swathed in the richest tints of scarlet and orange. A thousand colors lay on forest and lake. The mountain summits flamed. The sun, like a globe of liquid fire, quivering in the intensity of its heat, stood as if balanced on the western pines. Down into them it burnt its way. Pausing for a moment, and only for a moment, it poured its warm benediction upon the forest, sent a crimson farewell to each mountain-top, kissed the clouds around its couch, shook, quivered, dropped from sight! And there in the crisp air we three stood, and gazed in silence westward, until the shadows deepened along the sky, the fog crept in and filled once more the valleys at our feet; and the wilderness which had been to me and mine a nurse and home, and which we feared we should never see or enter together again, lay wrapped in silence and in gloom.